Kacey's Quest

David A. Byrne

DEDICATION

This book is dedicated to my dear parents. My mother Bridie was an avid reader who wore a permanent smile. Unfortunately she is now in a care home with severe dementia and no longer capable of enjoying the written word. My father has shown great strength and courage to cope with the separation of his beloved bride of 73 years.

Kacey's Quest

Kacey's Quest

Acknowledgements

Gordon Mills:

Cover design

Beth Field:

Editing and constructive input

Courtney, and Frederick Byrne: My beautiful children, and my inspiration to succeed as an author

David A. Byrne

David, a father of three, spent most of his career navigating the complicated world of investments. Since semi-retirement from a forty year career, mostly in the city of London, David has used that knowledge, along with his experience of travelling the globe to embark on his passion of becoming an established author. David's first three books have received much acclaim.

Money to Byrne: 2018

A true story of fraud and corruption involving the organised theft of billions of dollars.

Who's the Hangman: 2020

A gripping psychotic thriller involving a viscous serial killer, Peter Wheaton, who is hell bent on eliminating an unsuspecting group of individuals before he succumbs to his terminal cancer. The victims are unaware of the long lasting effects their bullying had caused to a young man all those years ago. Can detective Anthony Mazur and Agent Salonge Dupree catch him in time.

Letters to my Sister: 2021

The second book in the Mazur-Dupree series. After the success of their partnership during the 'Hangman' operation, the pair are seconded into a new Agency known as AICAC. A criminal gang from Eastern Europe have now expanded into the UK, and have ambitions to cross the Atlantic; they must be stopped.

Kacey's Quest is yet another demonstration of David's ability to change direction and tackle a completely different kind of storyline.

Kacey's Quest

Prologue

Kacey was walking home after celebrating her 21st birthday. Well, it was not so much a celebration, but the final shift of her bar job which had helped put her through university. Yeah, she'd had fun with friends, besides being the server, but had to leave immediately after last orders to catch up on sleep. Kacey was going to visit her grandad early the next morning. She had graduated from Oxford with a master's in history and, although her uni was close to where she lived, she had always felt very alone. Grandad was her best friend and the person who instilled in her an insatiable interest in all things past.

Up ahead she spotted them again, two local thugs from her early school days who had amounted to nothing. There were two more louts with them on this occasion, perhaps running away would not be an option. Back as early as pre-school Kacey, then enrolled under her christened name, Keith Chapman, had shown some effeminate tendencies; Keith had been born with a condition now referred to in the medical profession as intersex, previously known rather insensitively as a hermaphroditism, named

3

after Hermes and Aphrodite, the Greek God, and Goddess of Love.

The father had wanted a boy but everything in the mother's instincts told her that this should be a girl; the father won the argument. By junior school Keith had been caught on a number of occasions dressing in his mother's clothes causing ballistic arguments between his parents; the ignorant, homophobic father blaming this effeminate abomination on Keith's mother. He eventually left the family home and Keith's mum went into a severe depression. She too left Keith, but to an overdose, not by walking away. Having been brought up by her grandfather, upon his sixteenth birthday, Keith Chapman had undergone surgery forever more to be known as KC, or Kacey; the initials being the only remnant of her male past.

"Look who it is." Shouted one of the louts, the others spreading across the street blocking her path. Then Kacey heard more voices behind her and spun around towards the sound. Another two faces appeared from the shadows; also idiots from her early years but she couldn't remember their names. Kacey ripped a three-foot post from a dilapidated fence and charged the larger group, waving the makeshift weapon like a medieval long sword. Two minutes later all four boys blocking her escape had been felled, clearing the way. Instead of running, Kacey turned slowly to face the two boys at her rear.

"You may retreat with dignity, and I shall spare you a thrashing." Said Kacey. "Be gone!" She roared.

With that her pursuers turned on their heels and ran. Kacey was laughing all the way home, now using her fake sword as a rambler's walking stick.

When Kacey's mother had died, her father sold the family home and sent her 50K from the 280K sale price; he didn't even write a note. It was then that she moved in with Sir Grandad, a play on Sir Galahad as she sometimes affectionately called him. A year after Kacey went to university grandad decided to go into private care; his dementia was getting worse, and they agreed it would be the safest option. He had also sold his house and bought Kacey her own apartment, so she had no financial worries.

She would miss him though. After her visit tomorrow she was going on an adventure, or as other ex-students call it, a gap year.

Chapter 1

A Sad Farewell

I had accepted the £3,900 offer from webuyanycar.com, even though I could have got nearer four and a half had I held out for a private sale. The little red Fiat had served me well over the past three years and a small tear found its way down my cheek as I handed over the keys. I knew that this was not the only occasion when I would cry today, I had to say goodbye to my beloved Sir Grandad.

I packed the clothes I thought would be best for a year-long adventure with no precise agenda; some warm pullovers, some light t-shirts ... no bikini though. I'm not much of a beach person ... never have been. The rest of my stuff had been vacuum-packed to keep dust or hungry mice at bay during my absence. I placed my camera, phone charger, iPad, paper, and pencils into my backpack along with my Eurostar ticket to Paris and also my passport. I figured I would begin my adventure there and just go where the wind takes me. My phone pinged. (*Your cab is outside.*)

I picked up the wrapped gift for Sir Grandad and went down to the awaiting taxi. It was a new iPad, minus all the apps and confusing stuff. I was certain that, although he hated all things modern, grandad would make the effort to master facetime enabling us to stay in touch during my travels.

I entered his room at the care home and as usual his face lit up. Once the hugs and 'how are you's' were out of the way, and I had gone over the facetime instructions a couple more times, Sir Grandad put the kettle on; it was story time. Even though his mental faculties were fading, sometimes not remembering the names of his carers, he never forgot the storylines from tales of a time when chivalry and honour were the standard. Since I was a tiny child, he had been recounting endless exploits of bravery from times long past, and I had never tired of them. The ritual was always the same. He would unlock his private chest, remove the fake chainmail, the knight's helmet, and plastic sword. Sir Grandad would then close the chest, place a cushion on top and get comfortable with a hot cup of tea before beginning the stories. He was not crazy, just delightfully eccentric. As usual Sir Grandad opened the three padlocks, lifted the lid, and removed his costume. This time though he did not put them on, but instead laid them carefully on his bed. He returned to the chest and removed a false bottom, retrieving a small box which I had never seen before; I was both baffled and curious. Sir Grandad closed the chest and paused before slowly turning towards me with an unusually troubled look on his face. He gingerly took to his makeshift padded seat and placed the box by his side.

"Tell me Kacey. What do you know about Joan of Arc?"

In my final year I had completed a ten-thousand-word dissertation on the subject, so I didn't need to dig too far into my memory bank.

"She was born in 1412 and died in 1431, having been captured and subsequently burnt at the stake aged 19. She was believed to be responsible for many victories towards the end of the *Hundred Years War* leading to the French reclaiming their country from the English. In 1803 she was declared a national symbol by decree from Napoleon Bonaparte. It was not until 1920 that she was finally canonized, becoming a Saint"

"Very good Kacey. But there are things that have been hidden from the history books...things that you have in common with her. You too have shown much bravery over the years, have dealt with difficult situations with dignity and determination, and you are also a devout Catholic."

I gave him a gentle smile. "Thanks for the kind words

Sir Grandad, but that hardly makes us similar. At least not in a way that could see me held aloft as a country's saviour, let alone a martyr!" I chuckled.

"You may think not." He said, half-heartedly joining me in a soft laugh. "Nevertheless, let me tell you a story."

My loving grandad, the only family member I have ever cared about, took on a serious demeanour as he contemplated how to begin. I had the feeling that this tale would be different to those he usually recited of gallantry or swashbuckling heroics. After what seemed like an age, he finally began.

"It was a stormy night some six hundred years ago in Domremy in the Vosges of northeast France. A peasant farming family were expecting a child. The delivery was usually handled by a nun from the nearby church, but the weather and knee-deep muddy roads made this impossible. Jacques and his wife Isabelle called upon a neighbour's wife, a good friend, to assist in the delivery. The birth went without a hitch but once born, their child could be seen to have both sets of genitalia. Back then, things like this would see the mother being accused of witchcraft resulting in her inevitable hanging, maybe even the guillotine. The neighbours of Jacques d'Arc and Isabelle Romee were horrified and ready to flee to the authorities until Jacques managed to convince them otherwise. Times were tough for everyone, including their neighbours, so he offered a deal in return for their silence. Jacques held a part time position as a tax collector. He promised to adjust their neighbour's levies due in return for keeping this event between themselves. They agreed and an oath was signed by all. Jacques d'Arc and his wife proceeded to remove the male genitalia and name their child Joan."

"Sir Grandad, really." I said, expecting him to give me a wink confirming that this was a fabrication of his extraordinary imagination. But this was not a jovial subject matter and his face remained deadly serious. "Your stories are usually so good, full of battles and bravery. This one is quite ridiculous." I said, trying to not upset him.

Sir Grandad was silent for a long moment, just staring down at the small box on his lap. "You may think so." He said. "But true none the less."

Sir Grandad opened the box and handed me a small piece of paper encased in plastic. Take this to your history professor and have it carbon dated. You will find it to be over six hundred years old. Once that has been confirmed, you may return to collect the remainder of these ancient documents inside the box, including the actual oath of silence."

"Grandad, you are serious, aren't you? This could cause absolute mayhem with the history books." I said. "How on earth did they come into your possession?"

"The similarities I mentioned between you and Joan of Arc are more than you know. These documents have been passed down from generation to generation. I think a time has come where the world is more understanding, and the truth of the past will be more readily accepted." He said.

"So, if these have gone from generation to generation, you are saying...?"

"Yes Kacey. The bloodline of Saint Joan runs through your veins. It is now time that this documentation, which has been secretly protected by our family, must pass down to you. And you, my dear grandchild, must follow its clues to reveal the undeniable truth of the past. It will be a dangerous task to take on, but one you must accept. Many people, including the Catholic Church and powerful members of French Society will try to stop you. Good luck my wonderful grandchild."

Chapter 2

What difference can a few days make?

My plans were now in turmoil, but a real-life adventure such as this was so much more appealing than just visiting museums or taking snaps of famous landmarks around the globe. I found it incredible that, if what Sir Grandad had told me were true, then a brave couple who lived over six hundred years ago had made the correct decision that my own modern-day parents could not. I returned home and changed my Eurostar ticket to one week later; it shouldn't take that long for my old history professor, Elizabeth Field, to carbon date the document. I called her cell phone but got no response. This usually meant that she would be engrossed in research at the university. Beth did not believe that modern devices such as mobile phones should be found at a place of study. That's not exactly true, they could be found there but woe betide anyone whose phone was still switched-on during studies. I called the university who confirmed that the professor was indeed in residence.

I checked her office as well as several other locations; the lab, the uni's private museum and the basement where objects still being verified were stored, but she could not be found. My last chance was the vast library. I entered the room and involuntarily inhaled the musty smell of ancient books which, as always, immediately evoked images of events from history. Professor Field was in the farthest corner of the room. I made my way towards her, doing my best to minimise the squeak from my rubber soled trainers on the highly polished parquet flooring.

"Is there nowhere in this godforsaken place where someone can enjoy the solitude of their own company?" She said, without looking up from her the object of her studies.

"I'm so sorry Beth." I said, feeling unaccustomed to addressing her using the familiarity of one who is no longer a student.

Her head snapped up, ready to give a verbal reprimand.

"Kacey my dear girl, how are you?" She said, her perceptiveness instantly recognising the look of urgency combined with excitement etched across my face.

"I'm very well Professor Field." I said, feeling the need to correct the liberty I had taken with my tutorial mentor.

"I can see you have something of great importance to discuss. Let's go to the cafeteria, we can't talk in here." she said, grabbing her coat and bag.

Beth had been more than just a history professor. She had always been a sympathetic ear when the bullying and jibes about my gender reassignment had been the most popular activity on campus, and I could tell that she believed this to be the reason for my visit. Beth was a workaholic, so much so that whatever free time she had outside of the ludicrous hours she worked at the uni, Beth spent volunteering as a counsellor for abused children. My old professor ordered us some coffee and sat down without saying a word; her experience in social work having taught her that it was best to let the other person reveal their troubles first. I gave Beth a warm smile, reached into my bag and retrieved the document Sir Grandad had given me. The professor could read French and Latin as easily as English, and this document was made up of the first two. She reached for her glasses and studied the wording with great interest.

Finally, I said. "Do you think it is genuine?"

I had never seen Professor Field look so shocked and lost for words, her jaw dropping slightly as she searched for something appropriate to say.

"The paper, on first inspection, is of the period...the turn of phrase also. Where did you get this?"

I told her the whole story and asked if she could accurately verify the age of the document.

"Give me a couple of days Kacey. If this is a real document, you may well be about to change history. Let me make a call, how can I get hold of you?"

I gave her my mobile number as well as a big hug and left for home. I couldn't wait to call the care home and tell grandad. The next two hours were the most traumatic and horrific time which I had spent on this planet. As I walked into my apartment I was gob-smacked. The entire place had been trashed; clothes scattered everywhere; the vacuum packs torn open. Vases were smashed and the drawers and cupboards were hanging off their hinges . My phone pinged to say that I had a voicemail. I hit the play button to hear a frantic Professor Field.

My dear girl. When we were at the cafeteria, I could swear people were watching us. As you left, one of the men followed you and the other, I am sure, is following me now. I left my bag behind at the uni on purpose and then rang Maria the tea lady to retrieve it and keep it safe for me; your document is inside, and I said that you or I would call in to collect it.

I then heard a man's voice in the background. The diction was very precise and easy to hear the clipped English with a French tinge.

"Give me the document Professor, and I will not hurt you."

"What document, I don't know what you are talking about?"

"I shall ask once more professor, hand it over."

"I don't have any…".

I then heard the most dreadful, blood curdling scream. My first thought was to call the police but found myself punching in the number of the care home, some instinct telling me that Sir Grandad could be in danger. Everyone knew me at the home but the voice who answered was no one I recognised.

"Ah Kacey, we were just about to call you, my name is PC Carrow. I suggest you get to accident and emergency at the John Radcliffe hospital, your grandad has had an accident, I will meet you there."

"What sort of accident?" I said, knowing that it was

no such thing.

"Just meet me there and I will fill you in."

"He has been attacked, hasn't he?"

The phone was silent for a moment. "What makes you say that? She said. "What do you know?"

I hung up and called a taxi. When I arrived at A&E there was a woman standing outside the entrance monitoring every arrival. Even though she was not in uniform I knew it to be PC Carrow.

"What's happened to my grandad?"

"I am not at liberty to say too much I'm afraid. But I can tell you that he has been attacked and his room ransacked. You seemed to know something about it!"

"I want to see him, is he ok?"

Kacey, on the phone you said, 'he has been attacked'. How did you know?"

I needed to think quickly. "What I said was, has he had a heart attack, you must have heard wrong."

I could see in her eyes that she didn't believe me but also the realisation that I was in no mood for a debate. I was sure, however, that they would check the phone tapes later. She let it go and led me to the trauma centre. My pace quickened as we approached the double doors and I burst through without a thought for any unfortunate on the other side. A doctor glared at me, clearly not impressed with my inconsiderate, and uninvited entrance. I spotted Sir Grandad looking deathly grey, tubes hanging from his arms, his nose at an impossible angle and eyes well on the way to becoming panda-like.

"Excuse me miss; you can't be in here." Said the white coated doctor.

"You don't understand." I said. "That's my grandad!"

The doctor approached and confronted me, calling for security as he did so. PC Carrow produced her ID, her reassuring look of authority causing the doctor to abort his call for assistance.

All of our attention was caught by my grandad's voice, louder than that which should be possible from an old man at death's door. I was permitted to approach his bed and I immediately reached for his frail hand.

"Kacey my dear. I don't know how, but they are onto us...the danger has begun. I am so sorry."

"What has begun grandad? I asked.

"The people who wish the truth to remain secret have started their search for our documents. Anyone you have spoken to of this is in great danger. Kacey my child, you should not return to your apartment if at all possible. There is only one way forward now, you must begin your quest to uncover the truth. The answers are all in the chest, I do not believe that they found them. The men who attacked me were trying to find the rest of the documents as well as the maps, but they failed."

Grandad's voice was now all but a whisper, every utterance seemed an extreme effort. This was only partially true as I now realised it was also to keep our conversation out of PC Carrow's earshot.

"What other documents, and what are these maps you speak of Sir Grandad?" I said in an equally soft delivery.

"I only gave you one parchment for the purpose of verifying its age. I have much more for you to read including maps describing Joan of Arc's movements and battle plans. There are also clues as to where she hid evidence of the truth about her life. You must take on this most dangerous quest to uncover this truth. It is said that there are treasures of immeasurable value waiting to be uncovered, not diamonds and rubies, treasures much greater than mere trinkets."

I could almost see the life draining from my dear protector's body, fear and pain consuming every part of me in equal measures.

"Stop talking grandad." I said. "Let's get you well and we can go on a brave expedition together." I just managed to make the words audible between sobs. "We will both embark on a great crusade that would make Sir Galahad's adventures read like a boring Sunday picnic."

Grandad smiled. "That would be wonderful Kacey. However, I am not long for this world. Go to my dressing gown laying on the chair behind you. In the pocket you will find a piece of paper wrapped around a key. The key does not look like a key, it is a wooden wedge which you must insert into a slot in my knight's chest at the care home. The intruders have smashed the chest to pieces but have not, however, found the secret compartment containing the remaining documents and maps. You will need help to achieve success on our family crusade. The piece of paper enveloping the wooden key has a phone number. It is that of a distant relative, Salonge Dupree. I had already appraised her of the situation before the attack, sensing that things could escalate quickly, and you would need help. This cousin of yours was born in France, grew up in Quebec, then moved back to France to work for Interpol as head of cybercrime. She later transferred back to Quebec upon where she was subsequently inducted into the Chicago FBI in a collaboration between the two organisations. She is now living with her husband in Thailand heading an International Intelligence Agency. You will need her assistance, skills, and resources. You must leave for Paris as soon as you can. She will meet you in the George V on the Champs Elysée this coming Saturday."

I was barely holding myself together as I watched this gentle old man struggle for breath but wouldn't allow myself to completely breakdown in front of him. I would not permit any weakness of mine to be his final memory on this earth. He seemed to be gathering all of his strength for one final statement.

"Kacey, my dear dear Kacey. This is all very real and far more dangerous than I ever anticipated. The wheels are now in motion and cannot be stopped. You must not be sad, but instead promise me that

21

you will channel all of that energy into bringing the truth to light. Only then can I rest in peace."

"I promise Sir Grandad. I love you!"

I felt Sir Grandad's gip weaken on my fingers. I could hear a faint rattle as the last oxygen left his lungs, his chest and ribs retracting for the final time.

Chapter 3

Things to do

PC Carrow surprisingly allowed me to go on my way saying she would be in touch in a day or two. I left the hospital and to my surprise was filled with anger and determination, not sadness. I was angry at the people who did this to my grandad and determined to fulfil his dying wish. I figured that it would be too dangerous to go home and, although I needed to retrieve the document from the uni's cafeteria, going there was also out of the question. I took a chance and headed to the care home. I guessed that the police would still have a presence given the fact that this was now effectively a murder case, not just a burglary.

When I went through the doors several of the carers came over to console me. I asked if I could collect some of my things from grandad's room but was told that I would need to ask the police; they were still fingerprinting his room. I stood in the open doorway and could not believe the carnage in front of me. His chest of draws and wardrobe had been ransacked and his clothes were strewn everywhere. Grandad's mattress was in the middle of the room and the base of the bed had been tipped on its side. There were two men in white suits kneeling with small brushes and plastic bags filled with various items of grandad's. The chest was mostly smashed into splinters, but I could see that the two-inch base with the false bottom was still intact.

"Excuse me." I said. "I am Kacey Chapman. I am the granddaughter."

One of the forensic detectives rose to his feet, the other just gave a brief nod and continued looking for evidence.

"We have just heard your sad news Ms Chapman." Said Crime Scene Officer Price. "We shall do our best to find these bastards...I mean culprits."

"Don't apologise, you were right first time." I said.

"Ms Chapman, do you have any idea what these people were looking for? They were clearly after something. Did he own any items of great value, and if he did, where do you think he would keep them?"

I took a chance. "No not really. His most precious items were some photos of grandma, but he kept them in the draw of his bedside table. I guess if there were anything of value, he would have put it in the secret compartment of my chest. It's what I am here for, to collect my study work about Joan of Arc."

"A secret compartment." He said looking at the broken chest. "It doesn't look like there is anything secret left of the box."

"May I come in and take a look. I always keep the key with me." I noticed the strange look on the officer's face when he saw me produce the odd wooden wedge from my pocket. I walked over to the box and found the slot and slipped the key into it. The top of the base sprung open.

"I'm sorry miss, but I will need to take a look first." He said.

He retrieved an A4 sized brown envelope with my name on the front. The officer slid out a wad of photos. He was looking at them one by one, occasionally glancing in my direction.

"I guess it will be ok for you to take these." He said and handed them to me.

There were pictures of me as a baby and also as a young boy, but the officer didn't seem to make any connection. The photos were of my every birthday right up to present day, all of them with both grandad and me in the frame. This time I could not hold back the sobs. I looked up through misty eyes to see the officer holding open a heavy folder, flicking through the documents, all encased in protective plastic.

"It's ok to take this too I guess." Said Officer Price. "It says Kacey's history project."

"Thank god, there is over four years of my research in there." I lied. "I am due to leave for France this weekend to trace Joan of Arc's journey of six hundred years ago. Will I still be permitted to go?"

"Well, you are hardly a suspect young lady." He said. "Just leave us your e-mail address and mobile number in case we have any questions."

I felt guilty about not mentioning the worrisome call from Beth, but if something had happened to her there is no way that I would be allowed to leave the country.

....

I stepped outside of the care home for some privacy and called my friend, Johnny Valatone. Johnny did his own pirate radio show from his garden shed during the day and was the resident DJ at my previous employer's where I, until recently, tended the bar. His parents wanted him to give up the dream of being a top DJ, but he had stuck with it and was beginning to get a serious following. There were rumours of an approach being made by Thames Soul Radio.

"Johnny, it's KC."

"Hey babe, what's goin on." He said, in his best 'I'm in the music business' voice.

"I need your help, and its urgent." I immediately heard him talking into his mike.

"Ok Kids, Johnny is gonna have to leave you hangin for today. I've had a tip off that the fuzz is in the area tryin to shut me dowwwwwn. Here's one last vibe for ya."

In the background I could hear the unmistakable gruff voice of Joe Strummer of The Clash. *'I needed money cause I had none, I fought the law and the law won!'*

When Johnny came back on the phone he spoke normally. "KC, you sound scared to hell. What's happened?"

"Johnny, my grandad has been murdered and I think that something awful may have happened to Professor Field. I need somewhere to crash for a few days before going to France."

"No problem." He said. "You can have my room and I'll hit the couch. This sounds like heavy shit KC, whats it all about?"

"I'll catch a cab and should be with you in about fifteen minutes. I will tell you all about it then." I said. Something snapped me into alert mode, maybe it was Johnny's last words before he hung up. I had not been concentrating on my personal safety and there was more than a strong possibility that I was being watched. I scanned the carpark and noticed a black Mercedes sitting with its engine running; not a typical scene you would expect at this location. I went back into the home and told the uniformed officer that there was a strange vehicle in the carpark. I pointed the car out to him, and he unclipped his radio to do a registration check. Immediately the tyres of the Merc began to screech, and it sped off, almost taking the carpark barrier with it as the rear wheels mounted the curb.

The police officers radio began to crackle but I couldn't hear what was being said. However, I could see his face visibly relax as he re-holstered the communication device.

"Miss Chapman, the vehicle has diplomatic plates registered to the French Embassy in London." He said, giving me a sympathetic look. "You have had quite a shock and maybe should not be on your own right now. You are bound to feel a bit paranoid. Is there anyone who you could stay with for a few days"

"Actually there is." I said, giving the address of the closest Sainsbury's superstore to Johnny's house."

"I can drop you there. Let me just tell the guys." He said.

The officers face looked confused as we approached the super store. "Have you got the address right miss?"

"Oh I am sorry." I said. "My friend only lives around the corner, but he works here. I am just going to collect the house keys."

"Would you like me to wait?"

"No." I said, a little too eagerly. "I will be fine from here."

"Ok Miss. Don't worry, we will catch these people and I am sure you have nothing to worry about personally.

Once he drove off, I headed to Johnny's house on

foot knowing he was waiting, having never worked at Sainsbury's.

....

Johnny was sitting speechless on the couch, hardly able to believe what I had just told him, even though I had only relayed a watered-down version of events and little of the quest. I was also only too aware that I could be putting him in danger by divulging too much information.

"Johnny, I understand if you want me to leave."

"No way José." He said, his eyes conveying a different message.

"Thanks Johnny. There is one more favour which I need to ask of you. Professor Field has left a document for me with Maria at the university cafeteria. Could you possibly collect it for me?"

"Sure thing Kacey, I can go and get it now. Make yourself at home."

When Johnny drove off to collect the document, I quickly scanned the contents of grandad's folder. All papers save one were encased in protective plastic. The single item which was not looked to be every bit as old; there must have been a reason. On closer inspection I could see that this parchment had been deliberately aged and was no older than ten years. It was written, as were the others, in a mixture of Latin and French. It began with some useless blurb about the 100 years' war, but then suddenly changed. I took out my pencil and pad and began to translate the section obviously meant for me.

There is a safety box at London St Pancras, number 4018. There is also a lady's purse in the station lost and found. Inside this purse are personal items including bills with your current address. You must bring identification and claim back this lost item. Inside the the small zip compartment you will find the key to the safety box. Inside the box you will find a new passport and a Eurostar ticket to Paris, both in the name of Kacey Dupree, the pre-marital surname of your elder cousin. You will also find ten thousand euros and a platinum credit card providing access to any amount of money which you may need to fulfil your task.
God speed my wonderful granddaughter. I will always love you and watch over you.

Johnny returned from the university and was visibly shaken.

"What's wrong? I said. "Did you get the document?"

"Oh I got the document alright. I was grilled by the police for half an hour. They believed my story that the paper was just some research which you needed before going to France but asked when and where I was to meet with you."

"What did you say?"

"I told them we were due to meet at the pub this evening. I think they are going to arrest you. The professor's classrooms have been ransacked as has the library."

"That's terrible." I said.

"No that's not terrible." Said Johnny, clearly deliberating on how to deliver the next snippet. "What's terrible is that your old professor is in intensive care after someone tried to bludgeon her to death. You are my best friend Kacey, but I think you should leave; this shit is too heavy for me."

I was already on my way out the door, destination St Pancras.

Chapter 4

Salonge Dupree-Mazur

The life of Salonge Dupree had been eventful to say the least. Born in Arcachon, South West France, growing up in Quebec, then finishing her later education at the University of Bordeaux studying IT. Her talents had been spotted by Interpol and she soon became their youngest ever head of cyber-crime. Her family had relocated; first to Paris where her father built a reputable perfume production company, and then back to Canada as the business became internationally recognised.

Salonge had been so successful in her crime fighting role, particularly in North America, the FBI negotiated a deal whereby she would join that organisation creating closer collaboration between Interpol and the United States intelligence community. On one of her first assignments, she was sent to Chicago to investigate a major cyber-criminal and subsequently became embroiled in the hunt for a serial killer. It was during this mission that she met, and fell in love with her husband, Chicago Detective Anthony Mazur.

Working closely together, they had proved such a phenomenal team that they were commissioned to take on the task of shutting down an Eastern

European Crime gang who had expanded into the UK and were intending on further expansion into the US. This too was a success, culminating in a 'right to the wire' conclusion in Thailand, where they now lived.

Far from being a destination for them to lounge on the beach every day, they were now husband and wife, and the most senior operatives of a covert anti spy outfit called AICAC, The **A**gency for **I**nternational **C**ollaboration **A**gainst **C**rime. It had been a tough year in many respects, but also a successful one. Salonge was owed some well overdue leave, so when she received a call from her uncle's elderly father for urgent assistance in Paris, she jumped at the chance to visit the homeland.

Although never having met him, she had heard stories of this gentle old man. About how he had single handedly brought up his granddaughter, (originally born a boy, or something like that.) The old man had said that Kacey, the girl whom he thought of as his own daughter, would soon make contact, and that it was of vital importance that Salonge assist her in any way she can. Salonge had agreed to meet Kacey in Paris, but just to hear what she had to say and could not promise much more than that. Salonge figured that the limited information he divulged was just the paranoid ravings brought on by old age. Nevertheless, it would be nice to meet this younger cousin who had apparently had such a rough life thus far. Perhaps she could bring some joy to the girl's world in the form of some good Parisienne food along with a healthy side of retail therapy.

When Salonge received the first direct text from Kacey Chapman, the old man's ravings took on a far more serious note.

My Grandad had been murdered in his care home. My old history professor has been attacked, and I have been followed by a car registered to the French Embassy in London. Please confirm that you will meet me in Paris. Kacey.

Salonge confirmed that she would be waiting.

....

I was as scared as I had ever been, suspecting that every stranger on the train was paying me undue attention. This feeling of being watched increased immeasurably as the train entered the fifty-kilometre tunnel beneath the English Channel. I was starving but convinced that the girl serving in the buffet car was waiting to put drops of cyanide onto any delicacy I chose to order. I stayed rooted to my seat in the last row of the last carriage, able to see anyone approaching with my back set firmly against the rear partition of the train; no passengers behind me waiting to sink a syringe into my neck. I nervously reached into my rucksack and found the two plastic zip bags which could give me courage. Concealed within these were two of Sir Grandad's personal belongings. One contained his flat cap, slightly raised on one side to resemble a beret but not quite, and the other his silk neck scarf. By just unzipping the bags and inhaling felt as if grandad were there with me; the first emitting wafts of his Brylcream, passed involuntarily from head to hat, and the second his Old Spice aftershave. The effect was far more calming than breathing into a paper bag; the common prescribed method for averting a panic attack.

My relief was palpable as natural light once again flooded the train, French countryside rushing by the windows. I managed to regain my composure, remembering tales of bravery told by Sir Grandad, and the fact that I had to keep it together to honour his final wish. His memory and my pledge to him gave me a strength previously unknown to me.

I guess that I had been brave of sorts my whole life, facing down teasing bullies with make do swords, or simply ignoring the strange looks and whispers when I finally summoned the courage to go out wearing girls clothes after the operation. But this was a far more dangerous situation. There were now people who were willing to kill in order to thwart my quest for the truth. When the tannoy sounded announcing our imminent arrival at Gare du Nord I was desperate to meet my resourceful relative whom grandad obviously had so much faith in.

....

Salonge had checked into a suite at the George V feeling so good to be back among such culture and elegance. It was not that Thailand lacked culture, far from it. It was just the comforting feeling of that which is familiar and cosy; something of the homeland instilled in one's fibre at a young age. The suite had two bedrooms with an adjoining door; Salonge figuring that this young relative, who is clearly in distress, would want to feel safe but also maintain some privacy and not feel smothered by a relative stranger.

Salonge had unpacked and lay on the bed intending to watch some television and catch up on the latest news of her homeland. Instead, she just rested silently, admiring the class of the décor, something she honestly believed was magnificent and only capable by the French designers. The room emitted an elegance and style that modern imitators, and the even old Masters of Interior Design from Italy, could never quite achieve. The duvet cover was of a white linen with the classic Toile de Jouy pattern printed in a type of watered-down ink blue colour. The curtains had the matching print in miniature with the most delicately woven silk tiebacks. The cabinets and dressers were mostly Rococo in style with marquetry and shelled feet and the occasional marble inlay, whereas other fittings were more in the style of the Renaissance revival.

Salonge thought she best call her husband to let him know she had arrived safe and well.

"Anthony, it's me. How are you?"

"Hey babe, I'm good...and you." Came the reply.

"Agent Mazur, I am far from a babe as I no longer wear diapers, nor do I have collogen in these lips or plastic breasts. And yes, I am very well. I have a marvellous room at one of the world's most prestigious hotels. There is no mess to be found anywhere, and there is no Chicago Cubs on the television, and no messy American husband."

They both laughed.

"Anthony, I need you to do me a favour. Could you contact our London people and ask them if there have been any travel searches for a Kacey Chapman at the airlines or Eurostar."

"Sure, I will call you back." He said.

"And Anthony, make it quick. She arrives at ze Gare du Nord in about one hour."

Salonge hung up and took a shower. She had originally intended to put on her gym clothes and complete four circuits from the hotel to the Arc de Triumph, along the Champs Elysée, around the Place de la Concord, and back. However, jetlag had set in, and a day of self-pampering was more appealing. As Salonge was drying off she heard her room telephone ringing. The display indicated that there had been four missed calls, all from Anthony. She picked up the receiver knowing that her husband had something urgent to divulge; he usually waited for her to call back.

"Hello, Anthony, is that you."

"It's me alright, how long do you spend in the shower for heaven's sake? Now listen carefully. For the past week, our intel says that there have been over two hundred searches for a Kacey Chapman. Most of them from IP addresses traced to various French official residences and get this, one of them was from an unregistered number in the United States. The last search was from a number linked to the Suisse Guard at the Vatican in Rome."

"Did they discover when she will be arriving in Paris?" Said Salonge.

"Probably. They would have found no Kacey Chapman, but a Kacey Dupree will arrive at the Gare du Nord at six this evening."

Salonge looked at her watch. That was in forty-five minutes.

"Anthony, listen carefully. Contact Charles Worwood at MI6 in London. Tell him I need an urgent patch through to the security cameras at Gare du Nord"

"Wouldn't it be easier to ask your French contacts? He said. "Or even Interpol."

"I have an instinct that this is the last thing I should do."

"Ok, boot up your PC and I will get it sorted." Said her husband, suddenly regretting not having joined his wife on this trip.

Salonge turned on her monitor whilst getting

dressed. It only took a couple of minutes for it to begin showing incredibly clear images of the arrivals at the main station in France. Salonge had no doubt that Sir Charles Worwood, head of MI6, and the most senior member of the AICAC International cooperative, as well as the best man at their wedding one year ago, had pulled some strings. Salonge was able to zoom in and out to every area of the vast station but concentrated her efforts on the people awaiting the arrival of the Eurostar from London. Suddenly her blood ran cold. A face she thought she recognised was standing there, clearly trying to avoid the cameras. His complexion was ghostly white, a ghost from her past. This man, supposedly retired, was a deadly assassin used by rich businesspeople and governments to eliminate irksome problems. Considering what her young cousin had told her, her grandad's murder, the attack on her professor , the Mercedes that sped off from the care home using French diplomatic plates, , Salonge had an awfully bad feeling.

Salonge sprinted out of the door hoping that she would be in time to save her young cousin's life.

……………….

After exiting the train I hung back on the platform, taking my time getting to the ticket turnstiles. I took another long look at the most recent head shot picture Salonge Dupree had sent me and felt sure that I would recognise her. However, I felt it best to let the crowds thin out first making it easier for us to spot each other, me having sent her my mugshot too. By the time I passed through the ticket barrier the crowds had thinned out but there was no sign of my cousin. A man in a dark hoody began walking in my direction. As he raised his head, I could see a smirk across his red lips, accentuated by his incredibly white face. As he reached within three feet of me, he was suddenly poleaxed from the side. In a matter of seconds there was an incredibly beautiful woman straddled upon his chest with a knife held to his throat. Suddenly, a lady immediately behind me began screaming, drawing the attention of everyone in the vicinity.

"Someone is attacking my husband!"

The next thing I saw was my cousin helping the man to his feet whilst profusely apologising. The woman behind me was now shouting for the police. I joined Salonge with the apologies and things eventually calmed down.

Salonge scribbled a note and handed it to the couple telling them what hotel we were staying at, declaring that she would gladly buy them dinner and compensate them for any inconvenience they had incurred. Salonge then grabbed my wrist, propelling me towards the exit and into a taxi before we could be apprehended

Fifteen minutes later we were drinking coffee in our two-bedroom suite at the George V. Salonge suggested I take a shower and make myself comfortable before we go through the whole story again. Only then would we carefully examine the ancient paperwork in Sir Grandad's folder.

Chapter 5

Protecteurs de la France

The secret organisation named 'Protecteurs de le France' had called an emergency meeting. The highest members were ancestors of the men who orchestrated the storming of the Bastille in July of 1789, but the organisations roots went back to the 1400's. Some attendees were associated with the right-wing French national front group once headed by Jean Marie le Pen, and subsequently by his daughter. Others were patriots from other political parties, as well as high officials in the French courts, police, embassies, and even the French Secret Service. The final four seats were reserved for representation by Catholic bodies from America, the United Kingdom, Spain and finally Rome.

"Ladies and gentlemen. As you know there is a grave situation facing us. The legend of Joan of Arc must remain as it is. We cannot allow France, or the Catholic Church, to be tarnished by fabricated claims in the documentation which has recently surfaced. Of course we knew of their existence, however, the fact we know that the providence of their age alone, written by heretics of old, could convince some historians that their content be true. I shall let Pierre update you on the current situation.

Pierre Cardout had a brilliant brain which was off the scale when tested against anything Mensa could offer. However, academia is where his accolades ended. He was a racist, a chauvinist, a homophobe, and a thug. He was also a senior member of the DGSE, Direction Générale de la Sécurité Extérieure, the French Secret Service.

Pierre began. "My loyal French patriots and esteemed Catholic guests. I have much news to disclose, some good and some bad, so please do not interrupt. The documents of whispered legend have finally surfaced and must be destroyed. It has emerged that they had been handed down through generations, most recently to an old Englishman of French descent. He has now been dispatched."

Everyone in the room let out a cheer.

"Please do not drink your Merlot before I have finished speaking. As I said, it is not all good news."

The room went silent.

"We did not recover the documents. However, we believe that he has already passed them to his granddaughter with a directive to make their contents known."

"Do we know where she is at this time?" queried the representative from Rome.

Pierre gave a hard stare. "I beg that you let me finish monsieur. Our people at the French Embassy in London travelled to Oxford where she lives and eventually made visual contact at the grandfather's care home. His room had already been searched by our people and the grandfather was interrogated, but the old fool would not cooperate. Our Embassy colleagues believe that they were compromised in the car park and had to exit that location before she could be extracted. We have since discovered that she would be arriving at Le Gare du Nord earlier this evening, and it is highly likely that she has the documents with her. Two of our agents, one on the same train, and one waiting on the platform were to engage her. This is where things took an unexpected turn. A stranger intervened, somewhat aggressively I might add, someone who we now know to be an ex-Interpol and FBI agent. Her name is Salonge Dupree. Dupree thinks she had made a dreadful mishap of mistaken identity, and by way of an apology has invited our two assassins to dinner at her hotel this evening. I have instructed them to accept this invite but only on a fact-finding mission. We cannot eradicate them until we know the whereabouts of the papers. If Kacey Chapman has assistance from an experienced agent, which she clearly has having used a fake passport with the surname Dupree, then we must assume that the documents may well already be hidden in a secret location. I have a feeling that this unexpected complication may well prove troublesome.

The usual closing toast of VIVE LA FRANCE followed by, FOR GOD WE SERVE, was deemed inappropriate on this occasion. In all, fourteen grey faced men and women drained their glasses in silence and left the room. Two of them headed to their hotel to dress for dinner at the George V, relieved that Pierre had not identified them as the failed assassins at the station a short time ago.

……………….

Regardless of the ever-lingering sadness over the death of Sir Grandad, and the obvious dangers which lay ahead, I had never felt so comfortable and secure as I did right now. Salonge, my distant cousin, although being eighteen years my senior felt more like a protective big sister; we had bonded so quickly. We were of a similar size so I couldn't believe it when she said I could choose anything I liked from her case to wear at dinner this evening. We giggled about what that event would be like. The wife of the man whom she had poleaxed earlier had called to say that they were both fine and would be absolutely delighted to take up the offer of dining at the George V.

Whilst I was ironing an elegant peach all in one, Salonge was separating the contents of Grandad's documents onto the bed. To the left was the fake aged document giving me my instructions. To the right were the genuine, ancient articles. Above those was one which I had not noticed, it was blank.

"Kacey, why would your Grandad keep a blank document locked away?" She said.

"I have no idea." I said. "Don't you think that you should concentrate on the things which actually have words written on them?"

"Salonge passed me the blank document. "No Kacey, there is a reason for everything. Look at it carefully."

I stared and stared but it was just a blank piece of paper. "Means nothing to me." I said and handed it back. Just then the steam from the iron went up my nostrils , telling me that I had the temperature too high and could potentially ruin the garment that Salonge had lent me. As I pinched my nose to catch the sneeze there was a distinctive smell of citrus coming from my thumb and index finger.

"Quickly, pass the paper back to me." I said. "When I was just a child and having told Grandad that I believed I was a girl, we used to communicate using lemon juice with a quill. Once heated in the oven or in front of the fire, our secret conversations would reveal themselves."

We had no such oven in the suite of the George V, but I did have an iron. I carefully placed the sheet of paper onto the ironing board and repeatedly floated the surface of the iron gently across blank document. After the fifth sweep, writing began to appear.

My Dear Kacey

You must read paragraph four of document five in the folder very carefully. If I am correct, you will be the only mortal who can read a secret message polished within the breastplate of Joan's armour. This will reveal another secret as to the whereabouts of the proof behind the greatest secret in history. All I do know is that Joan of Arc's armour is being displayed at a rare outdoor event on the 21st of June at the Musée de l'Armée Invalades, Paris. You must go there!

I will always watch over you

Sir Grandad.
xxxxxxxxxxx

Salonge was listening to me mouthing the words as I read the zesty message and already had the required document five to hand.

 "I am afraid that I do not read Latin., but the 21st of June is tomorrow" she said, and handed the relevant page to me. I counted down to the appropriate paragraph four and began to translate the ancient script.

These words are true as God be my judge

No single man nor woman can reveal the secret, only man and woman as one. Upon my breast is a message for only the chosen to read. At the brightest moment, on the longest day of the year, a person pure of heart shall discover the secrets which reveal my true story.

Joan d'Arc

"What do you think that it means?" I said.

"We shall find out tomorrow." Said Salonge. "Right now, we have to get ready for an embarrassing dinner."

I went through the adjoining door bringing my borrowed peach garment with me. When I was satisfied of looking my best, I knocked on my cousin's door. Salonge was wearing exactly the same outfit but in a soft lilac colour; she looked spectacular. She had applied only eye makeup with a hint of foundation on her face. It was so subtle it made me feel a tad clown like, the peachy blusher and matching lipstick looking like an Andy Warhol creation. Salonge saw my concern and sat me at her dresser. As she cleaned my facial pallet and began a softer creation, I could tell she had something of importance to say.

"Kacey, may I ask you a question?"

"Of course you can, silly."

"If I had rugby tackled you at the station, jumped on your chest and held a knife to your throat, would you report it to the police or would you instead decide to accept an invitation to dinner with a lunatic?"

"Oh my god, it's them isn't it...the people who killed Grandad?"

"There is no doubt that they are involved, but I feel that these are just pawns and not the main people we need to find."

"We have to get out of here." I said, rushing towards the adjoining door to pack my things.

"No Kacey. We shall enjoy a fabulous dinner and see what we can find out. They will not cause us any harm tonight, not until they have retrieved the folder."

"Oh my god, the documents, where should we hide them?"

"I shall keep them with me. The best hiding place is in plain sight. Besides, I have no doubt that before we have finished the foie gras they will have thoroughly searched our rooms and belongings, and we will have extracted much useful information. I have also set up surveillance cameras allowing my husband will find out who these people are. Men do have some uses!" Salonge laughed.

Any elements of fear and doubt which had furrowed its way into my head disappeared in an instant. Salonge Dupree, my beautiful cousin, was every bit as brave as Joan of Arc, or any other heroic knight from Grandad's stories. Together I felt like we could achieve anything.

I puffed out my chest and turned to Salonge, feeling suddenly brave. "We shall make these vagabonds talk my cousin, even if we have to place them in stocks and thrash it out of them."

"Calm down my brave English Lioness. I said we would find out what we can, not beat it out of them."

Chapter 6

How the other half live

As we entered Le Cinq restaurant, I once again felt nervous and intimidated. I would far rather be yielding a sword against impossible odds than panicking at the vast array of of cutlery, china and crystal glasses arranged at each table, and the quandary of which ones were used for what. We were shown to our seats and ordered some sparkling water whilst we awaited the arrival of our guests. The sun bursting through the window made the whole restaurant seem impossibly clean and white, apart from the tablecloths which displayed miniature rainbows of diffracted light through the crystal. When the waiter returned Salonge began speaking French whilst shielding her eyes with one hand, like a 17th century sailor scanning the horizon from the crow's nest of a galleon. I can translate any document written in French, and more than get by when asking for directions in that tongue. But this was my first proper visit to France, aside from a day trip to Calais as a twelve-year-old, and the speed at which they were conversing meant that I could only get the basic gist of the conversation. As we were shown to the adjacent table, I was relieved to know that I had interpreted the discussion correctly; Salonge had requested that we be moved to a table out of direct sunlight.

"Why did you move tables?" I asked. "It's a glorious day, but the sunshine is hardly strong enough for us to require factor fifty."

"My dear Kacey, the light was just strong enough to obstruct our view of the street and also to make our silhouettes a perfect target. With our backs against the wall we can see our dinner guests whilst knowing that they cannot signal to any accomplices and in turn, those accomplices cannot prevent us finishing our meal courtesy of a bullet."

"A chill ran down my spine at the realisation of how unequipped I was to manage this task alone, grateful that my cousin with all of her experience was here to help. I wondered what kind of situations this beautiful, resourceful woman had dealt with in the past. As usual, grandad had been wise to ask her for assistance and I had the feeling that he knew some of the answers.

I spotted two people enter the restaurant. There was no doubt that it was the couple from the Gare du Nord, but they looked the oddest match. The seemingly young man who had worn the hoody, and was poleaxed by Salonge, was wearing a black tuxedo making him look closer to his real age, at least ten years older. His frumpy wife from earlier was now wearing a beautiful Chanel number, her hair pulled up in an elegant type of bird's nest; not too messy, but not manicured to perfection either. I saw the waiter gesturing in our direction, but the man was now gesticulating in quite an animated manner.

"Look." Said Salonge. "The gentleman is questioning why we are not sitting at the window seat. It was a wise decision to move tables."

The couple approached our table and offered their hands whilst making formal introductions. Their faces held the warm smiles, a message which their eyes failed to convey.

"Thank you so much for coming." Said Salonge. "I would not have been surprised if you had declined after my appalling behaviour at the station."

"I must admit." Said the man who had introduced himself as Julien. "We did ponder the wisdom of doing so."

"I'm still unsure if the wiser decision would have been to call the police." Said the lady we were to address as Sophia. "Even so, we were intrigued as to what made you act in such a way only to discover that you had made a dreadful mistake."

"It's a long story." Said Salonge. "And one which you will forgive us for not elaborating on. Now let's place our order. The food here is absolute perfection."

The man stared at us both for a moment. "It is a shame you cannot explain why you tackled me in such an aggressive manner. I would have thought that this would be the least you could do. Besides, the explanation could be helpful to our work."

"And what work is that?" I hissed, just managing to refrain from asking if their last job was to murder Sir Grandad.

The couple looked at each other and then back at me, sensing aggression in my tone. It was Sophia who replied first. "We are mystery writers and a situation like this draws us like moths to the flame."

Then Salonge said something which both stopped my heart momentarily and changed the tone of conversation.

"I suggest that this flame is too hot for mystery writers. Even hotter than those which engulfed our famous heroine, Joan of Arc."

"Ah, our beloved Jehanne d' Arc." Said Julien, using

the medieval pronunciation. "The Maid of Orleans, her armour even brighter and whiter than the magnificent silver cutlery in this fabulous restaurant."

Julien and Salonge were then locked in a long stare before Sophia broke the stalemate.

"So Kacey... that is what you said your name was, wasn't it?"

"Yes."

"What brings you to France?" She said, an ugly knowing smile forming across her face.

"I am just catching up with my cousin before completing a history project."

"Ah, how interesting." She said, an evil grin etching onto her lips. "My own Grandfather was fascinated by history. Unfortunately, he passed away just a few days ago in the most disturbing circumstances."

I was ready to explode even though I knew that I should not. She was baiting me, and it worked. I reached for the knife, ready to lunge, using it like a miniature pike, but Salonge grabbed my hand.

"No Kacey, that is a steak knife, the rounded one is

for the butter." She said, smiling at our dinner guests. "My young cousin is still learning the etiquette of fine dining."

That only served to infuriate me more, but my hand was welded to the table. I couldn't believe that that much pressure could be exerted by such delicate fingers.

Although no open admissions had been made, the testing innuendo confirmed that the pretense and charade being acted out by both parties was pointless, so we turned our attention to the menus. I ordered the line-fished sea bass with caviar and buttermilk to start followed by the lightly cooked blue lobster in chestnut crepes. For dessert I chose the iced dark chocolate with roasted peanuts. My order alone totalled over two hundred euros and, having insisted on paying, hoped that the platinum card provided by Grandad would work. Once I saw the price of the Petruse which Salonge had requested, I really really hoped that the card worked.

Our guests, staring vacantly at the fayre, had either lost their appetite, or were contemplating their next move. I spied Salonge's hand slide silkily into her bag and grip the handle of a gun.

"I am so sorry." Said the now agitated Julien.

"Something urgent has come up and we need to leave. Enjoy the rest of your trip. I hope your rooms here are satisfactory, I am told the suites are fantastique!"

"They are indeed." Said Salonge. "But I'm sure your friends will give you a full appraisal of our accommodation as soon as you leave."

Julien gave a half bow and clicked his heels in a manner more associated with the Third Reich than that of a French patriot. Sophia was already heading for the exit without so much as a goodbye.

....

"That was fun." Said Salonge.

"Fun?" I said with a confused and questioning stare. "Fun would have been stretching their limbs on a torture table at the Tower of London until they told us everything. Right now we have learned nothing, and you just let them walk away!"

"On the contrary my dear cousin." Said Salonge as she slipped Julien's knife and Sophia's fork into her bag. "I now have our guests fingerprints and my husband will be searching a facial recognition data base for the people who have no doubt searched our room. I suggest you enjoy this delicious meal, Kacey. And by the way, you will be relieved to hear that I shall be paying."

It took at least another two hours before we had finished our dining experience. Well it was an experience for me, Salonge looked totally at home. I was absolutely full to the brim, not so much by the volume of food, but the richness. So, when the leather L'addition booklet was opened disclosing the bill I was ready to project the contents of my dinner onto the white tablecloth, it was over a thousand euros.

"Do me a favour my young cousin. Do not stress about this money, it was my pleasure. If you really wish to repay me then please go to le tabac on the corner and buy me some Gitanes. I will see you back in the room. Do not fear, they will by now know who I am and will not harm you."

"Why is that?" I said. "Is it because they believe you are in possession of the documents, not me?"

"No my dear cousin. It is because they believe that they have recovered them.

....

Julien and Sophia, along with the search team, were sitting in their vehicle watching the exit to the George V, waiting to see if either Kacey Chapman, or more likely, Salonge Dupree would have tried to follow their dinner guests.

"I take it the documents were nowhere to be found." Said Julien to the driver; a statement not a question."

"No Julien, the room was clean." He said.

Sophia chirped in. "Whilst we dined, Dupree was protecting her bag like a mother hen, she must have them on her person."

The male driver continued, addressing Julien not Sophia, her being of a lesser rank of the two and equal to his own, not his superior. "We spotted some surveillance cameras in the room. They were very well concealed, but we used it to our advantage. We stealthily smeared a knockout agent onto her computer keyboard whilst blocking the cameras with our backs. As soon as she logs in to see who we are, her fingers will absorb the agent rendering her unconscious."
"How long for?" Said Julien.

"At least thirty minutes." Came the reply from the man in the drivers r seat. There had been a long-standing rivalry between Marcus and Julien, both attaining the same rank within their organisation, and certainly no love lost.

"What about the Chapman girl?" Said Sophia. "It is likely she will not go near the computer keyboard and will therefore be conscious."

"If she is, then we just subdue her and see if the documents are in Dupree's bag. If they are, we retrieve them and get back to the car."

"Look!" Urged Sophia. "The girl is leaving the hotel, but she is carrying nothing.

"Ok." Said Marcus, as he exited the car. "I will go to the suite and hopefully Dupree will be incapacitated. You three wait here and stop the English bitch if she returns before I am back."

....

I bought Salonge a box of two hundred Gitanes; it was the least I could do. I also stopped at the resident Chocolatier in the lobby of the hotel and purchased a box of chocolate truffles, box being the operative word. It was perhaps twenty centimetres square and forty centimetres high. But at 100 euros, I was shocked to see the inner space of the elaborate container loaded with far more tissue paper than delicacies. I exited the elevator and slipped the room card into the separate entrance to my half of the suite, and then did a *'Ta daaa'* bursting through the adjoining door laden with gifts. Salonge was slumped across her computer; her bag lay open on the bed devoid of any contents.

Chapter 7

Salonge comes clean

I was at a loss as to what I should do, having no medical training and not knowing whom to trust. Then I remembered that Salonge had given me the number for her husband in Thailand. At the time I thought it a strange thing to do, but now I was glad that she did; he answered on the second ring.

"Anthony, it's Kacey."

"Oh hi Kacey, is everything ok? He said, concern already revealing itself in his delivery.

I began spurting out the events at dinner...going to the tobacconist and the chocolatier...coming back to the room, and so on. I'm sure that I wasn't making much sense, but he got the general gist.

"Kacey, just calm down, I'm switching to video chat."

After a second or two his face appeared on the screen. He had a rugged sort of look with slightly more stubble on his face than that on his head. He had kind eyes though and I could understand Salonge's attraction to him.

"Point the camera at Salonge."

She had not moved an inch and her keyboard was

repeatedly making a beeping noise where her cheek was pressed down on several characters at the same time.

"Listen carefully. Do you have a mirror like a compact or something?"

"No, I'm sorry, I don't."

"Is Salonge's bag still in the room?"

"Yes, it's on the bed but they have taken my grandad's documents."

"Don't worry about that. She should have a compact mirror in the side pocket, see if it's there."

I ran to the bed and dug through her handbag. "I have it."

"Now listen carefully. Place the mirror directly under her nose, hold it perfectly still for at least thirty seconds and focus your camera phone at the glass reflection."

I did as her husband instructed and immediately realised the purpose. Every two seconds the glass would mist up and then clear; she was breathing steadily.

"Ok, now how long do you think she was in the room before you returned?"

"I'm not sure. Maybe thirty minutes."

"Right, I need you to carefully look over her body, anywhere where there is exposed skin. Start at the face and neck, then the wrists followed by the ankles. Make sure the camera follows your eyes."

"What are we looking for?" I said.

"Well, there are three possibilities. One is that someone was waiting behind a door and used chloroform, but I doubt that is the case. They probably know who she is by now and would not want to tackle her at close quarters. Given her position it is more likely that they either used a dart gun, which is what you are looking for now, or put some agent on the keyboard and possibly other items in the room, so be incredibly careful what you touch.

I gently lowered the collar of her lilac 'all-in-one' but could see nothing. I pulled back her sleeves and then each trouser leg, again there was no feathered implement visible.

"Kacey, go to the bathroom and get plenty of tissue. See if there is any bleach or household cleaner under the sink unit. If not, just soak the scrunched-up tissue with perfume. Gently lower Salonge to the floor and scrub the side of her face first, then do the same with the pads of her finger. As soon as you have done that, repeat the process with fresh water. Don't leave it too long between both procedures or her skin could become permanently damaged."

As the last digit of her left hand had been cleansed, I saw Salonge's eyes flicker, and she let out a slight groan. Anthony saw it too from my phone now perched against the skirting board.

"Well done, Kacey, she should come around quite quickly but will be disorientated. Do you think you can get her onto the bed?"

"I think so." I said as I raised her back from the floor, slipped my arms underneath her armpits, and tried to lift. Although slender, the dead weight of her unconscious body was proving difficult. I managed to drag her towards the foot of the bed and sat on the edge, my arms still tucked beneath hers. I then launched myself backwards in a Judo type manoeuvre whilst clinging on for dear life. The cantilever effect was instantaneous and and we both ended up in a heap, albeit in the desired location. I shuffled from beneath my now groaning cousin and slipped a pillow under her head.

"Good." Came Anthony's voice from across the room. You now need to run to a pharmacy, get some anti-inflammatory pills, some antihistamines, and a couple of litres of water. The medication will ease the reaction and the water will flush out the toxin. If all goes well, she should be back to normal within the hour. If there is any change for the worse...any at all...you must call me back immediately."

A girl in her early twenties running through the corridors of the George V was not something that they were accustomed to and there were many disapproving looks, but I didn't care. I was back in the room within ten minutes and was surprised to see Salonge had propped herself up with the full complement of pillows behind her back.

I ran towards her but held back from giving her a hug, the alarm in her eyes at my approach telling me that she was still feeling particularly delicate.

"I hope yo have brought some pain killers." She said, forcing a smile.

"I've bought the whole contents of the pharmacy next door."

"For god's sake pass me the water." She said, glaring at the Evian labels showing through the ultra-thin plastic bags. "My tongue feels bigger and fluffier than these goose down pillows."

I sat with her for another half an hour, waiting for her to feel better before addressing the subject at hand.

"Salonge, I thank you so much for coming to help me. But the whole quest has finished before it has begun, they have taken the ancient parchments. You could have been killed, and for what? A bunch of old documents!"

"My dear Kacey, you couldn't be more wrong. Our quest has just started, and they have already made three monumental mistakes."

"I don't understand." I said.

"Firstly, Anthony will now be able to use the camera footage and identify them. I guessed that they would try to drug me but knowing, as I am sure they do, that I am ex Interpol and FBI, would not risk a fatal attack... they just wanted the documents."

"And they have them." I said, in a sombre tone, thinking of how quickly I had failed my grandfather. Actually, how I had failed generations of my family within a few days of the documents being passed to me.

"So what was their second mistake?"

"That was their second mistake Kacey. Before I checked in to the hotel, I had previously booked another room disguised as a rich, single old woman. She is staying in a smaller suite below this one, and that is where your grandad's documents are."

"But I saw them in your bag." I said, now totally confused.

"No Kacey. What you saw, and what they now have, is a Latin translation of last season's Chicago Cubs games. That was Anthony's idea, it's his favourite team. We work closely with British intelligence who expertly mocked up the fake documents making them look like they are hundreds of years old. They were expressed here from their British Embassy whilst we were dining. When I excused myself to use the bathroom I sprinted to my room, switched the documents, took the real ones to the suite below, and returned.

I let out a loud laugh. "So what was their third mistake?"

"Ah, their third mistake was pissing off two strong, brave women with more brains than Albert Einstein and more tricks up their sleeve than Harry Houdini.

"So what is our next move?"

"Our next move is to get some well-deserved sleep. Don't forget, the armour mentioned in your grandfather's documents is being displayed at the rare outdoor event in front of the Musée de l'Armée des Invalades here in Paris tomorrow, June the 21st. Anthony sent through some information about the armour which you should hear.

There is some dispute as to the authenticity of the display being Joan's actual armour. It was purchased in 1996 by an antiques dealer named Pierre de Souzy from a Parisian collector who claims it was in his family for two hundred years. It was only when this petite suit of armour was modelled by his fourteen-year-old daughter, and his wife whimsically stated that she looked like Joan of Arc, that he decided to investigate. The armour itself is of the correct date, and the damage to the metal is consistent with her reported battle wounds, but many historians believe it not to be Joan's. Even so, it is a starting point, and we should be there. If your grandad is correct, and this is the genuine article, then something should be revealed to you on the longest day of the year."

"This really is a true quest of bravery and honour, isn't it Salonge."

"Yes, it is my brave young cousin."

Salonge slid gingerly off the bed, saying that she would retrieve the genuine documents and fetch them back to our room.

"Be careful." I said. Should I come with you?"

"No that's fine. At the moment I think that our intruders will be getting an ear bending."

"Oh, and Salonge."

"Yes."

"Anthony... I see why you married him. He's quite cute in a big cuddly bear kind of way."

"Hands off, he's way too old for you."

I drifted into a deep sleep long before Salonge had returned. I dreamt that Salonge and I were charging across fields at an invisible enemy, mounted upon magnificent horses whose shining armour matched that of our own.

Chapter 8

A good year for the Cubbies

Marcus was feeling rather pleased with himself as he returned to the front passenger seat of the Peugeot, eager to show Pierre what he believed to be the genuine ancient parchments. His accomplice in the earlier room search was still in the passenger seat, occasionally smirking in the rear-view mirror at Julien and Sophia's glum faces.

Julien was silently chastising himself for being so naively receptive to the invite for dinner by his attacker at the Gare du Nord. It was obvious that his cover would be instantly blown by so readily agreeing, and Pierre Cardout would not be happy at how Sophia and he had handled things. Worse than that, his rival within their organisation, and a person he despised, had completed his task perfectly and would be relishing every moment as he handed over the documents to their superior.

Julien considered Marcus a stupid, uneducated buffoon. But being Pierre's nephew, he had been fast-tracked to the same status as himself in half the time, something Julien had protested against vehemently. Since that moment they had butted heads regularly and there was no love lost between them; this would be a mighty victory for his adversary

For the first twenty minutes of the journey to the Chateau de Breteuil, no one had spoken a word. Marcus was concentrating on the roads which were becoming rather difficult due to the grease caused by fresh drizzle on the previously baked tarmac. The Chateau, home to the Marquis of Breteuil for generations, now widely opened to the public as an attraction, was another forty minutes outside of Paris.

The silence was eventually broken by repeated comments spoken by Marcus, innocently speaking his own thoughts aloud, but really intended to irritate Julien and pique his curiosity.

The teasing increased. "This is fascinating...simply incredible...ah, and these must be coordinates, Pierre will be pleased." Marcus turned to the passengers in the back. "With any luck my uncle will be so thrilled with these recovered documents he may go lightly on you two for your incompetence."

"What is so fascinating? Said Julien. "Do the papers have pictures because you can barely read French, let alone Latin."

"I may not be able to read Latin but there is no doubt about the age of the documents and there are clearly coordinates which will lead us to some great treasure. Also, even I can see that there is reference

to great victories of battle. Take a look for yourself."
Marcus passed the papers to his rival.

Julien's face dropped in shock as he stared at the first
page causing Marcus to to stretch his wicked victory
grin even wider. But the shock was a mixture of
emotions for Julien. He was elated that these were
obviously fake, and the smile would soon be gone
from Marcus's face, but it meant that Kacey Chapman
and Salonge Dupree still had the real items.

"May I take a picture of this first page?" Enquired
Julien. "I can try to translate during the rest of the
drive."

"Mon pleasure." Said Marcus. "Do let me know
what it says though. I should be the one to tell my
uncle, not you."

"Oh I wouldn't dream of doing such a thing. You
should definitely be the one to read the contents
aloud."

The first line of the first page translated as: *It has
been a steady year so far for the Cubs battling to
thirty-four victories, twenty-six losses, an average of
.567, slightly better than last year with an average of
.519.*

"I am having some difficulty translating for you." Lied
Julien. "Perhaps you should just let Pierre read them

for himself."

"Perhaps you are right. I suggest that you allow me a private audience with my uncle. Should you be required I shall summon you."

Julien no longer felt any pity for the smug idiot soon to be on the wrong end of a verbal eruption of Krakatoa proportions. Julien looked at the picture on his phone again. Marcus had been correct about one thing. There were definitely map coordinates identifying lines of longitude and latitude. He punched the numbers into the sat nav app on his phone.

Lat N 41 56 53.241

Lon W 87 39 22.864

The tiny map zoomed in on Rigley Field, home of the Chicago Cubs.

....

We had checked into a double room at the Hotel Muguet, a ten-minute walk from the *Musée de l'Armée Invalades*. It was a reasonable distance from where we had been staying, but closer to the Eiffel Tower, the peak of its iron structure visible from our window.

Grandad's papers were now in the safety deposit box

of the fictitious old lady in the room below ours at the George V. Salonge assured me that they would more likely follow us than suspect that we would leave them in the hotel under a different name. Even though the cleaning staff would be curious at the room not being used, the bill had been paid for one week in advance so they would be unlikely report anything until after that date.

I had spent the morning reading up about the outdoor exhibition set among the sculpted conifer trees in front of the Museum's grand arched entrance. The museum had been founded after the French Revolution and housed both modern and historic militaria, including the tomb containing Napoleon Bonaparte's ashes. I made a mental note to return one day, providing we survived this quest.

As we approached the magnificent building, we could see an unprecedented amount of police and security surrounding the event. This made us feel calm to a degree, but a little nervous that one or more of these officials could be on the payroll of our pursuers. We gingerly walked to the entrance and produced the e-tickets on our cell phones and passed through without hassle. There were concessions placed here and there where people were sampling delicacies and, unusually for the French, washing them down with bottled water as opposed to wine or coffee, today being incredibly hot and the longest day of the year. We spotted a spare white painted table of wrought iron with two empty seats and ran to occupy them seconds before an old lady and gentleman could steal our ideal vantage point . The couple gave us a disgusted look of disapproval, as did other visitors who saw us deprive the old couple's legs of a much-needed rest. Salonge queued for some refreshments, and I was surprised to see her return with two cups of English tea. I had made a handwritten copy of the instructions from grandad's document and retrieved it from my bag. I read the Latin transcript again, loud enough for Salonge alone to hear.

These words are true as God be my judge
No single man nor woman can reveal the secret, only
man and woman as one. Upon my breast is a
message for only the chosen to read. At the brightest
moment, on the longest day of the year, a person
pure of heart shall discover the secrets which reveal
my true story.
Joan d'Arc

"Kacey do not expect too much. The transcript indicates that there is a message on Joan's breast plate, but this exhibit may not be her genuine armour."

"Grandad, and now it seems you, are both assuming that I am pure of heart. I am not sure that I am worthy of that assessment. Even if this is Joan's actual armour, I may not be worthy of reading it. Besides, this all sounds like magical hocus pocus. How could I read, or see something that no one else can? It's a bit far-fetched, don't you think?"

"We shall soon find out." Said Salonge as she reached for my hand and gave it a reassuring squeeze.

"I am guessing that you know the relevance of, *only man and woman as one*?" I said, feeling my cheeks begin to flush.

"Yes, I know of your history from birth Kacey. In many ways Joan makes sense. Why should one sex be classified as pure? We are all God's creations, so perhaps one born with this gift is indeed the purest of all."

"So you think it was a gift and not a freak of nature?"

Salonge smiled and pecked me on the cheek, confirming her opinion without the need for words.

"It is now 11.40 am Kacey and, if your grandad was correct, all will be revealed in approximately twenty minutes." Said Salonge, a look of encouragement in her eyes combined with not a small amount of trepidation at my potential impending disappointment.

We made our way to the central exhibition area. There were glass cases displaying Napoleonic uniforms and armour. Others showed the crude, handmade weapons used by the revolutionaries who bravely stormed the Bastille. But there were two areas attracting the most crowds. The first was a group of reenactors creating scenes from history. The second was on a central patch of lawn with a sign saying, *'Armour of Joan d Arc.'* We maneuvered our way to the front receiving disapproving glances for the second time that morning. It was now five minutes to twelve and my pulse was racing. Each time the sun burst through the clouds Joan's armour gleamed and appeared almost white; a technique of polishing which had confused the English during the hundred years war, adding fuel to the the rumour that she was some sort of divine soldier from God.

The skies were getting ever darker, but with just thirty seconds to go, as if by another act of divine intervention, the clouds miraculously parted; the bright rays of light bouncing fiercely off the armour causing most visitors to avert their eyes. Mine however were transfixed on the writing which appeared before them. I grabbed Salonge's arm and urged her to look at the breastplate.

"What is it Kacey, I can see nothing."

"The writing silly, look at the writing! It has revealed itself to us, the righteous defenders of all that is good."

"It's no time for all this chivalrous banter, what are you talking about?" Said Salonge, angling her head this way and that whilst squinting at the polished metal.

I grabbed my phone and took a snap pf the script. I checked the image, but the picture showed no writing. I saw a young girl of about ten years of age making a crude sketch of the armour.

"Excuse me little one." I said. "Could I borrow your pencil and paper please."

"The girl tugged her mother's sleeve. "This nasty lady is trying to steal my drawings."

The girl's mother drew her daughter to her side. "What is going on mademoiselle?"

Salonge realised that I needed to write something down and urgently intervened, knowing time was of the essence.

"Madam, I will give you one hundred euros for your daughter's pencil and pad." She said, thrusting the note towards her.

The lady's hand flew out to grab the notes faster than a lizard's tongue snapping up a fly, ripping the pad from her daughter's grasp, thrusting it towards Salonge before she changed her mind.

"Now give the nice lady your pad and pencil and I will buy you an ice cream.."

I could hear the girl crying profusely but, with pad and pencil in hand, began to copy down the words which apparently only I could see.

As we headed back to the hotel, I explained to Salonge what I had seen and also that, although in French, it was in an historic format of speech not familiar to me so we may need help to translate.

We upped our pace, anxious to know what the message would reveal. I was so excited that I had not noticed the lady following us her, minus her daughter.

We turned the final corner before the Hotel Muguet, and Salonge told me to continue on whilst concealing herself into a shaded alcove.

"What is it Salonge?"

"Get back to our room and lock the door. It seems that the lady at the museum has decided to let her child buy her own ice cream and follow us instead.

....

The young girl was sitting alone on a seat beside the ice-cream concession, tears streaming down her face when the female gendarme spotted her. The official began striding towards the child, dragging an inconsolable women by the hand.

"Antoinette, where have you been, I thought I had lost you?" Said the frantic woman breaking free from the officer's grip.

The little girl ran to her real mother. "Momma, I couldn't find you. A nice lady said that I should stay with her and pretend to be her daughter., She took me to see the display of the tiny girls armour."

"Where is she? Can you point her out? What was her name?" Questions spurting from the gendarme's mouth, radio at the ready to catch the little girls abductor.

"She promised me ice cream, but she just ran off and left me on my own. Another lady stole my drawing pad and pencil."

"Please Antoinette, try to remember the lady's name...what did she look like?" Sobbed the mother, relief now being replaced by anger.

She said that if I called her Momma, she would let me have ice cream with chocolate sprinkles too, but she just ran away.   I want my ice-cream!!!"

9

Shambles at the Chateau

Marcus, having given the wheel to his subordinate midway through the journey, instructed her to pull up at the service entrance to the Chateau De Breteuil, deep in the beautiful Vallee de Chevreuse, thirty-five kilometres outside Paris. Sophia, being the less senior of the passenger team was sure that Julien would take most of the chastising from Pierre Cardout. However, there was no guarantee that Marcus would not stir things and throw her onto the pyre just to complete his triumph. Sophia could see that Julien was looking nervous too, but the little squeeze of her knee, and the sly wink told her that he had something up his sleeve, something which would turn the tables on the smug Marcus and his partner.

The gatekeeper had recognised Marcus as they approached, and the electronic barrier had almost fully opened by the time they reached the gatehouse. Marcus passed his identification to his partner, and she lowered the window.

"That will not be necessary monsieur et mademoiselle, Pierre is waiting to receive you all in his private chambers."

"Thank you, Antoine." Said Marcus, before silently

using a pointed finger to indicate the intended route along the stone pebbled driveway that his partner should take. They parked the car and Marcus led the way to Pierre's private rooms. He tapped three times on the enormous oak doors and waited until he heard a harsh *'you may enter'* from within. Marcus turned to his mini entourage with an evil victory grin.

"Oh, do not look so worried. If you are lucky my uncle will be so pleased with my achievements, he may forget about your bumbling efforts."

 Nobody spoke as they followed Marcus into the room . The grey faced senior enforcer, and overall number two in the Protecteurs de la France, was sitting behind a functional modern office desk, as opposed to something centuries old like the historic furnishings which filled the public areas of this tourist attraction. Four seats were arranged at the back of the room and one further chair was set in front of Pierre's desk. It was clear to all that they were to occupy the four seats until summoned forward, one at a time; Julien was called first.

"So Julien, would you like to explain the incredible inefficiency which gave away your identities, or at least your intentions, so speedily?"

"I'm sorry Pierre, it was my fault alone. Sophia was

just following my instructions... it won't happen again."

"Oh, of that I am certain." Said the enforcer. "So if I am to forgive this display of incompetence, I should like to know how you would do things differently, given the chance."

"I, I, I think I would have refused the initial invite to dinner." Stuttered Julien.

"And you think they would have called again? No they would not. They would have been relieved that the whole situation was over with and moved on. However, you and Sophia would then be of no use to the operation as they would recognise your faces."

"I'm sorry Pierre, I did not think."

"Let me tell you what you should have done. You should have reported it to the gendarmerie. They would have arrested the two females and you would have been summoned to press charges. At this point you could have said that you were not hurt and understood their mistake and do not wish to proceed with any action. And what do you think the result of this would be?"

"We would have gained their trust."

Pierre began to clap. "Ah, the penny drops. "So, when they then invited you to dinner as a way of thanks there would have been no suspicion whatsoever."

"I see that now Pierre." Mumbled a sheepish Julien.

"Well there is something else you do not see. If they had been arrested immediately, then we would have obtained the ancient documents straight away. Thank the good lord that my nephew was in a position to rectify your stupidity."

Julien did not need to turn around to imagine the smug smile on Marcus's face in his mind's eye. This was confirmed as Pierre, with a dismissive brush of the hand, indicated that Julien should return to his seat.

Pierre gave a warm smile to his nephew. "Marcus, please come forth. I assume you have the documents with you?"

"Indeed I do Uncle." He said, placing the folder on the desk. Marcus could not see the excitement which Julien was trying to contain at what he knew was to follow.

Pierre was proficient in many languages including Latin. He reached for the folder, holding it slightly aloft, midway between the desk and his nose, seemingly enjoying the musty smell of the ancient parchments before absorbing himself in the revelations held within. He almost ceremonially placed them back on his desk, poured himself a brandy, adorned a pair of white document gloves and placed his varifocals upon his nose. Pierre took a sip of the liqueur and opened the folder, delicately reaching for the first page. Marcus was so full of his achievement, and victory over his rival, that the moment almost reached one of sexual satisfaction; it did not last. Pierre's face looked incredulous as it turned ashen white, and his hands began to shake.

"What's wrong uncle, is it not good news?" Said Marcus, all his previous bravado having instantly left the room.

"Good news...good fucking news!!!" Hollered Pierre Cardout. "It's exceptionally good fucking news. That is if you are a fucking Chicago Cubs fan. Apparently 2021 could see them outperform their previous two seasons in the American Major Baseball league."

Pierre leaped from his seat sending it crashing into the wall behind him, tearing the fake documents into shreds and subsequently thrashing his nephew with the empty folder. He eventually regained his composure and picked up his thankfully, still functioning chair. He then pressed a security button hidden beneath his desk summoning two burly guards into the room.

"Yes sir." Said the first muscle bound Gorilla holding his snub-nosed pistol at the ready."

"Take those stupid bitches at the back to the waxworks."

The subordinates of Julien and Marcus were pleading for mercy as they were pistol whipped and carried out of the room. Julien and Marcus just stared at each other in disbelief.

The outbuildings and gardens of the Chateau were transformed into scenes from fairy tales by Charles Perrault for the enjoyment of the paying public, Little Red Riding Hood, Puss in Boots and so on, as well as historic scenes. The static wax figures that completed the scenes had an exceptionally good reason for seeming so lifelike. Encased within the coloured wax were many bodies of failed employees and enemies of the organisation ... there would soon be two more.

Pierre waited until it was just the three men left in

the room before continuing. "I am sick of the rivalry between you both. Even more so that this rivalry is now starting to affect the efficiency of our organisation. This must now stop! You two are now partners and I implore you to make things work or the consequences will be severe, even for you." He said, making a particular point of staring at his nephew. "The latest additions to the waxworks within the chateau grounds will be of the revolution...in particular, the cleansing of French imperialists via the guillotine. We shall of course need to test the working contraption on some dummies. However, I will not hesitate to make these tests on real life subjects, and at this moment you idiots are prime candidates. I need not tell you who will be the grieving sisters at the exhibit, they have just been carried to the waxing facility. Go to your rooms and I shall give you your next instructions in the morning. One of our agents has located the French traitor bitch and her young cousin at the Musée de l'Armée des Invalades. I am expecting some good news from her at any moment.

Chapter 10

Time for some Answers

Salonge was pressing herself as hard as she could into the alcove. The sun was creeping around the corner reducing the available shadow in which to conceal herself. She was counting the paces in her head, calculating the seconds before her pursuer should emerge, but that time had passed ten seconds ago. She was contemplating if she should risk revealing herself and peek back around the corner. Just as she was about to step into the light, the shadow of a head revealed itself onto the footpath, inches in front of her toes; the east west movement of the solar body now working in her favour. Two seconds later the woman from the exhibition came into view. Salonge held her breath for another few seconds until the woman had just past the alcove without noticing its inhabitant. Salonge leapt out, as if propelled from a Nasa launch pad, linking the targets right arm with her left, simultaneously thrusting the Glock gripped in her right underneath their knotted forearms concealing the weapon.

"How was your daughter's ice cream?" Said Salonge. "I'm sure you have been briefed as to who I am so it would be foolish to try and break free. I am also sure that, given your brief, you will believe me when I tell you that I have a real gun pressed against your ribs."

Her prisoner was silent for what Salonge correctly guessed would be around fifteen seconds. Salonge displayed a warm smile for the benefit of passers-by who would undoubtedly perceive the scene to be that of two close friends out for a leisurely stroll, linking arms as females of all ages often do. She was used to this period of contemplation from compromised assailants. The first three seconds was always shock. The next seven were anger at being outwitted. The final five seconds would see the captives body tense as they weighed up their chances of breaking free or overpowering their captor before relaxing again in acceptance.

"What do you want with me."

"Oh I think that is the question which I should be asking you." Said Salonge. "You shall walk calmy with me to my hotel. You will not try to cause problems, and you will not try to break away. I am disgusted that you used a child in your sick games. So make no mistake, I will shoot you without hesitation, and at this range I would not rate your chances of survival very highly."

....

Pierre thought his day had been bad enough, but this

was tipping him over the edge. The last communication he had just received from Adele, his most creative operative and mistress of many years, confirmed that the two girls who had deceived them were already getting closer to their prize.

Pierre, the two targets turned up at the exhibition as you predicted. I seconded the cooperation of a stupid child who had lost her mother, it was perfect cover. The younger girl from England seemed to see something on the breastplate of Joan's armour, which I could not... It was probably the angle of the sun. She was rapidly writing something down on a pad she borrowed from the brat child. I am now following the targets to their hotel and will try to retrieve the message which she was scribbling down. Here's the weird thing. I managed to take two photos. One of the writing pad and the other of Joan's armour...both pictures show as blank screens on my I phone.

Within a couple of minutes Pierre received another distressing message, this one from his DR man at the scene. DR stood for disaster recovery; this was only activated when situations went bad.

"Sir, it would appear that Adele has been compromised."

Pierre's pen snapped in half, succumbing to pressure from his shaking, adrenalin induced powerful fingers. "Explain."

"She is linking arms with Dupree. It is my opinion that she is being led to the Hotel Muguet under duress, probably a concealed firearm."

Pierre knew he could afford no more mistakes. Even he had higher entities to whom he had to justify any failures. During the following few seconds Pierre tried to process his possible alternatives but could find none. Another ten seconds passed, and several rare tears rolled down his cheeks before he sent the message which he knew he must, the most difficult of his life so far.

"Take out the asset. She must not be questioned by her assailant...she knows too much."

Pierre opened the draw to his bureau and withdrew a box of tissues along with the engagement ring with which he had intended to propose to Adele this coming weekend.

....

"You may as well shoot me now." Said Adele. "I congratulate you for outwitting me. But contrary to your obvious first assessment of me, I am a consummate professional and I shall reveal nothing to you."

"Oh you will talk alright." Said Salonge, jabbing the gun into Adele's ribs. "You will be our guest for a few hours until my delivery arrives. There will be no torture or threats, just a simple truth serum."

Adele stiffened again which gave Salonge a feeling of satisfaction. This woman had dealt on the dark side, but had not used, or been subject to, the most modern methods of extracting information. Salonge halted just before entering the hotel.

"May I remind you, should you misbehave, I will have no compunction about putting a hole through your intestines."

Adele turned to face Salonge with a look of defiance, but also one of resignation. Suddenly Salonge was staring at a pair of shoulders with a ragged mess where her neck once provided support to a missing head. Red spray and bone filled the air and subsequently decorated the cobbled pavement long before the rest of Adele's body realised that it should no longer be standing.

Salonge allowed the woman's arm to slip from hers and immediately knew what had happened, and also what the scene would look like to passers-by, her gun now in full view. Fortunately, there were no passers-by and the shooter had obviously used a silencer, so she just walked into the hotel and through the lobby to the elevator as if nothing had happened.

I was sitting at the tiny bureau having just translated the wording which appeared to me during the midday sun, when Salonge burst into the room.

"Get your things, we need to leave."

"Whats happened?" I said, still sitting motionless as she threw her case onto the bed and began piling the few items she had unpacked onto those still neatly folded.

"Now, Kacey. Move, move, move."

It was the first time that Salonge had spoken to me in such a terse manner, but it had the desired effect. I sprang from the chair and began packing if you could call it that. Within three minutes I was following Salonge along the corridor to the emergency stairwell. Salonge scanned the door and the push-bar, first checking that it would not trigger an alarm. We scampered down several flights of steps, our cases bouncing behind us as we went, until we finally exited at the back of the hotel. I spotted a taxi across

the road, its driver sitting on the bonnet sipping
coffee from a foam cup. I took the lead, heading
towards it at a rapid pace. I could hear Salonge
following close at my heels and felt pleased that she
clearly approved of this course of action. A police
car, siren screaming, came speeding towards us and
Salonge urged me to slow down. We both halted and
watched with fake curiosity as the vehicle sped past
us, just as you would expect from your average
rubber neckers hoping to witness some macabre
scene or spectacular crash; the official behind the
wheel gave us no regard. We continued towards the
taxi and Salonge took over, smiling warmly before
addressing the owner in her native tongue.

"I wonder what has happened. "she said. "I didn't
hear any crash or accident."

The driver shrugged his shoulders. "Probably some
degenerate stealing something from an American
tourist." He said. "The police in this sleepy own get
very excited when they have the chance to use their
sirens." The driver popped the trunk and loaded our
travel cases into the back. "Where can I take you
young ladies?"

"The railway station s'il vous plait." Said Salonge.

"Where are you off to?" He enquired.

I was about to answer, eager to test my French when Salonge jumped in, sensing that I had a location in mind revealed by my translation from Joan's breast plate and, if that were the case, didn't want the true destination revealed.

"We are heading to Bordeaux for a wine tasting weekend." She said.
"Things are incredibly quiet for me. I could make you an exceptionally good price to Paris Montparnasse. How does thirty euros sound?

"Parfait." Said Salonge.

I searched my bag for my pencil and pad and scribble a note.
We need to go in the other direction, northeast not south!

Salonge took the pencil from my hand and scribbled a reply whilst engaging the driver in pointless banter.

What destination do we need to head? Was it something translated from the armour?

The pencil came back to me.

To Compiegne, in Burgundy. And yes, from the

message on her armour.

We arrived at Montparnasse train station and retrieved our bags from the trunk. Salonge paid the driver and stood waving him off before hailing another taxi back to the Gare du Nord via a short stop at the George V.

Chapter 11

They can't just disappear

The man in the suit standing outside of the Hotel Muguet looked nothing like someone who had recently been peering through the sights of a sniper rifle. As the police car pulled to a screeching halt the man approached the officer, showing his secret service ID as he did so.

"Officer, I have managed to secure the area and borrow a blanket and some screens from the hotel. I urgently need to speak with your superiors on the radio."

The officer reluctantly allowed the man to sit in his car and use the communications device. Having worked his whole life in this relatively small town, the officer had never seen Secret Service ID and just hoped it was genuine.

"I need to speak with your chief of police." Said the man into the handheld radio.

"To whom am I speaking, and where is officer Fabron?"

"I am an agent of the Secret Service who will have

your badge and throw you in jail if you do not get your superior on the phone immediately."

The radio went silent for a moment followed by a crackle before a different man's irritated voice came through the speaker.

"This is the Chief of Police for Vallee de Chevreuse. Who is this, and where is my gendarme?"

"You can just call me Agent, monsieur. Now I urge you to listen carefully."

The man gave the Police Chief some instructions along with a phone number to call and told him to call back as soon as he was satisfied that the Secret Service would be taking over the scene and all trains leaving the local railway station were to be halted. A very humble Chief of Police came back on the radio within a minute.

"You have full control of the scene agent. How else may we be of assistance to you?"

"I require an ambulance to come and take this body to the morgue. I need a full alert to be circulated for the apprehension of two females. The first is French, aged thirty-nine with dark hair and green eyes. The second is English, twenty-one with light brown hair and blue eyes; he neglected to give the Chief their names.

The French Secret Service Agent, and also one of the Protecteurs de la France, knew that these country bumkins would have little chance of apprehending an ex-FBI Agent. He also knew that there would be nothing of use to be found in their hotel room, but he would check anyway. And truth be known, his superiors at the secret organisation did not want the girls harmed or even caught by legitimate authorities; at least not until the Protecteurs had retrieved the documents. The main reason for the instructions was to put Dupree and Chapman under pressure; people under pressure made mistakes, and they would hopefully be no different and reveal the whereabouts of the ancient papers.

....

The taxi pulled up at the George V and Salonge told the driver to wait. Kacey remained in the car, so he had no worries about the fare not returning. Even if the car were left empty, it would be most unlikely that someone picking something up from one of the world's most prestigious hotels would not come back. Salonge strode straight to the reception desk and produced her fake identification and checked out. The hotel day-manager did not notice that the attractive lady in front of him looked nothing like the old one who had checked in to the suite below our own accommodation He retrieved the documents from the safety deposit box and handed them to Salonge, wishing her a safe onward journey. She thanked him for a wonderful stay and left the George V, returning to our taxi oblivious to the concierge frantically punching the buttons on his mobile phone.

"Pierre, the woman of interest has just walked into the George V and retrieved a folder from a safety deposit box. The thing is it was for a different room to that which she had occupied."

Pierre immediately knew that the clever bitch had rented two rooms: so simple but so effective. He mentally chastised himself for not thinking of this. That didn't matter now. They had been spotted and there was no doubt that the genuine documents were now in her possession.

"Quickly Renaat." Urged Pierre. "They must have a taxi waiting outside. Get the vehicle's registration and hire company name... HURRY!"

The concierge sprinted to the revolving doors, pushing the vacuum restricted turnstile as hard as he could causing a rich elderly lady to stumble; something which would surely be reported to his manager. He had neglected to fetch a pen and pad but luckily was able to take a snap of the vehicle's rear on his mobile phone. His relief was absolute when he enlarged the picture by spreading his fingers across the screen to see a perfect image of the car's details. He forwarded the message to his superior via the encrypted WhatsApp type app; far more secure than that of the social media appliance.

Within seconds Pierre had established their destination and sent two agents to intercept the bitches who wished to change history and embarrass his beloved France and the Catholic Church.

....

As soon as they rounded the next corner, Salonge told the taxi driver to pull over and paid him for the full fare even though they had not completed the paid journey.

"What are we doing?" I said.

"Wait here. In five minutes hail another taxi...not the same company as the last one, I will be right back."

A few minutes later I spotted a private hire firm, a Mercedes, drop off a passenger on the other side of the street. I ran across and asked if he would take us to Gare du Nord, but I needed to wait for my friend.

The driver smiled, not wishing to be rude.

"I think that this particular taxi may be a little out of your price range mademoiselle. There is a taxi rank on the next street."

I didn't know what Salonge was up to, but my instincts told me that this private car would be a good choice and she would approve.; I needed to secure our ride.

"My dear sir." I said, lifting my chin and confidently raising my nose into the air. "It is a grave mistake to make assumptions. I am from a great noble family and am more than capable of meeting any such price for transit in your modest carriage."

The man smiled and leapt from the driver's seat to open the passenger door for me, bowing in a chivalrous, semi apologetic manner as he did so. I was proud that I had exuded such an air of authority which forced him to change his behaviour towards me. I then noticed his attention being drawn to something else. In fact, it was more transfixed, almost mesmerised. Even passing traffic had stopped to allow my cousin an unhindered, safe passage across the road. Salonge Dupree was gliding towards us, her hair bouncing gently off her shoulders. Even I was captivated at how she could look so attractive and elegant after a hectic day devoid of any preening. Ten minutes later, after exiting the vehicle, we were heading to the ticket office at the Gare du Nord and my whole world collapsed.

Both Salonge and I simultaneously felt hard objects pressed against our backs. I had never been in a situation like this, but the look that Salonge directed at me told me that these were handguns, and I should do as instructed.

"It is very simple." Said the man behind Salonge. "Just hand me the folder in your bag and you will be permitted to go on your way unharmed."

Salonge did as instructed, allowing her shoulders to slump in defeat. I could hear the man behind me tearing the manilla envelope open which contained my Grandad's folder.

"It's all here." He said to his accomplice.

"Please remain static and continue to face front. Do not turn around or move from this spot for five minutes." Said the other man standing behind my cousin. "It has been a great pleasure to meet you ladies. And thank you for allowing me to take these documents and undoubtably receive a great reward."

The tiny circular pressure on our backs disappeared and we stood motionless. Tears were welling up as I looked to the heavens, silently apologising to my Grandad. I turned to my cousin expecting her to have a look of sympathy and regret for being so easily compromised, but she was smiling.

"How can you smile?" I said. "We have failed so miserably in such a short time."

"My dear pure, innocent Kacey. You have much to learn about the methods of my strange profession. Our quest is still very much alive my little brave one." Salonge held my hand and thirty minutes later we were on our way to the place of Joan's capture in Burgundy.

....

Pierre was elated when he received the message that the ex-FBI agent and the young bitch from England had been compromised and the documents were now in the hands of the Protecteurs de le France.

Pierre sent a group message to all members of the secret organisation.

There will be a gala dinner tonight at the Chateau de Breteuil. 8 pm for aperitifs', dinner at 9pm…all must attend. The honour of France and the Catholic Church has been preserved.

Chapter 12

72 hours head start

Thankfully, the train was fairly empty, and we managed to find seats far from anyone's earshot.

"Ok, I think we have much to tell each other." Said Salonge. "Shall I begin, or would you prefer to start?"

"I think you should go first. You have obviously played another one of your spy tricks on our pursuers. The upsetting thing is that you never trusted me with your plans. They are my documents…given to me by my grandad, passed down through generations of my family. What gives you the right to play your silly games with them?"

"I am so sorry Kacey. I was only trying to protect you, and your inheritance. If they caught you, they surely would have made you talk and then maybe even killed you."

"Well that is my decision if I should take the risk or not." I said, but understood where she was coming from. "But what if it were you who were caught and murdered. My documents would have been lost to me forever if I have no idea where they are."

"No Kacey. My husband would have contacted you with their location."

"Oh, I see." I said, beginning to allow my blood to come off the boil. "So where are they now?"

"The first fakes looked real enough, but the only information they contained was the last few seasons results of the Chicago Cubs baseball team. I'm sure the people who stole them will now be in deep trouble. It was good to teach them a lesson not to mess with us. There were two sets still left in the safety deposit box at the George V. The real set have been sent by recorded delivery to a colleague of my husband in Thailand. Anthony will collect them and keep them safe. He will have them translated and keep in touch with us whenever we need to review their contents. That is where I was when we changed taxi's... I went to the post office and sent the real ones to Thailand."

"So the ones they took from us at the Gare du Nord were also fake?"

"Yes Kacey. However, these will be perceived as real. Much of the content is close to the truth but locations and items we need to search for have been altered. At this very moment they will be arranging for a team to head South West towards Bordeaux, not North East. If they translate the documents correctly, within the next few days, and after much misdirection, they should have retrieved a memory box which I hid in a barn when I was just ten years old."

Finally I allowed a smile. "What will they find?"

"Oh, I think I have some pictures of some boys I had a crush on. I am quite certain there is a poster of Plastic Bertrand along with a twelve-inch coloured vinyl of Ca Plane Pour Moi, their only chart success."

"What or who is that?" I asked, not knowing who Plastic Bertrand were, but guessed they were a group; I was correct. By now we were both giggling.

Salonge brought us back to the real world. "Do you have the little girl's pad with the notes you made? What was it you saw; I could see nothing?

"I fished into my bag and took out a folded sheet of paper. "As the midday sun hit the breast plate of Joan's armour, writing appeared as clear as day, you must have seen it?"

"I saw nothing Kacey, nor did anyone else."

"How do you know that?"

"Whenever there are inscriptions on historic items, there are always people holding up the queue until they have read every word or taken a snap of the writing to read at their leisure. You were the only person transfixed on the breast plate."

"I saw the woman take a picture with her phone!"

"As did I Kacey. But she is now dead, and her phone is in my bag."

Salonge, my wonderful friend and cousin never ceased to amaze me; I so wanted to be like her. I began to read the transcript as Salonge took notes, hoping that my translation of the old tongue was accurate.

I am proud to be French and Catholic, but even more proud to be what I am: A champion of all that is good in both men and women. As the siege of Compiegne becomes desperate, I fear my life's journey is close to an end.

A true account to secrets of my life's journey will be taken and buried for one true of heart to discover. It will be concealed fifty gallops north from the the mightiest tree in view of the place of my incarceration, wherever that may be.

"So, through your studies at university, I am assuming that you know where she was held captive?" Said Salonge.

"Yes, she was only eighteen when pulled from her white steed. The town had been under siege by the Burgundian's, allied to the British fighting against King Charles VII. When Joan's forces tried to break free from Compiegne she was captured and taken to Beaurevoir Castle, not far from where we are heading. I am afraid that there is only the small keep remaining of the original structure, atop a motte. But it is called the Joan of Arc Tower, so it's our best bet."

We were both silent, knowing that the likelihood of finding anything using these vague instructions, especially after the passing of six hundred years was, at best, extremely minimal.

"Salonge broke the silence. "It will be getting dark soon and we are almost at our destination, so I suggest we find some accommodation and take a look in the morning. Do not lose heart my brave cousin. I have a feeling that there are forces of good that will assist you."

Salonge did not seem to me like the superstitious type, but her words were nonetheless encouraging. And I knew she believed that I had seen the text on

Joan's armour, invisible to all but me.

....

Limousine after limousine was pulling into the
grounds of the Chateau de Breteuil. All were black
Mercedes with tinted windows concealing men in
black tie, and their partners in expensive designer
wear, halfway between cocktail dress and ball gown.
Once parked, the guests were offered hors'd oeuvres
with champagne and invited to enjoy the waxwork
attractions throughout the grounds, paying tourists
having long since gone. There was considerable
interest at the newest exhibit, a guillotine situated in
a miniature scene of the Bastille. The sculpted
models looked eerily realistic, especially the newest
looking young females mourning their recently
decapitated loved ones. It did not go unnoticed that
Julien, one of the enforcers for the Protecteurs de la
France was holding the hand of one female waxwork
whilst wiping a tear from his eye with his other.
There had never been anything other than respect
between him and his recently breathing partner; she
was more like a little sister come protégé than who
evoked carnal desires.

Four trumpeters emerged onto the grand entrance
and an announcement was blasted from the
loudspeakers. "Ladies and gentlemen, I urge you to

join in as our musicians play La Marseillaise."
Everyone stood rigid and and gave their best rousing,
patriotic performance of which even the anthems
composer in 1792, Claude Joseph Rouget de Lille,
would have been proud.

The guests were then led into the main dining hall
which had had its usual wax guests removed; their
historic information cards having been replaced by
name cards for the real-life diners. Pierre instructed
everyone to be seated as he announced the entrance
of their leader; a person whose face is globally
recognised but his name never mentioned by
members of the secret organisation on pain of death.

*"Ladies and Gentlemen, a warm welcome to you all
on this glorious evening. I am pleased to announce
that we believe we are now in possession of the real
documents whose lies could have caused so much
embarrassment to France, and potentially irreparable
damage to the Catholic Church. We shall be selecting
a team from amongst the distinguished guests
gathered here tonight to leave in the morning and
uncover the so-called secrets of Joan. But for now,
please enjoy the wonderful food, and the fabulous
entertainment. But first I should like to make a toast.
For God and France."*

For God and France, came the simultaneous response

from all those gathered.

....

Once off the train we were fortunate enough to hail the solitary taxi before he apparently called it an evening, this being the last arrival bar one at the station that day.

"Where can I take you to on this fine evening." He enquired, obviously happy to squeeze in one more unexpected fare."

"We were hoping you may suggest a local hotel or guest house." Said Salonge.

"What type of accommodation are you looking for." He said, rubbing his thumb and two digits together prompting us to give an indication of our budget.

"Oh, anything within reason that has good food and a comfortable bed." Said Salonge. "But we were hoping to find somewhere which has stables, we are keen horse riders."

I know just the place." He said, crunching the old Peugeot into gear. "It is a farmhouse not far from here. They used to keep many horses, but over time there were more horses than paying riders, so they converted half of the stables into simple hotel rooms.

The accommodations are basic, but the food is excellent."

"That sounds perfect." Said Salonge. "Do you know if they have vacancies?"

"If the rooms were full then my wife would have called me to say so and I would not still be in my taxi." The man laughed. "It is my family home. When things are not so busy, I provide a different kind of horsepower to tourists in the form of my old taxi. I would much prefer to go riding with you lovely ladies than sitting in this petrol driven monstrosity, but one must make ends meet."

Ten minutes later we pulled into a gravel yard with an imposing whitewashed farmhouse sitting square in front of the gates through which we had just passed. As we exited the car there was an overpowering, but pleasant smell of the countryside, mingled with the unmistakable aroma of horses, chickens and probably a few pigs. A cherubic lady came out of the front entrance and made her way towards her husband and gave his cheeks a squeeze before turning to face us.

"He really does work too hard you know." She said, holding one straight hand to the side of her mouth giving the impression that there was a secret she did not want her husband to hear. "I think he drives his taxi to avoid doing repairs around the farm or mucking out."

The red cheeked lady showed us to our room which, although a converted stable, was comfortably furnished and had a surprisingly modern wet room with shower, sink and toilet concealed behind a repurposed oak door. There was a wood burning stove against one wall with a small fridge at its side containing fresh milk and still water. Atop were two cups and saucers with spoons and some bowls with sachets of coffee, tea bags, and sugar.

"Excuse me madame, how far is the keep of Joan?" Said Salonge.

"It's not far at all. My husband could drive you there in the morning."

"Do you think it would be too far to ride there by horse?"

"Not at all." Came the reply. "At the back of the farm there is a bridle path that will take you directly there at walking pace. We only charge twenty euros per hour for the horses, and that includes riding hats and boots."

"That would be wonderful." Said Salonge. "Shall we say eight o clock in the morning?"

"No problem mademoiselle. Now I must get back to the farmhouse and prepare you some food. It's fresh eggs scrambled with spring onions, red peppers, and some secret herbs. It is an old family recipe; you will love it."

When the lady left the room, I asked Salonge what on earth she was thinking. I said that I had never ridden a horse before and quizzed her as to why we could not go via a comfortable...ish, taxi.

"First of all young cousin, if you cannot ride a horse, it's about time that you learned. Secondly, there is another particularly good reason for this mode of transport."

"And what's that?" I said, waiting for some jovial wind up.

"Your translation from Joan's breastplate stated that the secret which we must find is measured in horse paces, not feet, gallops to be precise."

I went through the transcript in my head, having memorised every word.... *It will be concealed fifty gallops north from the the mightiest tree in view of the place of my incarceration, wherever that may be.*

Chapter 13

The Professor Recovers

Professor Field had had the best night's sleep since the attack. The tubes had been removed from her arm and the headaches had ceased. The stitches on her temple still hurt though, and she hoped that the eyebrow hair above above her right eye would grow back. The doctor was doing his rounds, saving Beth for last, giving the two plain clothed officers who had been camped outside her door time to ask any questions. They had been there every day and night since the attack, waiting for her to awake from the drug induced sleep. It wasn't quite the deep coma that trauma patients are placed in when the brain has swollen beyond its available space in the skull, but it was a close thing, and she needed the rest.

"And how is my patient today." Said the doctor.

"I'm feeling much better thank you. Do you think I will be discharged today?"

"I think that is entirely possible. Let me just take your blood pressure and temperature Your injuries may look quite nasty still, but the swelling has reduced considerably

The doctor went through his procedures, taking notes as he did so.

"It would seem that all of your vital signs are well within range, including your blood pressure, which is a bit of a surprise."

"Why is that doctor...why would my blood pressure be high?"

"Oh, it's just quite a common phenomenon when an attack victim is questioned by police. Having to recount the whole nasty business gets the heart pumping a bit faster."

"I've not been questioned by anyone."

"How very odd. Two officers have been a permanent fixture outside your door since you were brought in. I just assumed that they would have some questions. Not to worry , I'm sure if they need to speak with you then they have your address. I am pleased to say you are free to leave. You will obviously require a chaperone to take you home. I will double check, but your young nephew should have been notified that you may be discharged and is no doubt on his way to pick you up."

Beth was confused, her mind wondering why the police would stand vigil only to disappear once she had awoken. And what was all that about a nephew, I don't have a nephew, she thought.

The doc looked up from his pad. "The nurses said that he was a very pleasant young man. He left those flowers for you last night along with a note."

"I'm sorry, who left a note?" Said Beth, still in a state of confusion.

"Your nephew, Johnny Valley something or other." Said the doctor."

As the left the room a different uniformed officer was walking towards him.

....

The previous evening Johnny Valatone had been relaxing in his apartment, smoking a spliff after a particularly good set on his radio show when he got the text message from Kacey.

Hi Johnny.

I can't tell you where I am, only that I am ok. This situation is more dangerous than you can imagine and has escalated. I need you to do me a favour.

Please check to see how Professor Field is. She needs to be warned to not trust anyone, even the authorities. I know you two have not met but I have spoken about you many times. Tell her you collected the item for me from Maria at the Uni Café and she will trust you.

Love KC

Johnny text back.

Sure thing Kacey. It's the least I can do. I feel so bad about asking you to leave my apartment.

....

The two diplomats were on their way back to the French Embassy in London. They had received a message that the documents were safely back in the hands of the Protecteurs de la France and there was no longer any need to interrogate the professor. It was a great relief for them both, having made a number of mistakes which did not go down well with Pierre in Paris. The first man had been a little overzealous in his attack on Elizabeth Field; he was only meant to scare her and obtain the ancient document. The other mistake was being spotted when they were parked outside Kacey Chapman's grandfather's care home.

....

Beth reached over and grabbed the tiny envelope perched perilously within the stalks and petals of the Tesco supermarket bouquet. For a moment she thought that she would not make it back to the laying position as her head began to swim and pains shot up her bruised arms; some from the beating and some from the injections and medication. She could see the silhouette of the doctor talking to someone in dark clothes and a peaked hat through the frosted glass, obviously a policeman. Now back in the almost horizontal, Beth opened the supposed get well note.

Hi Beth

I hope you are well. The radio station is going really well. You should tune in whilst you are recovering. I'll even play a request for you. Kacey said your favourite songs are Silence is Golden by the Tremoloes, and Dont Speak, by No Doubt. I collected your message for our friend from Maria at the Uni Café. Our friend has taken it on her travels. I have asked the hospital to call when you are being discharged and I will come to collect you.

Your loving Nephew

Johnny

Beth tucked the note beneath her nightgown whilst taking a long swig of water to clear her head. Could Kacey really be suggesting that she should hold information back from our own police? She decided that the best course of action was to fake amnesia, at least until she had discussed things with her 'new nephew'.

....

"Ah, you must be here to interview the professor." Said the doctor to the new man in blue. "She is well enough to be discharged but don't expect too much just yet, her memory could still be somewhat confused."

"Don't worry doctor, it's just a few routine questions. These random muggings are rarely solved. We just want to know what was stolen and if she can describe her attacker. ."

". "Oh I see, It's just that I thought that this was something far more sinister, with your superiors placing two plain clothed officers outside her door for the past week."

"I'm sorry...what plain clothed officers? Whoever they were, they were nothing to do with the Oxford

Constabulary."

The policeman rushed into the professor's room, pulled up a chair and looked long and hard at the patient.

"I don't know what is going on Ms Field, but I have a funny feeling that you know something and will say that your memory has not returned."

"I'm afraid not officer. Perhaps you could give me a few days to recover, and we can speak again."

The officer could tell that she was lying but opened his pad and began the routine questions anyway...has anything been stolen...did you recognise the perpetrator...do you have any enemies.

Just then the door to the recovery room opened and in walked Johnny Valatone.

"Well, well, well. So what have we here?" Said the officer.

Johnny's face went white, instantly recognising the man who had quizzed him when he had picked up the document from the university...the very officer who was to intercept Kacey at the pub later that evening when she never showed.

"Don't move a muscle young man. When I saw you at the University Café, you were picking something up for a person of interest in a murder case. And, if I'm not mistaken, it was some sort of historical studies about Joan of Arc."

His head turned slowly back to address Professor Field. "And wasn't it you who had left them there for her. Ok, I think you two better let me know what the hell this is about."

Chapter 14

A White Steed

The whole thing seemed so surreal given the overall situation; the tranquility of the farm, the cockerels and peacocks screeching out natures morning alarm call, and the waft of fresh coffee drifting to my nasal cavities from the pot atop the wood burner.

"So, sleeping beauty finally awakes." Said a smiling Salonge.

"What time is it?" I yawned.

"It is almost 7am. You must have slept for ten hours!" She said. "Take a quick shower, we have been invited to the main building for breakfast. I do hope it is not a mound of eggs again. And those secret herbs with spring onions gave me indigestion all night."

"Shouldn't we just get going, we have lots to do." I said, silently chastising myself for having wasted so much time on sleep.

"I understand your anxiousness, Kacey. But the brain is far more efficient when the stomach is fed. Even Napoleon said that an army marches on its stomach.

131

Besides, we would not wish to upset, or even give our hosts cause for suspicion. Trust me, it's better we play the tourists for a short while, we have time on our side for a change."

We trudged over to the farmhouse to find the door slightly ajar, steam spilling from the gap. Even before we knocked a voice invited us in. The husband, our driver from last night, was pouring coffee whilst his aproned wife was filling the table with bowls of bacon, more eggs, sausages, and some sort of sliced sauteed potatoes swimming in butter; it all smelled delicious though. The *piece de resistance* was the freshly baked bread.

"Please take a seat and help yourselves." Said the lady of the house. "Don't be shy, the Burgundy countryside followed by horse riding requires a hearty breakfast."

We all tucked in, and I was amazed at the mountain which Salonge had piled onto her plate. I thought she was just being polite by demonstrating the irresistibility of the morning feast prepared by our hosts, but having watched her devour every morsel, and then reach across for seconds, I was gobsmacked.

As eager as I was for us to be on our way, I was

stuffed and thought it best to allow the food to settle.. Besides, jogging along on a horse so soon after breakfast did not seem like a good idea. Also, I could tell that the innocent banter which Salonge was instigating was a fact-finding mission; do many people come here to ask about Joan of Arc; have you had many guests here lately; are any other guests due in the next couple of days?

"It's been particularly quiet lately. Said the husband. "The horses will be glad of a run out. If you are staying for a few days, it would be a great favour if you could rotate your mounts as opposed to picking a favourite."

"How many horses do you have?" I said, thinking it best to join in.

"We used to have twelve, but now we have just six. Only five of those can be ridden though."

"Why is that?" I asked. "Is it an old horse?"

"It's actually a story that may interest you." Said the cherubic wife. "He's a marvelous stallion of eight years old. He looks such a fine specimen we occasionally use him for stud with other horse owners in the region. He is a precocious animal though...a real handful. He stands at eighteen and a half hands and is of the purest white. It is said that his bloodline comes down from the horse from which Joan of Arc was pulled by the Burgundian archer before her capture. I wouldn't even recommend that you stroke that wild one, never mind ride him. Jacques, why don't you take our guests to get kitted out and choose their mount ."

As we approached the stables, we could hear the horses stirring, followed by a loud clattering which could only be that of hoofs against wood.

"That will be him, Vaillant Blancheur. I told you he was a wild one. Did you know his name t means Valliant Whiteness?"

It was obvious that he had said this for my benefit, Salonge being of French origin. The previous evening she had suggested the that I pretend to have little to no command of the native language, other than oui, no or merci; it was another trick of her dark profession. She explained that tongues loosen considerably if they believe that they cannot be understood.

We entered the stables the huge troublesome stallion immediately stopped misbehaving and looked directly at me, almost beckoning me towards him. On my approach I could swear that he was getting excited, in a happy way, not in anger as before. I grabbed a handful of hay and continued on, ignoring Jacques' pleas to be careful. The giant beast then stood still, like he was made of marble. He was just magnificent, and I knew that no other horse would do. I held my hand flat and Vaillant gently took the grass-like treat whilst I stroked his mane.

....

The head of the Protecteurs de la France had been first to leave the Chateau de Breteuil in the early hours of the morning. He needed to fly to Rome and report the good news to their man in the Vatican. He guessed that the Pope would also be appraised but, as was the case with himself, would never openly be connected to an organisation such as theirs. He also doubted that most at the Vatican cared too much about the pride of France, but the integrity of the Catholic Church was another matter.

Pierre was back in his private meeting room sitting behind his large modern desk. Three of the four chairs at the back of the space had been removed and one had been placed alongside what had been the single chair directly opposite his own. Julien and Marcus were summoned in and took to the vacant seats. The two men remained silent, patiently awaiting Pierre's instructions.

"I do hope the pair of you have had time to reflect on recent events and also your long standing, childish rivalry?"

"Yes Pierre." Said both men in unison.

"And you are both committed to working together harmoniously for the good of the organisation?"

Again, both men spoke at the same time. "Yes Pierre."

"Very good, now down to business. I have been awake since the early hours studying the contents of the folder. It would appear that all of the documents and maps represent a series of challenges. The second challenge can only be addressed once a clue has been revealed by discovery of the preceding one. Once you leave this room you will fly directly to Bordeaux. There will be a hire car waiting which you will drive to the Hotel Le Dauphin at 7 Avenue Gounod, Arcachon, 33120, Gironde. You must go through the check-in procedures, but this is not where you shall be staying, at least not for the whole duration."

"Do you have any idea what it is which we must find? Said Julien.

"The translation indicates that a treasure which reveals the true dreams and plans of a special child can be found at this location. I am guessing it is some kind of box or chest. It obviously refers to Joan d'Arc."

"Whatever it is, we shall find it my uncle." Said Marcus.

"Stop groveling you stupid man. Make no mistake, if you fail in this assignment then I would suggest thinking carefully about the wisdom of returning to Paris. From what I can ascertain, there is a village some fifteen minutes' drive north of Arcachon named Lacanau. There is a lake there of the same name, and on the north shore of this lake is an old house which, if I am correct, is the place where you must begin your search. Although hundreds of years old, it is still in use by the owner of a campsite within the grounds of which the property stands.

The first document says that the treasure can be found buried beneath the centre stone of the barn of this very house, which according to local surveys unfortunately may not still be fully erect, but its footprint should still be visible. Even though you have accommodation booked you may need to stay on the campsite in order to complete your task under cover of darkness. The necessary camping equipment will be in the trunk of your hire car. If you are successful, then you must return to the hotel and await my arrival, but under no circumstances must you open the box! Now be gone, and for your own sakes I pray that you are successful.

....

When Salonge was just a child, there was an elderly couple who worked for her parents. Both the old man and his wife had been active, and extraordinarily successful members of the French Resistance during World War II. In later years they cooked for her family, took Salonge to school, and even helped her with homework. As Salonge's father's fragrance business grew, and they uprooted to Paris and later Quebec, her father gave the family home, and its substantial grounds situated on the shore of lake Lacanau to the loyal servants. The old lady had long since died, but the old man, along with his own children and grandchildren, now ran a successful family campsite. Raoul was overjoyed when Salonge had called to see how they all were but was bemused by her request. She had asked if her old memory box was still in the storage room. He said that indeed it was. He stated that it, along with other items of her family's, had been well looked after and asked if she would like them shipped somewhere, not knowing where she currently lived. It was then that Salonge had made the strange request. She asked Raoul to bury the box in the centre of the old barn and to make it look as if it had not been disturbed for many years. She also said that men would come to the campsite soon to search for it. He was to allow them to make the discovery and leave with it in their possession. She also said that they were extremely dangerous people, so he must not intervene or cause them reason for suspicion. Raoul was excited. He knew some details about his benefactor's line of work, and even liked to think that tales of his exploits in his past were, in part, the reason for her decision to enter the world of espionage. Although now ninety-one years of age, he was excited to be given a task of such importance. Raoul grabbed a shovel and headed to the barn to create an ancient hiding place for the memory box.

Chapter 15

The real search begins

Jacques' wife went back to the farmhouse, mumbling to herself that allowing the young guest to ride the white beast was a mistake. Jacques too had more than a few misgivings about the wisdom of allowing this, but the young English girl was insistent, and they could ill afford to upset potential return customers. Jacques approached the stallion holding its saddle and bridle to be greeted by frenzied looking eyes and hoofs being raised into the air in defiance.

"I really do not think this a good idea mademoiselle."

"It will be fine." I said. "Give the saddle to me."

Salonge was also concerned but, knowing my determination and stubbornness, addressed the situation tactfully. "Do you even know how to secure the equipment?"

"Just pass it all to me and tell me what to do ."

Once I took the heavy leather saddle and bridle from Jacques, the horse immediately settled down, eyes turning calm and all four hoofs settling safely on the ground, unmoving.

"That is incredible." Said Jacques.

I walked forward as Vaillant lowered his head, seemingly inviting a pat or stroke along his mane. A couple of minutes later I was sitting upon the stallion's back, not remembering how I had secured the saddle or its spaghetti like strips of leather which completed the tackle .

"Open the stable gate kind sir, I have a quest to fulfil." I galloped forth as if I had been born in the saddle.

Salonge urged Jacques to prepare the chestnut mount as fast as he could and was soon racing after me. The sun was beaming directing along the bridle path which I had taken. Salonge reared her horse to a halt and squinted into the distance with one hand placed strategically above her brow. Powerful rays of sunlight were causing her pupils to contract, restricting her view of the way ahead. High upon a mound, some four hundred meters ahead, Salonge could just make out the outline of a magnificent horse and rider surrounded by a white halo of light. . The person in the angel like vision appeared to be wearing a knight's helmet. Salonge encouraged her mount forward at a slow pace, not quite believing what she was seeing. As she drew closer, and her eyes adjusted, the image became clear to her. . My elasticated topknot had forced my riding hat to sit unusually high, creating the illusion of a knights helmet. A trick of the light completed the illusion.

"What's with the strange face?" I said.

"It's just you were...I mean you were wearing...I thought you couldn't ride?"

"I didn't know that I could." I said, only now realising what I had accomplished.

"Ok." Said Salonge. "Let's go find Joan's keep. And I am taking the lead young lady... no more riding off."

We meandered along, Vaillant behaving as calm and obedient as a show horse, and his gait every bit as elegant. We passed through meadows and along shaded wooded paths, occasionally ducking our heads beneath low hanging branches. The events of the past week seemed like a distant memory. After a delightful forty-five minutes without so much as a mention of Joan D'Arc, I began to feel nervous, something which Vaillant could sense. I instinctively gripped the reins tighter and leant forward in the saddle, digging my heels into Vaillant's hind quarters as I did so. The reaction was instantaneous, and we bolted past my cousin into an open field. Vaillant continued to gallop until we reached a crest in the rising landscape. Once at the top and stationary again, another mound came into view in the distance, but this one had an old stone keep at its peak. My heart was pounding more furiously than I had ever experienced before, and my ride was frantically marking time whilst snorting the delirious sounds of a warhorse going into battle. I dismounted and gave Vaillant a reassuring pat on the cheeks at which point he immediately calmed down, as if knowing that this action signified no danger ahead. Salonge came alongside and also dismounted. In the distance we could see tourists busily taking photos of each other wearing gift shop plastic armour depicting Joan's coat of arms whilst wielding children's toy swords. We covered the eight hundred yards to the keep on foot so as not to spook the visitors, but as we did so Vaillant was repeatedly pulling to the right, trying to lead me to some other location in the vicinity. Once we reached the keep Salonge began visually scouring the landscape with her back to the keep.

"What are you looking for?" I said. "The instructions are quite simple. We just gallop fifty yards north from here."

"Read the instructions again my impatient cousin. It actually says fifty gallops north from the mightiest tree in view of the place of my incarceration. So there are four windows high up on the keep, each facing different directions. We have to take a view from each standpoint and assess which is the mightiest tree in view. It is from that point which we must begin our fifty gallops north."

"Well that's an easy one." I said. "There are no trees in view from the woodland from whence we came as the mound is obstructing the view, so that's one window we can discount."

"That is true Kacey, but don't forget, we are at ground level, however, Joan would have had a viewpoint from some fifteen meters higher. Did you not do trigonometry at university?"

I felt suddenly stupid, but also grateful that Sir Grandad had arranged Salonge's assistance.

"There are two more things to consider. Firstly, the mightiest tree may not necessarily be the tallest. It may be one of great design and stature...or even girth."

"I didn't think of that Salonge. What is the other consideration?"

"Trees, although having an exceptionally long life, can sometimes be removed because of development or disease."

We spent the next two hours sat upon our horses just
scouring the terrain for evidence of knolls or circular
undulations in the landscape which may reveal the
previous location of a once mighty oak or some such,
but to no avail. Although not a major problem,
Vaillant continued to encourage me in a different
direction to that which I intended, the result being an
overworked right arm, having to continuously tug on
his reins. Not only that, but my derriere was also
beginning to feel like it had been slapped a thousand
times with a cricket bat. It was now well past
midday, so we headed to a mobile concession selling
snacks and soft drinks as well as souvenirs. Neither
of us said a word but our demeanour told each other
that we were beginning to feel that this was a futile
mission. Then Salonge jumped to her feet and
approached the old lady behind the concession.

"Excuse me Madame. How long have you worked at
this monument?"

"More years than you are old Mademoiselle, and my
mother before that, and hers before that, and so on."

"Could you tell me if there was once a great tree
within view of the Keep?"

"Ah yes indeed. It was called the Tree of Injustice."

The old lady pointed in the general direction and said to look for the white flowers. I could see the urgency in my cousin's eyes as she rushed back to me and told me to remount.

I was suddenly full of energy again, even my behind refused to acknowledge the soreness. We set off at a cantor and were rewarded almost immediately. A large ring of daisies came into view, perfectly encircling a deep hollow which could only be the base of where the roots of a great tree once stood.

"This has to be it." I said. "All we have to do now is make fifty gallops north...but which direction is north?"

Salonge removed her watch and held it up to the sun.

"What are you doing Salonge? That is a watch not a compass. We can work out roughly where north is just by looking at the sun and the time. You really must begin trusting in my methods young cousin. This is something we were taught in survival training at the FBI. You hold your watch horizontally and align the 12 o'clock marker with the sun. The point between the 12 o'clock marker and the hour hand is precisely north. We need to be accurate unless you wish to spend months digging holes across the entire meadow.

I felt that we were finally we were getting somewhere. We made several runs north from the daisy ring using both horses to get the best average for the most likely location of our prize. Vaillant continued to pull, suggesting that we should be looking elsewhere.

Chapter 16

Field finds the correct Field

Johnny Valatone had accepted Professor Field's invite to stay for dinner after collecting her from the hospital, stopping to restock her fridge and cupboards on the way home. Beth had given him her debit card and pin number with which to pay the bill, still feeling too weak to trapse around a supermarket. Johnny had initially refused the offer, insisting that it was a favour to Kacey and besides, the professor must be tired. However, once she gave him the scribbled grocery list, consisting of many fine ingredients as well as a case of Malbec, he changed his mind; there would be a price to pay though.

"So, Johnny, do you know how to cook?"

"Of course I do." He said sarcastically. "You peel back the foil lid, boil the kettle and pour the hot water on the noodles."

"Ok young man, I get the gist, but it is time you learned. I have some research to do and am still feeling decidedly tender, so why don't you tell me precisely what Kacey divulged to you, and in the meantime, I will give you culinary instructions."

Johnny began his chores as instructed; peeling potatoes and slicing a couple of leeks whilst trying to figure out what a garlic crusher looked like. As he slowly familiarised himself with the alien environment of a fully equipped kitchen, Professor Field began firing questions.

"Your last contact from Kacey said that the situation had become even more dangerous, if that were possible, but she gave no indication where she was?"

"No, nothing. But I am sure she is in France on the trail of Joan of Arc."

Beth didn't want to chastise him for stating the obvious, so continued on.

"Right then, as the document Kacey showed me is back in her possession, I think the best course of action would be to trace the journey of Joan D'Arc from birth to death. Kacey must currently be at one of these locations. Now, Joan was born in Domremy, we should start there."

"No disrespect Biffy, but I think that you are wrong!"

Beth had to do a double take to be certain she had heard correctly. "Did you just call me Biffy?"

Johnny immediately realised that his DJ intuition had made the instinctive decision of applying a name which he felt more trendy or suitable.

"Didn't mean to freak you out Biffy. It's just that you are too cool for a name like Elizabeth, or Professor Field. You just got attacked by assassins and were then put in a coma by these doctor brainiacs. When you left hospital, you were like... 'let's get these dudes...they don't scare me! You are defo a Biffy not a Beth... a bit like Buffy the Vampire slayer."

Beth had no idea who Buffy was, but now felt strangely flattered by her new handle, and buoyed by the fact that a relative youth thought her cool. After a brief moment of wallowing in the flattery Beth snapped back into the mind frame required to assist Kacey.

"What do you mean that you think tracing Joan's journey from birth is wrong?"

"Let's put it this way Biffy. If you asked me what I did last week I could tell you. And even if I couldn't, there would be some evidence in the dishwasher or in the trash."

"Well remembering what you ate wouldn't be

difficult Johnny." Chuckled Beth. "You would only need to recall which flavour pot noodle you ate. What's your point?"

"That was not cool Biffy. What I meant was, I would start at the place of Joan's known death and work backwards. Kacey will have more chance of picking up clues by beginning at the end if you get my drift.

"Mr Valatone, you are a brilliant young man...that is how Kacey would do it, and also how the documents would be laid out.

Beth needed to concentrate, so printed off the final instructions for Johnny to complete the chicken and leeks with pancetta in a bechamel sauce, smothered with mashed potatoes, topped with a gruyere and parmesan crust.
As Johnny placed the food on the table, convincing himself that it was all of his own creation, Beth made a proclamation; "I know where she is. However, she may well be looking in the wrong place."

"What have you found?" Said Johnny, realising that he should run and get some placemats before the hot plates cracked the glass table.

"Joan's body was burnt at the stake in Rouen, Normandy, and the remains scattered into the Seine.

Some of her innards survived the first burning, so they torched them twice. Therefore, I can see no point in Kacey or anyone else searching at a location where nothing can be found. However, prior to her death, Joan had been incarcerated for one year in a keep at a castle in Compiegne, Burgundy. Tourists and school history classes visit this monument every year, but it is not where she was imprisoned; well not exactly."

"What do you mean by not exactly?"

"There once stood a great castle of which the current structure was just one of many towers which fortified the outer wall. As this is the only remnant left standing of Beaurevoir Castle, people renamed it Joan of Arc's Keep. The actual place in which Joan was held crumbled to the ground centuries ago and would have been located somewhere behind the line of defence. If you are correct young man, and Kacey is tracing Joan's journey in search of some secret, then it is here where I believe she may be.

"But I thought that she was later sold by the Burgundians to the English and taken to Rouen. But even before that wasn't she transferred to a town called Arras after making several attempts at escape from Beaurevoir?" Said Johnny, much to Biffy's amazement.

"Very good young man. Where did you study history? I don't remember tutoring you at the university."

"I never went to university. It's just that when Kacey told me about her grandad and all, I figured that I should do some reading up in case she needed my help."

"Well, your research is correct young man. But by that time, she would have been very closely watched and most likely had any possessions or writings on her person confiscated or destroyed. I am certain that it is Beaurevoir where our dear Kacey is likely to be. We need to send her a message with the information about the keep, but it needs to be coded in some way."

"Leave it to me." Said Johnny, taking out his cell phone. "Tell me what to say and I will use DJ speak...Kacey will work it out."

....

Our day had been fruitless. We were both exhausted and to some degree felt defeated, sure that we only had one more day before our pursuers discovered the deceit of Arcachon. I suggested that Salonge shower first as I was in no mood to even attempt raising my torso from the bed. I could hear my cousin talking to someone on her cell phone and had no doubt that it was her husband. The peacocks and cockerels had long since retired for the night, so it was difficult to avoid involuntarily intruding on Salonge's private conversation. I am embarrassed to say that as the conversation became more animated, I took a coffee cup and held it to the wet room door. When Salonge emerged from the plastic bathroom, wrapped in a bath towel, it was all I could do to swallow the cold coffee, pretending I had just boiled the kettle and was not earwigging.

Salonge looked towards the heating utensil knowing that it had not recently been in use. I sat expecting to be chastised, feeling stupid at using such a naïve ploy against an ex-FBI agent.

"My dear cousin." Began Salonge. "I was only speaking to my husband. I would never keep anything from you, so there is no need to drink cold coffee or hold your ear to the door."

"I'm so sorry Salonge." It is not something which a brave person of honour should ever do. Sir Grandad would be most disappointed in me. It didn't sound much like mushy stuff, you know, I miss you too and all that so it must have been about the quest."

"Anthony said that he has safe custody of your grandfather's documents and is in the process of getting everything translated. I also told him that any other help or information he can uncover is desperately needed as we appear to be at a dead end."

I was about to cry, yet again feeling that Sir Grandad had misjudged my ability to fulfil his dying wish. My phone pinged indicating that I had a message; it was from my friend Johnny Valatone.

Collected Biffy from the vet and she's doin fine. Gonna play some toons for you today. Slow down at the castle by Saint Etienne, Keep passing open windows by Queen and So close by Hall and Oats.

Salonge could see by my face that my brain was doing overtime. "What is it, Kacey?"

"It's a message from Johnny, but it's cryptic."

"May I see?" Said Salonge. Even better, just scribble it down. It is easier sometimes to play with such messages on paper. Besides, two minds are better than one."

We sat in silence for a moment before my cousin

broke the silence. "Didn't you say that you asked your friend Johnny to collect your old professor from the hospital. Could that be the reference to the vet?"

"Of course." I said. "Her name is Beth, but it would be typical of Johnny to rename her Biffy. The first song title, Slow Down at the castle by Saint Etienne...they know we are at Beaurevoir, and he is saying that we should stay here, I'm sure of it."

"And the second title." Said Salonge. "Keep Passing Open Windows by Queen, it must be telling us to ignore the existing keep."

"Yes, and the final track indicates that we are close to where we should be."

Salonge was silent for a moment. "What we need is a map of where the old castle buildings stood. Perhaps there is a local library."

A thought suddenly sprang to mind. "Salonge, could you ask Anthony to identify the maps at the back of my grandfather's folder. One of them must the layout of old Castle Beaurevoir."

There was a polite knock. "Mademoiselles, will you be dining with us tonight or eating in the room?"

Said a voice from the other side of the heavy oak entrance.

Salonge opened the door to see Jacques holding something behind his back. "I think we shall just dine in our room thank you monsieur."

"I thought that this would be the case, so I brought you a nice Burgundy as an aperitif. My wife will bring your food in about half an hour. It is roasted free range poulet."

"Merci beaucoup." Said Salonge, expecting him to turn and retreat to the farmhouse. "Is there something else Monsieur?"

"My wife was wondering how many nights do you intend staying? You have not said."

"We shall probably stay only one more night monsieur. And we should also like to go riding again in the morning."

"Excellent, excellent. I will go by the henhouse to collect some eggs for breakfast. Tomorrow you shall sample my wife's speciality; a six-egg omelette with peppers and shallots. "

Salonge closed the door and turned to face me with a

worried look. "I do hope the six-egg omelette is to share and not per person."

We both burst out laughing, feeling happy and positive once again.

Chapter 17

Sharing the Glory

The drive from Bordeaux to the Hotel Le Dauphin had passed relatively pleasantly, aside from the odd snipe about each other's driving skills. When Marcus was at the wheel his passenger would be watching the speedometer, stating that they would need to arrive in one piece if they were to complete their mission. When it was Julien's turn to dive Marcus would keep tapping the clock on the dashboard making huffing noises whilst mumbling that they had just been overtaken by a horse and cart. The hotel eventually came into view, and they parked the hire car in a secluded spot under the shade of a tree.

"Good afternoon gentlemen, if you could please sign the register and I will show you to your room." Said the young, but officious young lady at reception.

"Did you say room?" Said Marcus. "There must be some mistake."

She flicked through the booking register. "No, there is no mistake. One room, twin beds, shower with separate toilet…breakfast only. I remember taking the booking myself from a Monsieur Pierre Cardout. I assure you that I do not make mistakes monsieur."

Both men's shoulders were slumped, more from the
thought of sharing a room than the weight of their
overnight bags as they were led along corridors and
up two flights of stairs. As they followed, the lady
went through her practiced information routine.

"Breakfast is served in the orangery between 7.30
and 9.30. Unfortunately, we do not provide room
service for le petite déjeuner. There is no booking
required for lunch, but the evening reservations must
be made two hours in advance along with any special
dietary requests."

"Thank you, mademoiselle." Said Julien. "But I fear
our days and evenings will be really quite busy. It is
likely that you will see very little of us during our
stay."

"Oh I see." Said the young hotel manager as she
demonstrated the key card entry mechanism to their
room. "Are you here on business?"

"Actually, we're making a report on the area for the
tourism department of the French government." Lied
Marcus.

"Oh, I see." Said the manager, straightening invisible
creases out of her perfectly starched uniform.

Julien burst out laughing. "Take no notice of him. We are on a friendly fishing expedition. You know how it is with us fishing enthusiasts; up early, fishing all night, and so on."

The mademoiselle resumed her air of superiority as she did an about turn, clearly not impressed, and marched back the way they had come."

Once in the privacy of their room Marcus rounded on Julien. "What was all that about? If we had stuck to my story, then she would have bent over backwards to assist in anything we needed."

"Precisely you fool. She would notice everything we did and everywhere we went, trying to make a good impression: Knocks on the door with complimentary wine or chocolates, saving the best table in the restaurant just in case we made a booking."

Marcus realised that Julien had been correct to change the story so just went about checking out which bed felt more comfortable, choosing the one closest to the window.

The hotel manager returned to the front desk and made a note for housekeeping to double fumigate the bedding in room 214 once the smelly fishermen had checked out. It was odd though, she thought, they neither spoke nor looked like any fishermen she had ever encountered.

....

Pierre was tucked up in bed and sleep should have come easy, but that was not the case. The Chateau was silent now that the Protecteurs de le France and their companions had left, and the tourists would not be spilling through the main entrance again until 9am. He guessed that it was the excitement of the discovery which he was sure that Julien and his nephew would soon make; they wouldn't dare let him down again. Pierre used the in-house communications system to call his manservant to order some warm milk containing a generous shot of brandy. Another two hours passed, and he was still wide awake, this could only mean one thing...he had missed something important. Pierre rolled off the giant four poster which had once provided comfort to Napoleon himself and began slipping his arms into a silk night robe as he headed back to the study. He poured over every report since the whole emergency came to light but could find nothing, aside from too many mistakes; the overzealousness which caused the girl's grandfather to die; his men being compromised at the care home; Adele having to be terminated due to the interference of the FBI agent who seemed to have outwitted them so easily on a number of occasions. The last thought stayed with him for several minutes. Could this Salonge Dupree Mazur have tricked them yet again? ...Impossible! Pierre began to relax, putting everything down to excitement but, just in case, sent a blanket message to all of his minor agents in the field; the ones in corner shops or hotels that were just his eyes and ears and played no major active role in the organisation.

The PDLF is interested to hear of any sightings of two females travelling together showing a particular interest in the history of Joan of Arc. For those of you situated close to monuments or museums, please commit their descriptions to memory.

1.   Female, 21, English, 5'7, brown hair.
2.   Female, 39, French, 5'9, brunette.

Report sighting directly to me.

Pierre returned to bed and drifted into a deep uninterrupted sleep.

....

The old lady who worked the concessions van at Joan's keep near Compiegne was having another restless night courtesy of her crippling arthritis. She was taking another scoop of her medication, one more than the four suggested on the prescription, but tonight the pain was particularly excruciating. She would need to get the dosage increased at her next visit to the doctor on her rare day off. As she swallowed the disgusting fluid, she heard her phone vibrate; the dresser where it rested acting as a kind of amplifier. Her husband had been a loyal member of the PDLF but had long since died. As a reward for his service, they had continued to supplement her income long after his death. She remembered two girls that fit that description from earlier in the day but decided not to reply just yet; she could ill afford to send the organisation on a wild goose chase and risk losing the extra income if they were genuine tourists. She decided to see if the females returned to the monument in the morning. The old lady kissed the photograph of her husband and smiled whilst whispering a message to him, believing that he could hear her prayer.

My dear husband.

I think I have some information which our beloved Protecteurs de la France may find of great value. I do hope so my love. I fear that my aged bones cannot continue the gruelling task of standing all day to sell coffee and pastries to ungrateful tourists. I have decided to verify their identities tomorrow and then talk to Pierre. If I am correct, then the PDLF will surely pay me a handsome reward .

We shall be together soon; I can feel it. But a few extra euros to make my last years a little more bearable would be most welcome.

Wish me luck my love.

....

Jacques had brought the meal to our room along with another bottle of Burgundy. I can take my drink, although since leaving uni I had spent more time serving alcohol to others as opposed to consuming it, but a second bottle of red was making my head a little woozy. I was aware that Salonge tactfully filled her glass slightly more than mine on each pouring, noticing my developing slur. The chicken, served with roasted peppers and more home baked bread was delicious. I was still feeling tense though, waiting for confirmation that one of the maps in grandad's folder was the old layout of the castle. Salonge could sense my tension and tried to lighten the mood by stating that, with one less chicken in the pen, the breakfast may contain less eggs; it didn't work. Her face then turned both serious and also sympathetic at the same time.

"Kacey, Anthony will be doing everything he can, but it is now 4am in Thailand and we should get some sleep. By the time we wake in the morning I am sure he will have something for us.

Chapter 18

Back to the Keep

The next morning I was first to rise, deliberately clattering cups and saucers as I made the coffee, anxious for Salonge to open her eyes.

"What time is it...why didn't you wake me?" Said Salonge as she rushed to her bag and retrieved her laptop. Once it was booted up my cousin looked angrily in my direction before her face softened. "It's 5.30 in the morning Kacey!"

I gave her my best apologetic look. "Not in Thailand." I said. "I am so sorry Salonge. Last night I was so eager to hear news from Anthony , I set my watch to Bangkok time. It says it is past ten thirty there now, how silly of me." I grinned.

"Don't get smart with me young lady." Said Salonge checking her secure e-mail whilst attempting to conceal a smirk. "You were right Kacey, one of the maps in your grandad's folder shows the original layout of Beaurevoir Castle. The current monument stands on what was the south east corner of the structure and is marked with a small red X. The place where she was most likely imprisoned was in the centre of the castle, approximately one hundred meters north west. The plans indicate that this structure was square and not round, which is most helpful. And the four walls faced the compass points which is also convenient,

"That makes sense." I said, eager to demonstrate some knowledge which could be helpful. "In the summer months meats and perishables were stored in the rooms facing north, whilst the living quarters were situated on the south side.
But how does that help us ?" I said.

"Well, if it were round, and we have no idea where the windows were placed, we would need to search a full three hundred and sixty degrees in every direction for any possible tree of great stature. We now only need study four compass points from the real keep: North, East, South, and West. When you consider that the windows would have been quite small, and set a reasonable distance in from the corners of the structure, we have reduced the search area considerably."

Adrenalin was now pumping through my veins and, as if triggered by telepathy, I could hear Vaillant Blancheur excitedly braying in the distance. There was some kind of connection between us that could not be easily explained, but it was definitely present .

....

The old lady had barely slept, but not because of her
aches and pains; she had never felt more alive. Never
the less, she took one quick swig of her painkilling
medicine directly from the bottle and headed out to
her 1950's Citroen HY van. The old maid wanted to
get to Joan's keep early for fear of missing a life
changing bonus opportunity from the PDLF. Less
than an hour later she had breakfast baguettes
underway in her mobile kitchen and a pair of
binoculars tucked beneath the counter.

....

We were both ready to go by six am, but when we
heard the clucking of hens, we realised that we were
not the first to rise. Salonge ran to the door signalling
for me to join her. Our eyes strained in the dim dawn
light and followed the sound until Jacques silhouette
came into view, stooping inside a mesh pen filling a
basket with the days fresh, yolky produce. .

"Hello mademoiselles. You are up bright and early."

I took the lead. "Being our last day, we thought we
would get a full day of riding in."

"Morning is my favourite time of the day, especially

for riding." He said. "I have a little surprise for you after breakfast."

"And what would that be monsieur?" Said Salonge.

"You just wait and see. Come on, let's get ourselves fed."

At this sitting it was me racing to devour the food, hoping that the faster the bowls were emptied, the sooner we could get going, regardless of indigestion, or worse. Jacques left the kitchen table first and told us to join him in the stables when we were ready. When we arrived, there were three horses bridled and ready to go, but Vaillant was not one of them.

"What's going on?" I said, a little too curtly.

"I am sorry mademoiselle, I just thought that I could join you and show you young ladies some of our beautiful countryside."

I pulled myself back in check, prompted by a nudge from my cousin's foot. "That is very considerate of you kind sir, but my quest here only concerns the keep."

"A quest is what you are on, is it?" Said Jacques chuckling.

This time Salonge almost broke my toe indicating that I was divulging way too much information.

"My young cousin has a very important set of history exams coming up, and I am afraid she spent too much of the early summer at parties instead of doing her research. I brought her here to help get her back on track."

"I didn't mean to intrude. If it's ok, I shall just ride along with you to the old concession van and deliver this basket of food and then be on my way." Jacques gave a warm smile. "Oh to be young again. Anyway, there is an old lady that sells food at Joan's monument. Once a week I drop off bread and eggs along with some sausages and bacon. I will ride with you to that point and then leave you to your own devices. .   The poor thing has found it hard since her husband died."

I tried to recover the situation. "We saw her yesterday." I said, now smiling to make recompense for my earlier outburst. "It would be our privilege if you would join us, at least to the keep."

"And it would be my privilege to join you, mademoiselle."

"Just one thing kind sir. As fine a specimen of horse this is, it would be a great favour if I were permitted to ride Vaillant again."

The huge white stallion began prancing on the spot and I could swear that he was smiling, if horses could do such a thing.

....

Julien and Marcus were up bright and early for their so-called fishing trip to the campsite on Lake Lacanau. It was just as well that the rest of the guests at the hotel were still asleep, or they would surely have drawn plenty of attention to themselves. At this time of year most locals, and even seasoned fishermen visiting the area, simply wore shorts and plenty of sun cream. However, Julien and Marcus looked as if they had just bought the entire catalogue from Anglers Weekly; waders, wax jackets, wide brimmed hats with fishhooks attached, the whole shebang. At six in the morning the roads were clear, so it took just fifteen minutes driving on a semi-major road, followed by five minutes on a dirt track before the entrance barrier to the campsite and the owners old house came into view.

....

Fudge, Raoul's French Bulldog was, as usual, the first to hear the approach of any vehicle coming along the driveway. There were no new campers due to arrive until just before midday, so Raoul guessed that it would be the visitors looking for Salonge's memory box, although he was sure they believed it to be something quite different. He reached for his binoculars which hung beside his bed (a habit from his resistance days) and focussed his attention on the two men talking animatedly in the front seat of a rental parked some fifty yards from the barrier; it was definitely them. Raoul didn't bother getting dressed, or even comb what remained of his hair, wanting to look disturbed by the unexpected guests. He did, however, place his old homemade, snubbed nose pistol in his dressing gown pocket remembering Salonge's warning. Raoul allowed the doorbell to ring for a third time before he ambled downstairs, rubbing his eyes as he greeted the two men.

"Gentlemen, you must forgive me. I am not a young man anymore and I do not recall you having a booking. Let me go and get the register."

"You are not so old monsieur, and you are correct in assuming that we have made no booking." Said Julien. "We were just hoping that you may have a space to camp for a night or two and perhaps do some fishing."

Raoul had the whole conversation planned out in his head certain that he would be convincing, and things would undoubtably go according to plan. Besides, compared to being interrogated by SS soldiers during the war whilst concealing secret messages in unmentionable places, this was a walk in the park.

"I am afraid that all of the fishing swims around the lake are already occupied, or will be by tomorrow afternoon. They have been pre booked you see. You are welcome to camp anywhere close to the house though and use the designated communal fishing areas such as the jetty."

Marcus pitched in. "That will be fine. Is there a bait shop on the site?"

"I'm afraid not. The serious anglers, searching for big carp and so on, bring their own. The ones that fish for fun just dig for worms in shaded areas where the soil remains damp."

"I see that you have a barn." Said Julien. "Is it old?"
"That depends on your definition of old, young man. It is certainly older than you, but definitely younger than me. Both myself and the barn have unfortunately seen better days."

Julien's heart momentarily sank before a question from Marcus surprisingly rescued their hopes.

"Your house is charming but appears to be many hundreds of years old. Is there another, perhaps rundown barn which is no longer in use? Rotting wood and so forth are like five-star hotels for worms, slugs and many other kinds of bait."

"No, that is the only barn. Or should I say, that is where the previous barns have always stood. I find it quite incredible how talented the craftsmen of years gone by were. Do you know that barn sits on the same footings which were laid God knows how many hundreds of years ago? And that goes for the clay floor tiles too. Although they are in a sad state of disrepair, can you believe that they are the very same tile flooring laid when the first structure was built some six hundred years ago?

Both men looked at each other; *it has to be buried there.*

If it is ok with you Monsieur." Said Julien. We would like to pitch a tent close to the old barn and dig around inside for some fish food for the morning."

"Please yourselves." Said Raul. "But it will still cost you 40 euros per night."

Raoul took their money and closed the door, rushing to the monitor beside his bed; this would be far more fun than reality tv, he thought. Fudge, his loyal companion, leapt onto the space beside his loving owner and also stared at the screen, maintaining a low grumble of dislike towards the new guests.

Chapter 19

Staying Ahead, or just about.

Jacques could not believe what he was witnessing. Vaillant Blancheur was leading the trio of horses, demonstrating impeccable behaviour, an elegant gait, and a proud demeanour. The young English girl who sat high in his saddle looked like a person of nobility at a royal parade but there was something else, almost an air of fearless determination.

As we emerged from our wooded canopy for a second time my white steed reared up on his back legs and then began a full-on gallop towards the ruins. It was all that Salonge and Jacques could do to keep us in sight never mind match our pace; it was exhilarating. Vaillant was again doing his best to veer in a different direction from that which I was aiming, but I eventually won the battle, and he reluctantly obeyed my tugs on his reins. When the others eventually joined me I dismounted and suggested we have a coffee and order a couple of baguettes for later as we would most likely be out for quite some time. Besides, the sad story of the old lady at the concession van having lost her husband, and subsequently struggled financially, made me feel that we should support her in some small way. There was another, more important reason though. I wanted Jacques to be well on his way back to the farm before we resumed the search for one of Joan's treasures...or at least another clue. When the old lady saw the three of us together her eyes lit up and a wide smile spread across her face.

"Please mademoiselles, you must allow me to pay for your refreshments and le déjeuner as it is included in the price of your stay." Said Jacques.

"Merci beaucoup." Said Salonge, her eyes telling me that a refusal would most likely offend.

Jacques approached the large square hole in the side of the Citroen van which acted as a counter for the concession and handed over this week's donations from his farm.

"Thank you, Jacques. What would I do without the kind help of you and your lovely wife?"

"It is our pleasure, Madam Dupont. How is the arthritis?"

"It is getting worse by the day. However, there is a possibility that I will not have to work these gruelling hours for very much longer."

"Oh, that is good news." Said Jacques. "Have you won the lottery, or come into some great inheritance without telling us?" Laughed Jacques.

Madam Dupont beckoned Jacques closer by repeatedly bending her index finger, indicating that she had something of great importance to discuss which must not be overheard. "I see that you have guests. I would say that the older one looks to be around thirty-nine and undoubtedly French."

"Yes, she is French, and I assume that you are probably fairly accurate with the age, but I would never ask a lady such a thing."

"Of course, of course. And am I correct in assuming that the younger girl is English and has a great interest in researching Joan of Arc?"

"Once again you are correct Madam Dupont, but what is this all about?"

Madam Dupont beckoned him even closer. "Jacques, you were once a member of Le Protecteurs de le France, and you had very good reasons for leaving. But I have received a message from the PDLF that they are urgently seeking the whereabouts of two such ladies, and a high price will be awarded for information regarding their whereabouts. Tell them that the baguettes are with my compliments. How long are they intending to stay with you?"

"They leave in the morning."

"Jacques, they must not leave. Keep them at the farm as long as you can. I shall report the sighting."

Jacques felt awful. He loved France, and also the Catholic Church, but the PDLF were ruthless. How could these young ladies be a threat? If he had not previously been a member of this organisation, then his own daughter would be alive today; she would have been around the older girls age, and they were so alike.

Jacques was walking slowly towards us with a troubled look on his face.

"Are you alright monsieur?" I said to Jacques, as Salonge angled her head towards the old lady who now appeared to be suddenly very preoccupied.

"Yes, I'm fine." He said, although his eyes did not support that statement. "Here is your lunch and some bottled water. I must be on my way."

With that he rode off.

"Something is wrong." Said Salonge. "We need to find this next clue, and fast."

Madam Dupont was frantically looking for her cell phone and finally located it hiding behind the bread bin. She pressed the button with which to send a message to Piere , but a blank screen stared back at her. She shook the tiny, dated Nokia and tried again. This time she was rewarded with two seconds of a small red bar and the words *'Low Battery.'*

The old lady put up the 'closed' sign and rushed the final orders to the waiting customers, many of whom mumbled displeasure at the slap dash presentation of the food. Dupont battened down the hatch and leapt like a gazelle, not an old lady, into the driver's seat and struggled to slot the key into the ignition, excitement causing her aged hands to shake uncontrollably. Madam Dupont was furiously pumping the gas pedal, so when she finally engaged the engine, it backfired and let out a vast plum of black smoke from its rusted exhaust.

....

"What's wrong, Jacques. You look like you have seen a ghost." Said his wife.

"It is our two guests."

"They are wonderful young ladies. How can they be

the cause of such a worried look on my handsome husband's face?"

"Madame Dupont has said that the Protecteurs de le France are urgently looking for two people fitting their description."

"You must warn the girls. You know what will happen if those beasts get hold of them."

"But what will happen to us...to you... if we do warn them? Madam Dupont will surely tell the Protecteurs that the girls were our guests and that she told me to keep them here."

"My dear Jacques, the so called Protecteurs did not think twice about sending our daughter on an impossible mission knowing that she would probably die. They only allowed you to resign from your commission because they thought you were too emotionally scarred to be of any more use."

"My dear wife, don't you see? They will hurt you, not me, if I assist these girls. Anyway, I hardly know them, and they may well be guilty of something terrible for all we know."

"That is ridiculous Jacques, and you know it. If you allow those young ladies to be harmed then you are not the man whom I married."

Chapter 20

Another clue, another location

Raoul was laughing uncontrollably watching the two fake fishermen trying to erect their tent. Luckily, he had already made a flask of coffee and selected some snacks for potentially his longest night of tv in years. There was also a bowl of water on the floor and some doggy treats for Fudge.

If these people, as Salonge had intimated, were a danger to him, then it was a mystery as to how. They were tripping over guy lines, pushing each other in the chest whilst animatedly gesturing as to the correct way the structure should be erected. Having said that, Raoul had learnt long ago that more deaths and injuries are caused by incompetent fools; an accidental discharge of a weapon or setting too short a time on the fuse. However, the darker haired of the two appeared more capable. He had those ruthless eyes too; the type which had belonged to many of the SS all those years ago; the type that appeared dead, and only came to life when observing or inflicting pain.

Now that the new guests were safely inside their tent, Raoul decided to have a final bathroom break before episode two began. He also thought it best to allow his dog to enjoy the same pleasure outside; he couldn't afford the scene to appear too quiet for fear of arousing suspicion at the lack of normal activity. Fudge was pleased at being permitted to conduct later than usual ablutions, and eagerly scampered out of the door to investigate if trees smelt differently at night. After having watered the base of several bushes, Fudge then lowered his head and cautiously approached the newly erected canvas: canine curiosity getting the better of him. Raoul could hear one of the men shooing Fudge away; *Get lost you smelly mutt...fuck off, sniff somewhere else*. Fudge stood defiantly by the zipped entrance to the temporary shelter, challenging their rights of residence on his favourite patch of grass. Eventually one of the men opened the zipped slat in an attempt to appear more forceful, at which point the little French Bulldog cocked his leg and sprayed the final remains of his bladder into the man's face. Raoul ran across the cool grass to retrieve his pet, apologising to the occupants inside the tent. He picked up his beloved dog and verbally scolded him whilst simultaneously stoking his head and feeding him some treats. Raoul and his pet returned to the comfort of the bedroom and set the motion alerts in the old barn to active.

Fudge was soon fast asleep, curled upon the spare pillow beside his owner, comforted by the warmth of

Raoul's bowed arm and familiar smell. His owner was at the point of joining his little friend in the land of sweet dreams when the monitor bleeped and sprang to life. The image on the screen was initially totally black and then suddenly bright white. Raoul was cursing whilst waiting for his eyes to adjust and his mind to reengage. Seconds later the screen became clear, and Raoul made sense of the confusion. As the men had entered the barn in total darkness the infra-red cameras had engaged, having detected motion. . When one of the men had turned on his torch it momentarily caused a white out effect on Raouls monitor; eyes and lenses now adjusted, the men's images became clear. A second torch was lit making the scene appear as if in daylight. The slightly shorter, lighter haired of the two was carrying a bucket and a small hand trowel, obviously using the props to back up their wormy bait searching alibi should they be disturbed. The taller, more dangerous of the two was carrying a crowbar and a shovel, pacing back and forth in a grid type formation, repeatedly banging the shovel on the floor tiles hoping to identify a hidden chamber by the change in sound.

"Marcus, over here. I think I have found something."

Julien tapped the gardening implement on four large tiles encircling a centre one. Each time he tapped the outside clay, there was a dull thud. When he pounded the tool on the centre tile there was a perceivably higher-pitched noise, almost an echo.

"Here, take this." Said Julien, handing him the crowbar. "Try and wedge it under this tile."

Marcus began eagerly scraping dirt out from around the four-foot square floor tile until he could eventually see its bottom edge. He then forced the crowbar underneath and applied all of his weight. As the gap widened, Julien slid his shovel in beside the crowbar and managed to lever the tile to one side. Both men shone their torches into the cavity before them and turned to each other with genuine smiles.

"This has to be it." Said Marcus. "It's a little smaller than I anticipated but it definitely looks to be old enough."

"Agreed ." Said Julien. "This is where Pierre's documents told us to look, it does appear to be very old, and it has been well hidden. Let's lift it out and get back to the hotel."

Raoul watched as the men briefly examined their discovery, happy that he had replaced Salonge's original memory box with a much older relic, placing her knick-knacks inside before attaching the oldest rusty lock he could find. Raoul rolled out of bed to fetch his binoculars and made his way to the landing window at the top of his staircase and waited. The two men carried the box and placed it in the trunk of their car. They then drove off leaving their entire camping and fishing equipment behind. Raoul was most pleased with himself. Not just with his deception, but also that he had placed one of the tracking devices from his static caravans underneath the back wheel arch of their vehicle. He knew that it was a rental, and that they would have used fake ID, but it could prove useful to know what their movements were after finding the box.

Raoul sent a message to Salonge.

The rats have taken the bait!

....

(Earlier that day at the keep)

We watched as Jaques disappeared over the crest of the hill above the woods, increasing to a gallop as he did so. The old lady in the food van was bunny hopping down the road, tooting her horn at ramblers blocking her exit.

"I think we should go." Said Salonge. "If this clue, or

treasure, has remained hidden for six hundred years, then it will be safe until we can return."

"No, we must find it today!" I said through gritted teeth.

Salonge thought for a moment and glanced at her watch. "Two hours... then we go."

She pulled out the map containing the footprints of the old castle.

"I suggest we do a cantor around the circumference to see if we can spot any other evidence of where a large tree once stood. We then, one by one, try to ascertain if it could have been seen from the castle, agreed?"

"Agreed." I said.

Just then Salonge's phone buzzed; it was a message from Anthony.

We have managed to get some more information which could save you lots of time. One of the documents is a transcript of a letter Joan wrote during her first days of incarceration at the castle. (See below)

Every morning when I wake, I stare out of my window at the great oak in the distance, knowing that I must be that strong. The fierce winter winds assaults its back, yet it stands firm. The baking summer sun beats on its chest, and still it stands firm. At midday I shall leap from this window into the moat hoping that the shadow of the castle, please God, will assist my escape.

Kacey must know that this is one of many escape attempts which Joan attempted, this one causing some significant injuries. But that is not the important bit. The information as to the weather tells us that she was in a south facing room of the keep. I have obtained a satellite image of the terrain and can identify the stump of a huge tree that once stood in view of the castle, and it's to the south. Here are the coordinates.

"Kacey, get the horses. My wonderful husband has come to the rescue."

We began trotting due south whilst Salonge monitored her GPS, making slight tugs on her horse's reins as she did so. The strange thing was, Vaillant Blancheur was consistently pre-empting her movements, getting ever excited with each manoeuvre, instinctively knowing where we were heading. After just a few minutes, the stump of a tree came into view. Its circumference must have been at least twelve metres.

"This has to be it." I said, a look of hope and excitement becoming obvious across my face.

"I agree." Said Salonge. "But fifty gallops north from this point takes us virtually back to where the old castle wall once stood."

"Perhaps the tried and trusted method of hiding things is plain sight is not such a new strategy." I said.

"Well let's find out my brave little cousin."

We set off in silence employing an even pace, counting the gallops in our heads. As we reached the count of fifty, an old well came into view, now filled to the brim with centuries of dirt. Vaillant was prancing frantically around the ancient watering hole, kicking at the crumbling remains of its stone rim. I dismounted in an attempt to calm the majestic beast, but to no avail. I stood back as he continued his assault on the crumbling stonework. Piece by piece, and brick by brick, it began to fall away. Suddenly a gap appeared between the inner and outer wall of the well and Vaillant stood still, as if his work was complete. I looked into the cavity to see a chain attached to a metal ring. I instinctively began pulling whatever it was attached to up to the surface. At its end was a lead box no bigger that trinket case. It had a solid crude fastener, but no lock. I undid the latch and opened the receptacle. Inside was some sort of muslin cloth wrapped around something which felt like a heavy stone. I unfolded the sacking to reveal a huge, blood red ruby. Well, I assumed it was a ruby, but one cut in such a way which I had never seen, not like a typical gemstone. The base was perfectly flat, and the cylindrical sides contained dozens of unusual etchings. What I assumed to be the top had been cut to form a jagged edge like the end of a Christmas cracker. Salonge was holding the muslin in her hands and was squinting over her shoulder whilst silently mouthing words.

"Salonge , Joan has written a message, but it's extremely faded."

"What does it say?"

I pray that this has been found by one pure of heart and an equal as both man and woman in the eyes of our lord.
This blood stone was given to me by Archangel Michael when I was thirteen, informing me that I will become a warrior of the Church, and for France. He told me that I would die for the cause and that my final

stand and capture would be here on this very spot in Compagnie.

A second stone was given to me by Saint Catherine; a blue sapphire representing water, earth's life source. She decreed that I would win a great victory at Orléans for the glory of my Lord, the Catholic Church and my king, Charles the VII. I placed this stone neath the arch of a foot by the church of Mary the Virgin in a town on the Loire, just east of Orléans named Gien. If you are truly the chosen one, and pure of heart, it will know you and seek you out.

May god be with you
Joan D'Arc

We rode in silence back to the farmhouse. I was having a conversation in my head with Sir Grandad; you were right about everything. I promise I will not stop until our quest is complete...I know you can hear me...I love you.

Salonge looked deep in thought, and I could tell that she now knew this to be something of far greater magnitude than she could ever have imagined. Even before the old farmhouse came into view, we could hear animated, raised voices reaching across the breeze; our hosts were arguing vigorously. Salonge began a pointless conversation in a raised tone solely for the purpose of announcing our arrival; it had the desired effect. The door opened and the lady of the house emerged.

"Bonjour mademoiselles, just leave the horses in the stable. Jacques is not feeling too well, so if it is ok, I will bring your dinner to your room."

"That will be fine madam." Said Salonge, as she gave me another worried look.

Once inside Salonge told me to pack but leave some clothes laying around to disguise the fact that we had done so.

"What is it Salonge?"

"Something is definitely wrong. The way Jacques behaved today and also the lady at the concession. We may need to leave secretly tonight after dark."

"How are we going to do that, on horseback? We are miles from the station, and we don't have a car."

"Well we may have to borrow Jacques' vehicle. I will send him some money in the post."

Less than half an hour later the old lady brought our food. She was very edgy, but there was a soft look of concern in her eyes. As she was about to leave the room, she turned to face us.

"It has been so nice to meet you wonderful ladies, but you must leave tonight. You are in great danger. The keys to my husband's car are in the breadbasket. I will make sure he has plenty of cognac before bed...he will not hear you leave."

With that she left the room and closed the door.

Chapter 21

No pop stars in the 15th Century

Pierre was being chauffeured to Arcachon in his black limousine and, although sumptuously fitted with every possible comfort, he was unable to sleep regardless of extreme fatigue. The head of the Protecteurs de la France had called him from Rome, screaming that he would now look like a fool if he did not report to their man at the Vatican that the first treasure had been uncovered. Pierre had received a message from Julien and Marcus that it was, in fact, in their possession and he had left Paris immediately to join them. However, as instructed by him, the discovery was not to be opened until his arrival. There were three things causing Pierre overwhelming anxiety. The first was that it was his understanding that the head of the PDLF, his only superior, answered to no one, and that their relationship with the Vatican was simply a cooperative in the interests of the Catholic Church; their last telephone conversation indicated otherwise. His second concern was the repeated ineptitude of Julien and his nephew; had they actually recovered a genuine treasure, or a box of rubbish? The final, and probably most significant development was a text message from the old lady who sold snacks and coffee from a concession van at Joan's keep in Compiegne. What was the French bitch and her English cousin up to by visiting the monument? Was it that they had made a second copy of the documents and were still searching, in which case, why did they not follow the trail to Arcachon? The only conclusion he could reach was that the PDLF had been sold yet another dummy.

Julien and Marcus had both showered and changed and were sitting on their hotel balcony sipping champagne, despite the fact that it was now almost two in the morning. The box had been placed on the bed alongside a pair of small bolt cutters ready for Pierre to do the unveiling. The two men had never got along so well, laughing about the old man and his stupid dog. They were even congratulating themselves on what a great team they made and perhaps should request that it be made a permanent arrangement.

....

Salonge and I had been taking turns looking through our window to see if the farmhouse lights were still on, which they were. But the couples' conversation was far more muted now and this was an indication that the cognac was taking effect. At around half past midnight Salonge received a message from a family friend named Raoul. It simply said, *'The rats have taken the bait.'*

"Get your things Kacey, we have to leave."

"We can't, the old man is still awake."

"That's a chance we shall just have to take." She said, still staring at her cell phone.

What was that message about?"

"Any time now our pursuers will discover that Joan of Arc liked 1980's pop stars and keeps her posters and old records in a box. They will be back on our tails in no time, and my guess is that Jaques may well have alerted them, despite his wife's protests.""

"If that is the case." I said, "then we must make haste and face our adversaries another time...when the conditions of battle are in our favour. I have an idea!"

"What is it Kacey?"

"The dirt road from the house to the road is downhill. Why don't we release the car's handbrake and coast to a safe distance before firing the engine?"

"That's brilliant Kacey, you are a saint!"

With those words a shiver ran through my whole body, and I swear I could feel a vibration coming from the ruby in my shoulder bag. We slipped out and crept towards the vehicle. I moved to the rear of the car as Salonge tried the driver's door and immediately smiled, giving me the thumbs up. Although no words were exchanged, I could tell that we both assumed the old lady had unlocked the door for us. I placed both hands on the trunk, dug my heels in and began to push. Salonge was doing the same with one shoulder against the doorframe whilst gripping the steering wheel with one hand. For a moment or two our efforts looked to be in vain as the underinflated tires refused to budge from their muddy bed. We began a pulsated coordinated rhythm of pressure and release causing the car to rock back and forth. Eventually the old jalopy lurched out of its resting place causing me to lose my footing and crash my head on the bumper before falling face first into muck and horse faeces. I looked up to see Salonge now trying to halt the cars momentum down the hill. I leaped to my feet, sprinted to the passenger side, and jumped in. Salonge slipped into the driver's seat and guided us towards the exit from the farm. When we reached the road gate, Salonge slipped the key into the ignition and jump started the vehicle, simultaneously flicking on the headlights as she did so. I looked over my shoulder to see the old lady waving and blowing us good wish kisses from her doorway.

....

"After you." Said Marcus. "No, after you." Replied Julien, in response as to who should open the door for Pierre. This newfound camaraderie between them felt natural and genuine, both looking forward to successful and equal ascendancy within the ranks of the Protecteurs de la France.

"Come in uncle, the treasure is on the bed."

"Is it indeed. Which one of you would like to open it?"

"It is your triumph Pierre." Said Julien. "After all, it was you who deciphered the documents regarding its location."

Pierre was fully aware that, if this were another deception by the FBI bitch, he would also be held to account by his only superior. But, thought Pierre, the Vatican's puppet would not be delivering any punishment to him. It was time that a true Frenchman led the organisation. The Protecteurs de la France should be led by one who answers to his country and God alone, someone like himself. Pierre walked slowly to the bed and picked up the bolt cutters.

"I would like some privacy." He said. "Both of you continue to discuss your newfound friendship on the balcony. I see by the champagne that you have been celebrating. I do hope it was not premature."

Pierre applied pressure to the oversized secateurs and the rusty lock easily gave way. He positioned himself beside the box on the soft mattress and tried to control his breathing before lifting the lid. Staring back at him were some pop star posters, fluffy toys, and a collection of brightly coloured vinyl records from the days before downloads and Spotify.

Julien and Marcus were anxious to know what glorious artifacts they had recovered but dare not turn around, Pierre insisting on privacy. For a full twenty minutes neither man could hear any sound emanating from the bedroom. Eventually Julien plucked up the courage to take a peek. The room was empty, that is aside from the open box, a scribbled note, and a pistol.

What can I say? This time your joint efforts have culminated in the biggest fuck-up to date. There is a pistol on the bed containing one bullet. Only one of you will be permitted to leave this room and return to Paris.

Good Luck.

On his way down to his limousine Pierre sent a text to the old concession lady.

Call Jacques at the farmhouse. On no account must his guests leave the premises.

....

We needed to get to Gien, just outside Orleans, one hundred and ten kilometres south of Paris. We had a full tank of petrol but there would definitely be an all alerts out on our vehicle before we covered that distance. We decided that we would drive to Paris and take the train. We would abandon the car at the Gare du Sud and take a taxi to Gare du Austerlitz for the one-hour rail journey.

Thankfully, the country roads were deserted, and we were tempted to take a south easterly route through open country and small villages, but this would have doubled our journey time. Instead, we chose the main A1 motorway which, although busier, would be less conspicuous at this early hour, especially if we could lose ourselves amongst the tourist vehicles and caravans who also chose ungodly hours to travel.

We kept to the slow lane, which was not really a choice at all as the temperature gauge on Jacque's old taxi immediately went into the red each time the speedometer breached the 60 kilometre an hour mark. Regardless of this, we were still making reasonably good time, that is until twenty kilometres outside Paris. Traffic began to slow and eventually adopted a stop and start rhythm; people occasionally stepping out of their vehicles to peer up ahead on tiptoes. Salonge edged our vehicle into the middle lane and, as she did so I could spy blue flashing lights in the distance; it was a roadblock.

Chapter 22

A Cull and a Capture

"Where is Pierre?" Enquired Marcus.

"He has left. It would seem that our treasure chest was not quite what he was expecting."

Marcus walked towards the bed and looked into the old box. Having seen the posters and memorabilia of a young girl fixated on pop stars and cuddly toys, he just slumped onto the ruffled duvet. Unable to remove his gaze from the disastrous discovery, he addressed Julien in a defeated tone. "Well it looks as if we are in serious trouble."

"One of us most definitely is." Said Julien, his voice returning to the spiteful, clipped tones which, until recently, he had always used when speaking to Marcus.

"Well blood is thicker than water my friend." Said Marcus in his most sarcastic tone. "I suggest you start looking for cheap properties in the Caribbean, or any other small corner of the earth. I shall be fine; my uncle would never hurt me."

"No he wouldn't." Said Julien as he raised the pistol with its silencer extended barrel. "But I would."

....

Pierre was back in the limo heading to an apartment on the Champs Elysees deciding that that would be a better location than the chateau from which to manage the situation. Upon hearing of the girls appearance at Compiegne, he had arranged for roadblocks at all routes into Paris, and for PDLF eyes to be alert at all major train stations. Wherever they were heading next it was more likely that they would need to travel from a location with multiple options such as central Paris. Pierre constructed a single text message and sent it to two separate phone numbers knowing that only one would respond.

Which one of you is still with us?

.....

Julien read the message and wondered what the reaction would be when Pierre discovered that it was he who survived the ultimatum and not his nephew.

....

There is only one of us remaining Pierre. I am truly sorry about Marcus, but your instructions were clear. Should I return to the Chateau?

....

No, Julien. I have fresh instructions for you. Do not concern yourself about Marcus, he was a fool and a

liability. You have a final chance to redeem yourself.
You must fly to Charles de Gaulle and check into the
airport Ibis Hotel. You will find everything that you
need in room 269 which has been pre booked in the
name of Thiery Vendome. The head of the
Protecteurs de la France has betrayed us. He arrives
back in Paris at 7.50 in the morning on Air France
AF2666 from Rome. He must not leave the departure
area, or ever even step foot on French soil ever again.

Juliens face turned white. He had just been told to
assassinate the chief aide to the President of France.

....

As we got ever closer to the checkpoint my heart was
racing. I looked to Salonge for reassurance, but her
focus and calmness only served to increase my
anxiety. The police officers were not searching every
vehicle, so it initially appeared to be somewhat
random. Two consecutive cars would be thoroughly
examined, including the back seats and trunk, then
four or five vehicles would be waved through.

"They are only stopping cars occupied by two
females." Said Salonge. "Jacques' car must have
been reported stolen and we can assume know that
our adversaries have discovered the deception by
now regarding my old memory box."

"So we stole a car. We can just take the penalty with dignity and pay the fine. We can also offer to compensate Jacques and his wife in return for them dropping the charges."

"My dear Kacey. Do you not see? The police would never set up roadblocks for the theft of a single motorised rust bucket. Someone much higher up must be pulling the strings."

"Well we should just charge through the barrier and be on our way."

"We could never outrun them Kacey, and they may well decide to pepper this death trap with bullets instead." Salonge was clearly wracking her brain for an alternative method of escape."

"Surely the French police would never do such a thing?" I said.

"Kacey, the people we are dealing with are ruthless and obviously have some serious connections. Remember, wasn't the black car at your grandfather's care home registered to the French Embassy in London? And if they can murder your dear grandfather, and beat your history professor to within an inch of her life, then I think we should play it calm and await an opportunity."

We inched forward, hoping against all hope that the

roadblock was for some other reason than our capture when Salonge told me to hold the steering wheel whilst she messaged her husband. She then reached over to her handbag and and pulled off one of the studs whose job was to secure the handle. I was in total confusion as her hand slipped inside the front of her trousers and her face began to contort.

"It is a transmitter." She said. "As soon as I unclip it from my handbag it begins emitting a signal which Anthony can trace. I doubt very much if they will discover its new hiding place. It also transmits my pulse rate informing the recipient if I am in duress or, in a worst-case scenario, still breathing."

Sure enough two police officers waved us to the hard shoulder, one of them resting a hand on his holster whilst the other was talking animatedly into his radio; there was no doubt we were their intended quarry. Salonge re-took control of the car and followed the hand signals indicating where we should pull over. Both officers turned their backs to us and signalled for the roadblock to be removed whilst vigorously urging the remaining queue of traffic to be on their way. As this was all in motion Salonge once again reached into her handbag and tore through the lining to retrieve a short blade knife.

"I had hoped to see you produce another modern spy gadget, not a child's penknife. What good will that do?"

Salonge ignored my derogatory comment and began prising the back cover from her cell phone. Once off, she placed the device on the centre consul and drove the stubby knife into the centre of the lithium battery. Within seconds I could hear a fizzing noise followed by tiny swirls of smoke twisting towards the roof of our car. Moments later the phone was in full flame and the acrid smell of burning electronics was making me gag. I managed to avoid asking the obvious, realising just in time that Salonge was destroying her contact numbers as well as any messages regarding the true content of Sir Grandad's documents sent by Anthony. Suddenly there was an almighty crash as my window exploded and a truncheon smashed into my ear. The officer lunged through through the jagged aperture and grabbed for Solange's burning device , yelping as it glued itself to his flesh. The screaming uniformed man shook his hand vigorously until the melted blob detached itself and fell to the floor.

I looked to Salonge whose face was displaying a series of emotions all at the same time. I could see satisfaction at her having destroyed the cell phone, combined with an element of anger and defiance, but also an air of defeat and concern. I felt a need to be the positive, stronger member of the partnership for a change.

"My dear cousin, Joan of Arc was also captured, but her actions resulted in a unanimous victory. And as far as I know, being burned at the stake is no longer a popular punishment in France. Besides, once we are at the police station I shall demand to speak with the British Embassy."

Salonge's face softened. "My dear brave young cousin. I fear we shall not be taken to any police station.

With that, we were both unceremoniously dragged from the vehicle, placed in handcuffs, and bundled into the rear of an unmarked car.

....

Anthony was sitting by the pool in the hills above Pattaya when he received the message from Salonge. He immediately ran back into the villa, his wet feet almost causing him to slide straight across the teak flooring and into his workstation. He booted up his computer and activated the tracking app.
Immediately a flashing dot began creeping along one of the major routes into Paris. As the dot passed the last possible exit before entering the city, the map zoomed in to show a more detailed picture of the road network within its boundaries. Anthony was

chastising himself for not having put a contingency plan in place when Salonge had left to rendezvous with her young English cousin. However, at that time it had just seemed like an innocent trip to discover their family history, not a deadly game of cat and mouse. The flashing dot became stationary around halfway along the Champs Elysees and the screen once again enlarged to show a plush block of early 19th century apartments; then the flashing stopped.

………………..

Salonge was doing her best to look confident and calm. However, even though only knowing her for a short time, I could tell that she was extremely concerned. There was what looked to be a bullet proof partition between us in the back of the vehicle and the two men up front, but there was no doubt they would be listening to any conversations. Even so, I needed to ask.

"It can't be that bad Salonge. If they were going to hurt us they would have driven us to some deserted spot, not the centre of Paris."

"Salonge gave a weak smile. That's the problem Kacey. We have not been blindfolded and I am an operative of an international joint government agency. I am also ex Interpol and FBI. If I were released and divulged this location and the identity of the person I am sure we are soon to meet, then there would be devastating repercussions. I am afraid that they intend to interrogate us and then make us disappear."

Everything momentarily went pitch black as the vehicle glided down a slope into an underground car park. After a few seconds, as our eyes adjusted, we could just about make out several executive cars, Rolls Royce's, and security vehicles. Our car came to a stop at the farthest end of the cavernous space and sat idling as a camouflaged type of panel in the wall slid to one side revealing two burly men. Each went to the rear passenger doors and gestured for us to accompany them. Once inside the secret cavity the door closed and one of the men pressed the elevator button. There was a buzzing noise, and we could feel an electronic pulse fill the room. The second man smiled.

"It's nothing to worry about. It will just disable any devices which you may have hidden on your person."

The elevator slowly ascended its shaft and eventually bumped to a gentle halt. When the doors parted there was an elegant man in a blue suit with a red tie and crisp white shirt. He bore a cross of the crucifixion as a tie pin and the French flag as a lapel adornment.

"Mademoiselles, my name is Pierre Cardout. Pleased to finally make your acquaintance.

Chapter 23

Interrogation

Anthony was pulling his hair out (or would have been had he not sported a close crop since leaving high school.) He had placed a number of calls to a select few heads of global government agencies whose resources he and Salonge had access to and often relied on to complete their dangerous missions. Unfortunately, this not being a sanctioned assignment, they were unable to offer help of any great significance. One did respond with information as to the owner of the building on the Champs Elysees where the tracking device had stopped working. They confirmed that the vehicle from where the signal had been emitting did enter the basement car park of that specific building before it stopped transmitting and had not left that location. The problem was that this residence was owned by a Gabriel Abadie, chief aide to the President of France, and as such was off limits to any operatives including Anthony. In fact, the direct head of his own organisation, although a close friend and sympathetic towards his situation, had expressly forbade Anthony from flying to Paris but promised to do all he could to help, whenever possible.

....

Julien had checked into the Ibis Styles Paris Charles De Gaulle hotel as instructed using the name Thiery Vendome. Once in his suite he was surprised at the amount of equipment and weaponry laid out on the bed. There were two types of handguns complete with silencers, a medical case with several syringes of what he assumed to be a deadly liquid, a stiletto knife and even a magnetic bomb which could be attached to their leader's car. The fact that the proposed methods of dispatch were all designed for close quarter work confirmed to Julien that he was not expected to survive the assassination; everything wreaked of a set up.

'So, it seems you intend to kill two birds with one stone do you Pierre, I do your dirty work and then get arrested for murder...or more likely shot by security...I don't think so.'

Julien only had a few hours to decide his next course of action before Gabriel's plane landed. He lay on the bed and mulled over recent events. He had long suspected that Pierre had ambitions to take the helm of the PDLF, and claiming that Gabriel was a traitor who needed to be assassinated would serve that purpose. But what proof was there of this betrayal?...none! Julien also knew that he had fallen out of favour in recent months and couldn't figure out why he had been given the chance to escape punishment in Arcachon. Then the answer suddenly became obvious. Pierre wanted them both dead but didn't have the stomach to kill his own nephew so had him do it instead.

....

"Please take a seat mademoiselles." Said Pierre. "Or should I say madam and mademoiselle, as I believe the elder of you is married. No?"

Neither of us furnished him with a reply.

"Come come ladies, this will be much easier if you cooperate. It would be such a shame to see two such pretty faces contorted in pain."

"You do not scare us sir." I said through gritted teeth. "I take that back. Calling you sir implies that you are a gentleman, a man of honour, and clearly you are not."

"Ah, the spirited little English girl breaks the silence." He said, picking up a file from his desk. "Oh silly me, I have made yet another faux pas. First of all I call a married lady a girl, and now I am calling a boy in girls clothes a girl. You were born a boy were you not Kieth."

A lump rose in my throat, and I clenched my hands as tight as I could, ignoring the pain caused by the restraints, determined not to cry, but he had virtually broken me in less than a minute.

Cardout smiled at me in mock sympathy before his eyes returned to my medical report. "Now this is interesting. It says here that you have a perfectly formed uterus and womb. Just think, had you not had your man parts removed it is entirely possible you could have somehow impregnated yourself. It is claimed that one of your sort actually achieved this in the Philippines."

With that I burst into tears, years of pain and suffering brought to the fore with one vicious sentence delivered by a homophobic beast. Salonge, still handcuffed to her chair, leapt forward like a deranged panther sinking her teeth into his hand. Pierre began to scream for his guards who came rushing into the room.

"Don't just stand there. Get this crazy bitch off me."

The two burly men from the elevator struggled for half a minute before one of them pistol whipped my cousin causing a spray of blood to eject from her skull and onto his desk.

....

Julien recognised one of the PDLF's junior soldiers waiting at arrivals wearing a chauffeur's cap, eagerly scanning the passengers exiting the customs area; the man recognised Julien too.

"I take it you are here to drive Gabriel to his apartment." Said Julien.

"That is correct sir." Said the young man.

"Something important has come up. Give me your hat and car keys with the parking ticket. You can take the rest of the day off."

The junior soldier reluctantly obeyed his superior knowing this to be a rather strange request and outside of normal procedures.

Julien sensed the man's trepidation. "Is there a problem?"

"No sir, sorry sir...here you go."

"That's more like it, now be on your way."

Julien briefly watched the man head for the exit displaying the taxi rank sign before returning his gaze to the passengers arriving from Rome.

"Sharpen up young man." Said Gabriel. "I have been standing beside you whilst you were staring in the other direction."

Julien raised his head to reveal his face from beneath

the peaked cap. "Welcome home Gabriel. I'm afraid that there have been some rather disturbing developments since you have been away, hence my reason for being here in person."

"Developments, what sort of developments?"

"Pierre Cardout is trying to seize control of the Protecteurs de la France and sent me here to kill you. I, on the other hand, am loyal only to you."

"Where is the treacherous pig now?"

"I believe he is in your apartment on the Champs Elysees sir."

"Take me there now and call every soldier of the PDLF whom you trust."

....

Salonge had just regained consciousness when Pierre Cardout came back into the room, his hand completely bandaged like a boxer before slipping on his gloves.

"You stupid bitch. You almost bit off my thumb."

"I wanted to bite off your dick but figured it would be too small to get my teeth around." Spat Salonge.

"I do not have time for this ridiculous banter so I will

cut to the chase. It has long been rumoured that Joan of Arc has a bloodline in existence. It has also been rumoured through the ages that Joan was in fact a boy, or possibly a disgusting abomination such as yourself." He said, looking directly at me hoping for more tears.

"Kacey is a beautiful young lady." Said Salonge. "If you wish to see a disgusting abomination, then I suggest you go and look in the mirror."

Pierre regained his composure. "Mrs. Dupree-Mazur, if it were not for the fact that I am certain it was you who has hidden this fake bullshit evidence, you would already be dead. I have a simple proposal for you. Deliver the documents to me and there will be no further pain for anyone. We may even pay you a handsome fee and even commission a wonderful marble headstone for young Kacey's grandfather."

It was my turn to lunge, although he was ready for me and produced a pistol whist simultaneously rolling his chair out of striking distance.

"I can see that you do not intend to accommodate my proposal, in which case I can assure you a most painful and unpleasant stay with us."

The telephone on his desk began to ring and Pierre winced as he attempted to grab for the receiver with his damaged hand.

"Excuse me ladies, but I have been expecting a call regarding an unfortunate event at Charles de Gaulle airport. I see no reason why you should not hear the conversation given your predicted short life span." Pierre pressed the speaker button.

"Hello, Pierre Cardout speaking."

"Pierre Sir, it's Antoine."

"What is it Antoine, I am very busy at present?" He said, preparing his act of pretence at being shocked when told that Gabriel Abadie had been killed.

"It's just that Julien relieved me of my duties. I thought it strange so decided to check with you."

"Where are they now?"

"I slipped back into the airport and followed them to the car. I thought I heard Julien say something very odd."

"What is it Antoine, out with it man."

"I thought I heard him say that you had ordered him to kill Gabriel."

Pierre hung up and told his guards to get us to the vehicle immediately.

Chapter 24

Divine Intervention

We were both thrown into the back of the limousine accompanied by one of the guards brandishing a gun. Our hands were still handcuffed but they had taken a moment to secure them behind our backs rendering us defenseless. The second guard jumped into the driver's seat whilst Pierre occupied the passenger side.

"Get us to the Chateau as fast as possible."

The wheels of the limo began to screech on the slippery carpark flooring as we lurched towards the exit ramp and the slowly ascending security gate. As we reached the speed hump at the top of the ramp the car literally took off, our heads hitting the roof at the same time as the top of the car hit the not quite fully retracted gate.   The vehicle flew through the air and out into the sunlight and I could hear the driver shouting as he flung his arms up to protect his face. I just caught a glimpse of the advertising on the side of the white coach blocking our path. It had a picture of a female medieval knight sitting upon a warhorse. Above this were forty or more tourists screaming silently through the windows as we pierced into the luggage compartment of the tourists transportation . The words beneath the image on the side of the coach said Joan of Arc tours.

When I opened my eyes both Salonge and the man guarding us were unconscious. Blood was running down their faces and smeared in unusual shapes all over the partition glass. The airbags in the front had successfully deployed, but neither Pierre nor his driver were moving; I assumed they must have clashed heads. I had no idea how long I had been unconscious, but as I surveyed the scene I could see two ambulances arrive and the fire service was already spraying the smoking undercarriage of the now empty coach. A medic appeared in the window and was gesturing for me to move back towards the other door. He was also acting out some sort of mime indicating for me to drag Salonge away from the door too, his voice unable to penetrate the bullet proof glass. Suddenly there was a loud bang and the door exploded open.

"Are you ok Kacey?" He said.

"Yes, I'm fine." I said, wondering how he knew my name.

"Can you get yourself into that ambulance whilst my colleague and I follow along carrying Salonge?"

I didn't know how or why, but the fact that the medic was virtually trampling on the guard to reach Salonge told me that these must be good guys and I should trust them.

....

Julien was taking every back street he knew in an attempt to avoid the traffic in and around the Champs Elysees. As they drew closer to Gabriel's apartment block they could hear sirens and see billows of smoke rising into the air before diffusing and drifting over the rooftops.

"Pull over Julien." Said a concerned looking Gabriel Abadie. "We can walk from here. I have a feeling that this incident is no coincidence. Are you armed?"

"To the hilt." Came the reply. "Two pistols, a stiletto, two syringes of poison, and a small incendiary device."

"Leave the little bomb but bring everything else and pass me one of the guns."

As the two men neared the scene, they could already hear people crying above the sound of impatient drivers tooting their horns. Once they rounded the corner both men recognised the diplomatic vehicle embedded in the side of a tourist coach.

"Look." Said Julien. "That's Pierre in the passenger seat. He looks to be unconscious, or even dead ."

"Well let's make sure that he is. Follow me and have the syringe ready."

Gabriel strode toward the firemen trying to cut an opening in the crumpled doors of the limo.

"Gentlemen, my name is Gabriel Abadie and that is a diplomatic vehicle. The man in the passenger seat has highly confidential government documents on his person. I insist that my colleague retrieves them before you remove him from the vehicle."

Every rescue and medical worker instantly recognised the chief assistant to the President, negating the need for him to produce identification.

"Please be quick monsieur. We have no idea how bad the injuries are."

Gabriel whispered into Juliens ear. "Use the needle."

Julien walked calmly towards the vehicle and leant through the window, pretending to rifle through Pierre's jacket pocket. As he did so Pierre's eyes opened with a look of horror.

Pierre tried to call for help but there was just a gurgling sound coming from his throat and blood-filled lungs. Julien angled his body to restrict the view of any onlookers and held his hand over Pierres mouth, simultaneously inserting a needle into his neck.

....

We were speeding away from the scene with sirens blaring and lights flashing. The medic was inspecting Salonge's wounds after having cleaned away the blood and had attached an oxygen mask making her condition look somewhat more dire. I was now full of questions.

"Who are you? Where are you taking us? Why did you leave the injured man behind?"

"All in good time Kacey. Let's get your cousin stable first."

The medic was no longer speaking with a French accent, it was distinctly American. Solange's eyes began to flicker, and she let out a groan. She was staring intently at the man tending her wounds, clearly trying to focus. After a moment or two I could see a smile appear behind the plastic cup covering her mouth. The man gently removed her mask and smiled back.

"You tell that husband of yours he owes us one. What the hell kind of a mess are you into this time?"

"Thanks Jack, I will."

"Could someone please tell me what is going on?" I said.

"My partner and I worked alongside Salonge for a few years in the FBI. We still work for them, but Salonge moved on. We got a call from Anthony saying that you two ladies needed help. I pulled some strings with my boss, but it's only limited I'm afraid. You can stay in our safe house for one night, maybe two, and then you are on your own.

....

Gabriel and Julien walked back to their car and headed for the Chateau de Breteuil.

"How many of our people do you think were behind Pierre in his scheme to gain control of the Protecteurs de la France?" Said Gabriel.

"I don't think he confided in any of them, nor divulged his plans to anyone but me. I think he figured that with you gone, and me no doubt in prison or worse, he would have been considered your natural successor and suspected of nothing."

"So if he thought you would assassinate me at the airport, I would imagine that he had arranged for our members to gather at the Chateau this evening, or tomorrow at the latest, for another of his lavish gala dinners."

"I agree Gabriel."

"What news of the two females causing us so much trouble?"

"I believe they were captured and probably brought to your apartment. I also have reason to believe that they may have been in the destroyed vehicle."

"What makes you say that Julien."

"When I was injecting Pierre with the poison, I could see a lady's jacket in the back of the car."

"Check the hospitals and police reports. Find out where they are."

....

We pulled into yet another underground carpark which gave me the jitters, more from flashbacks of the recent events than any mistrust of our hosts. Four men in overalls came running out of the shadows, two carrying jet hose equipment, one holding a bundle of rolled plastic paper, and the final one carrying new number plates. The back doors to the fake ambulance swung open and number plate man stepped in and removed our handcuffs with some bolt cutters. Jack suggested that I stretch my legs for a moment whilst he tends to Salonge. I stepped out of the ambulance and was instructed to stand back whilst the team got to work; I was immediately mesmerised. The official medical signage was peeled off and then the white paint fell away under pressure from the hoses. Old plates were removed and replaced with new before all four men ran around the vehicle brandishing chamois leathers. Satisfied that the van's natural deep blue paint was sufficiently dry, the rolls of plastic were unveiled and adhered to the sides of the vehicle; they depicted logos of a home delivery service. Twenty minutes later we pulled into a courtyard in the Latin quarter on the Southbank of the Seine and shown into the safehouse.

Chapter 25

My First Sleepover

Our safe house was on the top floor of an ornate, but semi gothic apartment block complete with a small railed balcony, although this one gave us no access to the outside space due to the French doors being permanently fastened shut. Special Agent Jack, Salonge's old colleague and our saviour, had given us a brief tour of the accommodations including where the panic buttons were located as well as the various monitoring devices covering the elevator, stairwell, and courtyard. It consisted of a comfortable lounge adjoined to a small kitchen separated by a breakfast bar. The long narrow corridor contained three doors; the one at the very end being the bathroom and the two facing each other on opposite walls being the bedrooms. The two rooms were identical in size with basic furnishings and neutral, almost bland décor. However, the left bedroom had closets filled with varying sizes of men's clothes, whilst the other had an assortment of basic women's attire along with a dresser and vanity mirror. As both bedrooms had twin beds, we decided to share the same room which gave me a further feeling of security. I took the opportunity for a quick shower whilst Salonge familiarised herself with the surveillance and alarm systems. When I came out wearing the surprisingly soft and fluffy white bathrobe, and an equally soft towel turban around my head, Salonge was dozing on the sofa.

"How do you feel." I said softly just in case she was in fact asleep.

"How do I look my brave young cousin?"

"Bloody dreadful." I said unable to contain a nervous laugh. Her eyes looked like a Panda's caused by smashing the bridge of her nose against the car partition, and there was a small bag of ice perched upon an egg sized lump on the side of her head where she had been pistol whipped.

"I ran you a hot bath whilst I was in the shower. Why don't you go and have a long soak and I will prepare us some dinner? Your friend said that the fridge here is usually fully stocked."

"That sounds wonderful, you are a true saint."

That was the second time in as many days that Salonge had called me a saint, and the second time that those words had sent a shiver across my whole body. The first time was when we were stealing Jacques' taxi from the farmhouse shortly after we had discovered the blood ruby. At that thought the shivers immediately stopped and were replaced by a feeling of gut-wrenching panic and despair.

"The ruby, where is the blood ruby?"

Salonge forced a smile and withdrew the stone from her pocket. The relief was overwhelming.

"Thank God, how on earth did you conceal it?"

"My dear Kacey, surely you didn't think that it was the small transmitter making me wince when I slipped my hand down my trousers at the roadblock."

This time I let out a full-blown laugh and ran to give her a hug, but the alarm in her eyes reminded me that she was still in a delicate state.

"What do you fancy to eat?" I said.

"Surprise me." Said Salonge. "But if my memory serves me correct from my days in the FBI, supplies in their safe houses requires quite some imagination in order to create a pleasant culinary experience."

With that Salonge pecked me on the cheek and meandered down the corridor towards the bathroom.

I opened the top section of the fridge freezer and understood precisely what she meant. There was a six pack of Jupelier, a six pack of Leffe Blonde, one bottle of absolute vodka and three one litre bottles of diet coke. I turned my attention to the cupboards only to be confronted by another source of disappointment; twenty different varieties of pot noodle, ten varieties of flavoured chips, plus a multitude of cookies and confectionary. My final hope was the freezer, but by now my expectations had been considerably lowered. The first draw contained stack upon stack of microwave meals, none of which looked particularly appealing. The second draw, although not exactly Michelin star, was a vast improvement. I selected two medium sized pepperoni pizza's, a melt in the middle chocolate pudding, and a tub of orange sorbet. I gave it thirty minutes before placing the pizzas in the oven guessing that Salonge would spend at least forty-five minutes in the tub; I was correct. When she finally emerged, I had our meals set on two trays and suggested we eat in bed. I was so pleased when Salonge agreed; it felt like my first girls sleepover.

"You look so happy Kacey. Have you not done this before?"

"No, I was never allowed. Well, that's not entirely true. When I was very young I often ate in bed when my parents would argue, but never with the company of a friend."

"Is that before you had the corrective procedure?"

I was so glad about my cousin's choice of words. She could easily have said 'was that when you were a boy?'

"What were their arguments about?"

"Mostly about me. I think my mother knew that I was a girl, despite…you know…additional parts. It was my father who insisted that I should be a boy. But when my behaviour was not the macho image that he had hoped for I think that I just disgusted him."

"How old were you when he left home?"

"It was my twelfth birthday. I was just about to wash before going to bed when he came into the bathroom. I tried to cover myself with a towel, but he just shouted that I needed to know how a man should clean his parts and whipped the towel from my grasp; he left our house that night."

"If this is upsetting you then we can change the subject. I just think that it is good to talk."

It was the first time that it felt right to let everything out so, for the first time in my life, I did.

"When my father ripped the towel away he could see that I was in the early stages of developing breasts. He looked at me like I was some kind of animal and threw up into the toilet. He then began to run a sink of hot water and I thought he only needed to clean his mouth and face. Instead he grabbed the back of my neck and forced my face under the water. I honestly think that I only had seconds to live before my mother burst in and attacked him with a kitchen knife, screaming for him to leave me alone."

Salonge got out of her single bed, piled all of her food onto my tray and snuggled in beside me.

"Ok let's talk about something else and eat." Said Salonge. I'm sorry to have brought it up."

"No, I want to talk about it. I never have, not even to grandad."

"Ok angel but stop if it gets too emotional."

"My father (I never called him dad) punched my my mother and left home that night; I never saw him again. My mother was never the same again and, although she never said it, I could tell that she blamed me for his leaving. With his income gone, and her losing her job shortly after, depression set in, and she took an overdose."

"Kacey that's terrible."

"You would think so, but the following years living with my grandad were the happiest of my life. That's why this quest is so important to me."

Our conversation was broken by a telephone ringing

in the lounge area. Salonge leapt from the bed and ran to the source of the sound. Neither of us had noticed a new mobile on the coffee table with the note telling Salonge it was her replacement device and perhaps she should call her husband.

Salonge punched in the numbers. "Well thanks for letting me know you are ok." Said Anthony.

"I'm so sorry darling, I fell asleep and was just about to call you." She fibbed.

"Oh, and thanks for saving my life Anthony." Came the sarcastic response. "Seriously hon, are you ok. This is getting really serious, and I don't know if I can organise another stunt like this one. Why don't you come back to Thailand and bring your young cousin with you?"

"That is impossible Anthony, I have to see this through."

"I thought you would say that, so I have got something for you. It's from the old documents. It is the genuine original charges that Joan was accused of before her execution. I think that you will find them quite extraordinary and certainly explains why many people would not want them revealed, let alone proven."

"That's amazing, thank you Anthony, I love you."

"I love you too."

Chapter 26

Leave no stone Unturned

The forty members of the Protecteurs de la France were, as was the norm, gathered around the exhibits at the chateau sipping champagne and cocktails, waiting to be summoned, but things felt far from normal. This was the first time in the organisation's history that they had been called to attend two grand meetings in the same month. Favourite colleagues were congregating in groups of threes and fours, whispering to each other with quizzical looks on their faces. Eight buglers emerged onto the terrace wearing their usual, military style red uniforms with elaborate gold braiding, but this time they were brandishing highly polished rifles instead of shiny instruments. Julien savoured the increased buzz emanating from the crowd as he, not Pierre, emerged onto the terrace.

"Our leader requests your presence in the main ballroom." Said Julien in a loud and authoritative voice.

Julien turned on his heels as the entourage silently followed in single file. Once inside the ballroom the electric buzz of anticipation increased again as Julien took to his seat at the top table next to Gabriel Abadie. Four armed buglers positioned themselves either side of the entrance doors as the other four took corresponding positions on the outside before locking the guests in. Gabriel rose to his feet and raised his arm with his palm facing outwards as if taking an oath; all present recognised the command for silence.

"Dear members of the PDLF, I have some rather unfortunate news to give you. Earlier today Pierre Cardout was tragically killed in a car accident close to my apartment on the Champs Elysees."

Gasps of shock reverberated around the room.

"Alas, I feel no sadness as Pierre was not the friend and colleague I believed him to be. It was brought to my attention that this traitor had ordered my assassination upon my return from Rome this morning. He intended to place himself at the head of the Protecteurs de la France. Thankfully, Julien ignored the order and informed me of the plan."

Gabriel paused for a few seconds to allow the statement to sink in.

"It is obvious to me that he could not have achieved such a feat without some collaboration and assistance from others within the organisation. I request that those of you who supported this treacherous attempt to usurp me as your leader make yourselves known now. I promise that no harm will come to you by my hand. You will, however, be expelled from the organisation, never to return."

Gabriel slowly scanned the faces of all in the room hoping to see a glimmer of betrayal in their eyes. Suddenly he heard the loud scaping of a chair to his left as one elderly member stood defiantly, pointing a bony finger in Gabriel's direction.

"I did not know of the assassination order, but I did support Pierre in his ambition to become leader. We both felt that you are a mere puppet of the Vatican and not worthy of the position as leader of the PDLF."

"I see." Said Gabriel smiling. "Are there any others here present who feel the same way?"

Silence.

Gabriel clicked his fingers and one of the buglers raised his rifle and shot the man in the centre of his forehead. The deceased man stood motionless for what seemed like an eternity before collapsing to the floor.

"I did keep my promise as it was not my hand which pulled the trigger. Now, down to business. Julien will take over Pierre's position as head of operations and enforcement. Any objections should be made known now."

Once again Gabriel scanned the room for signs of dissent; there was none.

"We have evidence that Pierre had captured the two females who wish to bring disgrace to our own history and that of the Catholic Church. Unfortunately, due to his underhand plans and the subsequent accident, it seems that they have managed to escape. The limousine in which Pierre died was fitted with a black box system, similar to those found on aircraft, which records video footage of the car's movements as well as recordings of conversations within its interior. Unfortunately, unless you are interested in a video of the burning undercarriage of a tourist coach, the video is not of any use. The voice recorder, however, reveals something of far greater interest. A medic can be heard giving the women assistance and even tells this Kacey child to head for the ambulance whilst he and his colleague carry her cousin. This is where it gets interesting...the medic was speaking in an American accent. Not only are there no American medics working for the Parisienne ambulance service, but no genuine official at the scene treated the two women. We believe that they had assistance from the FBI for whom the elder of the two once worked. A complaint has been made to the American Embassy and an investigation is under way. I urge you all to enjoy the sumptuous dinner which awaits you but

please be frugal with your consumption of wine.
These females need to be caught as a matter of
urgency and we must leave no stone unturned.

....

Dr Gunter Schmidt is recognised as one of the world's
most respected neurosurgeons, and also one of the
wealthiest private practitioners in France, servicing
the needs of the rich, the powerful, or both with
utmost discretion. It had not always been that way
though. The garage to his mansion in Grecy is larger,
and more comfortable than the grey concrete one
bedroom apartment in Berlin where he and his family
had spent most of their lives. In 1989, when Gunter
moved to Paris after the deconstruction of the Berlin
wall, western doctors and scientists had been
astounded at his revelations. They were well aware
of the performance enhancing drugs administered to
athletes from the eastern bloc, but Gunther shed
light on far more extreme activities for which he was
responsible. One was the use, or restriction of, a
neurotransmitter chemical called glutamate. This
allowed athletes to ignore pain levels and push
through previously unattainable barriers. The other
was the experimentation with dopamine, a natural
chemical produced in the brain which, when
overactive is believed to be associated with
schizophrenia and psychotic behaviour.

"Ah Gabriel, it's good to see you. What seems to be the problem, is it the headaches again?"

"No Gunther, the headaches are fine, but I am worried."

"What is it, are the behavioural issues increasing?"

"Yes, yes they are."

"What has happened, is it another prostitute? You know that my professional oath of patient doctor confidentiality means that you can tell me anything."

"There was a problem with a prostitute in Rome, but she deserved what she got. She recognised me and thought that I should buy her silence through bribery...I silenced her in a more efficient way."

"Oh I see. What else is troubling you?"

"Someone whom I thought was a friend betrayed me. He had an automobile accident but would have survived had I not ended his life."

"Gabriel, a man in your position in government, and at the helm of such a secret organisation, sometimes has to take extreme measures. This does not sound like something which would usually worry you, is there more?"

"I'm afraid so Gunther." Gabriel was rubbing his

head ferociously, unable to look Gunther in the eye.

"Gabriel, if I am to help you there must be no secrets."

"The PDLF had an important dinner last night. Before I went to the chateau I was in a rage. I arranged for the dead traitor's body to be taken from the morgue to a butchers shop owned by a loyal member in my organisation. I had it deboned and the meat processed and packaged into a gift box of cutlets, sausages, burgers and so on. I then arranged for them to be delivered to the parents of the dead man as an anonymous gift."

"That does seem to be an acceleration of extreme behaviour Gabriel. Perhaps we should book you in for another scan to see how the tumour is?"

"I can't, not yet. There is an urgent situation which needs to be addressed."

"There is something else troubling you Gabriel, you must not hold anything back."

"After the business was concluded at the chateau I retired to bed. The next morning, when I awoke, I was not at the chateau."

"Where were you?"

"I was in the back garden of Pierre Cardout's parents

house. I was peeking through their window at them eating the sausages made from his buttocks...I had been masturbating."

"Jesus Gabriel, we need to do that scan and possibly operate."

"I told you, I am too busy right now. Tell me, if you do not operate, then how long have I got?"

"Without a scan it's hard to say. Best case scenario one year...worst case, three months. However, this latest development in your behavioural patterns is most worrying."

"Thank you Gunther for your candour. I will be back as soon as possible. Goodbye my friend.

Chapter 27

France and the Vatican

(Two formidable opponents)

We were sitting at the breakfast bar of the safe house eating microwaved Mac & Cheese for our petit déjeuner. The texture in my mouth felt like lumpy wallpaper paste but, in all honesty, it didn't taste too bad. Salonge activated the Bluetooth on her new phone and and linked it to the printer. The swelling on her face had subsided but her eyes were more like a panda's than a panda. She poured more coffee and popped a couple of painkillers before sitting back down with three documents sent by her husband. We both sat in silence as we absorbed their content. The first was the eventual twelve charges on which Joan of Arc was sentenced; whittled down from the original seventy-two. The second document was the literal translation from medieval French into English. The third was the most interesting. This document was produced by a close friend of Salonge's who worked for Interpol in Quebec. Anthony had been introduced to him some time ago by Salonge, then his fiancé, and he remembered that the man's speciality was languages, both new and old, so decided to confide in him. The feedback had questioned the interpretation of the literal translation from ancient French.

Dear Salonge

This really is a fascinating story which Anthony has relayed to me regarding your young cousin, and it is not without substance, especially as he assures me as to the authenticity of the documents and their age.

Most of the 72 charges against Joan by the Burgundians and the English were discarded as they contained too many embarrassing accounts of her victories across France and her success in reclaiming the throne for King Charlese.

They then focussed on her visions, as they called them, and her supposed meetings with Saint Michael and later with Saint Gabriel in a corporeal form, she claiming to have had physical contact with both, kissing their hands and so on. This is mentioned in article one of the final twelve charges.

The following five or six articles of accusation again relate to her visions and question her sanity. Joan gives details of her many discussions, dreams and visits from Saint Margaret and Saint Catherine.

Things then take a turn when they focus on claims that she was instructed by God to assume a man's role in this struggle for the liberation of France and wear clothes befitting a knight in battle, and a man's attire at all other times. Her accusers claim that she be a witch, thus demanding she be burned at the stake. But in the 1400's witches were believed to be non-virgins, having slept with many men, including the devil himself.

This is where is gets interesting. The common interpretation of the old tongue reads that she was requested by the angels to remain forever a virgin and interact with no man, as is the wish of God. However, this can also be read as 'you must remain a virgin as you be neither a man nor a woman, as with God's vehicle on earth .'

One last thing which may be of help. In Joan's testimony she maintains that many of her early visions appeared to her at the foot of a tree beside a spring. It was called the 'The Fairy Tree' and is believed to be still standing in the village where she was born. Anthony mentioned that you have discovered something of great interest in a water well close to a tree in Compiegne.

I did some further research and uncovered many accounts of Joan seeking privacy and solace by sitting alone under trees close to water. I would suggest that you pay close attention to places which fit this description during your continued search.

Good Luck and stay safe xxx

P.S Anthony mentioned that your young cousin has a history professor back in England. You may wish t to get a second opinion and see if she concurs?

"What do you make of that oh wise cousin?

"It seems to be implying...I mean inferring that God was...is..." Salonge was searching for the right words.

"It's ok, you can say it. It implies that God was like me, you know...both man and woman."

"Or maybe not. " Said Salonge, wanting to reinforce her support for me. "Why should it be a man that is solely accredited with all creation? But what if God's vehicle on earth was referring to Mary. If you think about it, it throws a whole new light on Mary, Jesus, and the immaculate conception. Take a look at article six of Joan's charges. It says that on many of Joan's letters, they were signed, or displayed a signature, Jhesus Maria...Jesus Mary???"

As Salonge stood to open the blinds I took the blood ruby from my bag and held it up to the bright morning sunlight now eagerly bursting into the room. The beautiful stone instantly turned from a deep dark crimson to a mesmerising cherry colour with a crystal type clarity only spoiled by the strange etchings on its outer surface. Salonge turned to face me and was immediately frozen to the spot; her eyes were focussed above and behind me. My heart rate increased tenfold believing that someone had breached the security and entered the room. For a second my mind convinced me that Salonge was pointing a gun, but on the second take I realised that it was just her hand pointing towards the wall behind me. I gingerly turned to where her index finger was suggesting, and my jaw dropped. There was writing being projected onto the cream wall. I did not initially recognise the language and there also appeared to be intermittent words missing. Below the writing was the outline of a person with no detail or features, similar to the chalk marks scribed in chalk by homicide detectives in the United States. I was still staring at the projection when I heard Salonge asking me to keep my hand steady. With each movement of the object I was holding, the writing would move across the wall and fade in and out of focus. I steadied my arm by placing my knee upon the coffee table, and my elbow on that knee. There were three fast flashes as Salonge recorded the image on her phone.

"I've seen that type of script before." I said.

"Can you read any of it?"

"I'm afraid not, but I have a feeling it is Aramaic."

"Is that a dialect of Arabic?"

"Sort of. It's a bit of a mish mash of middle eastern dialects combined with words and terms no longer in use."

I turned back to address Salonge; my face having turned white. "It is the language believed to have been used by Jesus."

"We need to get these images and the documents from Anthony over to your Professor Field."

"Of course. That's where I have seen this wording. She is an expert on ancient text, and I attended one of her seminars on the subject."

Our train of thought was interrupted by the ringing of Salonge's cell phone.

"Salonge, it's Jack. How are you feeling?"

"Not too bad, thanks Jack. My eyes look dreadful but are not too painful, certainly not as bad as my stomach feels after enduring two subsequent meals from the FBI food reserves."

"You need to leave the safehouse immediately I'm afraid."

"Why, what's happened."

"What's happened is that some powerful people in France have made an official complaint to the director of the FBI and if you don't leave then my arse is toast...in fact, it's already sitting in the toaster and I'm trying to convince my boss not to hit the power button. I guessed that your bruising would be worse today so public transport is out of the question. Ive arranged a rental which should be outside in five minutes. Sanitise the safe house including prints, hair from the shower drain, DNA from cutlery...the lot, and get yourselves outta there."

"Thanks Jack. I hope I haven't just blown your pension."

"Don't worry Salonge, I'll be fine, but if you wanna help then get a move on."

Salonge ran to the washing machine and pulled out a small sack containing latex gloves, cleaning fluids, and a bottle of clear liquid in a squirty bottle. She threw a pair of gloves in my direction and told me to grab some FBI standard clothing from the bedroom and, once done, not to touch anything she had cleaned on my way back from the bedroom. I grabbed what I figured we could manage with for a day or so before we could go clothes shopping and waited by the exit for Salonge to finish sanitising the apartment. She stood in the centre of the lounge area, her head scanning the room for anything she may have missed before throwing our gloves, along with the duvet covers and pillowcases, into the separate tumble dryer. Salonge then squirted the clear liquid into the cylinder and closed the door of the appliance and pressed 'quick dry.' The circular window flashed bright red as she grabbed my arm and thrust me down the emergency stairwell.

"It's an incinerator, not a tumble dryer." She said, understanding the confused look on my face. "Ok Kacey, where do we go, Gien? Or should we look for a tree by a brook in Joan's home town?"

There was no doubt in my mind. "Gien." I said. "There are two more stones to find first and, don't ask me how, I just know that they will be needed for whatever we discover in Joan's village."

Chapter 28

A profound message from the Past

Professor Field was due to begin a lecture in the auditorium in less than an hour when she received the message from Kacey.

Hi Beth

I have a favour to ask, but totally understand if you wish to have no part in my quest.

Kacey my dear, are you ok? Of course I will help you.

I have one document from grandad's chest which has been translated by a friend. I have included his comments and observations which question the accepted interpretation. Could you give your opinion on this?

The second attachment is a picture taken on my cousin's phone of some Aramaic writing projected onto a wall. There appear to be words missing but do your best.

And Beth, for your own safety, tell no one about this!

I will do my best for you my dear. Stay safe xxx

Professor field had no trouble reading the ancient

French without the aid of any reference books. She was also familiar with the twelve articles upon which Joan of Arc was ultimately charged. She was, however, surprised at the logic of the alternative interpretation on the notes and wondered why this had never been questioned before. For the next task she would need to rely on many reference books but by the time she had collated as many as she could it was time for her lecture. For the next hour Professor Field was unusually impatient with her students, chastising people for for asking what she considered to be pointless questions to which they would have known the answers if they had been paying attention. There were no complaints from the auditorium when she said that she was feeling unwell and made her apologies before calling the tutorial to an end a full fifteen minutes early. Beth rushed back to her office, locked the door, and made a fresh brew of Earl Grey before getting to work on the Aramaic projection. Two hours later, after several re-checks, Beth was satisfied that she had managed to produce an accurate translation, even though the script didn't make any sense with so many words missing. There was certainly enough to suggest that, when complete, it could reveal something of great historical importance. Professor Field saved the document and did one final check before sending it back to Kacey.

....

Julien was admiring the new solid gold door plate inscribed with his name. It covered the faded patch where Pierre Cardout's old brass one had once greeted terrified members of the PDLF who had been summoned to his office at the chateau de Breteuil. The brass nameplate which had been replaced sat in the draw of Pierre's mammoth desk, but Julien had urgently commissioned the precious metal version from his own pocket. He entered his new office and surveyed all before him with contempt; *Cardout really had no taste or style when it came to furnishings or décor he thought, but putting his own stamp would have to wait*. Julien sat in his new seat of power as head of operations and stared at the telephone, impatiently tapping his fingers on the desk imploring the device to ring with some news of the two bitches. He was just about to hurl a crystal ashtray at the ugly pendulum clock in an attempt to silence its annoying tick tock when the nineteen sixties communication device let out its piercing ring. Julien cursed as his hand became entangled in the plastic-coated coiled cable as he reached for the cumbersome receiver.

"Julien Thibaut speaking."

"Sir, I think we have something. We have managed to obtain CCTV footage of the fake ambulance leaving the scene of the accident and entering an underground car park behind the Arc de Triomphe. No ambulance was discovered in this facility, nor did any ambulance come back out."

"So what are you saying? A fucking 2000kg vehicle disappeared into thin air?"

"Of course not sir. There is evidence of white paint on the floor inside the facility, and a blue vehicle of the same dimensions was seen leaving the carpark."

"Did you trace where that vehicle went?"

"Yes sir. We have traced it all the way to a block of apartments in the Latin Quarter."

"Is it still there?" Said Julien, feeling his pulse rate begin to race.

"No sir, it stopped there for around ten minutes and then left. We followed it on camera until it entered the grounds of the American Embassy."

"Well this is interesting. They know that we can't enforce a search of those premises, however, as I believe this to be unsanctioned assistance by the elder woman's previous colleagues, I doubt very much if they would be holed up inside an official residence. Do we know anything about the apartment block where the vehicle stopped?"

"Yes sir. One of our inside men at the Embassy said that the shit has hit the fan about the unauthorised use of a safe house in the Latin Quarter by an FBI operative."

"That has to be it! Get every man and vehicle to that location. We won't need to raid the apartment; we can just wait them out. They can't stay in there forever , and even if they did, at least they would not be advancing in their mission to ridicule France and the church. Besides, we could always arrange a fire in the building to flush them out. The cladding and century old timber can be quite hazardous I am told."

....

I could sense, as opposed to see Salonge's whole-body tense as we approached the first set of traffic lights. She reached into the side pocket of the door and pulled out two baseball caps, donning one and throwing the other onto my lap.

"Quick, put this on, tuck your hair inside and keep your head down."

"What is it?"

Salonge was now angling the rear-view mirror to focus on some activity behind us.

"Two black cars have just entered the apartment

gates, and another has parked up outside. There are two more vehicles of the same type approaching on the other side of the traffic lights ahead."

The black cars paid us no heed as they whizzed past and screeched to a halt either side of the entrance from where we had exited only seconds ago. The traffic was painfully slow until we eventually crossed the Pont Notre Dame leading towards the bastille area. It then only took us another fifteen minutes before we were heading south on the Route de Chartres towards Orleans and Gien.

I checked my messages. "Beth has just sent me an e-mail with an attachment. She concurs with the possible interpretation which your friend sent us.

She assures me that it is accurate, but there are too many words missing from the Aramaic projection pictures for it to make any real sense. I think that we need all three stones to uncover its full content."

"You are probably right my clever young cousin. Indulge me if you would, I am somewhat of an expert at cryptic messages and codes."

"Really, you think you can make sense of this random mess?"

Salonge glanced at the image on my cell phone.

"Actually, it looks like your professor friend has accurately spaced the missing words, although it could be misleading if the English substitution is a much longer or shorter word in Aramaic. Read it to me anyway Kacey."

As soon as I began to recite the broken text the words magically began pulsating in the same colour red as the blood ruby.

I,   of God hereby   those born as

both   woman shall   God as the

saviour   Only one   the

virtues   can truly   good, and

the   the earth.   for

                    burden of our weaknesses

the   comes when   wins

through. Only then can the world live in harmony.

My   Mother be   and in one

are the   things. I deliver   to

you,   in the form   stones.

You must   until the day

that   and of your bloodline, shall

reveal   Only when   joined
together,   crystal font
your   can this message be   and
truly understood.

Your quest   the words
my messengers   Arcangel, Saint
Catherine of   and Saint   They
will advise   the suffering
oppressed in your land,   many
years   . There are three orders which
you must obey   be accepted into
our creators   You must lead the
                      dressed in manly   You
shall remain   either man or
woman. You   ultimate
sacrifice, as did I.

Many   when one of your
born in the bodily   will
the truth   the world.

Amen

"Well I must say, making sense of that will be a tough one regardless of my training." Said Salonge. "There are certainly enough key words there to safely assume that it directly relates to Joan and your quest."

"I agree, but the further into this we get, the more confused I am as to how all of this relates to me. If Joan was somehow special, and it is true that she was born like me, how does that prove that we were related?"

"That's what we are here to discover Kacey. I have a feeling that we have not even scratched the surface."

"What more could there be? She did have three older brothers, and a much older sister, but little is known of them."

"Perhaps that is what needs to be discovered. Don't forget, there is still a number of untranslated documents in your grandfather's folder. Once we get to Gien I will call Anthony to see if he has made any more progress."

"Do you think the bad guys will be watching out for us in Gien?"

"Somehow I don't think so." Said Salonge, proudly demonstrating her recent efforts to brush up on history. "Gien is only mentioned briefly as a short stopover before Joan liberated Orleans."

"Yes that's right, I am impressed my wise old cousin. Joan stayed there briefly whilst organising a gathering of troops on the west of the city. Once all of the English barricades and soldiers were diverted towards that threat, Joan simply marched in through the east gate of the city with food and provisions. The English then withdrew with their tails between their legs."

I could tell that Salonge was taking everything in, but I could also detect a frostiness in her demeanour. "What's wrong Salonge?"

"Using the term older cousin is fine. Wise is ok too...but old...really???"

"Oh I see. I meant it as a compliment, as in wiser than your years. In truth you look around my age!"

Salonge let out a real belly laugh. "Now you have gone too far the other way. Apology accepted."

Chapter 29

Upping the Ante

Special Agent Jack Nichols had had his worst dressing down to date. He had been told in no uncertain terms what his future would be if he ever tried a stunt like that again without the proper authorisation . His boss screamed that US Agency safe houses were for official assignments only and not for him to use in the assistance of friends, even if they were ex colleagues of the same agency. He was instructed to make sure the place was sterile as there was a remote chance that they would have to give access to the French authorities to search the premises . The FBI had of course denied any knowledge of assisting two women or giving them bed and board for the night, but the French were insisting on full cooperation.

Jack Nichols drove the delivery van into the courtyard and immediately spotted the suspicious dark vehicles parked along the street by the entrance to the FBI's safe house apartment block. Jack exited the vehicle and retrieved a box from the rear, pulling the peak of his Amazon cap a little lower as he did so. He ambled over to the entrance door and punched in a code which automatically gave him access without the need for someone to press a buzzer from inside the apartment. Jack faked a conversation with the intercom and held the Amazon box in front of the tiny camera as if being requested to so by the occupant. Once inside Jack sprinted up the stairs, avoiding the elevator, and began searching for anything Salonge had missed when sanitising the place before they had left.

....

Julien's phone buzzed.

"Julien, it's Antoine, we have a show at the safe house."

Even though Antoine had been the one to inform Pierre of Julien's betrayal, he thought that he was only doing the right thing by the organisation and, as such, Julien decided to give him another chance.

"Have you spotted the females?"

"No sir. But a delivery man from Amazon turned up at the safe house and we ran his picture through facial recognition."

"And."

"And it's a match for the medic at the crash scene."

"If he exits the building, you must follow him but leave two cars at the residence." Ordered Julien before hanging up and punching in Gabriels cell phone number."

"Gabriel, it's Julien. The mysterious medic who rescued the girls has turned up at the FBI safe house."

"Send in a team. Incapacitate the bastard and tell them to take him to the Chateau, I assume that is where you are calling from."

"Yes sir, I'm in the office. But Gabriel, we are talking about abducting a probable FBI Agent."

"Of course he is a fucking FBI Agent, but this is France, not America. I will meet you by the waxworks at the rear of the grounds this evening, and make sure that the Yankee fucker is with you."

Julien's face turned white as he redialled Antoine and gave the order.

....

Gabriel's tumour was making itself known, but the throbbing pain was exhilarating for a change, not the dull ache which usually presented itself. He felt sure that this was God's way of rewarding him for his courage and for making bold decisions.

Yes, that's it. I need to be far more assertive if I am to protect the honour of France and the Catholic Church.

Gabriel picked up the phone to his PDLF members working at the French consulate in England.

"Just listen carefully and do not speak." Said Gabriel along with the password which identified him as the head of the PDLF. "There is no doubt that the professor in England is a friend of our quarry and has probably had contact. Shake her up and see if we can rattle out some information of use. Scare her a bit before you confront her. Shoot her dog or something."

Gabriel hung up and everything went black.

....

Professor Elizabeth Field was exhausted as she loaded the shopping into the back of her twelve-year-old Ford Focus. It had been a particularly draining day at the university, but it was the various aches and pains which still remained since her supposed full recovery from the beating a few weeks back that were causing her most aggravation. The groceries consisted mostly of salad ingredients and were no real problem to lift from the trolly. It was the last few items which caused her to involuntarily wince, the surprisingly heavy flour sized bags of bird seed, the tins of cat food, and the grotesquely huge bag of contents for the litter tray.

Beth entered her apartment expecting to hear the tweeting of her cockatiel defiantly teasing George the cat as he sat on the arm of the chair considering the conundrum of how to breach the feathered pet's impregnable cage, but all was silent. Beth looked into the empty cage and became even more confused by the still securely fastened door. She walked into the kitchen and plonked the bags onto the work surface, a ritual that usually resulted in George emerging from his hiding place to worm in and out of her legs expecting to be fed, but nothing. She then detected an unusual smell, half burnt Sunday roast, or half singed hair caught in a pair of faulty GHD straighteners . Beth noticed a post-it note stuck to the oven door which was beginning to brown and curl due to the heat of the appliance.

We wanted some answers from your pets regarding a particular ex history student of yours, but your animals refused to talk. We shall visit you soon and anticipate far more cooperation. If not, the same fate could befall you!

Beth's eyes began to well up as her shaking hands opened the oven door. The heat, and rancid billowing smoke hit her face in waves until she finally had a clear view inside. Staring back at her from within the 220-degree crematorium were the shrivelled, dehydrated eyes of her beloved pets, bodies bare of both feather and fur.

....

Gabriel woke with a start. He was naked and there was, once again, evidence of self-sexual satisfaction dispersed around his office in the Elysee Palace. Jesus Christ, he thought, the President of France is in the next room. The door was locked but what if he had demanded that it be broken down, he thought. Gabriel looked at his watch calculating that he had blacked out for over three hours. He quickly dressed and left the room to see his secretary looking up quizzically from her desk.

"Gabriel, you have ignored the last five calls, I was getting concerned."

"I was on my private cell phone...personal business."

"Oh dear, is everything alright?"

"Yes, it's fine. Would you tell the President I have had to leave on a domestic matter?"

"The President has gone for the weekend and, if it is ok with you sir, I would like to leave also."

"Yes that is fine Ines, have a nice weekend. Oh, and Ines."

"Yes sir."

"I have important and confidential documents splayed around my office and have no time to put them away. The door is locked and should remain so. No one is to enter, not even the cleaners."

"Understood sir. They don't have a key to yours or the President's room, only me"

"Very good. See you on Monday."

....

Jack was pleased with what he had found, or rather not found in the safe house. Salonge had been as thorough as ever, and his special torch had picked up no missed fingerprints or hair fibres. She had even remembered to burn the bed linen in the tumble dryer, come incinerator. He had one more visual inspection of the premises before opening the entrance door and stooping to remove his blue plastic shoe coverings. As he did so, the light spilling from the room produced a second shadow to join his own and he instantly felt the prick of a short needle puncturing the soft skin at the side of his neck.

....

Gabriel's headaches were coming and going with increasing frequency. When he awoke from the latest blackout at the office, he had felt almost rejuvenated. But the traffic on his drive to the chateau brought on a migraine as severe as he had ever experienced. As Gabriel's destination eventually came into view he felt the infliction ease, and by the time he had parked and entered the wax work facility it had all but gone.

The four soldiers from the PDLF had enough knowledge of the equipment in order to get the wax in the vats to boiling point. They were not required to learn the skilful process by which the regular employees turned moulds into lifelike characters to populate the chateau's exhibits.

Gabriel walked in and was satisfied with the scene; the bubbling wax, the wooden chair with restraints attached to a pully and chain, the single light with its silver reflector dish, and a 200-watt halogen bulb beaming towards the interrogation seat. The one thing which was missing was the occupant from whom he would extract information. It was the rhythmic throbbing in his temple which indicated Gabriels heart beginning to race as he fumbled for his phone yet again.

"Antione, where the bloody hell are you?"

"We will be with you in five minutes sir."

"And our guest, did you successfully extract him from the safe house?"

"Yes sir, he's sleeping like a baby."

"Excellent."

Chapter 30

Finally the Odds Improve

Sir Charles Worwood, head of MI6, as well as chair for the International Crime Fighting Cooperative known as AICAC, was disturbed by the developments that had emerged over the past few days, but also glad that these developments meant that he could now sanction some much-needed assistance to one of his main agents and her young cousin.

Although made up of representatives from most western powers, only Charles and the US representative, FBI Director Al Vicarrio, was present at this meeting.

"Please take a seat Al. Can I get you some coffee?"

"Two shots of espresso with two shots of brandy...actually, skip the coffee and make it four shots of brandy Charles. And whilst you are at it, try to think of a good reason why Salonge, one of our top two AICAC Agents, is running around France causing mayhem with some young, distant relative?"

"I have no idea what you mean. I did sanction her request for two weeks annual leave."

"Bullshit Charles, we have known each other far too long. What is God's name is she up to?"

Charles let out a puff of resignation as he slumped into his seat and joined his colleague in a ridiculously large brandy.

"I'm sorry Al, the first part about sanctioning leave is true, but things have developed at quite some pace."

Al reclined his chair in anticipation of full disclosure. "It's best you give me the whole shooting match Charles because I have a disturbing revelation also."

"Well it all began rather innocently actually. Salonge's young cousin from England was given some ancient documents by her grandfather which claim that she is related to Joan of Arc. This young girl, Kacey Chapman, began life as Kieth Chapman and, after a tortured upbringing, underwent the necessary surgery to...shall we say, correctly align her body with whom she really is. The documents also claim that Joan of Arc lived and died having been born with a similar physical predicament, something which the French, and the Catholic Church are hell bent on preventing from becoming common knowledge."

"There has to be more than that Charles."

"Yes, I fully concur. But what that may be, I have no idea. All I do know is that the Kacey's grandfather was murdered, both she and Salonge have been vigorously pursued across France without regard for their wellbeing, and there has been another development over here on British soil, but that issue could be a pure coincidence."

"That's more bullshit Charles, you don't believe in coincidences...what's happened?"

"Now you must believe me Al, this most recent information has just come to light. I decided to do a search on Kacey Chapmans relatives and friends to see if they had been receiving any undue attention. Her old professor at Oxford was assaulted two weeks ago. It was initially reported as a simple mugging but since then her apartment has been broken into and a threatening note left on the door of her oven. Inside the oven were the cremated remains of her pet cat and parakeet. The lady in question, a Professor Field, has been suitably spooked to the point where she has finally revealed to police that all of these events are indeed connected and relate to Kacey Chapman and the documents.

"Is that everything Charles."

"Absolutely old chap, on my honour."

It was now Al Vicarrio's turn to make some revelations. "Well hold on to your shirt tails because this shit has just become a whole new ball game."

"Oh I see, please go on."

"It seems that one of my FBI Agents in France decided to offer Salonge some unsanctioned assistance. Not only did he commandeer a vehicle and use our resources to dress it up as a French ambulance before rescuing our heroines, he also, again without permission, gave them overnight bed and board in one of our safe houses."

"Surely you can clear all of that up Al, and just give your agent a wrap on the hands proportionate to his misdemeanour. Are the girls ok?"

"We think that the girls are ok. Where they currently are I have no idea. Something which is of more concern to me is that the French authorities are demanding access to the safehouse. We sent Special Agent Jack Nichols back there yesterday to sanitise the safe house. He has not been seen since."

"That certainly does change things, what?" Worwood had a habit from his old Etonian days of ending a sentence with a question, which was not a question. "I suggest we call an emergency AICAC meeting to sanction our direct involvement."

"No, we can't do that Charles. Whoever is behind this obviously carry some clout at the highest levels in the French political system as well as their government agencies. Given the subject matter, it is entirely possible that their tentacles reach to Rome and several other locations. I suggest the British and Americans go alone on this one. More accurately, I think at stage one we provide Anthony Mazur with some resources and send him to Paris to help his wife."

"Don't you think that he, being Salonge's husband, is too close emotionally to handle this?" Said Worwood, involuntarily expressing his thoughts aloud ."

Al dismissed the statement . "They are the best team I have ever seen. Each of them are singularly extremely talented... together they are formidable."

"Agreed." Said Charles as he clinked gasses with Al and swallowed the remainder of his brandy. "I shall liaise with Anthony and make his travel arrangements. I assume that he can rely on the cooperation of your people on the ground in France?"

"You will have absolute and unlimited cooperation from the FBI, and if they have harmed Special Agent Jack Nichols then there will be hell to pay.

"Thank you Al. Fortunately, I am in a position to immediately sanction MI6 involvement. I shall get my best digital intelligence man, Billy Agoba, onto this and see what we can find out in cyber space.

These people must be communicating somehow and if anyone can find them then it's Billy.

....

Jack Nichols nasal senses were the first to come alive; pungent fumes from the burning wax beginning to sting the inner reaches of his nostrils. Next to reengage were his eyes, but his brain seemed to be lagging behind, unable to comprehend the visual messages being sent along its optical nerves. From his slumped head viewpoint it was obvious that he was sitting on a wooden chair, legs dangling over the seat ledge, feet swinging loosely some three feet off the floor. As his ears finally began to register sound, Jack could hear a squeaking noise from somewhere high above him, perfectly timed with the gentle to and fro movement of his chair. He quickly guessed that he was suspended from some kind of metal pully.

He initially attempted to raise his head, but it felt like a ten-ton weight. The FBI agent then remained as motionless as possible, trying to survey as much as he could from his peripheral vision before his abductors realised that he was conscious. Suddenly a hand grabbed his hair, wrenching several follicles from his scalp as he was forced to face his abductors. In front of him were four people in smart suits (one clearly a woman) wearing grotesque WW11 type gas masks.

Gabriel spoke first. "Ah, I see that you are awake Special Agent Jack Nichols."

Having been drugged and now being restrained in a type of Witching chair, Jack knew all too well that a painful interrogation was imminent; the heat from the huge bubbling vat to his right being the most likely method for encouraging his cooperation. Jack said nothing, fully aware that unless there were a rescue team on its way then he would not be leaving this factory.

"I can see that you are mentally assessing the situation, however, I assure you that the outcome could be far more favourable than your training would suggest."

"Enlighten me." Said Jack in a mocking tone.

"It's quite simple really. You were unconscious when you arrived and, providing that you cooperate, can leave in much the same way without being harmed. You will have no clue as to this location and our identities are concealed by these rather ugly masks. All you need to do is tell us all you know about your ex-colleague and her companion along with their whereabouts."

"Go fuck yourselves."

"Now now Agent Nichols, you do disappoint me."

"I'm not telling you shit. There are moulds in the corner, a door marked costumes and wigs to my left, and a cauldron of boiling wax to my right. If you let me go then we would have this place nailed within the hour. I can already make a couple of educated guesses."

"Of course you are correct Agent Nichols. I apologise for underestimating your intelligence. Please allow me to offer you a more realistic alternative. Tell us what we need to know, and I will give you a swift death with a bullet to the back of your head. If you refuse, then you will be lowered into the vat of wax inch by painful inch."

"Salonge needed help...I gave it...end of story. I know nothing more."

Gabriel gave a signal and the man standing behind Jack Nichols, the same one who had grabbed his hair, began to turn a crank. Very slowly the chair started shifting both vertically and horizontally until Jack was eventually situated high above the centre of the boiling wax.

Chapter 31

Johnny's dream Job

Johhny Valatone was sitting in his high tech shed playing some of his favourite tunes across the airwaves when the door burst open and in rushed two enormous men clad in black. It was only when his eyes adjusted to the invading sunlight that he could just make out blackened eyes through the tiny letterbox slits in their balaclava's.

"Oh man, it's a bit over the top, don't you think?"

"Shut up and put this over your head." Said the first man throwing him a black hood without the the slit for viewing."

"This is bollox. I don't even make money from doing this man, I just love playing music."

Johnny began broadcasting rapidly into his microphone. *Ive just been busted by some police thugs trying to shut me down. It's an abuse of my human rights and I want my listeners to.....*

Suddenly there was an explosion of noise as his equipment flew off the desk, blown into a million pieces by the bullets erupting from the barrel of the second man's semi-automatic.

"Jesus Christ, you could have killed me!"

"Put the hood on now."

A terrified Johnny did as instructed before being led to a black vehicle and bundled into the back. For the first fifteen minutes of the journey he remained silently shaking whilst trying to figure out whom his abductors could be. Worryingly, he had already figured that these were not police chasing pirate radio operators, and he was also sure that his abduction was linked to Kacey. Johnny summoned the courage to begin asking questions, convinced that Kacey would forgive him for divulging what he knew, which was very little anyway.

"What do you want with me? If it's to do with Kacey I know very little."

Nothing.

"Just pull over and ask me anything. If I know the answers I'll just tell you...I promise." He pleaded.

Nothing.

"That was ten fucking grands worth of equipment you just demolished."

Nothing.

What he guessed to be more than an hour later he could sense that they were in a tunnel, a car park, or some other type of underground space. The hood he was wearing was impervious to light, but the strange echo of the engine and wheels entering a confined space was the giveaway. Johnny was gently assisted out of the vehicle and taken into an elevator. (This was now even scarier, if that were possible) After a brief but swift ascent, the doors opened, and his hood was removed. The two SAS like men pressed an intercom button on the wall.

"Sir, the package has arrived."

The door opened and a smiling Charles Worwood offered his hand.

"Do come in young man. I must apologise for the method of this inconvenient visit, what. But you see it was necessary for your own safety to be transported here to MI6 headquarters as soon as possible. I believe you know Professor Field."

Beth's face looked ashen, but her warm smile immediately put Johnny at ease.

"Please take a seat young man. Can I get you some refreshment...some soda perhaps?"

"I'll take a double vodka and coke along with a cheque for ten grand to cover a smashed deck and a vintage MB C540 microphone if that's not too much trouble."

Worwood laughed. "Ah, I am guessing that your DJ equipment was damaged during your extraction."

"Blown to smithereens would be more accurate."

"Don't worry young man. I have a job for you whereby you will be employed to head up a new London Radio Station. It has the latest thingamabobs used in your trade which will be yours to keep when this mission is over. Professor Field here will also be assisting us, and you both shall be remunerated handsomely for your assistance. Now, let me get you both up to speed, what."

....

We had driven through Gien, and Salonge said that she could detect no signs of unusual or suspicious characters lurking about. We checked into a small motel on the outskirts of the town and began our research. I was starting to feel rather despondent having discovered that the town had been sacked and rebuilt many times over the centuries. It had also been mostly destroyed by bombing during WW11. Joans message wrapped around the blood ruby said that a second stone, a blue Saphire would be found, or rather, would find me from its hiding place beneath the arch of a foot. Any statues dating from the early fifteenth century would surly have been destroyed by now. And the church where it resided would long since have crumbled to dust. I looked up to see that worried look on Solange's face again.

"What is it cousin? No lies please."

"It's Anthony. I have sent him at least ten messages during our journey here without a single reply."

"Perhaps he has been assigned a new mission by Ailac?"

"It's AICAC, and no. He would have got word to me somehow."

It was then that her phone made a ping, and I could see the relief on her face followed by disappointment and confusion.

"Who is it?"

"I don't know...I don't recognise the number."

"What does it say."

"101.7 FM, that's it."

There was a retro style, Bakelite radio sitting on the bedside table. I ran across the room and twisted the circular dial to the appropriate position. Straight away I could hear my friends voice and recognised his style of delivery, but the DJ said his name was Tony

Alva.

"Turn that rubbish off, I'm trying to think!" Said an irritated Salonge.

"Be quiet." I snapped. "That's my DJ friend from England."

Suddenly the tough plastic box had taken on a whole new level of importance.

That was the fabulous 'One night in Bangkok' by Murray Head and it goes out to my good friend Anthony who has just spent one night in that crazy city before boarding a flight to meet his lovely wife who is visiting relatives in France.

Salonge smiled and began scribbling some letters onto paper. "It's Worwood at MI6. He's using your friend to send us messages. What was your friends name again, it was Valatone wasn't it?"

"Yes, why?"

"Tony, given some license, could be spelt Tone. The DJ's last name is Alva...jumble them up and you have Valatone."

The retro box now had our full attention.

This next song goes out to that very lady. Sit back and relax to the slick and soulful delivery of 'Until

Morning' by James Vickery.

"It's Anthony, he's coming to France to help us. We have to let him know where we are!" Said Salonge, once again looking troubled.

"What's wrong now?" I said. "Turn that frown upside down...surely that's good news?"

"Yes, yes of course it is. But why hasn't my husband returned my messages? He must have had time between flights to respond. I think that they know that the people we are up against have connections at the highest level in France and think any communication may be compromised."

The solution came from the Bakelite speaker.

So you lucky young lady, if you want to reciprocate by sending your devoted husband a dedication, you can e mail me on Soulalva@radmusiclondon.com, or send an SMS to 1396629.

Again I saw a big smile appear across Salonge's face which filled me with both jealousy and sadness. Since Sir Grandad had died she was, although a recent acquaintance, the closest family I had left in the world. I was also jealous that I couldn't imagine, even in my wildest dreams, ever attaining what they have together.

"I am happy that Anthony is on his way. And God knows we could use all the help we can get, but can you concentrate on the quest at hand and not your potential canoodling and special cuddles. Don't worry, I shall give you both your space when the moment arises."

I instantly felt guilty at the clipped and spiteful undertone of my delivery. Salonge, however, reached for my hands and kissed each of my cheeks.

"Dear Kacey. The SMS code is 1396629. The letter 'M' is the 13th letter of the English alphabet. 'I' is the 9th letter, and 6 stands for what it is. Then we have the second part. 'F' is the 6th letter of your alphabet followed by '2', representing 'B' and finally '9', once again representing 'I'. If you put it all together we can be assured that MI6 and the FBI are now supporting us."

I sank my face into the crook of my cousins neck and began sobbing uncontrollably, the pressure of the situation combined with a mixture of emotions suddenly becoming too overwhelming to keep in. Salonge began stroking the back of my head and manoeuvred her mouth towards my ear, whispering words of comfort.

"My dear Kacey, I can promise that we shall complete your grandfathers dying wish, but I cannot guarantee that what we find will be of any comfort to you. I can make you one guarantee though. As sure as the French produce the best chefs in the world, you too will find that special someone. And when that happens, it will be he who is the lucky one."

Chapter 32

Julien made a Mistake

Jack was sweating profusely and didn't know how much longer he could keep his legs stretched out in front of him. The pully suspending his chair had been lowered to the point whereby if his legs were not held horizontally they would have been submerged into the boiling wax almost to his kneecaps. The process to reach this perilous position had taken almost an hour. Up until now only one of his abductors has been speaking: Where are the girls? Where are the documents? Why did you help them? What did they tell you? Each time Jack responded with 'I don't know' the chair was lowered another couple of inches. He did divulge that he assisted them in response to a call for help from Salonge's husband, and that he was more than willing to help as they had been colleagues some years back. That was the only occasion when the pully had been raised back up as a demonstration of how the game would work.

As the muscles in Jacks legs and stomach were beginning to give way he heard the agitated voice of a second man. He feigned no interest, pretending to focus on his immediate predicament and wanted to convey that he had no understanding of French. However, he understood the words coming from the second man's mouth, even though they were muffled by his mask, and understood they were his only hope.

"Sir, we cannot kill an FBI operative. Please raise the chain, it's clear he knows nothing!" Said Julien.

The man whom he was addressing dropped to his knees and pressed his hands against his temples, obviously in pain.

"Do not presume to tell me what to do. If we kill him they will surely try to hunt us down, this is true. But if we let him go then they are sure to find us." Said Gabriel whilst trying to return to a standing position.

"Are you ok sir? I beg you, please come outside for some fresh air and hear my reasoning." Said Julien, guiding Gabriel out through the huge sliding doors.

Julien continued. "The man was hooded and drugged for the complete journey here and we can do the same again... just dump him somewhere in Paris."

Gabriel was still massaging his temples when he replied. "And then he contacts his agency, and they raid every waxworks within an hour's radius of Paris of which, may I remind you, there are only two."

"My suggestion is that you leave for your apartment now. The other three can drug the agent and deposit him on a Paris street. Fifteen minutes after they leave here, I will call the police and say that we have had a break in at the waxworks."

Gabriel seemed to be in increasing pain. "Do as you wish Julien, but if this goes wrong then it will be your turn to become an exhibit."

Julien watched as Gabriel walked gingerly to the trunk of his car and took out a bag. He appeared to be taking some medication before sliding into the driver's seat and speeding away.

....

Anthony Mazur passed through customs at Charles de Gaulle without any problems and turned on his cell phone. His ears were bombarded with message alerts. Most were from Salonge saying that they were fine and not to worry, but sensibly she gave no indication of their whereabouts. She did say, however, that if he should become bored with French music that he should tune his rentals radio to 107.7 FM for some English lyrics...*They have so many hidden meanings lol.* Muz knew straight away that Charles Worwood, their immediate boss at AICAC, had set up some sort of communication channel.

Anthony produced his false documentation and filled out the insurance forms for the young man at the Avis rental desk. He asked for the address of the best three, five-star hotels close to the Arc de Triomphe. The young man offered to check availability for him, but Anthony said that he preferred to drive by in person as the pictures always overstated their opulence. "Besides, he said with the confident wink of an experienced traveller, "you sometimes get better deals as a walk in."

Anthony headed to the parking bay where his compact was waiting but he would not be heading to the Arc de Triomphe. He had already booked a small hotel close to the Pigalle but wanted to cover his tracks. Once in the car he tuned his radio to 107.7 to hear the unmistakable banter of a London DJ who called himself Tony Alva.

That last tune was for my dear American friend Anthony. Hope you had a safe flight from Bangkok. This next song, 'Come to me,' is from the fabulous musical Les Misérables and goes out to JN who is currently in the American hospital of Paris after an unfortunate run in with an ambulance whilst on holiday. If you are listening Anthony, perhaps you should pay him a visit and bring some grapes. After all, he is one of your countrymen.

Anthony processed the information and was soon screeching out of the section of carpark reserved for the rentals: The man who he had asked to help Salonge and her cousin was currently being treated in hospital. He knew that as an ambulance was mentioned, it meant that the two were connected and Jack Nichols had been injured.

....

Julien was exhausted as he contemplated taking a quick shower to rid his skin of dust and the smell of bubbling wax. During the fifteen minutes before calling the police to report the break in, Julien had turned off the burners, scrubbed the wooden seat of any DNA and detached the chain pully. He had then gone to the walk-in costume closet and cast medieval clothes and props around the floor of the wax factory before taking a quad bike fitted with a trailer to retrieve empty wine bottles from the chateaus cellar. This was to complete the scene he had described to the police of some youths breaking in to have a raucous party. The head of the Gendarmerie had wanted to send some men over immediately despite the hour. However, Julien had told them that they could take a statement in the morning as nothing appeared to be irreparably damaged or missing. If the FBI agent described his interrogation Julien would suggest that his abductors must have staged the fake scene.

Something was keeping Julien glued to his office seat. Why did Gabriel drop to the floor holding his temples? The heat emitting from the vat was not excessive at the distance they were standing, and the fumes were evident, but not overwhelming with the extractor fans efficiently sucking air out through the chimney. Gabriel also appeared to be enjoying the prospect of submerging the FBI agent in boiling wax. A thought came to Julien. What if Pierre had uncovered some condition which Gabriel was hiding and that was why he wished to usurp him as leader. Pierres belongings were still boxed in the corner of the office waiting to be delivered to his estate. Julien paced around the cardboard stacks of labelled containers; photographs; suits; ornaments; certificates/accolades; private desk papers and diaries.

It was the final, and smallest box which caught his attention... Diaries!

Julien slipped the knife out of his Churches Chelsea boot. He hated the English, but this traditional shoemaker produced the most comfortable and subtle slip-on ankle boot he had ever worn, and they were easily adapted to conceal weapons. He sliced through the duct tape with ease, and he scanned the folders and books held within. He trained his eyes to search for more personal documentation as opposed to official looking papers and was rewarded with three promising candidates. The first was a large leather-bound book emblazoned with the words

'Work Diary.' Julien flicked through this with abandon, stopping randomly to read a few lines of exactly what he had expected to see; July 16th, meeting with Gabriel and the President; August 21st, envoy arrives from Saudi. He discarded that and reached for the next item marked private diary. Julien spent barley thirty seconds on this one; September 5th, daughter's birthday; December 1st, Anniversary. His third choice was smaller, but much thicker, containing many more pages. He eagerly tried to pull the pages apart, but the crocodile skin cover would not separate. Julien inspected the booklet to reveal a solid gold, ornately engraved block at the base of its spine which had a tiny keyhole in its centre. In total frustration he reached for Pierre's solid crystal ashtray glistening from within the depths of the box. Julien grabbed the object and smashed it against the ornate locking device which broke apart with ease.

The pages within were structured similar to that of a private telephone directory, or of the now outdated Filofax with silver ringed loops allowing for more pages to be inserted, the letters A-Z cascading along the right-hand side. Instinctively he opened at the pages marked A.

It has pained me so much to give the order to assassinate my love, Adele. I so wish that I had been brave enough to leave my wife and marry this angel sent to me from heaven. However, for the good of France, and the preservation of the Catholic Church, I had no choice. This pain in my heart shall remain until my dying day.

Realising that these were Pierre's most secret and personal thoughts, Juliens thumb flicked immediately to the letter J.

Julien is one of my most loyal and trusted soldiers. I realise that I am particularly hard on him, but this is necessary if the Protecteurs de la France are to survive. He has made many mistakes over the years, but never repeated a single one.. He is truly special, and I think of him as the son I never had, unlike that buffoon of a nephew Marcus. I will need to reveal all to him sooner rather than later as Gabriel is fast becoming a liability.

Juliens eyes began to well up, knowing he had made a dreadful mistake. This time his fingers almost refused to obey as he hesitated over the letter G, for Gabriel.

This was the third time that Gabriel had taken on a strange persona whilst we were on PDLF business abroad. He has always had a penchant for ladies of the night following a successful meeting. But this time, in the back room of a nightclub, he murdered a girl. I tried to stop him when I heard her screams, but he had an inhuman strength running through the sinews of his arms and his eyes were that of a delirious madman. I managed the situation satisfactorily, but when we spoke of it the next morning he had no recollection of the event and even suggested that it was I who required psychiatric evaluation. Please God, with a heavy heart, I pray that Julien is successful in stopping this beast and joins me at the helm of the PDLF. The order to assassinate Gabriel is absolutely necessary, I just hope that my good friend Julien completes this difficult assignment . My investigations uncovered that Gabriel has an incurable tumour which will increasingly produce psychotic behaviour. Once I divulge this to Julien he will understand what appears to be a strange order.

Julien sank to the floor. "What have I done?"

....

Anthony was expected by the FBI Agents guarding Jacks private room at the American Hospital in Paris.

"How's it going Jack?" Said a sheepish Anthony.

"How do I look?"

"At first glance, I would say...medium rare."

"F-You." Said Jack Nichols. "Give my wife a helping hand you said. Should be a walk in the park, you said."

"Sorry bud. Let's go get these bastards. Any idea when you will be discharged?"

"Get my clothes."

Chapter 33

I've seen the Light

We had had a good night's sleep, feeling confident that our pursuers had no idea where we were. Salonge popped out to buy some croissants, cold meats, and fruit. Our simple room did have a kettle along with sachets of coffee, sugar and mini, foil covered tubs of milk.

"I have been asking around and initially the vendors in the shops were confident that there are no churches left standing in Gien which date back to the early 15th century."

"So our trip here was pointless and the quest is at an end." I said, feeling a wave of despair wash over me.

"Not so fast my young cousin. The old concierge downstairs said that the old castle was completed towards the end of the fifteenth century."

"So you are saying that Joan came back to life and hid the blue gem there?" I said sarcastically."

"Dear Kacey, you are usually so mature for one of such a young age and, quite frankly, I would prefer it if you could maintain that persona as opposed to one who conjures up these sulky attempts at sarcasm."

"I'm so sorry Salonge. It's just that the emotional

rollercoaster of euphoria followed by despair is becoming unbearable."

Salonge placed a sympathetic arm around my shoulder. "Do you think I would say what I just said if there were not some encouraging news?"

Instantly the roller coaster was on the upward track again. "What is it? What have you uncovered?"

"There is a church which forms part of the castle. It was not completely destroyed, and the later structure was sympathetically attached to the original place of worship...It also overlooks the Loire. Remember what my contact at the FBI said?"

"Yes, that during our search we should pay particular attention to places that are close to, or overlook, water."

"There is more. We are looking for a stone hidden in the arch of a foot. This implies that the sapphire must have been concealed inside the foot of a statue. The old man said that many treasures and statues from around the area were moved to the cellars of the castle for safe keeping. I am going to see if the priest would allow me a viewing. I know that you would like to come along Kacey, but don't forget that they will be looking for two females: one of them English. It will be easier if I go alone."

Once again I felt the beginnings of a sulk coming on, but managed to hold it in.

....

Anthony Mazur and Jack Nichols were in a pokey bedroom overlooking the Pigalle. Jack was lying face down on the bed in his boxer shorts allowing the salve to sink in to his blistered calves. Anthony was sitting at the two-seater table trying to fold a map in such a way as to still be of use whilst making room for his laptop.

"So, what's with the 'Anthony' business all of a sudden. I'm sure that Salonge used to call you Muz."

It happened when we moved to Thailand with AICAC. The Thai's rarely use the letter Z and had trouble pronouncing my name. It didn't matter how many times I told them; they would always call me Mush."

"And that bothered you?"

"Not really, it's when Salonge started using that name that I insisted on being called Anthony."

Jack laughed. "Have you found any waxwork candidates?"

"There are only two that look to be possibilities, given the size of the facility you described."

"It was only a guesstimate...I was hooded and drugged don't forget."

"The first is part of Disneyland, to the south near Marne a Vallee, and the other is a place called Chateau de Breteuil."

"It has to be the latter." Said Jack as he rolled onto his back wincing as the muscles of his legs caused the taught crusty skin to crack. "I remember hearing the crunching noise of rubber tyres on cobbled stones when we approached, and the drugs were wearing off. I have taken the kids to Disneyland a dozen times and don't recall any cobbled approach roads."

"Great work Jack. Let's see what we can find out."

Anthony began punching his keyboard until the screen was populated with the Chateau's website. He then clicked the *'about us'* icon.

"Chateau de Breteuil has been in the family of...blah...blah. The house is packed with historic paintings and furniture dating back to...blah blah. The estate is currently managed by Pierre Cardout who's expertise in Fr...."

Jack sat bolt upright. "Say that name again."

"Pierre Cardout."

"Jesus, he was the guy who just died in the car crash

on the Champs Elysee. The same one that I rescued the girls from!"

"Best we pay them a visit in the morning."

Anthony then returned his attention to his keyboard and googled the feed from Thames FM radio.

"Seriously, you are listening to some English music channel. You could at least tap into some blues from Chicago."

"It's a communication vehicle set up by MI6. Anything important will be looped every hour, on the hour and its almost nine o clock."

Tony Alva's voice crackled out from his laptop.

Hey Anthony. I hope your friend is recovering well. I have a message from your wife. She arrived yesterday at Nigel's place down south...or Nige as he likes to be called. She requested this song for you. So lay back and listen to this classic by Mike Waters...I'm doin Fiiiiiine.

Anthong focussed his attention back on the laminated map.

"I have it...I know where the girls are. Down south means south of Paris. Nige is an anagram of Gien. It's where Joan of Arc prepared for the liberation of Orlean.

....

Salonge had just completed her second circuit around the circumference of the castle and was back at the entrance to the oldest part of the structure; the inadvertently annexed ancient church.

"Can we help you young lady?"

Salonge spun around a little too alarmingly, but quickly regained her composure. Standing in front of her with broad smiles were two priests clutching bibles. One looked to be at least ninety, whereas the other appeared to have left school before the required age.

"I'm afraid that this particular church is not for general use, but I would be happy to show you around. Or is it the architecture of the castle which brings you here?" Said the older gentleman.

"That would be wonderful." Said Salonge. "It's both really. I have a great interest in the church and also ancient architecture, but it is mostly statues that are my real calling. I am told that, over the centuries, many artifacts were taken to the cellars here for safekeeping."

"This is true young lady. I think that I could arrange for a quick viewing. However, as it is unofficial, it would only be a whistle stop type of affair."

The younger man spoke for the first time and Salonge's senses went into high alert. "Are you here alone, or do you have a friend who may also like to take the tour?"

As he said this the young priest dropped his bible and tripped on his slightly too long set of robes whilst attempting a fumbled recovery.

"Please forgive my young charge. He is true of heart but, as you can see, a little clumsy."

The young priest now held his head low in an attempt to conceal his blushes which encouraged Salonge's senses to relax once more. She was chaperoned with one priest at either side through a door marked 'Authorised personnel only.' They emerged into what must have once been the castles great banqueting hall. There were coats of arms, tapestries, and banners draping from the walls above the heads of shining suits of armour.

"Quite magnificent isn't it?" Said the older priest. "Please follow me.

They proceeded down the centre isle until confronted with a heavy oak door. The younger of her escorts withdrew a huge brass key from a pocket concealed within his oversized robes and inserted it into an equally huge keyhole.

"Would you be so kind as to assist Father Brech down the stone stairway? They are rather steep for an older man to negotiate, and the steps are very worn. It is a rule that the door must be secured at all times so I must lock it behind us."

Salonge carefully, but firmly, gripped the old man's arm and began guiding him down into the musty crypt. Suddenly she felt a firm hand pushing on her back. As she tumbled endlessly through the air she could just make out the sound of the young priest laughing. Salonge hit the floor with a bone crunching thud but was more or less unhurt, unlike the smashed and bleeding head of the gentle old man. She rolled over to see the evil smile of the apparently not so young innocent priest gloating at the top of the stairway.

"I saw the alarm in your eyes when I asked if you were travelling alone. Did you not think that the Protecteurs de la France would not be watching this place?"

Her assailant once again slid his hands beneath his robes, but this time to produce a revolver, not a brass key.

"Tell me where the English bitch is and the blasphemous documents...You have ten seconds."

Suddenly the old wooden door burst open sending splinters of varying sizes into the priests back. There was a flash of light as a mighty sword came slashing down vertically into the man's shoulder. Salonge stared in disbelief as the chain mailed figure removed the knights helmet. Both items fell from Kacey's hands as she dropped to her knees with a look of shock and terror on her face.

"God forgive me, I think I have killed him."

Salonge fought against the pain in her bruised, and most likely cracked ribs to ascend the stairs.

"What are you doing here?"

"I just had a feeling that you were in danger. I had a vision of you being shot at the foot of a stone stairway. I followed you here, and when I saw them leading you down these stairs I grabbed some of the display armour...you know, just for protection."

Salonge squeezed me tight. "He was going to kill me Kacey, he deserved it. I know this must feel awful right now, but you had no choice...thank you my brave young cousin."

Salonge did her best to lighten the situation. "When I looked up the stairway I was convinced that it was Joan of Arc herself who saved me."

I looked sincerely into her eyes and spoke honestly.
The words which left my mouth were somehow not
of my own construction.

"Maybe it was!"

Chapter 34

Revelations

Jack Nichols contacted his boss, Al Vicarrio at the FBI, informing him that he was safe and well and was now staying with Anthony Mazur in a hotel apartment overlooking the Pigalle. He reported that the pair of them were confident that the location of his interrogation was almost certainly the Chateau de Breteuil. Under normal circumstances allowing the FBI MI6 or AICAC to the interrogate the manager of the family estate of the aristocratic Breteuil family would not have been granted. However, due to the fact that Jack had been abducted from a US safe house meant that the French authorities were reluctantly cooperative.

Every fibre and desire in Anthony's body was urging him to head in the other direction towards Salonge, the love of his life, but there were three things driving him north of Paris towards the chateau. The first was that his wife was more than capable of looking after herself. The second was that if he and Jack could apply pressure from their end, it would give Salonge and Kacey some much needed space. The third was that every instinct told him that the chateau, or employees at that estate, held the key to finding his wife and cousins ruthless pursuers.

The hybrid car he had switched to made no noise whilst cruising at slow speed, apart from a gentle crackling of tyres on pebbles which they hoped would not alert the new estate manager, Julien Thibaut. He was expecting them of course, but they had arrived early to find the main gates open, and the gatehouse keeper absent from his position. They parked at the farthest end of the car park from the great house and proceeded to have a look around on foot. Once through the first arched hedgerow Anthony jumped as his torch hit the face of an exhibit.

"Jesus Jack, look at that."

"What did you expect? It says that the grounds are full of waxworks, or have you forgotten why we are here?"

"Of course I haven't smartarse. But look at the face, it's so lifelike."

They both moved their torches in broad low circles keeping the beam below the hedgerows and out of sight of the house. A guillotine came into view with a terrified face anticipating the dropping of the blood drenched blade.

"Jack, hold my torch for a second and shine both at this contraption."

Anthony quickly scaled one of the execution posts to

get a clear view. To the right he could see bright lights flooding from the chateaus many windows out across the manicured lawns. To his left was the blackened outline of a large building with just a feint crack of light escaping from its entrance.

"This way Jack, I think I have spotted the wax factory. We should have about half an hour to look around before they are expecting us."

Jack was struggling to keep up as the fast-stooping pace which Anthony had set was causing the damaged skin on the backs of his legs to pull taught. By the time he reached the large shed Anthony was urging Jack forward indicating that the building was empty. As soon as they entered, Jack was overcome by a feeling of nausea as the smell of burnt wax caused a barrage of flashbacks.

"Are you ok Pal ?"

"Yes I'm fine buddy, let's have a look around."

Jack walked straight over to the large vat and looked up expecting to see the pully system, but all that remained was a single steel hook. At first glance it looked to be unused and rusty, but upon closer inspection Jack could see the gleam of shining metal where a chain had passed across. He scanned the room searching for the wooden ducking chair, but all he could see were costumes and discarded wine bottles.

"This place has not only been cleaned and sanitised, but then staged to look like the scene of a drunken party." Said Anthony holding aloft a clear bottle of alcohol."

"Let's look in the backroom marked props, perhaps they have missed something." Said Jack.

"Like what?" Said Anthony.

"Like the chair and chain that hoisted me above that vat."

Both men entered the prop room and, seeing that it had no windows decided to risk turning on the light. The whole right side of the room had reproduction clothes from across the centuries drooping eerily from wheeled hanging rails. To the left were at least two dozen hard props of which at least half were wooden chairs. Jack walked over and began inspecting them when a voice roared from the doorway.

"Officer, arrest these trespassers." Said a raging Julien Thibaut to the gendarme standing at his side.

"Hold on there Mr Thibault." Said Anthony, stepping forward whilst producing his ID. "We arrived early and thought it would be alright to have a quick look around. After all, perhaps we could assist in finding the intruders."

"Well it is not alright. I informed your superiors that we had a minor break in by some youths and this is not the scene of some fantasy abduction. I did, however, offer to speak with you at the main house and did not give permission for you to go snooping around the estate. That courtesy has now been withdrawn. Now this officer will escort you from the premises and I shall be making a formal complaint."

"Just hold on there Mr Thibaut. My colleague here was almost murdered in a waxworks two days ago and ..."

"It's ok Anthony, let's go." Said Jack Nichols taking Anthony by the arm. "There is nothing here that strikes me as familiar."

An angry and confused Anthony followed his colleague to their car.

"What the hell was that about Jack. You had a hood on. How on earth could anything seem familiar?"

"This is the place, and Thibaut is involved."

"Explain please."

"First of all, when I was stripped and strapped to the ducking chair they removed my watch but not this diamond ring. The funny thing is the watch was a fake Rolex and that was not returned. My ring, however, is a family heirloom and worth tens of thousands. I managed to scratch an ex into the underside of the left wooden arm of the chair. That chair is in the prop room."

"Anything else."

"I recognised Julien Thibaut's voice. He was present that night.

....

"Quickly Kacey, give me a hand. We need to get this door back up."

"How can we." I said. "The hinges are hanging off and panels are splintered."

"We need some time to sort out this mess and have a look around. If we can just get it leaning, then from a distance people may not notice the damage."

As we struggled under the weight of the door I could tell that Salonge was wondering from where I had summoned the strength to kick it clean off its hinges; I had no idea either. Once satisfied that it was leaning in as good a position as we could hope for,

Salonge did a quick check of the old priests pulse and as expected, he was dead. She picked up the discarded sword and placed it in his hand producing the oddest scene of a fight between two men of the cloth. However, as the younger was obviously part of the criminal gang who were chasing us, Salonge figured that the deaths would somehow be covered up. If we were lucky, perhaps they would be fooled into believing that there had indeed been some sort of altercation between the two.

"Kacey, we don't have long. Forget about what has happened and lets find the blue gemstone."

We both instinctively headed for the open arch at the far end of the room. As we approached, the dusty smell of confined spaces harbouring ancient artifacts attacked our nasal cavities. There was a long corridor flanked by cloister type arches. Flickering electric flames mimicked the original oil fed torches which once adorned the walls above each arch to provide adequate light. Below the first torch was a plaque revealing a date...***1801-1900 AD.*** Salonge and I walked into the cavernous space to see stacks of religious paintings, gold icons, statues of Jesus and old trunks with heavy metal locks. We left that space and continued along the corridor. The following arch was dated ***1701-1800 AD.*** We looked at each other with excitement and a realisation that this search could have suddenly become much easier. We hurried deeper into the cellar until we found the date which corresponded to, and encompassed, Joan of Arc's time on this earth...**1401-1500 AD.** This space appeared even bigger than the first and was packed floor to ceiling with artifacts. Lying flat, side by side towards the back of the room were four life sized statues: Saint Joan, Saint Catherine, Saint Margaret, and the Arcangel, Saint Michael. Salonge picked up a heavy gold candelabra.

"I hate to do this Kacey, but we have no time."

Salonge fought her way over stacks of obstacles and gave me a brief smile before smashing the candelabra into the arch of each statues foot. As they succumbed to the vicious assault my heart sank ever lower; there was no hidden gem concealed within.

Salonge dropped the heavy golden object to the floor.

"Kacey, there is nothing here...we have to go."

"We cant." I said. "It has to be here somewhere."

"Even if it is, it could take hours or even days to find."

The torment of this emotional roller coaster was once again becoming unbearable. I had just murdered someone, and almost in an instant brushed aside this terrible thing which I had done in the interests of completing my quest...what type of ruthless creature had I become? My only selfish thought was to recover the blue gem and perhaps find another message from my ancestor, Joan. Was I becoming possessed to the point where death no longer mattered to me?

It all seemed so futile, such a waste of life. After coming so close, we now had to flee empty handed for fear of being captured and tried for murder. We retraced our route back into the first chamber where the two dead men were staring into each other's eyes. I had to turn my head towards the wall as we stepped over the still warm corpses. Salonge was already peeping through the cracks in the door to make sure that the way was clear.

"Ok cousin, let's move this heap and get the hell out of here."

My feet were frozen to the spot as if some invisible force were preventing me from leaving.

"We have to go back." I said.

"Kacey no. We need to leave now!"

"When you were smashing the statues I stepped on a loose stone by the entrance to Joans cavern. I felt a strange trembling rise up through my legs from the large slab beneath my feet. I thought it was just nerves or adrenalin, but it wasn't. It was Joans sapphire calling me... I know it is there.

"Kacey, you have just killed someone, and your emotions are playing tricks with your mind. We have to go now!"

Suddenly everything became clear. A voice in my head was telling me to think laterally in respect to the old French translation. "That must be it." I said. "It's another translation issue from ancient French. *Hidden in the arch of a foot* could mean *Hidden in the foot of an arch!* I turned and began hurrying back into the cellar, regardless of Salonge's pleas. I shone my torch at the one metre slabs at the entrance to Joans cavern and spotted one which appeared to be ever so slightly raised. I planted one foot on the slab and the trembling once again began rising up my leg. It was not visible like adrenalin, it felt more like an invisible electric current. I began searching for anything which I could use as a lever to dislodge the stone and spotted two long metal rods which looked to be spares for an iron railing.

"I'll get them." Said Salonge. "Take this knife and try to dig the dirt out from the edges so that we can gain some purchase."

I dropped to my knees and was about to begin scraping away when I noticed a tiny engraving in the top left corner of the slab. There was a sword pointing from the hilt upwards and upon its tip was the resting crown of Charles V11. Either side of the blade were two Fleurs-de-Lys. I instantly recognised Joans coat of arms given to her family by the King of France. I began scraping away vigorously until there was a large enough gap for the iron rod. Salonge forced the pointed end into the gap and began leaning her full weight onto the opposite end of the makeshift excavator for maximum leverage, but the heavy stone would not budge. I dug the second rod into the gap beside Salonge's, but she let hers fall to the floor.

"It's no use Kacey. The stone is far too heavy. It would take ten of us to move this even an inch." Said Salonge as she stroked my hair. "Come on young cousin, we did our best, it's time we go."

Her words of consolation and sympathy only served to fire my resolve. I took a deep breath in preparation for applying every morsal of strength in my body to the task. Before I barely even applied any pressure the stone began to lift as if someone were pushing from below. I manoeuvred my rod and the stone slipped gently to one side. Moving the object was no harder than steering the the rudder arm of a small sailboat. We both stood silently staring into a square, jet-black abyss.

"How on earth did you do that Kacey."

"I don't know, it didn't feel like it was me doing it."

We dropped to our knees and shone our torches into the space, but the range of our beams faded before they could reach the bottom. I shone light onto the upper face of the four confined walls and discovered that one of them had foot and hand holes dug in, descending at alternate distances for the left foot and then the right. Suddenly we heard a loud crash from the main room followed by a woman's scream and the shouts of at least two men; get security, call the police.

We looked at each other in horror knowing that there was no other way out. Salonge went first and I quickly followed. We knew we would have to throw caution to the wind and make as much headway as we could before the passageway was discovered. The square of light above our heads was getting smaller but I could not yet see any inquisitive, angry heads searching for us. My heart froze as I heard a scaping noise and I looked up once and swear I could see the stone sliding back into place of its own accord

Chapter 35

A dead end for Anthony but not the Girls

Julien Thibaut was back in the office at the chateau feeling both angry but also concerned. He was certain that he had detected signs of recognition in Jack Nichols eyes from when he had raised his voice urging Gabriel to spare the FBI agents life. He had prepared for the interview with the agents by introducing subtle changes to his vocabulary and its delivery. But when one of his groundsmen had reported them snooping around the factory he had, through anger, reverted to his usual manner of speech. Julien slammed the desk at his own stupidity and knew that action, including a diversion, needed to be put in place. Julien looked at the diary of his direct superior and chief aid to the president of France, Gabriel Abadie. He spent hours going through the various pages reading accounts of debauchery and murder as well as an emotional account of Gabriels latest meeting with a Dr Gunter Schmidt. It told harrowing details of the incurable tumour and likely increasing occurrence of Gabriels blackouts and associated psychotic behaviour.

Julien reached into his pocket and withdrew Jack Nichols Rolex. He had retained the item feeling it may be useful for the very reason he had decided upon now. Somehow he would need to place this evidence somewhere amongst Gabriel Abadie's belongings and then make an anonymous tip off to the Americans. It would be for the good of the Protecteurs de la France and besides, the man would be long dead before he went to trial.

There was a knock on the door.

"Would you like a night-time Cognac sir? I assume you will be staying at the chateau tonight.

Julien, being so recently promoted, did not yet recognise the voices of his man servants or their names.

"That sounds like a fabulous idea." He said whilst twirling the watch in a hoopla type rotation around his index finger.

The door opened. "Surprise!" Said a naked Gabriel Abadie balancing a solid silver tray in his right hand, fingers spread for stability like an upturned spider. Two perfectly cut crystal glasses were filled to the brim with the finest cognac.

Gabriel brought his left arm into view which had been folded behind his back like a servant preparing to bow before his master; in his hand was a revolver. Julien was desperately trying to think of something to say which could reach out to this madman.

"Gabriel, I know that you have an illness, we can fix it."

Gabriel laughed. "I see that you have been reading Pierre's diaries. I did have a suspicion that he had discovered my tumour and that it is inoperable."

"Think of your family...think of France and the church. If you have to leave this earth, then do so with dignity and pride, not as a murderer."

"I also see that you have the FBI agents watch. I'm sure that you can afford your own Rolex, or did you have another reason for retaining it...a keepsake perhaps? Or were you thinking of employing it in a more devious manner...to frame me perhaps?"

Juliens mind was racing, trying to think of another approach with which to disarm the situation, but his thoughts were disrupted as the madman approached. He didn't know how, but this was the first time that Julien noticed the naked man wearing a bow tie around his genitalia. As he drew closer, blood could be seen oozing from both nipples which had been recently pierced by Gabriels usual lapel pins, the French flag, and a religious cross.

"So the cat who was a kitten such a short time ago now believes he is a tiger and, like Pierre, intends to be rid of me."

"Of course not Gabriel. I thought we could use the FBI man's watch to frame one of our enemies and divert attention from us."

"Very good Julien. Very clever, but not true. Perhaps I should call you a hyena, not a tiger; sly, devious, ready to take advantage of others hard work. Now take out a pen and your personal stationary."

Julien opened the draw, withdrew his gold pen, and embossed paper wishing that he had not discarded Pierre's desk pistol.

"Now take this down."

This is my confession and my dying wish.

Julien was forced to confess to the killing of the old man in England, for using his influence to appropriate resources of France for his own personal goals. He was made to admit hiring assassins to find and kill an innocent girl from England, Kacey Chapman and her cousin on the basis of a rumour that they wished to degrade the history of France and the Catholic Church.

The letter concluded:

I have done great wrongs and wish to apologise to my family and my country as well as anyone I have harmed. I leave this world now and must face the ultimate judgement from our Lord.

Sincerely, and remorsefully

Julien Thibaut

"That is perfect Julien. I must admit, your penmanship is quite beautiful and far superior to mine. However, the leaning downward slope in your *S's* is said to be the trait of one destined to fail, or so it is said by leading graphologists. If you would be so kind as to join me in the centre of the room please. I recommend that you swiftly swallow both glasses of cognac, it may make the next part more bearable."

Julien gulped them down in one and slowly walked towards his aggressor and previous mentor, but now the most terrifyingly mad adversary he had ever encountered. Gabriel was holding a tiny remote-control device in his free hand and smiled as he pressed the down button. Instantly the giant crystal chandelier began its descent from its usual position some three metres above floor level. Until recently there was a pully system which allowed the thousand bejewelled glass decoration to be polished and cleaned, but this would take at least five members of staff. Now it was done electronically meaning that one person could raise or lower the mammoth light fixture. The chandelier was now so close above Juliens head that he could see the odd cobweb

waiting to be brushed away. Gabriel quickly fixed a
rope to the ornate object with a short length leading
to a pre-prepared hangman's noose.

"Place the loop over your head please Julien. Hurry
up now and I will give your legs a tug once you are
suspended to make your demise a quick event."

"And what if I refuse? You will have to shoot me
which ruins your suicide plan."

"Have it your way. I am dying anyway. But you are
too weak and scared to challenge me whilst I hold a
gun."

Gabriel walked behind Julien and slipped the noose
over his head to save time. He then pressed the
ascend button and laughed deliriously as the first
choking sounds left Juliens lips and his feet began to
kick. Before the corpses arms were out of reach,
Gabriel paused the remote in order to remove the
dead man's watch and replace it with Jack Nichols
Rolex. He then wiped the remote-control device
clean before pressing Juliens hand onto its casing and
his index finger onto the up button before allowing it
to drop to the floor creating the illusion of suicide.

....

Gabriel awoke and and tried to focus on the surreal
scene. As the fog cleared he could see Julien

Thibaut's body hanging from the chandelier and the events of less than an hour ago came flooding back with satisfaction. He looked down and began to flush with embarrassment at the dickie bow still tied around his private parts. His head was no longer throbbing, but Gabriel winced as he carefully removed the lapel pins from his nipples which displayed tiny rivers of dried blood mixed in with his chest hair. He leaped to his feet and ran to open the office door and was relieved to see his clothes undiscovered and laying in a heap below the do not disturb sign.

Gabriel dressed as fast as he could and made one final check of Juliens office before stopping off in the room which housed the security camera footage. He removed the tape of him arriving at the chateau earlier that day and also him returning a few hours later. Gabriel hoped that the police would somehow overlook protocol and just accept the scene of a suicide. Either way, no tape at all was better than his vehicle being spotted at the premises during the approximate time of death. He rushed to his car and headed for his office at the Elysee Palace to clean up the sordid mess from the previous day. Gabriel would also use an untraceable phone to tip off the police that Julien Thibault was missing; they would soon make the connection to the chateau.

Chapter 36

The second part of the Puzzle

The tunnels damp, stale air was causing Salonge and I to breath heavily, although part of the reason was due to the amount of fear and adrenalin rushing through our veins. The passageway was straight and narrow allowing for our torches to pick up the odd scuttling rat. We had initially heard footfalls above our heads as the old church annexed by the palace was searched, but thankfully there was no sound of a stone slab being pulled aside. As we continued forward there were new sounds to be heard; the occasional rumble of traffic mixed in with a gushing noise ahead which was steady and increasing in volume. After another five minutes the tunnel became narrower and shallower causing our backs to ache as we were forced to stoop. Eventually the beams from our torches hit a dead end and Salonge stopped in her tracks.

"We are trapped Kacey. The only way out is to go back and that means certain capture."

Something was telling me to continue forward. "No, look. There are drips falling from the roof, I think we are by the river bank."

"That makes sense." Said Salonge. "Once we

descended into the passageway it went straight south under the roads."

I ran forward and was soon standing beneath my own personal subterranean shower. I shone my torch up into the relentless torrent and could just make out the grimy outline of a stone slab similar to the one we had removed from the entrance. I slammed my foot into the muddy end of the passage to gain some purchase before seeing if I could budge the obstacle to our escape but let out a yelp as my toes hit a solid wall. A cascade of mud fell from the wall into the mini lake engulfing my feet. A giant engraving of Joan revealed itself. In her right hand was a cross, but her left was pointing towards a cavity dug out of the wall. I instinctively reached into the hole and my hand felt the cool surface of a second lead box and I instantly knew that I had found the blue sapphire.

....

Anthony Mazur and Jack Nichols were back in their aparthotel on the Pigalle waiting for permission from from Al Vicarrio to exert some pressure on Julien Thibault, but communication channels remained silent since the first reply instructing them to sit tight. Anthony was desperate to message his wife but knew that Charles Worwood would not have gone to the trouble of setting up Thames FM Radio if it were ok for him to do that. It was almost 9pm again so he turned on the radio in the hope of receiving a disguised message via Johnny Valatone.

This goes out to my good friend Anthony currently vacationing in Paris. Your father, Charlie in London wants to hear from you. It would seem that your recent problem is over, but he has not been able to inform your wife yet.

The blood drained from Anthonys face as Bob Marley began wailing from the radio.

Don't worry...bout a ting...coz every little ting... gonna be alright.

"Whats wrong buddy?" Said a concerned Jack Nichols.

"I need to call Charles Worwood. He's saying that the bad guys have been caught or are out of action."

"Well that sounds like good news to me, why the long face?"

"He's also saying that Salonge and Kacey are missing."

....

I opened the ancient fastener and prised the lid of the lead box. The object inside was of the same size as the blood ruby and was also enveloped in a muslin cloth. I unwrapped the prize and a blue light filled the passageway causing every puddle on the floor, and each particle of water dripping down to come to life. Salonge was the first to break free of the trancelike astonishment we had succumbed to.

"Kacey, put it in your pocket and let's get out of here."

Salonge dropped to her knees, and I instinctively kicked off my shoes before thankfully stepping out of the vermin infested water and onto her back allowing me to put all of the pressure from my own torso behind the task at hand. After several attempts, and a few groans from my cousin, the stone shifted aside causing a flood of water to slam onto our heads. Once the initial deluge had ended I was able to hoist myself up onto the riverbank. I sat panting for a few seconds before turning to offer my hand down to Salonge but, to my surprise, she had vaulted out of the space without any assistance.

Again I felt an energy pulsating through my body. But this time it was far more intense, and yet balance. It was as if the two stones were producing energy in unison. "Let's get back to our hotel and see what message is on the cloth as well as the script on the blue gemstone. It has similar etchings along its sides as the ruby."

"I think we should just collect our things and disappear." Said Salonge.

"Where to? The clues are right here in my pocket. These will tell us where we need to head next."

"Kacey let's just go and we can do all of that once we are safe. There could be an army on its way here to search for us. We can go somewhere remote which has no connection to Joan. Trust me, this is the right thing to do. Besides, I need to make contact with Anthony and Charles Worwood."

We headed back to the hotel and were relieved to find the old man at reception dozing at his desk. We gathered our belongings and Salonge left a more than sufficient amount of cash on the counter to cover our board and incidentals.

....

Anthony's Skype alert began beeping from his laptop. It was not the product used by businesses to host video meetings and share documents on screen, this was an encrypted version designed by Billy Agoba, head of cyber security at MI6.

"Dear Boy, how are you." Said Charles Worwood.

"How do you think I am Charles? Unless I am wrong your Bob Marley ditty indicates that Salonge and her cousin are incommunicado!"

"Well young man, I have some rather good news for you. In fact, two rather spiffing revelations to deliver, what."

Worwoods usually endearing vocabular habit of finishing a sentence with *what,* was on this occasion overwhelmingly irritating to Anthony.

"What the hell do you mean what? What does 'what' mean Charles. I'll tell you what, I would like to know where the hell my wife is and if she is alive?"

"I'm very sorry young man. It was inconsiderate and insensitive of me. I shall let this pass but please do not forget to whom you are speaking."

"I'm sorry too Charles. Is there any news of Salonge?"

"Indeed there is young man. I take it that you figured out her last location. It's ok, you can mention the name of the town."

"They were south of Paris in Gien."

"Indeed they were. Salonge and Kacey have moved on, to where I do not yet know. She left a song request for our resident DJ about an hour ago. It turns out that you two gentlemen were correct about Julien Thibault. He has decided to make amends for his misdemeanours by taking his own life. So it seems that the girls can continue their quest without interruption. However, there may well be some rogue operatives of his secret organisation who may wish to continue their pursuit. With this in mind I have not informed them of the suicide, and we shall maintain a stealthy method of communication until we are sure."

"That's great news Charles. Thank you."

....

We set off heading slightly north east of Gien, away from the Loire and deep into the Burgundy countryside. My instincts were telling me that we should be heading in the other direction, west along the Loire towards the area where Joan fought many of her early battles. However, Salonge said that our pursuers would be thinking the very same thing and we needed time to evaluate our discovery. I retrieved a wrinkled map of France from my jacket pocket and began searching for a destination in which to lay low, each suggestion being rebuffed by my cousin; it's too small, we would be noticed; it's too close to the outskirts of Paris etc. Finally I suggested Auxerre which Salonge immediately accepted.

"I know a vineyard there which produces the most

delicious Chablis and is surrounded by many guest houses and small hotels. Two females turning up unannounced for a couple of nights wine tasting would not look out of place. Did Joan fight any battles in that area?"

"Only one skirmish, but it is barely mentioned in the history books and besides, most of the Catholic structures were sacked and demolished by the Huguenots in the 16th century. I doubt if our enemies would expect us to be searching there for anything of great significance."

"Can you see the best route on your map?"

"Take the next exit for the D965. We should be there in just over an hour."

I reached into the back seat and hauled my bag through the centre consul and onto my lap. I undid the zip and stared with nervous excitement at the two objects wrapped in muslin cloth. I removed both items and turned my shoulder bag onto its side to form a makeshift desktop and placed them side by side. I could feel an energy penetrating my upper thighs and radiating throughout my whole body causing my heart to race. I slowly unwrapped each cloth to reveal two magnificent jewels. Each was formed into a cylindrical shape of around forty centimetres in length, both with a flat bottom and a jagged top. I inspected our latest discovery first and could see that the etchings were of the same Aramaic scripture as the blood ruby. A thought occurred to me that perhaps the two jagged edges were supposed to be slotted together like some sort of key. I gently lifted both coloured stones and began slowly bringing the uneven edges into alignment. As I did so my hands began to tremble, and I could feel a magnetic force repelling my actions. The closer they came together the stronger the rejection. Suddenly the car began to lose control and its interior became filled with blue and red flashing lights. I was transfixed by the pyrotechnic display but could also see, and hear, Salonge struggling to maintain control of the vehicle. The last thing I remembered was careering into a ditch beside the D965 motorway.

Chapter 37

The Observers

Anthony had had a decent night's sleep since the conversation with Charles Worwood but was still anxious to hear from his wife, Salonge. When he awoke there was a message from London that Worwood, through pulling a number diplomatic strings, had gained permission for them to revisit the chateau and the scene of the so-called suicide. Initially the French authorities were totally against the idea, almost to the point of blaming the two Americans for a respected citizens demise. It was only the surprise intervention by the French Presidents chief aide who finally gave the approval. In fact, Gabriel Abadie offered to meet them at the chateau personally.

Anthony produced his identification to the young man at the gate and was instructed to take the right fork off the gravel driveway towards the back of the chateau. As they approached the rear of the property they could see two police cars, an unmarked ambulance, and a black luxury Mercedes. Jack was first to exit their vehicle and approach the two officers guarding the tradesman's entrance, whilst Anthony looked on curiously as the rear door to the merc swung open. An elegantly dressed man emerged. His tall slender frame, perfect deportment, and crisply cut hairstyle exuded an air of importance. Anthony opened the driver's door and made his way towards the senior politician.

"Gabriel Abadie I presume." Said Anthony, feeling obliged to address the man in a formal manner.

"Indeed I am. And you no doubt are...wait, don't tell me...Anthony Mazur."

Muz knew that this was the man's way of letting him know that he had previewed their intelligence files.

"I see from your response that I am correct, in which case that must be Special Agent Jack Nichols."

"Correct on both counts. Thank you for coming in person. although it seems a bit unusual for a man in your position to attend a simple suspected suicide."

"On the contrary. This estate has been in the hands of a famous French aristocratic family for generations, and the current descendants are very close personal friends."

Gabriel Abadie led the way into the building, followed by Jack and Anthony who were also accompanied by two gendarmes. Abadie led the way into the office to reveal another two men in white overalls and blue plastic gloves operating a remote control which was lowering chandelier suspending the stiff corpse to the floor. The men removed the rope from the dead man's neck before stretching the body out flat on the parquet flooring.

"May we take a closer look?" Said Jack.

"Of course you may, but please do not touch anything."

Jack rolled his eyes in Anthony's direction indicating that this politician must think that they were stupid and had never managed a crime scene. Anthony's attention was drawn to something completely different. Gabriel Abadie's eyes were darting between a stack of boxes in the corner and a crocodile skin diary sitting open on the office desk. Anthony decided to test precisely how important these boxes were, having noticed that they had been packed and sealed, but the duct tape had been recently sliced open.

"May I take a look in the boxes?" He said.

"And why would you wish to do that?" Said an even more nervous Gabriel.

"I can see that they have been sealed but reopened. Perhaps there is more to this than a simple suicide."

"I am sorry but there may well be sensitive government documents inside. I'm afraid that I must deny this request."

"Why would a chateau, basically a tourist attraction, have government documents in their possession?" Anthony said, noticing the increased discomfort in Gabriels eyes.

Jack had been crawling around the body on all fours, getting as close a look as possible whilst avoiding the bodily fluids still escaping from the dead man's cavities. Gabriel Abadie walked over to the desk and picked up the small leather-bound journal, flicking through its pages with an attempt at indifference before slipping it into his jacket pocket.

Gabriel produced his best false smile. "Gentlemen, there have been three recent events which have led to us extending you the courtesy if visiting this fabulous estate for a second time, all of which I can assure you are unconnected...aside from Monsieur Thibaut's admissions. First of all, there was a break in at this establishments wax facility, probably by some youths. Second, this is not the location of your unfortunate abduction Mr Nichols. Lastly, this is clearly a suicide, and the dead man has admitted to taking extraordinary measures with which to cause harm to an ex-FBI agent and her cousin, for what reasons I have no idea."

Gabriel turned to one of the white suited men from

the coroners department. "Could you please give your assessment of what occurred in this office and the approximate time of death."

"Yes sir. Death occurred approximately twelve hours ago, circa 9pm last night. The dead man wrote the suicide note and proceeded to lower the chandelier via a remote control which activates an electronic pully. He then attached one end of a rope to the chandelier and the other to his neck and, using his right hand, raised the chandelier until he was suspended."

The man then lifted Juliens left hand and stretched out the digits.

"There is blood under the finger nails of his other hand and also on the man's neck indicating that he had second thoughts and tried to loosen the noose."

Gabriel put a hand over his mouth in an expression of shock. "How dreadful for poor Thibault ."

The fingers of the corpse had been ravaged so much in his desperate struggle that blood had ran down his wrist as far as his watch."

Jack gave no indication that he recognised his own timepiece caked in blood.

The white overalled man then walked around the

body and lifted the right arm.

"The remote control was found on the floor, two metres to his right. We can assume that he dropped the item and was unable to lower the chandelier."

Gabriel then looked at his watch before addressing Anthony and Jack. "I'm afraid that I must be on my way. I assume that you are satisfied with our cooperation and will now also leave this estate. As you can see, it was a simple suicide. Good day gentlemen."

Anthony and Jack followed Gabriel out of the building and watched as he appeared to have dropped something as he was getting into the rear of the vehicle. The chauffeur rushed to his side but was angrily brushed away.

"I wonder what he has dropped?" Said Anthony. "It certainly wasn't that book which he cleverly slipped into his pocket."

"He hasn't dropped anything." Said Jack. "Look carefully. The man is in pain...he is rubbing his temple."

"What makes you think that?" Said Anthony.

Jack let out a knowing laugh. "Because that is exactly what happened when he was interrogating me. And another thing. Did you notice how he tried to draw attention to Julien Thibaut's watch?"

"Yes, it seemed a bit odd to me."

"That's because he was expecting a reaction. It was the watch that they took from my arm during the interrogation."

"Holy crap. Are you sure?"

"As sure as the Yankees will beat the Cubbies again this year."

Anthony. being from Chicago and a massive Cubs fan, let the jibe from his New York associate pass. "I also noticed something odd. Did you see the ring on Thibaut's little finger?"

"Yeah...yeah I did. It was a small gold oval shape with some letters inscribed; PFS or something."

"It was PDLF." Said Anthony. "Abadie was wearing the same ring."

Anthony and Jack were as silent as the engine of their hybrid vehicle, deep in thought as they slowly rolled towards the exit barrier of the estate with its small guard house.

"Just run with me on this, I need to check something." Said Anthony.

He pulled to a stop at the guard house even though the barrier had been raised. Anthony lowered the driver's window and smiled at the young uniformed man. The man smiled back and approached their car and Anthony noticed him make an involuntary pat at the bulge beneath his breast pocket, obviously a gun.

"Can I help you monsieur?" Said the gatekeeper.

"I certainly hope so." Replied Anthony. It looks like our business here is concluded so we are heading for Charles de Gaulle. The problem is that we seem to have lost our road map. Would you happen to have a spare?"

"I'm afraid not monsieur. But I can write down directions for you."

The man went back into the stone hut and began scribbling a crude map with motorway exit numbers and approximate times for each part of the journey.

"There you go monsieur." Said Antoine, handing the piece of paper using his left hand keeping his shooting arm free. "You should make it in less than an hour at this time of day."

Merci beaucoup." Replied Anthony before driving away.

"Did you see it?"

Jack smiled. "I sure did. A signet ring with the letters PDLF."

Antoine watched as they drove away before hitting Gabriels speed dial on his cell phone.

"Sir, it's Antoine. It appears that you have satisfied their curiosity. They are leaving France."

"Are you certain Antoine, this is very important."

"Yes sir. They stopped at the guard house and asked for directions to the airport and virtually stated that their investigation was over."

"That's excellent news Antoine. Come to my apartment on the Champs Elysee tomorrow for a celebration dinner, and also receive your promotion. We now need to get the search for those irritable, blasphemous women back on track."

Gabriel Abadie could feel the pain from his tumour rapidly subsiding. The onset of the excruciating ache in his head had begun when the dumb FBI agent had failed to recognise his own watch, thus apparently scuppering the plan to frame Julien.

Gabriel decided he would treat himself to a whore at one of the more select brothels close to the Pigalle. After all, he told himself, "*I deserve it.*" Gabriel felt confident that this good news would help him perform very well, and hopefully the need for slapping and violence would be minimal in order to attain satisfaction.

Chapter 38

Everyone is searching for the Cousins

Billy Agoba had been called into Charles Worwoods office at MI6 on the banks of the Thames in London. His official title was head of Cyber Security which really meant Cyber Intelligence, or electronic spying.

"Something is very wrong Billy." Said Worwood, his eyes transfixed at a point on the wall somewhere above Billy's head.

"What is it sir?"

"It's Salonge and her cousin. They have not made contact since the brief message yesterday."

"Does Anthony know?"

"No, not yet. I have told him that they are fine as I need him to focus on a rather pressing matter; something that he and our American friend have uncovered. Successfully deceiving one's enemies is easy, and quite frankly rather enjoyable, but fibbing to one's colleagues is a part of the job which has never sat well with me."

"How can I help sir?"

"I have two urgent assignments for you, and both are of equal importance. I need you to infiltrate the data base of the French gendarmerie as well as that of their hospital network. I have the feeling that Salonge is in trouble or possibly injured."

"No problem sir." Said Billy whilst typing notes onto his laptop. "And the second item?"

"Anthony and Jack are convinced that Julien Thibaut's suicide was a sham set up by none other than the chief aid to the president of France. They believe that he, along with the dead man, and god knows how many others, are part of a secret organisation called the PDLF. See if you can find out what this organisation is."

"Sir, you do realise that my only starting point is to crack the chief aids personal e mails?"

"I'm fully aware of what I have asked of you, but we have no choice. Firstly, one of my finest agents, and very close friend is in grave danger. And secondly, if someone that high up in the French government has gone rogue and is running around trying to kill innocent British, French and god knows who, then he needs to be stopped.

………………..

I opened my eyes and immediately thought I had died. Everything was a misty white aside from one brilliant light in the centre of my blurred vision.

"Thank god you are awake Kacey." Said Salonge as she approached my hospital bed with a limp.

"Where are we...what happened?"

"Where we are is a small suburban hospital on the outskirts of Auxerre. As to what happened, well that's a bit of a mystery. One minute you were playing with the two gemstones, the next minute the car was filled with coloured lights and decided to do its own thing. How do you feel Kacey?"

"I have a thumping headache and feel like I've done ten rounds with Mike Tyson."

"You were barely conscious when the ambulance arrived, so they sedated you whilst they did some x rays and other checks, nothing is broken."

I was suddenly overcome with panic. "Where are the stones?"

"I have them here in my bag." Said Salonge, patting her Louis Vuitton. "Do you think you can walk?"

Salonge helped me to a sitting position at which point a wave of nausea washed over me. "I feel sick." I said.

"That's just the drugs wearing off. I'll help you get dressed; we need to leave. I gave the hospital some cash and a credit card, but they are insisting on seeing our insurance documents. The police also want to speak with us and are waiting until the medics confirm that you are awake. As soon as they file that report I'm certain that the bad guys will be here in a heartbeat."

Salonge opened the door an inch and peeked through the gap to gauge the human traffic in the long corridor whilst I tested my joints and balance by walking around the bed using it for support.

"Kacey, are you ready?"

"As ready as I'll ever be."

Salonge watched with with concern as I limped towards her.

"Give me your bag and link my arm. There is only one person at reception, so   just smile at whatever I say and keep walking no matter what."

We began strolling towards the reception desk and the double doors beyond keeping our pace steady but not rushed. The young lady at the desk glanced up from her computer and then back to her administrative tasks without paying us much heed. As Salonge hit the small domed green button that activated the automatic doors we heard the lady's alarmed voice.

"Madame et mademoiselle, where are you going?
You should be still in bed!"

Salonge first placed a single finger to her mouth
pleading for the receptionist to keep her voice low.
She then bounced two separated v shaped fingers on
her lips indicating that we were desperate for a
secret cigarette. The woman shook her head in mock
disapproval then tapped a finger on her watch face
telling us to be quick. We passed through a second
set of doors and were relieved to see several drivers
chatting beside their empty taxis. Two of the men
shook hands with a third who smiled in our direction
whilst indicating which was his vehicle.

"Where can I take you on this fine evening?"

"Auxerre-St-Gervais station please."

"Ah you are leaving us. I hope your visit to the
hospital was not a serious matter."

"Not at all, we were saying goodbye to my sister
before heading back to Paris." Smiled Salonge. "She
is a nurse and unfortunately could not take our last
day in Auxerre off."

I was about to ask Salonge why on earth would we go
back to Paris, but a squeeze of my knee told me to
hold my tongue.

....

The receptionists mouth was watering as she sliced through the game pie which she had just fetched from the oven; her husband had removed the cork had decanted a fine bottle of red wine. She had prepared the dish that morning, so when she had finished work a little over an hour ago it was just a matter of popping it in the oven and turning up the heat. It was their first anniversary and their physical attraction for each other had not abated one iota. She was flashing glances at her husband, full of promise of what lay ahead after dinner when the phone wrang.

Her husband watched as his wife listened and her face turned deathly white.

"What's wrong my love?" He said.

"That was the hospital administrator. I have to go back work. The police wish to speak with me."

It was only then she realised that it must be about the two patients who had not returned from their cigarette break.

....

I was sitting on the bed in our small hotel room in Loroche-Migennes doing my best to translate Joans faded message from the ancient French tongue to modern English. Meanwhile Salonge had drawn the curtains and was using her jacket to cover the bedside lamp leaving only one aperture of space at its rear to create a makeshift projector for the sapphire.

When we had purchased our tickets to Paris from the kiosk in Auxerre-St-Gervais station the gentleman behind the counter had told us that if we hurried we would be able to catch the non-stop service from platform sixteen. Salonge thanked the man and began rushing in the direction of the platform he had indicated. I was barely able to keep up as shooting pains travelled up my bruised legs. The gap between us was increasing despite my gargantuan efforts until I eventually lost sight of my cousin as she disappeared around a corner. I agonisingly pushed my limbs even harder, furious that my cousin would be so inconsiderate. When I rounded the corner Salonge was eagerly waiting and pulled me against the wall to divulge her plan. She explained that the police would soon find the taxi driver who took us to the station and subsequently the man who served us our tickets to Paris. She then led me to a different platform keeping well out of view from the ticket office. This service also went to Paris so our tickets would be valid. The only difference was that it stopped at a number of stations along the way including a change of train at Laroche-Migennes where we exited the station.

"We need to send a picture of this muslin cloth to Professor Field. There are details which I cannot understand. The one thing which I am fairly certain of is that the third and final stone is somewhere close to her house in Domremy."

"Are you sure Kacey?"

"I think so. How long do you think we shall be safe here?"

"They are pretty good at tracking us down and the pattern so far has been around two days. Let's project the writing from the blue stone onto the wall and send send both that, and the message on the cloth to Charles Worwood."

"Why would we do that? It's bound to be written in Aramaic again and my old professor is the expert."

"If I'm right, the bad guys will be monitoring her phone and e mail. Besides, I'm sure that he would have taken her under his wing for protection, which is obviously the case with your friend, Johnny Valatone. There's one way to find out."

Salonge grabbed her phone and sent an SMS to Thames FM Radio. She then opened her laptop and tuned into their dot net service; we were rewarded almost immediately.

Hi there listeners. I have a request from a young lady who would like to hear anything from the fabulous Professor Green.

The professor is in fine form and if you would like to hear more from my good friend, the prof, you can make another request through my six usual channels.

So relax and enjoy 'At your convenience.'

Salonge gave me an excited smile. "Kacey, it's good news."

"How is Johnny playing a song by a British rapper good news?"

"I substituted Field for Green hoping they would make the connection, and they did, and she's fine.

"Of course, that's brilliant."

"There's more." Said Salonge, barely able to contain herself. "Johnny said that any further requests could be made through 'my six usual channels'."

"What does that mean. I thought that you just had to send an SMS?"

My can be replaced by Mi, and six is for 6...MI6. It also means that we now have the full official support of my boss, and therefore can make contact at our convenience using the usual channels. Now let's take some snaps of these messages and send them to Charles."

Salonge placed the blue sapphire on the bedside table and switched on the lamp. The whole wall behind the bed lit up in a brilliant blue and the text came into focus.

Chapter 39

PDLF

"Whats the latest news Charles?" Said Al Vicarrio, FBI Director, and a senior member of AICAC.

"Our heroines are safe and well somewhere on the outskirts of Paris."

"I thought we agreed, no BS Charles. My sources tell me that they were in an accident and were taken to a hospital in Auxerre. Why are you holding out on me, don't you trust me or something?"

"Now now dear chap, there is no need for that tone. If you would be so kind as to let me finish. They were indeed in a car accident and subsequently taken to a hospital at the location which you stated. However, they discharged themselves and left that area. They made contact with our resident DJ via SMS but have wisely held back on their precise location for obvious reasons. I have since received a fascinating e-mail, the details of which I shall divulge shortly."

"So what's all this 'somewhere on the outskirts of Paris' crap, and holding back their location...where exactly are they?" Said an agitated Al Vicarrio.

"That, as I stated old chum, I do not know, and I think it's best if it stays that way, at least for the time being. In the meantime, regarding the e mail, they have found the second clue on the quest which is causing such a furore across the channel; Professor Field is translating it as we speak. The lady in question is currently our guest upstairs, as is Johnny Valatone our resident DJ."

"So is MI6 running an Air B&B these days? Wouldn't it be better to just provide protection or place them in a safe house?"

"On the contrary old boy. The young man has been temporarily seconded into our communications division and is working extraordinarily long hours. The Professor on the other hand has unrivalled expertise in Aramaic and could be needed at any moment."

"What news do you have of the pricks who abducted Jack Nichols?"

"I think it best you hear that directly from Mr Agoba."

Charles Worwood pressed a button on his desk and summoned Billy to his office. He entered the room within seconds carrying a heavy folder, his own office being directly next door.

"Please take a seat Billy, you know FBI Director Allesio Vicarrio?"

"Yes sir, but we have never been formally introduced."

Formalities out of the way, Billy began. "As I'm sure you know, Anthony Mazur and Jack Nichols are certain that Julien Thibaut's suicide was manufactured, and they are also certain that the waxwork factory at the Chateau de Breteuil is the scene of Jack's interrogation. They also believe that the orchestrator of both events was none other than Gabriel Abadie, chief aide to the President of France."

"That's preposterous!" Yelled Vicarrio, barely managing to remain seated. "I know you British don't have the best historic relations with the French, but implicating a senior minister in this debacle is going a step too far."

Worwood gave Vicarrio a serious look before nodding at Billy to continue.

"Anthony and Jack said that the dead man was wearing an engraved ring, as was the man at the gatehouse to the chateau. Gabriel Abadie was also wearing an identical ring."

"You can't be serious?" Said Vicarrio, letting out a sarcastic laugh whilst shaking his head incredulously.

Billy took several photos from the folder and handed them to his superior and the FBI Director. "These are blown up photos of the dead man's belongings. The ring in question shows the engraved initials PDLF with a minute crest at the top of the oval."

Billy then passed over another two photos. "When Anthony and Jack were leaving the chateau after visiting the crime scene, they stopped at the gatehouse pretending to ask for directions. Anthony managed to take a picture of the gatekeeper's hand using his phone. It's not the best quality, but there is no doubt that it is the same ring."

"Who gives a crap about the gatekeeper and the estate manager? That proves nothing." Said an irritated Vicarrio.

Billy then passed over another set of pictures. "We obtained these from the archives of Le Monde newspaper. They are snaps of Gabriel Abadie accompanying the French President at several publicity events. I had the images of his left hand enhanced. An oval ring displaying the initials PDLF with a small crest at the top can be clearly seen."

"And that's all you have?" Said Vicarrio, picking up his briefcase preparing to leave. "They could have gone to the same school... they could support the same soccer team...Like PSG, Paris St Germain.

"With all due respect sir, I'm not finished." Said a

blushing and nervous Billy Agoba as Worwood restrained a smile. Billy passed out more pictures. This first enhancement is a magnified picture of the crest. "It contains two tiny Fleurs de Lys dissected horizontally by a sword set upon the background of the crucifixion, the minute artwork engraved in gold is quite extraordinary."

Billy Agoba pushed on, sensing that another dismissive interruption from the FBI man was imminent.

"I have done some research on the crest and came up with a hit. An organisation was set up in the mid 1500's, shortly after the end of the 100 years' war and Joan's execution. Its name was The Protecteurs de la France...PDLF and it has precisely the same crest as the ring. They were renowned for being ruthless with their methods against anyone or anything which threatened the integrity of France or the Catholic Church. It is said that for centuries they delivered punishments and retribution which made the Spanish inquisition seem like a quiz show. It is thought that they were the main instigators of the storming of the Bastille in 1789, but once the French monarchy was deposed the secret organisation appears to have vanished."

"Well it would appear that they have reappeared, if they ever actually went away." Said a thoughtful

Worwood.

Allessio Vicarrio had turned ashen. "Thank you for the insights gentlemen. Now I think it's time that I consulted with my people in Paris."

Al Vicarrio left MI6 and headed for Heathrow airport for his transit to Charles de Gaulle.

"Is that all sir?" Said Billy.

"Yes that is all. Brilliant work young man, what."

He was just about to leave the office when Worwood spoke again.

"Billy, how did you think that went?"

"It went fine sir, that is once Al calmed down and accepted the evidence."

"But did he accept it or was there something else? Just for the moment, pass everything through me should Mr Vicarrio make any requests for information."

"Yes sir."

"And Billy, keep this conversation between us."

....

The receptionist from the hospital could barely see

the road through her tears. She had been grilled by the police for two hours and, just when she thought the worst was over, the hospital administrator called her into the office and gave her her marching orders saying that she had behaved irresponsibly and jeopardised the security and integrity of the hospital. She parked in the driveway and sat motionless thinking of ways that the couple could save money until she found another job; they would have to cancel the short vacation and send back the anniversary gifts which still sat unopened on the dining table. Eventually she gathered the courage to break the news to her husband. After wiping the streams of mascara from her cheeks and finished applying a fresh face of makeup, she entered the house and froze. Her husband was sitting in the lounge bound and gagged with blood caked around his nostrils. Next to him, in very much the same condition, was a taxi driver who serviced the hospital. A young man in a suit was standing beside them brandishing a gun. The receptionist glanced at the remnants of the smashed house-phone before turning to flee and seek assistance, but her path was blocked.

"Please take a seat young lady." Said a smirking Gabriel Abadie from behind the door.

The receptionist obeyed the pleas from her

husband's terrified eyes to comply.

"Who are you?...what do you want?"

"Who I am is someone that can cause you immeasurable pain if you do not answer my questions. Tell me about the two ladies who left the hospital."

"There is nothing to tell. They had been admitted the evening before my shift began. I had no idea that the police wished to question them. The lady who works the alternate shift forgot to update the admin file."

"And what is this person's name and address?"

The terrified receptionist was busy scribbling the details onto a pad when she heard an angry elongated growl from her husband and looked over at his distorted face, and then down to his clenched fists. She wondered what the point was, him being bound so securely. Her husband's eyes then rolled into the back of his head as he lost consciousness. The clenched fists unfurled to reveal eight bloody fingers but no thumbs.

"We had to be sure that your husband was not holding out on us. I have been kind enough to place the stumpy digits into your freezer so the tissue should be in a good enough condition to sew them back on. Now tell me what the two criminals said to you as they left the hospital. One of your resident taxi drivers was foolish enough to give them a ride. Unfortunately he has no information of any substance so is of no longer use to us." With that Gabriel nodded to Antoine who shot the man through the temple.

"We didn't actually have a proper conversation, I swear." Said the sobbing young woman. "The women gestured that they were just popping out for a cigarette. It's quite common for patients to do this and we usually turn a blind eye."

"Were you not curious as to why they did not return?"

"I forgot all about them. My shift was almost over, and it is our 1st anniversary. You must believe me...I know nothing."

"Fortunately for you, I do believe you."

Gabriel gestured to Antoine that they were leaving and turned for the door.

Recognition suddenly came to the receptionist and words began involuntarily leaving her mouth. "I know you...I've seen you on TV with the President. You are Gabriel Abadie."

Gabriel turned to face her. "I wish you had not said

that. Or more to the point, you should wish you had not said that. I am truly sorry young lady."

Chapter 40

The Creator Stone

Salonge's computer pinged, and we both sprang from the bed having been listening to Johnny Valatone's selection of soul records from two decades before I was born; there were no new messages though. Salonge began typing in a long series of numbers, letters, and characters onto her keypad.

"That noise means we have a message from Charles Worwood; the usual secure channels are back online."

"What does it say"

"Give me a minute. It goes through a series of encryption checks before I can read anything."

We both sat staring at the screen until what looked like a bad reception before the pixelization became clear and the message appeared.

My dear Salonge and Kacey, I do hope you are safe and well.

For the time being it would be best if you continue to keep your precise location to yourselves unless it is an absolute emergency. Anthony is safe and well as is your old colleague Jack Nichols and I am sure you will be seeing them soon. Regarding your old organisation, the FBI, I would refrain from passing any information to them for the time being. It may be nothing at all, but I feel it prudent to err on the side of caution.

Below I have attached the professor's translation of Joan's second message on the muslin along with the ancient Aramaic from the sapphire. It would appear that your next destination will be Joan's birthplace but, as mentioned above, keep this to yourselves.

Re developments: It has now emerged that a secret organisation called the Protecteurs de la France, or PDLF, are the baddies on your tails. What is even more concerning is that the head of this organisation could very well be someone at the very highest levels of politics in France. It would be inappropriate to name him at this point, just be on your guard.

Although this channel is back online, and you have our official support, please continue to us the Thames FM channel to pass on updates. BTW please inform Kacey that the professor and the DJ are well and send their best wishes.

The message on the second muslin cloth is self-explanatory. The blue sapphire message, as was the case with the blood ruby, was extremely disjointed. However, when the professor overlaid them, it begins to make sense. It seems logical to assume that the full document shall reveal itself when the third stone is discovered.

Good luck kiddywinks

"What do you make of that?" I said.

"It's bad news and good."

"How so?"

"For one, Charles instincts are never wrong. It seems there is a leak within the FBI. Secondly, a secret organisation headed by a senior politician in this country means that we are facing a formidable force."

"I see. So what's the good part?"

"The good part is that Charles is now on their tails, and I would pitch his courage and intellect against anyone or anything."

"Don't forget." I said. "We have the forces of good on our side, and we too, just like the noble knights of old, are also a formidable force. Let us open the first attachment and bring our quest to a successful conclusion."

Salonge hit the first tiny icon.

If you have found this blue sapphire representing water, the very source of life, then you are truly the chosen one and of my bloodline. Now that you have two stones you will be able to achieve things thought impossible for a mere mortal. Perhaps you have already experienced this.

It is believed that my beloved sister Catherine died in childbirth in 1429, this is not the case. Her child was born in our bodily likeness, and they feared persecution. She and her husband fled to England and assumed the name Chapman.

Our creator appeared to me prior to my execution and delivered incredible revelations which you must make known to the world.

I did not fear death, and nor should you. But you must find the third stone to reveal the truth.

I entrusted a close friend to hide the third stone, a diamond-like crystal, at the place of my birth. My true ancestor will feel its location.

I pray that the world is finally ready.

I was in shock. Sir Grandad was right, Joan is saying that I am of her bloodline. Seeing my surname, Chapman, staring back at me from a six-hundred-year-old muslin cloth message written by Joan herself was astounding.

"Open the second attachment and see what the blue gemstone has added." I said in a zombie like monotone.

I, the son of God hereby   those born as
both   woman shall   God as the
saviour   Only one who encompasses the
virtues   can truly   good, and
the bad which inhabits the earth.   for
       burden of our weaknesses
the   comes when understanding wins
through. Only then can the world live in harmony.

My Father and Mother be as one, and in one
are the   things. I deliver this message to
you, Joan D'Arc, in the form   stones.
You must hide them in separate locations until the day
that   and of your bloodline, shall
reveal   Only when   joined
together,   crystal font
your   can this message be read in full and
truly understood.

Your quest   the words

my messengers   Arcangel, Saint Catherine of Alexandria and Saint Margaret. They will advise   the suffering oppressed in your land,   many years   . There are three orders which you must obey   be accepted into our creators Heavenly Kingdom. You must lead the   dressed in manly   You shall remain   either man or woman. You   ultimate sacrifice, as did I.

Many years from now, when one of your born in the bodily   my mother will the truth   the world.

Amen

Salonge was studying the translation with pen and paper to hand, but no ink had touched the page.

"There are still too many gaps Kacey. One tiny misinterpretation could lead us to a completely wrong conclusion."

It's obvious." I said. "The third stone will fill in the gaps, but there are no solid clues as to its whereabouts."

"Joan said that you will feel its location, just as you did with the vibration of the stone in the crypt."

"So what do you suggest? I spend a year standing on every flagstone in Domremy until one begins to tremble."

"Kacey, I think the red and blue stones will assist you. Joan says that they have powers which may already have been of help. Are you forgetting that two-ton door which you smashed off its hinges?"

"Then I think we should head to her birthplace tonight."

"That's not a good idea Kacey. By the time we get there it will be almost midnight. Two females looking for accommodation at that hour would attract too much attention. I sincerely doubt that they have traced our movements yet so let's enjoy the space to get a good night's sleep. Besides, I need to organise another hire car."

I knew that it was sound and logical advice so just sat staring at the two magnificent gems standing base down on the coffee table beside the window. Suddenly they began to glow alternately; first red and then blue. It was very dim at first but gradually increased until the whole room was illuminated in the magnificent primary colours. I walked towards the table and picked them up, one in my left hand and the other in my right; I didn't want to cause another catastrophe by bringing them too close together. I was confused. Neither gem appeared to be emitting light, but the room continued to glow red then blue. It was then when I looked out of our hotel window that I saw the two police cars with their roof lights dancing.

Chapter 41

Two people to watch

Let's take the mood down now as I play 'Silence is Golden' for a gentleman who is making a surprise visit to his friends in Paris. Believe it or not listeners, he is a vicar from Rio. Yes you heard correct listeners...a vicar from Rio. Following that we shall edge the mood back up with a frequently requested song...Don't Speak, by No Doubt and the beautiful Gwen Steffani.

Anthony came running out of the shower wrapped in a towel. "Did you hear that Jack?" The only response was the sound of Jack's snoring. "Jack wake up. I think we have another message."

Even though most listeners tune into Thames FM on their radios, the show is also available via dot net which gives the option to freeze or replay the schedule. Anthony rewound and replayed from the start of the previous dedication.

"Jack wake up." Hollered Anthony.

"W..w..what's up?"

"We have a message, but I can't figure it out, have a listen."

Jack did so as he stretched and slid off the bed. "Play

it again." He said, yawning whilst grabbing a pad and pen.

"It's clear that they are warning us to be careful who we speak to." Said Anthony. "Silence is Golden is a new one one, but they have used 'Don't Speak' before which is unusual for Charles, it must be really important."

"Holy crap." Said Jack Nichols staring at his scribbles.

"What is it Jack?"

"A Vicar from Reo...That's my boss's boss at the FBI...A Vicar rio...Al Vicarrio. He must be coming to Paris. I guess that he's here to kick some French arse over my abduction."

"Maybe." Said Anthony. "But it's more than that. You may not know it, but Allesio Vicarrio is also a director of AICAC who Salonge and I work for. Why on earth would Charles be telling us both to keep tight lipped to whom we both, directly or indirectly, work for?"

"I don't know, but I don't like it." Said a thoughtful Jack. "What's more, I put in a request at the Bureau for any deep information on Gabriel Abadie's past. It was initially approved by my direct superior here in Paris and then immediately blocked by his boss, Allesio Vicarrio."

....

Al Vicarrio marched into Gabriels apartment on the Champs Elysse without knocking, much to the displeasure, and protestations of the guard at the door. The soldier did not know the identity of the uninvited guest, only that he was of great importance to the PDLF, so reluctantly stood aside.

"Good afternoon. How are you today?"

Gabriels head shot up. "Who let you in? I do no recall you requesting an audience."

Remember , Gabriel. You are only the figurehead of The Protecteurs de la France because we allow you to be. Without funding from America, you would be no more than a right-wing gang of lunatics with some aristocratic connections and a questionable, vicious foundation."

"Mr Vicarrio, may I remind you that I am not only the head of the PDLF, but also the chief aide to the President of France, and I object to your assumptions that our honourable society, which has been in existence for longer than the country of your birth, rely purely on the support of a capitalistic, greedy nation. We shall survive with or without the assistance of the Americans."

"Ok I get it. But at the rate that you are killing your

own members, there won't be any of you left anyway. How's the tumour?"

Gabriel's jaw dropped. "How do you know about the tumour?"

"We have our sources."

"Fucking Doctor Gunther Schmidt, I'll cut his balls off." Gabriel began massaging his temple.

"Don't blame him Gabriel, he had no choice. We have been following you to your consultations and decided to put a proposal to the old gentleman. He either breaks doctor patient confidentiality or we produce dozens of ex-East German athletes suffering from an innumerable amount of conditions in later life due to his experiments. He didn't much fancy the idea of spending his twilight years in a German prison. Tell me Gabriel, have you given any thought to your replacement? After all, you have eliminated Pierre Cardout and Julien Thibault. Perhaps there is someone whom you could mentor in the little time you have left?

"And who would you suggest? One of the decrepit old has-beens who turn up to our meetings because they are too stingy to buy a decent bottle of wine themselves. Or perhaps one of the new modern females who believe they are as intelligent and as strong as men?"

"Oh I think that you are doing both categories a great injustice and underestimating their capabilities. However, I was thinking of someone much closer to home."

"And who could that be?" Laughed Gabriel.

"Your son perhaps?" Said Al, knowing that this would confuse his verbal combatant.

"It is you who must have the tumour. Either that or the FBI really do need to shake up their intelligence sources. I have one daughter who is at finishing school in Geneva."

"Ah, that is what you really believe is it? One of the whores you took a liking to some thirty-two years ago, you know, before you began killing them after coitus, became pregnant. She had a son."

"Don't be ridiculous."

"Did you know that many illegitimate children in France made alterations to their cruelly allocated surnames from the universally allocated Batard, (I'm sure you know what that means) to more acceptable titles like Bouvard?"

"What are you saying?"

Al Vicarrio smiled. "Antoine, would you come in here please. I would like to introduce you to your father."

....

Earlier that morning

Anthony and Jack had been wondering what to do. Should they sit and wait to be contacted by Vicarrio, or carry on as usual with their investigation. If they did nothing it would seem strange and Vicarrio could get suspicious. Jack was dubious as to the possibility of someone that high up in the FBI being involved with the PDLF, but Anthony was adamant that there must be some substance behind the message from Worwood on Thames FM. The decision was made when Anthony received his first text from Salonge for over a week.

.....

"How are you my love? I have to keep this message short. I figured out that the warning which Charles sent over the airwaves was for you and Jack. Tell Jack to be careful, the man in question is ruthless and was an ass when I worked with him. We are on the third, and hopefully final leg of this quest. Please don't worry about us, but if you really want to help, then keep the bad guys busy in Paris.

S x"

.....

"Will do babe. Missing you like crazy.

A"

.....

Anthony showed the message to Jack Nichols before grabbing his coat and car keys.

"Where are we going?" Enquired Jack.

"We are going to keep them busy. Let's see what our Monsieur Abadie is up to."

"He could be anywhere."

"That's true." Replied Anthony. "But I have a feeling that if Vicarrio is part of this mess then the first thing on his agenda will be a meeting with the head of the PDLF, and they would hardly do that at the Elysee Palace."

"Abadie's apartment it is then." Said Jack. "I have an idea. Do we have time to stop at a print shop?"

"I guess so. What do you have in mind?"

After a flying stop at the printers, they parked their car two blocks from Abadie's apartment and walked to a café opposite the entrance to the underground car park. Anthony ordered the coffees whilst Jack walked over to the security man at the subterranean entrance. Initially the guard refused to allow Jack to distribute the leaflets onto the windscreens of the parked vehicles of the tenants offering a new bespoke valet service. Jack tested the man's resolve with the offer of fifty euros which was refused, but when he produced a second note of the same denomination the guard waved him through. Jack thanked the man and pulled the peak of his baseball cap a little lower whilst donning his sun glasses, hoping the man wouldn't find this strange given the low-lit area he was about to enter.

Anthony was nervously sipping his second coffee when he saw Jack jog back across the road and enter the café.

"Is Abadie there?"

"Yep, it looks like it. His car is in his personal space and the engine is cold. ."

"Ok, so we wait until he leaves and tail him, maybe to a rendezvous with Vicarrio."

"I don't think we have to."

"What do you mean by that Jack?"

"There is an FBI vehicle in the guest space. People in our game, even those not with the bureau such as yourself, can easily spot one of their vehicles. But what your average Joe doesn't know is about the plates."

"What's so special about the plates?" Said Anthony.

"Aside from the single screw fix on each corner, they also have additional screws top centre. One screw denotes a field agent. Two screws an operations manager and three screws for director or above. This car had three, it must be Vicarrio's."

"So I guess we go back to the car, wait for him to come out, and then see where he goes."

"That's about all we can do for the moment."

Chapter 42

Domremy

We continued to watch the police from our window as one of them began walking away from the first vehicle and around the back of our hotel to block our escape. The driver from the second vehicle was standing by his car door speaking into the radio; his partner had already entered the hotel; we were trapped.

Salonge grabbed her phone and began dialling a number.

"What are you doing?" I said. "Even if the Concord were still flying there is no one that anyone could get here in time to help us."

"Just keep watch and tell me what's happening."

Salonge began speaking to who I assumed to be a receptionist.

"Good morning mademoiselle. My husband and I spent a wonderful couple of days at your establishment last month and would like to pay you another visit. Could you tell me if room 252 is available? If I remember correctly, it was at the back of the hotel with wonderful views and devoid of any traffic noise."

I whispered to Salonge that a member of staff had emerged from the hotel with the gendarme and was pointing up at our room. Salonge silently mimed for me to quickly gather our things before continuing her conversation.

"252 is unoccupied, oh that is marvellous. Our names are Mr and Ms Dubois. We should be with you shortly after midday. Merci beaucoup."

Salonge replaced the phone and rummaged in her bag, eventually retrieving an odd-looking type of Swiss army knife. She opened our door and took two paces across the corridor to room 252. Seconds later both Salonge and I, along with all of our belongings were in a fresh location. We both had our ears glued to the door and soon heard footsteps.

"It's three men and one woman." whispered Salonge.

We could hear knuckles rapping on the door to our recently vacated room.

Pardon mademoiselles...housekeeping. (Silence)

I have fresh towels and complimentary refreshments for you. (Silence)

Then there was the crashing sound of a door being kicked in followed by men's agitated voices... They have gone!!!...They can't be far...

"Jean Paul, tell headquarters they have escaped but we have their vehicle so they can't be far."

We could hear the police asking the maid if any of the other rooms were occupied in case any of the guests saw us leave, but she said that most arrivals were due that afternoon. We then heard him tell her to gather all the staff in the reception. We had eluded them for the time being, but I was at a loss as to how we would get very far without a car, and the local gendarmes would also be on high alert. Salonge carefully peered out of the window of our temporary room using the flimsy curtain for cover. This rear aspect revealed the single policeman walking back to the front of the hotel passing several camper vans with the logo of our hotel emblazoned on the rear. The establishment clearly had a second source of income by renting out medium sized Winnebago's to the more adventurous traveller.

Salonge waved me over. "Kacey, I think we may have a way out of here. How are you at shimmying down gutters and drainage pipes?"

I walked to the window and followed her line of site to the cumbersome vehicles. I turned towards her in disbelief. "Are you seriously suggesting that we steel a motor home emblazoned with this hotel's logo, and accelerates from zero to sixty in around three hours? They would catch us in no time."

"That doesn't sound much like my brave young relative and descendant of Joan."

Salonge placed her palms on my cheeks and kissed my forehead.

"Dear Kacey, we are mice trapped in a corner by vicious cats. A mouse only needs to get out of the corner before it finds a safe hole in which to hide."

"I am brave like Joan D'Arc, not a mouse. We are together brave and honourable like Joan." And don't forget, if I am of her blood then somewhere along the line, so are you."

It was the first time that I had seen Salonge truly lost for words as the realisation of my statement hit home; it was no longer just about me, it was about our combined family heritage. We opened the stiff sash window and began our descent. We instantly regretted testing the aging pipework with our combined weight in one go, but time was of the essence. The retaining brackets were whittling out of the concrete walls throwing dust into our eyes; the odd bolt falling loose to the floor. Thankfully, once at ground level we sprinted unnoticed to the farthest Winnebago. Salonge again retrieved her Swiss like burglar kit and began working on the door. I couldn't help emitting a soft giggle as I opened the vehicle's unlocked door having seen the keys dangling from the ignition. We both held our breath as a throaty roar burst into the rear parking lot, so we instinctively dropped to the floor and rolled under the camper. A powerful Harley Davidson motor bike pulled alongside us. We could see one blue left boot at the front and one red left boot directly behind, both with matching leathers to the knee which was as high as we could see. Two female bikers began talking about the thrill of their new two wheeled cruiser. When they dismounted we could now see all four boots standing toe to toe. Their legs became intertwined and the sound of mouth upon mouth became obvious, the thrill of speed being their own particular form of aphrodisiac.

I love you...I love you too... said the female devotees

I was mesmerised by their excitement and obvious arousal as they removed their boots and full leathers. Inquisitiveness turned to understanding as they made the familiar grunts of people squeezing into skinny jeans and donning awkward high heels before a night out. We waited until the click clack of stilettos diminished before sliding out from the underside of the camper.

"I think we have just found a more stealthy and efficient mode of transport." Said Salonge.

She used her burglar's tool to good effect this time,

unchaining the two crash helmets and removing the girls' leathers from the panniers. We now had a super cool bike, a set of nondescript biker wear with colour coded crash helmets; the reflective mirrored visors completed our disguise.

"I haven't ridden a bike for some time Kacey, so hold tight."

"Well I have." I said, swapping to the main driver's position. "I ride my friend Johnny Valatone's bike all the time…it's you that should hang on. Now how are we going to get this thing stated?

"Kacey, just touch the two wires that I stripped and start her up… let's get out of here!"

Straddling the Harley I felt exhilarated by the engine's vibration which penetrated every bone in my body from head to toe.

It was only then that I realised it was the red and blue gemstones which were causing the tremble and not the engine. The police at the front of the hotel paid us no heed as we sped past. Rumbling down the road I was consumed by the thought that the girls who turned up in the red and blue leathers, facilitating our escape, were possibly modern-day angels summoned by the gems. I will soon have my answer, I thought.

If the two-wheeler is not reported stolen then our creator is truly on our side.

....

Anthony and Jack were sitting in their vehicle having watched FBI Director Allesio Vicarrio leave Abadie's apartment, park his car, and enter the safe house recently vacated by Salonge and Kacey. Jack's phone buzzed.

"Jack Nichols speaking."

"Special Agent Nichols, this is Al Vicarrio."

"Good to hear from you sir. How can I help?"

"You could help by getting yourself over to the safe house in the Latin quarter and bring your new sidekick with you."

"Yes sir. I didn't realise that you were coming to Paris." Jack lied. "When did you arrive?"

"I've just got here from the airport. We need to sort out this mess which you have created. Be here within the hour with some good answers."

"Some answers sir?"

"Yes, good answers such as how does a fully trained FBI agent with fifteen years' experience allow himself to be abducted and then throw accusations at the chief aide to the President of France. Answers such as, how has Anthony Mazur convinced the head of AICAC and MI6 that this ridiculous accusation has any substance? Answers such as, why is his wife running around France causing mayhem?"

"Actually, we can be with you sooner sir. We were just on hour way to stake out Abadie's apartment on the Champs Elysee. Should we abort and head to you?"

"Bloody hell yes. On no account are you to tail Abadie. Have there been eyes on him already?"

"No sir. This was to be the first stake out." Nichols lied for a second time.

The exhalation of breath indicating Vicarrio's relief at not being spotted was audible.

"ETA at the safe house in fifteen minutes sir." The phone went dead.

"I guess that answers our questions." Said Anthony.

"Im afraid it does. Vicarrio is up to his neck in this shit."

"Agreed." Said Anthony. "I need to let Worwood know. I'll send an SMS to Thames FM."

....

A certain Vicar from Reo made a request yesterday for two friends he is visiting in Paris. That's a first for me listeners. Apparently, they are meeting up later this morning and his friends have returned the gesture by requesting two songs of their own. You will love these classics by the king himself... Devil in disguise, and Suspicious minds.

....

MI6

"Surely you could have just relayed the SMS request to me instead of actually broadcasting the message?" Said an agitated Charles Worwood.

"Listen dude." Said Johnny Valatone. "I may be new to this game, but if I've sussed things correctly then Kacey and her cousin will want to know the lowdown too, and this is the best way to keep everyone in the know."

"That is a very good point Johnny, I apologise, what. Play a song for me if you will. It is called 'I'll protect you' by 888 Blue."

When Johnny returned to his decks he couldn't help but be impressed by Charles choice of song and the opening lines.

It's all scary but that's okay, it shall pass, yeah, rest for the day. You deserve the world, but it's on your shoulders...............

Chapter 43

The Quest Continues

It was the first time since Sir Grandad died that I had felt truly free. Of course, a Harley doesn't have the acceleration of a modern Yamaha R1, or a Ducati Panigale, but the roar as we cruised along the country lanes in our red and blue leathers was exhilarating. Passing the odd remote convenience store, groups of teenagers would stop drinking cans of coke to point as we whizzed by, looks of awe and envy on their faces. Sitting on their porches, the occasional pensioner would gaze at our ride, reminiscing about a time when style and craftsmanship were more important than pure speed; I'm not sure that they approved of the vibrant colours of our leathers and sparkling helmets though. We even got a wave from several police motorcycles travelling in the opposite direction, obviously tasked with scouring the local roads in search of two desperate females on foot.

For the next three kilometres our only audience was the wildlife being disturbed from their perpetual task of gathering worms, nuts, and berries to take back to their nests, dens, and hidey holes. We ascended a steep hill and emerged from a canopy of trees to halt on its crest affording a breath-taking view of the valley below. On a different occasion it would have been almost spiritual. Today, however, the fly in the ointment was a roadblock in the distance; there was no turning back, and a dash across the rolling countryside would be like sending a 'here we are boys, come and get us' message to the police.

We dismounted the Harley and rolled her back under cover of the trees. Our only hope was to hide it in the foliage and attempt an escape across country on foot, devoid of our brightly coloured leathers. Our solitary zippers to the protective overalls had barely reached our navels when all seemed lost.

"Kacey, can you hear that?"

"It sounds like an army division of tanks coming up the hill, who couldn't hear it?"

"I am going to make a run for the trees." Said Salonge, reaching into the left panier for her bag. "Stall them as long as you can."

"I understand your decision to abandon me my beloved cousin. This is my quest after all. I shall buy you as much time as I can, however, unfortunately I do not consider your chances of escape very high."

"I'm not abandoning you, you silly thing. I just need enough time to call Charles Worwood. If we send an SMS to Thames FM, the chances are we will be dead before the request is played. We need his assistance immediately."

I felt ashamed. Of course my wonderful cousin would not have abandoned me. How could I ever have considered that to be a possibility when this very person had put her entire life on hold at the bequest of Sir Grandad.

Salonge had barely tapped three buttons on her phone's keypad when our bodies were illuminated by the headlights of the vehicles approaching us; all was lost.

The headlights were all of a different size, and none were of an equidistant measure which would indicate a car. Added to this was the now unmistakable sound of multiple motorbikes. However, the combined glare of forty headlamps meant that we had no idea of who occupied the mass of vehicles. Almost at once, every light bar one was extinguished leaving the outline of a bear like individual with long straggly hair.

"Have you broken down mademoiselles?" Said a gruff voice.

The blue jeaned, leather jacketed man, wearing more jewellery dangling from one ear than Salonge and I owned together in total, stepped forward.

Salonge took a gamble. "Bonjour monsieur, we have aggravated the local gendarmes and it would seem that they have us in a trap. We can't go back, and as you can see; our way forward is blocked."

"Well that looks like quite a concerted effort by the police to capture two young ladies. It seems more appropriate for apprehending murderers. Perhaps we should assist them in their duty...unless you could convince us otherwise."

The relief at seeing that they were not the authorities diminished in a second. Salonge walked forward until standing toe to toe with the giant. With each approaching step my cousin appeared to be shrinking, he was humongous. Salonge showed no fear as her face contorted and her voice took on a vicious tone.

"My cousin and I are on a bike touring vacation. We stopped at the hotel a few kilometres back. This morning the concierge saw me go out for croissants because the breakfast there was shit. He let himself into our room when my young cousin was in the shower and tried to rape her. She held her own, but he began to get the better of her. Just as she was about to be violated, I returned and stuck a bread knife into his bollocks."

The big bear laughed. "I saw loads of cops back there. I guess you could do with our help?"

"What's the price?" Said Salonge. "We don't put up with rape, and we don't sell our bodies."

"Woohaaa there tiger. You girls are kindred bikers, and we always help each other, you should know that. One of you jump behind me and the other behind Robert. The crazy guy with one eye is Domonic, he will ride your bike through the checkpoint. He usually goes first and acts a bit crazy. The police always ask for proof that he is eligible to ride a motorbike with just one eye. Whilst he is showing them his documentation, we get waved through with our weed intact."

"That would be great." Said Salonge. "Where are you heading?"

"There is a bikers' convention at a campsite just outside Domremy. There will be some real enthusiasts there with amazing modified rides, you would love it."

"It must be sold out." Said Salonge. "And as I mentioned, we are not into doing girl favours for favours, if you get my meaning."

"Jesus, why do you think us guys all ride together? We are into each other, not girls. My brother owns the campsite, it's called Camping L'Arc En Ciel. Don't worry, there will be girls there too, if that's your thing. It's close to where Joan of Arc was born. They say that she was one of us of sorts, or even a bit of both.

I was already sitting at the rear of Robert's bike with my arms around his waist before Salonge had registered the leader of the gay Hells Angels statement.

Salonge smiled and gave me a wink before sliding onto the back of the gentle giant bear's bike.

Chapter 44

Questions and Mistrust

When Al Vicarrio had left Gabriel's apartment, he had placed an FBI file onto the desk leaving the two men to discover the evidence of their paternal links together. Gabriel's emotions were in turmoil; was this an imposter being maneuvered in place by the sly American or, after many fruitless years of trying for a son, was this young man really the product of his loins?

"When were you told of this ridiculous claim that you are my son?"

"I wasn't told Sir. I was sent an anonymous file some months ago which claimed to show irrefutable proof as to the identity of my father. His name was blanked out though sir. I received a second message yesterday instructing me to print the file and bring it with me today."

"So you believe that I am the man whose name was erased?"

"I don't know what to believe sir. The first thing I knew of the potential identity of my father was a few moments ago when Mr Vicarrio summoned me into your office."

"If the name in question was blanked out then what convinced you that the document delivered to you carried any credence?"

Antoine lowered his head in mild embarrassment. "Sir, my mother died shortly after I was born. As you can guess, I never knew my father. It could have been anyone as she was a..."

"She was a what...is whore the description that you are searching for?"

Antoine raised his head in anger. "Yes sir, she was a whore, as you say. She laid on her back and earned enough money from people like you in order to put food on the table." Antoine suddenly fell silent, hardly believing the words which had left his mouth. "I'm sorry sir, this is just very emotional for me. The only family I have ever really known were my grandmother who raised me, and the Protecteurs de la France. Please don't take the PDLF away from me. Can't we simply throw both files into the fire and continue as before. I will be the most loyal soldier in your whole organisation."

Gabriel couldn't help liking this young man, and considered that he would make any father proud. He also liked the fact that Antoine was content to carry on as before, and respectfully continued to call him sir, not father; hardly the behaviour or someone out for personal gain. Even though it was a humid afternoon, Gabriel opened the FBI file and began scrunching up the documents to form kindling for the fire.

"Antoine, why don't you join me in putting your documents into the fire as I am doing with my file and forget about this crazy American's claims."

In an instant the enormous tension in the room evaporated. Gabriel poured two large cognacs before beckoning Antoine towards the hearth's virgin flames. The young man received a warm smile from his superior as they clinked glasses, and each took a generous sip from their crystal fishbowls.

The flames grew in intensity, fuelled by page after page from each man's file. Antoine hesitated to destroy the final one, seemingly transfixed on a photograph of his mother holding her new-born son, a four-day old Antoine.

Gabriel walked towards the younger man to see what had captured his attention, instantly recognising the woman smiling for the camera. He immediately lunged towards the fireplace throwing a jug of water onto the flames. Plumes of smoke filled the room setting off the fire alarms, but Gabriel was oblivious to the piercing noise. He held the retrieved remains of his young self, kissing a beautiful woman, the same woman in Antoine's photograph.

That in itself was not what astonished Gabriel. It was the unmistakeable likeness of his own younger image in the picture to that of the person standing beside him.

"Antoine my son, we have such little time left. If only your mother had told me!"

Gabriel threw both arms around his child before the pain in his temple arrived like a battering ram causing him to release his embrace and crumple to the floor.

....

"Let me do the talking Anthony, we can't have you blowing off." Said a very tense Jack Nichols as he pressed the buzzer to the safe house.

"What's that supposed to mean?"

"Come on buddy. If this guy is behind the bastards trying to hurt Salonge and Kacey then it's just best that I handle it. We have to bide our time and nail him, not get ourselves in heaps of trouble by you punching his lights out."

The door clicked open but there was no verbal welcome crackling from the intercom. Both agents gave each other a knowing look as the mood for their meeting with Al Vicarrio was apparently already set.

Vicarrio was standing by the open door to the safe house as the elevator opened.

"Ok gentlemen let's make this quick. Do come in and take a seat and I shall give you your instructions."

"With all due respect sir, I take my instructions from Charles Worwood in London." Said Anthony whilst watching Jack raise his eyebrows, simultaneously producing a zipping motion across his lips with his thumb and index finger urging him to reign it in.

Vicarrio's head snapped in Anthony's direction with a look of fury in his eyes which rapidly softened. "Of course you do AICAC Agent Mazur. But FBI Special Agent Nichols does not. Also, Charles Worwood is, as you stated, in London and not here. I shall make my recommendations to Charles and I'm sure he will concur and instruct you accordingly."

"I wouldn't bet on it." Whispered Anthony to Jack through the side of his mouth.

Jack gave him a nudge in the ribs as they followed Vicarrio into the safehouse and took to their seats at the four-seater kitchen table. Two glasses were filled with chilled water, demonstrated by the moisture and droplets running down the outside. An equally chilled jug of agua was placed equidistant between the two. Across the table sat a quarter emptied bottle of Jack Daniels with an amply filled tumbler of the recently poured alcoholic beverage. A full bottle of diet coke was also present, but Anthony noticed an empty receptacle of the same mixer in the trash can, resting perilously atop two recently devoured pot noodles.

"So gentlemen." Slurred Vicarrio.

Neither man had initially detected the impaired speech or the smell of alcohol.

"Ok, now I want you to listen, and listen carefully. Gabriel Abadie is to be left well alone. What you may not know is that he is terminally ill, and to spend money and resources investigating these ridiculous claims of him being part of a secret organisation is pointless as he will soon be dead."

"It sounds like you know him well." Said Anthony.

"We have met on a couple occasions...of what importance is that?"

"Where did you meet him, at the Elysee Palace or his apartment on the Champs Elysee?"

Vicarrio was caught off-guard. "I erm, I can't remember."

"You can't remember? I thought that a highly enhanced memory function was a pre-requisite for any FBI Agent, let alone a director."

Anthony felt a kick from Jack.

"I'm sorry sir. I just thought that if you knew him well then it would give us some insight as to why you are convinced of his integrity. Please continue."

"Gotcha Agent Mazzzuuurrr , no problemo." Said a slurring, and less than observant Al Vicarrio , the obvious insinuation passing over the increasingly inebriated director's head. "What I believe we should do is find these girls who are causing mayhem with international relations and convince them to abort this ridiculous quest which they have embarked upon. Agent Mazur, I'm sure that you will have no objection to being tasked with finding your wife? In my day we knew how to keep our little ladies in check."

Anthony gripped the edge of the table with both hands, ready to tip it, along with its entire contents, onto the chauvinistic idiot sitting opposite. Jack lent forward exerting his entire bodyweight onto his elbows avoiding a catastrophic, career ending event. Luckily, the episode went unnoticed by Vicarrio.

"Now gentlemen, when I say find them, what I really mean is find their current location. I would suggest that you make contact with your wife Anthony.

When they have disclosed their current position, you are on no account to meet with them. You should notify me immediately at which point I shall send a team to extract them and deliver them to safety thus ending this ridiculous debacle."

"I'll try to contact her." Said Anthony. "But she has an uncanny knack of sniffing out a trap."

Vicarrio slammed the desk as Jack Nichols held his head in despair. "What on earth are you insinuating Agent Mazur?"

"I'm not insinuating anything sir. It's just that as experienced as she is, she is likely to show reluctance at divulging her whereabouts in case our communication channels have been compromised."

"Oh, I see, I apologise. For a moment I thought that you were...never mind."

"Is that all sir?" Said a relieved Jack Nichols.

"Yes, that is all. And bear in mind Agent Nichols, successfully bringing this craziness to an end may well be the very thing which makes me lose the file investigating your incompetence at being abducted from an FBI safe house."

Anthony was already heading for the door in disgust, determined to warn his wife about whom he now felt certain was at best an incompetent alcoholic, and at worst a traitor, when he heard the scarping of a chair followed by a crashing noise. Vicarrio had swivelled violently in Anthony's direction whilst roaring that he had not yet been excused when the legs of his seat buckled sending him sprawling to the floor. Anthony and Jack rushed to his aid, each taking an elbow and placing an arm around his waist before half carrying the director to the bedroom. An embarrassed Vicarrio thanked the men and said they were free to leave.

Once back in the car Anthony told Jack to drive to their aparthotel.

"This could be interesting." He said, holding a burner phone in his left hand.

"Christ Anthony, did you take that from Vicarrio?"

"When we were carrying him to the bedroom I could feel two mobile phones in his pocket. I guessed the larger of the two to be his FBI I Phone, but why would he need a smaller second means of communication?"

"Let's go find out."

....

We gently thundered down the hill towards the roadblock in a diamond display squad type formation, with the one-eyed rider at its pinnacle. As we arrived at the barrier another police van joined the four cars; eight gendarmes were already in place. The most senior officer stepped forward with his arm raised instructing us to stop. Domonic removed his helmet revealing his one good eye and a toothless grin.

"Ah, it's you Domonic." Said the lead officer. "Please tell me that I don't need to breathalyse you on this occasion."

"Non, monsieur. I have had only coffee today. The drinking will begin tonight at the party at which point I will have no intention of riding my bike."

"A party you say. I do hope that this raucous gathering is not on my patch Domonic."

"No, it is not monsieur. We are heading to Domremy."

"I am very pleased to hear it. Tell me, have any of you gentlemen seen two ladies on your travels. They are most likely on foot which would look most strange on these deserted country toads."

Dominic gave the man a wink with his one good eye, indistinguishable from a blink. "We did see some rather handsome young men a few kilometres back, but we rarely take notice of women."

The officer stepped closer. "I am well aware of your tastes and preferences, now get the hell out of my sight and practice your ungodly antics in another province."

Two of the police vehicles reversed a few yards leaving just enough room for us to proceed on our way in single file. My heart skipped a beat as I heard two of the officers laughing at me... the skinny guy in red leathers.

Chapter 45

Breaking the Codes

Anthony and Jack were back at their aparthotel on the Pigalle discussing who to give Vicarrio's phone to for deciphering. The fastest method would be for Jack to use FBI resources, but if this were a genuine business phone containing information above his pay grade he would be in serious trouble. Both agreed that the best person to handle this delicate situation would be Charles Worwood in London. However, getting the device there in a secure manner would take too much precious time. There was a slight rustling noise coming from one of the bedrooms, barely audible but unmistakeable to both professionals' trained ear. Anthony and Jack withdrew their pistols and tiptoed to the bedroom in question, one flanking either side of the door. Anthony took two steps back as Jack held up his hand with fingers spread wide. One by one a digit was folded down indicating a five second countdown. As his hand finally resembled a clenched fist Anthony booted the door clean off its hinges.

"My dear boys, so good to see you. I know that it is polite to knock but wasn't that a tad excessive...what." Said a yawning Charles Worwood stretching out his limbs after a catnap.

"Jesus Charles." Said a relieved Agent Mazur. "I could have shot you."

"Don't get all melodramatic on me Anthony. You are many things but trigger happy is not one of them. When this current situation has been dealt with you should, however, consider scheduling a basic training refresher."

With that Billy Agoba, head of cyber security for MI6 and AICAC, made his presence known having silently emerged from the second bedroom.

"Oh no." Said Anthony. "I've just been shot in the back with a memory stick."

Everyone laughed.

"What brings you here Charles?"

"We have been monitoring Abadie's communications as well as Vicarrio's FBI cell phone. You didn't hear that did you Jack?" Anyway, shortly after your scheduled meeting with Vicarrio he sent a message to Abadie enquiring if he had left his other cell phone in his apartment that morning. Knowing you as I do Anthony, I immediately surmised that you had somehow obtained the said device and would want me to analyse it?"

Anthony fished the cell phone from his pocket and

handed it to Worwood, shaking his head in disbelief at another display of the man's perceptive abilities and unequalled intelligence.

"Billy has brought along some gizmos and will have this thing deciphered in minutes. Now, tell me what was discussed at the safe house?"

Jack took the initiative this time. "Vicarrio told us in no uncertain terms to back away from Gabriel Abadie. He also said that the man was dying and any pursuit of him would be a waste of time and money."

"Did he indeed...anything else?"

"He said that we, or more to the point, Anthony, should make contact with Salonge and discover her whereabouts."

"And" Interrupted Anthony. "We were to inform him, and only him of their location, and I was not permitted to meet her. He said that he would send an extraction team."

"It's looking increasingly likely that he is up to his neck in this and would more likely send an extermination team. Sorry Anthony, that was insensitive of me. Can you get a message to your good lady?"

"I have no doubt she will contact me at some point,

but she appears to be changing phones fairly regularly."

"I see." Said Worwood scratching his chin in thought. "Well, the best we can do at the moment is send a message via Thames FM and hope she tunes in. That service has just about outlived its usefulness, so I suggest we play a couple of dedications using your real name and keep it on a loop."

"What do you suggest?" Said Anthony.

"Firstly, we want her to call you, at which point you must divulge everything; she needs to be fully appraised as to the level of danger they are in and from what source."

"That's an easy one." Said Jack. What about 'Call me' by Blondie?"

"Excellent choice." Said Worwood. "Until she calls, she must keep on the move. I would suggest we get Johnny to play 'Keep on Running' by The Spencer Davis Group; I rather like that one. You know chaps, a few days ago I was all for instructing Salonge and her cousin to abort this quest they have embarked upon. Now, however, I think it is serving a much bigger purpose by exposing some rather nasty individuals operating at the highest international levels."

Billy Agoba called out from the lounge where he had been doing his magic with Vicarrio's cell phone. "He is definitely involved with the Protecteurs de la France. He may not be an integral part of the organisation, but there is evidence that Abadie often seeks his approval and even takes the occasional instruction; read this...

First transcript:

The two females gave us the slip again...

How can this be? You appear to be protectors of nothing...

They won't get far Al

Ok, but no more slip ups Gabriel

Another transcript:

Jesus Christ Gabriel, not only did you abduct one of my operatives from our safe house, but you let him go. The least you could have done is put him with the other exhibits in the grounds.

Should we eliminate him now?

No, leave that idiot Jack Nichols to me.

"There are other messages of course but this last one is the only other which seems to relate to Salonge and Kacey." Said Billy.

**Can you please get your act together? Killing that
innocent nurse and her husband in Auxerre, all
because the females outwitted you again was
foolish, and it was me who needed to clear up the
mess. And while we are on the subject, stay away
from the whores. I refuse to send teams to every
location that you visit just to dispose of prostitutes'
corpses.**

I will stay away from ladies of the night Al, as long as
you stay away from the Jack Daniels. Think you can
do that?

**Be careful Gabriel. You would not be where you are
now if it were not for me.**

Jack had been pacing the room waiting for Billy to
finish. "So the bastard knew about the abduction and
wanted me terminated did he. Well I'm going to
terminate his career and make sure he spends the
rest of his days at our Federal Supermax prison near
Florence, Colorado, and that aint no holiday camp.

"All in good time young man. First Billy will put a
gizmo into this phone, and I will send someone to
Abadie's apartment to say that it was found on the
floor outside the elevator. This way we can follow
their every move just in case they trace Salonge and

Kacey before we do."

....

As we had travelled to the campsite at Domremy,
more and more bikers had joined our procession
along the way, so by the time we passed through the
entrance we must have been sixty strong. Some
were on super bikes, but most were riding Harleys
similar to our own; more than a few had guitars
strapped across their backs. The odd customised
three wheelers were also present, their back seats
filled to the brim with booze. This looked to be the
makings of a mini festival and not some weekend
break in the country. We dismounted our bikes,
removed our crash helmets, and joined every other
person who were all simultaneously massaging their
posteriors.

Salonge walked toward me and gave a wink. "This is
ideal Kacey. Nobody is going to suspect us hanging
around with this lot."

"I agree. But if you think I am sharing a tent with any
of those louts then you are sadly mistaken."

Salonge laughed. "Now that would take real courage
my brave young cousin. Go get our bike back. If they
ask where we are going, just say that we need to buy
a tent and are popping into the village. I want to

have a quick look around and also buy another burner phone."

Sure enough, as I maneuvered our Harley through the spaces between the other vehicles, one eyed Domonic approached us.

"Where are you two off to then?"

I responded as instructed by Salonge.

"There is no need to do that, I have a spare tent." Said one eyed Dominic.

"There are some other things that we need." I said, hoping he wouldn't ask for an inventory, having no idea myself what they could be."

"Don't you think you two should lie low for a couple of days? Give me a list and I will buy your necessities."

Now I really was stuck until Salonge came to the rescue.

"That is kind of you, but you see these items are very personal to the female genre."

"Fair enough, just trying to be helpful. You know me by now, good old one-eyed Dominic. What was it you said your names were?"

"We didn't." Said Salonge as she tapped my shoulder indicating for me to hit the throttle.

"Before you speed off ladies, you may want to reconnect the wires for the ignition, it having no keys and all. We may not like the authorities that much, but we despise motorbike thieves even more."

Feeling panicked I could think of nothing else to do other than compress the clutch lever and kick down on the starter. At first there was no response from the engine, but I continued to kick down in desperation. Suddenly a calmness came over me as I felt the energy building from Joan's gemstones hidden in the panier. Seconds later I could see a blue and red electric spark dancing between the disconnected wires. I kicked down one more time and much to my astonishment, and that of the dumbfounded Dominic, the engine roared into life.

As we sped through the exit gate, I could hear the gang's leader beckoning the one-eyed man to join the fireside party.

Domonic remained static though, involuntarily twisting the tiny gold 'Protecteurs de la France' ring which adorned the smallest finger of his left hand; he had an important call to make.

....

We cruised through the lanes at a steady pace for about two kilometres, avoiding too much use of the throttle with its resulting thunderous roar. We passed a small gas station, but had only recently filled the tank and were sure that this small outpost would not have the items which we required. A fork in the road appeared before us; the right fork indicated the village of Domremy-la Pucelle, whereas the left was signposted for the 'House of Joan', and the 'Basillique du Bois Chenu'. I knew from my studies at Oxford that the Basillique was of fairly recent construction, built to commemorate the spot where Joan is said to have received her first visions. Salonge projected her right arm and palm over my shoulder directing me towards the village. She rubbed two fingers and a thumb together indicating money followed by the bent pinkie and thumb meaning phone; I knew that she needed to buy the new burner and contact Anthony. I gave the handlebars a gentle turn and we headed in her desired direction, although every bone in my body was urging me to take me to my ancestor's home.

Chapter 46

The ancient Priest

Vicarrio was speeding over to Abadie's apartment relieved that his second phone had been found. His head was pounding and causing him to think irrationally about what he would do if the head of the 'Protecteurs de la France' had tried to access the device. (He would find no trace of interference given Billy Agoba's expertise.) He was also aware that he was effectively a functioning alcoholic. Having this knowledge and self-awareness was not a problem, he knew he was still brilliant at his job. However, other people knowing this was a weakness he could not afford... Vicarrio pressed the doorbell.

"Ah, I'm so glad that you are here sir." Said a worried looking Antoine. "My father collapsed. He is recovering well but I thought that he was going to die!"

"Unfortunately Antoine, your father will die soon, as shall we all. So you need to mature and learn at a faster rate than we had anticipated. Where is he now?"

"He is lying on the bed. Let me show you through. After his initial collapse I carried him there. A few moments ago he received a phone call from one of the older, lower ranked members of our organisation. It seems that we may have located the females."

....

Within thirty seconds of taking the right fork our engine died and the connecting spark for the ignition had disappeared.

"We have no choice." Hollered Salonge into the side of my helmet. "We will have to roll her back to the garage and pray that it is something simple to fix."

We both dismounted and struggled to push the Harley back towards the service station. (if you could call it that.) We once again came to the fork in the road and the engine immediately fired up and the fuel gauge returned to the full tank position. We both looked at each other in confusion and laughed, remounted, and set off back towards the village. For a second time in the space of five minutes the engine cut out, and we repeated the process, dismounting and walking back to the fork in the road. Again, for a second time the fuel gauge bounced back to full, and the iconic pistons began pounding ignited fuel out through the dual exhaust pipes.

"That's weird." Said Salonge.

"It's not weird at all. The stones are telling us that time is running out and we should take the left-hand turn towards Joan's house and the Basilica."

"What are you waiting for my magical, brave cousin. Let's go."

I was feeling my way as opposed to reading the signs, or perhaps the stones were guiding me. I can't really explain how I felt, it was almost a feeling of coming home after many years of travel, or even a crusade. I spotted a very humble white structure in the distance with an almost impossibly angled, slanted roof. I could just make out the bobbing heads of visitors above the hedgerow, queuing at the tiny farmhouse entrance. We pulled up at the gravel make-do car park and dismounted the Harley. I pointed the motorbike away from the tourists and historians whose attention had been grabbed by our throaty arrival and pulled on each side of the ignition wires to separate them and kill the engine, but the blue and red spark remained as bright as ever and refused to disconnect.

"The stones are telling us to move on." I said. "There is nothing for us here."

"Are you sure Kacey? I know that there is a bit of a queue, but the house is tiny. Shouldn't we at least take a look."

"I'm sure." I said. "Think about it...this place must

have been excavated many times, or at least scanned with those machines that archaeologists use. If the final stone were here, it would have been found already."

"That makes sense." Said Salonge. "Where do you suggest that we go?"

"I think we should try the Basilica. It's only a couple of hundred years old, but it was built at the place where Joan received her first visions."

We set off again, away from Joan's house and continued on only for the Harley to lose power again.

"Perhaps you were wrong Kacey, and the stones want us to go back."

"I don't think so." I said, pointing ahead to a tiny church. "This is where she used to go to pray. It is said that when she was as young as five years of age, she would kneel by her window and stare at the church for hours, praying in silence throughout the night. It is called Saint Remy Church and it is where she was baptised."

I turned the handlebars and pointed the front wheel towards the 13th century stone structure; sure enough, the engine spang to life. What was now becoming less surprising, as we pulled up at the old oak doors to the church the engine silenced. Out of respect to the institution, and to Joan, we removed both our helmets and our leathers. Salonge courteously stood to one side allowing me the honour of entering first. There was the instant aroma from centuries of burning candles and incense. Streams of coloured light were bursting through the stained-glass windows; obviously, a recent addition as they depicted images of St Joan. As my eyes adjusted to the contrasting shadows and sunlight I could detect movement in my peripheral vision and snapped my head towards a corner pew. A frail old man in brown robes struggled to his feet and turned to face us with a broad grin.

"Joan told me you would come." He said, shuffling in our direction. He appeared to be at least as old as the church itself.

I looked at my cousin, and then back at the old priest. "Joan told you?" I asked.

"That is precisely what I said. Surely it is I who should be hard of hearing, not a young brave knight such as yourself. Yes, Joan told me that you would come and that I should give you this." He said, handing over a small wooden box. "I believe there is a message for you held within. Please, make yourselves at home and read her words very carefully."

With that the old monk type figure shuffled down the

aisle and out through the door through which we had entered, his silhouette, outlined by the bright sunlight briefly casting a shadow throughout the centre of the church before disappearing.

Salonge was looking perplexed, twisting the box this way and that looking for its lid, or any other means of opening the ancient mini safe.

"I think it may be one of those Chinese puzzle type things. You have a go." She said, handing me the wooden jewellery sized box.

I presented my arms towards her, both hands turned palms up and joined together producing a flesh shelf on which she could place the sacred artifact. As the base of the box touched my skin, a lid, previously unseen, sprung open to reveal another muslin cloth message. I gingerly removed the document and began to read.

My Dear Kacey.

You are truly my ancestor, as no other mere mortal

could have made it this far; the first two gemstones would have prevented it.

The final stone is hidden at the place of my visions and must be joined with the others. Only then shall the truth, or the path to the truth be revealed. I cannot assist as to its precise location as much would surely have changed over the centuries,

Trust the stones, they will surely help you.

There will still be much danger ahead, and I fear that your quest has only just begun.

God shall reward you for your bravery at the time of reckoning.

Joan.

"This can't be real." I said. "How could she know the name of someone in her family who will not be born for another six hundred years?"

"I don't know." Said Salonge. "Why don't we ask the old guy in the robes?"

We both hurried down the centre of the pews towards the door, and as the heat from the sun hit our faces we both froze on the spot. Lying on the stone footplate to the church were a crumpled set of brown robes, slowly disintegrating. Sixty seconds later they were just a pile of dust being gently blown away to reveal a set of bones and a single crucifix which had, only moments ago, adorned the old monk's neck.

....

"How are you feeling Gabriel?" Said Al Vicarrio, watching the man rolling on the bed in an attempt to slide into his trousers using the one hand which was not massaging his temple.

"How does it look like I am feeling? It would seem that the bitches are in Domremy, Joan's birth place. It's so bloody obvious now. They have been tracing her life in reverse. I would have thought that your brilliant FBI brain would have worked that out long ago if it were not half pickled most of the time."

"Well, I thought that the Protecteurs de la nothing would have worked that one out also!"

"Enough." Shouted Antoine. "Can't you two grey haired children put your bickering to one side. We need to get to Domremy as soon as possible."

Gabriel smiled at his son's new found sense of duty and command of authority. An embarrassed Vicarrio patted the young leader in waiting on the shoulder and turned back to Gabriel.

"Do you have my spare cell phone?"

"It's in the top right draw of my desk."

As Vicarrio retrieved his device Antoine gently assisted his father in getting dressed before all three headed down to their Mercedes in the underground car park.

....

Anthony, Jack, and Charles Worwood were deep in discussion at the tiny four-seater table in the lounge of the boutique hotel when Billy Agoba rushed in from his makeshift control centre in the spare bedroom. He held an iPad sized gadget in his hand with a flashing green dot traversing along a road map.

"Guys, the compromised phone is on the move, and at a pace. The speed indicates that it is in a vehicle which just left Gabriel Abadie's apartment."

Worwood sprung to his feet like a Gazelle. "Come on chappies , the chase is on. Oh, and make sure you bring your pea shooters with you, what."

Chapter 47

The final Stone

I squashed the wooden box with its muslin message inside the panier along with the stones. The second storage box on the opposite side of the Harley was almost empty, but it felt right that her artifacts were kept together.

"Salonge, you will need to ask someone where the Basilica is. The only sign post that I noticed was way back at the fork in the road."

Salonge placed a gentle hand on my shoulder and twisted my body in the opposite direction. There before my eyes was a brand new, seemingly freshly painted post with a single direction pointer which read 'Basillique du Bois Chenu' 1.2 kilometres.

"I swear that was not here when we arrived." I said.

Salonge shrugged her shoulders. "I agree, but don't ask me to explain, I am just a mere mortal, not a reincarnated knight with some sort of guardian angel showing the way."

"As true and honest as your words are, you are my true guardian angel my cousin. Now let us complete our quest in the honour of Joan and my grandfather."

....

431

The large Mercedes-Maybach was travelling at a steady 100 kilometres an hour, less than half the speed that the powerful engine could deliver when they saw the first signs for Domremy.

"You do realize that if you push down on the right-side pedal this contraption will transport us there faster?" Said a frustrated Al Vicarrio.

"Or it could transport us into a skid and one of these boggy fields, assuming we do not hit a tree." Said the young Antoine at the wheel.

A smile appeared across the face of Gabriel, enjoying the way his new found son was demanding respect from the alcoholic FBI Director. Even the pain in his temples seemed to momentarily decrease. When they finally approached the town and came to a fork in the road, Antoine had to edge the huge beast of a car towards the drainage ditch as two people in red and blue leathers went roaring past on a Harley Davidson .

"Turn the car around." Screamed Gabriel. "That is them...it fits the description that Dominic gave."

The behemoth of a beast took five changes from forward to reverse in order to face the right direction in order to pursue Kacey and Salonge. Antoine turned off his headlights which, although still a bright evening, were needed to navigate the twisting, tree canopied dark lanes. However, the Harley's bright headlight up ahead shone, which forewarned Antoine of any impending twists in the road allowing them to cruise at a safe distance. It was only five minutes of careful squinting, with the odd twitch of the wheel to avoid a pothole, before they saw the magnificent 'Basillique du Bois Chenu'.

....

Billy Agoba was watching his screen resize and zoom out every few minutes as the green dot sent from Vicarrio's compromised phone kept disappearing from range. Anthony was engaging in the futile exercise of tooting his horn, along with other rush hour drivers, frustrated at the lorry which had jack-knifed disrupting all three lanes of the motorway out of Paris.

"Calm down kiddywinks." Said an equally frustrated Worwood, trying his best to be both diplomatic and pragmatic. "We know where they are heading now and, don't forget Anthony, your good lady wife is an accomplished agent in her own right who is capable of coping with any situation until we arrive."

Billy spoke again. "The vehicle has stopped at the Basillique du Bois Chenu'. That is close to where Joan of Arc was born and built on the spot where she is said to have received her first visions."

"Charles, do something." Pleaded Anthony.

Fifteen minutes later, with traffic at a standstill, the distant thwapping of a tiny, bubble glassed helicopter could be heard overhead. Tourists and commuters alike jumped out of their cars to take video and snaps of the three men who had abandoned their car and were boarding the fishbowl, motorised machine. Charles would instruct his MI6 team to recover the vehicle.

....

We dismounted the Harley and stared in awe at the magnificent basilica . The first thing that caught my eye was a statue of Joan in the grounds, staring at the pinnacle of the building which held a statue of St Michael upon its summit.

"I think we should go inside and bring the gemstones with us." Said Salonge.

I felt exhilarated and weak all at the same time. My hands were trembling, and my knees felt like they could give way at any moment. I fumbled with the latch of the Harley's pannier and removed the red blood, and the blue water source of life stones from their temporary safe. Even though buried beneath my pullover in a thick canvas bag, their glow was perceivably emanating through the sacking. We walked towards the entrance to the basilica and their energy began to fade.

"My cousin." I said. "What we seek is not in this place, it is by the statue."

The glow from my cheap canvas bag became impossibly bright as we again neared Joan's stone image. I stared with an almost impossible feeling of emotion at the defiant slant of Joan's mouth showing a determination to succeed. I folded my thumb and smallest finger and kissed the three remaining digits of my right hand indicating the father, the son, and the holy ghost. I then placed them on the lips of the concrete effigy of my ancestor. For a brief moment I swear the slanted lips turned to a smile.

"Did you see that?" I said.

The confused look on Salonge's face gave me my answer. I reached out and held Joan's right hand in a kind of handshake.

"Please help us find your last stone." I said, as if speaking with Joan herself.

With that the stone arm fell to the floor and shattered to reveal the brightest, most magnificent diamond tube I had ever seen. The lights from my bag were now dancing and I could feel an energy one thousand times stronger than that I had yet experienced.

"Salonge, we have found it. I could never have done this without you. I love you so much."

With that I flung my arms around my wonderful cousin, and we hugged so tightly that we could almost have morphed into one being. Then I felt Salonge go rigid.

"Kacey, run...run now for the trees and don't look back."

My first instinct was to be brave and face whatever was coming our way, but there was that professionalism in Salonge's eyes that told me not to question her instructions. The stones in the canvas bag clearly concurred as they appeared to be pulling me towards the woodland. I kissed her as passionately as I had ever kissed a woman and ran for my life. I chanced a brief look back to see two older men. One of the men, perhaps in his forties, was holding a gun in his outstretched hand. . The other appeared somewhat older and, although not certain, I could swear he was rubbing his temple as if in pain. I wondered if Salonge had injured him with some sort of projectile. .   Tears were rolling down my face as I reached the shadows of the trees which I believed would provide my escape when a much younger man appeared from their camouflage.

"Hand me the bag and I will let you live." Said a serious Antoine, showing a steeliness belying a man not too many years above myself.

"Be gone young soldier and I shall let you live." I said.

"Ah, I have heard that you are a feisty one. Let me put this another way. Hand me the bag and my friends will let your beloved cousin live."

I turned my head but could only see a heap on to the floor where the statue had once stood. I shielded my eyes from the fading evening sun and my heart sank; all was lost. It was obvious that Salonge had put up a fight, knowing that it was futile she was just probably buying me time. I could faintly hear her pleas to not worry about her and just run. I dropped to my knees and sobbed.

....

"The signal is still strong." Said Billy as they hovered over the Basilica. "But I can see no vehicles other than a single motorbike."

"Put her down." Said Worwood to his pilot. "Keep the rotors going though young man. I have a feeling our flight schedule is not yet complete, what."

Special FBI Agent Jack Nichols, Secret AICAC Agent

Anthony Mazur, and head of AICAC as well as MI6 Charles Worwood followed Billy Agoba and his gizmo to the source of the signal.

"There could have been a struggle here. But my feeling is that the desecrated statue, along with the broken phone has been staged to throw us off course. Vicarrio obviously discovered your tracking device Billy, and sent us on a wild goose chase."

"I don't think so Charles." Said a seething but tearful Anthony Mazur whilst holding the broken left arm of the statue. "The girls were here alright. Their motorbike is over there, and look at this."

Upon the second finger of the statue's left hand was Salonge's wedding ring.

Chapter 48

Back to the Chateau

We were sitting in the back of our captor's Mercedes, both of us with our hands tied impossibly tight behind our backs by nylon police restraints. Sitting between us was Gabriel Abadie wearing his evil grin, a hand on each of our thighs. The youngest man who had apprehended me was driving and someone who Salonge knew as Al Vicarrio of the FBI, was in the front passenger seat.

"So, Al." She said. "Since when did you become a traitor and begin hanging around with baby faced crooks and perverted ministers?"

"Now that is why I am an FBI Director, and you keep getting moved sideways. First Interpol, then the FBI, and now AICAC. You see Agent Dupree...oh I do apologise...Agent Dupree-Mazur, congratulations on your wedding. Anyway, you never have managed to see the bigger picture, or really understand the nuances of our business. It serves our country's interests to have friends, especially influential ones, even among some of the less savoury organisations."

"Could you tell this influential pervert to take his filthy hands off our thighs." I said.

With that Gabriel Abadie let out a hyena type laugh

and thrust each hand towards our crotch.

"I see that you recognise the chief aide to the President of France. He is very good at his job you know. He does, however, have a rather naughty side, especially when it comes to the younger ones. I'm sure he will want to have some fun with Kacey before you ladies are disposed of. I may be able to convince him otherwise should you choose to cooperate. Now let's take a look at what goodies you have concealed in this canvas bag."

One by one he removed the cylindrical stones with the Christmas cracker type ends and examined them with curiosity.

"What, may I ask, are these for?" Said Vicario holding the only one aloft which had two crimped ends, the one we had just found.

Salonge and I just stared in disbelief and confusion at the jet-black object. He then held the other two, now also jet-black.

"If I am correct, it looks as if they are meant to be joined ."

I held my breath as he slotted the three stones together, but nothing happened; there was no pulsating energy running through my bones and no interference with the cars electrics which was what I had hoped.

"Why would you be carting such useless objects around when you are supposed to be on a magnificent quest of lies?"

 For some reason he had decided to address me with that question.

"They are for my boyfriend. He is an abstract sculptor and needed these Onyx shapes cut. Paris has the only factory in the world where they can be cut as cleanly and precisely as this, so I said that I would get them done whilst in France."

I don't know where I conjured the answer from, but it seemed to satisfy Vicarrio, especially when Abadie threw his two dimes worth into the conversation.

"Our glorious France is the best in the world at so many things; wine, food, architecture...and now it seems we also excel at stone cutting."

Abadie reached for the items and examined their girth. "These are the perfect size to loosen your loins before I enter you." Once again the hyena laugh returned.

"Where should we head for Al?" Said Antoine. "We can't go back to my father's apartment."

"No, drive to the Chateau de Breteuil. We can

interrogate them there and then dispose of their bodies."

Gabriel Abadie threw the stones onto my lap and began massaging his temples. "Have you lost your mind? They have already been there twice and the arsehole Nichols who works for you is convinced that that is where he was taken after his abduction from the safe house."

"My dear Gabriel." Said Vicarrio whilst rolling his eyes. "That is precisely why they will not think to look there again. Just relax and play with the girls and leave the clever decisions to me."

With that an evil smile re-emerged on Abadie's face and his hands returned to our thighs...this time noticeably higher up.

Antione's mind was in turmoil. The man for whom he had worked since his teens turns out to be his father. Not only that, but this recent discovery also happens at a time when the man is found to be extremely sick...in more ways than one; Antoine was disgusted. His other concern was the frequency at which Vicarrio was sipping from his flask marked coffee. The aroma of the Jack Daniels was unmistakable even though he had cracked the window to the point where he thought no one would notice.

....

Billy Agoba and Charles Worwood had tactfully walked out of Anthony's earshot who was still kneeling at what he was convinced to be the scene of a struggle involving his wife.

"It doesn't look too promising, what."

"Sadly, I have to agree. If Salonge and Kacey were carrying the first two stones, and found the third one, then they would now be surplus to requirements." Said Billy.

"I'm not so sure." Said Worwood, scratching his chin. "They are no experts at ancient history, other than that of their own disillusioned organisation, and will want to interrogate the girls before disposing of them. Besides, the struggle may have taken place before the third stone was discovered."

Just then Anthony called them over whilst holding a shattered arm of the statue aloft.

"What is it Anthony?" Said Worwood staring towards him.

"The broken arm of this statue had something concealed within. It's looks to be the same size as the first two stones but the markings from where it was hidden indicate that both ends are crimped."

Worwood and Agoba exchanged sombre looks.

"What...what's with the glum faces?" Said Anthony.

"Well Anthony." Said Worwood. "We were rather hoping that the final stone had not been discovered."

"You think that they are going to kill them, don't you?"

"Unless we act quickly, that is a distinct possibility." Said a frank and honest head of MI6, used to delivering truthful statements regardless of the emotional attachment to his agents. "Let's be logical here. First, we should see what's been left behind. The motorbike looks untouched, and the PDLF may not have recovered the muslin instructions for the stones, in which case they may have no idea of the objects importance...hence they will not dispose of Salonge and Kacey...at least not yet.

"Well let's get moving." Said Anthony. "There are only a couple of roads out of here and they may have left just moments ago!"

"And they may have left half an hour ago and be almost anywhere. "Said a sympathetic but logical Worwood. "And what if we race off southbound and they headed north, what then? Are you willing to take a fifty-fifty chance Anthony?"

AICAC special agent Mazur's head dropped in defeat as Billy Agoba placed a hand on his shoulder. "Come on guys, let's get this whirlybird take us back to Paris. I need to look at my tracking devices."

"Hello genius." Said a sarcastic Mazur. "Your tracking device, along with Vicarrio's phone is in pieces by Joan's statue."

"Indeed it is, but things have become far more sophisticated these days. Not only do our so-called gizmo's track the phone in which it is placed. What they also do is send a signal to other cell phones which are in a close proximity to them, or are in regular communication with the compromised device. So, even though Vicarrio's secret phone is broken, we now have a Trojan horse tracking the other devices."

"Well what are we waiting for chappies, let's get back to the Pigalle, what.

....

We passed through a gatehouse and along a gravel drive. The sun had long since succumbed to the horizon but the delicate lighting illuminating the magnificent chateau left us in no doubt as to the size of this magnificent estate. Antoine turned off the engine; the sudden silence rousing Abadie from his slumber. Vicarrio turned to face us in the back seat.

"Now ladies. Please ignore some of the comments which I made earlier regarding your imminent demise. Tonight you shall sleep in one of these magnificent bedrooms and, but before that you shall be brought a meal of the highest quality. Tomorrow, all you need to do is tell us of your discoveries and promise to cease your ridiculous quest. If you do this then you shall be released unharmed."

With that Antoine and Vicarrio got out of the vehicle and opened one of the passenger doors.

"Gabriel, could you please climb over Salonge and join us outside the car."

Abadie took his time crawling over my cousin, hands pretending to slip as he groped every area of interest. The door was closed as the three men stood watching us in the back seat. The driver, Antoine pressed the key fob and the golf tee like buttons indicated that the vehicle was locked. He then pressed another button and gas began emitting from the air vents and everything went black.

....

The first thing I remember was a feeling of floating on a marshmallow. I struggled to open my eyes, but a torrent of light caused a searing pain at the back of my brain. I could hear someone talking, but that too was distorted.

"Kacey, wake up. Are you ok?"

I forced my eyelids apart and turned towards the source of the sound disregarding the torturous light. Salonge was laid next to me on the largest bed I had ever seen. Lying next to me was somewhat of an exaggeration. We both could have rolled our bodies four times in either direction and not plummeted to the floor nor clashed heads; the bed was huge. Our wrists were still tied but now secured to what appeared to be a solid gold headpost. Salonge twisted her head in an upwards direction whilst directing her eyes to a camera; we were being watched. Before any words could leave my impossibly dry throat, we could hear a key turn in the heavy door to the sumptuous bedroom. Gabriel Abadie walked in.

"Did you have a nice sleep ladies?"

"Fuck off." Replied Salonge.

"Now now, there is no need for such profanity. You must be hungry. We had the most delicious dinner earlier but have saved you some duck salad. I shall be back momentarily. Antoine, could you assist the ladies to the table but do not untie them. I shall feed them personally."

Gabriel left the room and his concerned looking son carefully maneuvered us one by one to the highly polished cherrywood dining table. He secured our arms behind our backs once again and left. Five minutes later a naked Gabriel Abadie wheeled a food trolly into the room. He was wearing a leather gimp mask and had a full erection. Placed upon the trolly beside our salads were the three gemstones and some lubrication oil; the stones were still black, and I wondered if they had somehow lost their power.

"Eat up ladies, it's delicious. You will need plenty of energy for desert...which is meeeee."

Abadie joined us at the table and began to masturbate. "Would you like some mayonnaise? I'm sure that I could produce some in a moment or two."

Antoine was in the next bedroom squashing pillows against his ears to avoid the nightmare from sounds of his father's twisted debauchery when he made a decision. Antione quickly slipped his trousers back on and steadied his nerves for what he knew he must do.

I did not hear nor see the door to our room open, only an explosion of noise followed by a dressing of bone and blood splattering our table. As the headless corpse fell to the floor, a sobbing Antoine dropped to his knees begging his father for forgiveness.

Chapter 49

Time is running out

Anthony, Jack and Charles were pacing the floor of the aparthotel on the Pigalle when a frustrated Billy Agoba came through from his temporary office in the spare bedroom.

"What seems to be the problem Billy?" Said Worwood recognising a rare look of irritation on his subordinates face at not solving a technical task.

"I have identified the devices which have the most contact with Vicarrio's secret cell phone, and also identified who they belong to."

"And who are they? Said Anthony.

"One is Gabriel Abadie's, and the other is owned by a certain Antoine Babin."

"That's great." Said Jack. "Can you locate them?"

"That's the problem." Said Billy. "It just doesn't make sense."

"What doesn't make sense?" Said Anthony as he took three strides across the room to grab Billy by the shoulders, barely managing to refrain from shaking the answers out of him."

"Anthony!" Hollered Worwood. "Please restrain yourself and let Billy finish. We are all on the same side here young man."

"I'm sorry guys. I just couldn't bear losing Salonge."

Billy continued. " Abadie's phone indicates that he is in Zimbabwe, and Antoines says he is in New York."

"That's impossible." Said Jack. "We know that Vicarrio went to Abadie's apartment to collect his spare phone not five hours ago. He couldn't possibly have made it to Africa in that timeframe. And, before that, when your fake delivery man dropped the compromised device to Abadie saying he had found it in the elevator, a young man answered the door. I bet my bottom dollar that he is this Antoine character...again, impossible for him to be in New York."

Billy looked at all three in turn. "It would appear that they have some sort of diversion, or displacement device inserted in their cell phones, a bit like when criminals on the web bounce IP addresses around the world to hide their actual location. It could take days to break the code as it seems to be a different setting for each phone...I'm sorry Anthony."

Anthony punched the wall before slumping into a chair in despair.

"Wait a minute." Said Worwood; his immense grey cells kicking into gear. "Is this tracker only efficient in real time or can we backtrack and see what location was indicated when we know Abadie, and Antoine were at the apartment?"

A light immediately came on in Billy's eyes as he rushed to the table carrying his laptop size gizmo and began tapping away.

"Can someone tell me where we are going with this?" Said a confused Jack Nichols.

Worwood smiled. "We know the GPS location of the apartment. Therefore, if we backtrack to that time and see what the displaced location said, we can work out their true location as of now. Billy, I take it that you are already making the calculations."

"Yes Charles, but I've not done this procedure before. It could take ten minutes, or it could be a couple of hours."

Anthonys head sprang up. "I thought we had a tap on Vicarrio's FBI phone. Why don't we just follow that. Even if he is not with them, he will know where they have taken the girls."

Billy replied without taking his eyes from the task at hand. "I tried that Anthony. He must be getting suspicious...his phone isn't emitting a signal."

....

I was still staring at the splattered remains of Gabriel Abadie when Salonge spoke up above the sound of Antoines sobs.

"I'm so sorry, we didn't know he was your father, but you did the right thing. He was clearly a very sick man and you have saved the lives of two innocent people."

Antoine remained on all fours with his forehead planted on the carpet, shoulders lifting and falling with each wail.

"Please untie us Antoine and end this crazy situation. Im sure that Kacey will speak up for you, as will I. It was a truly brave and painful thing that you have done."

Antoine slid his hands forward along the polished floor and began a press-up type motion, rising into a kneeling canine like posture. His dipped head slowly rose to reveal a face contorted in anger; a vicious sneer resembling that of a rabid dog.

"I didn't shoot my father to save the lives of two bitch whores who wish to deface the history of my country. I did it to save the honour of the Protecteurs de la France."

At that moment Al Vicarrio silently entered. "Jesus Christ, another fucking mess I have to clean up."

With that he walked across the room and shot Salonge equidistant between her shoulder and heart before placing the gun on the table. The force of the shot sent Salonge's chair smashing back against the wall which just managed to stay erect on its rear two legs. I jumped at the deafening sound and took a gasp of breath as my Jaw felt like it had hit the floor. My eyes began welling up and I could just make out face of my wonderful cousin gazing at the whole in her shoulder with its ever-increasing circle of blood expanding over her blouse. Salonge forced a smile before mouthing the words 'I'm sorry Kacey'. Her head then pitifully slumped to one side.

"Your cousin is not dead mademoiselle Kacey, but she will surely bleed out in the next hour or so. If you wish her to live then I suggest that you cooperate fully."

I fought against my restraints which just served to

amuse the beast in front of me. "You are a despicable force of evil and I shall tell you nothing. I may appear in your eyes to be a young child, or perhaps a helpless damsel in distress, but if you dare to untie me, then as God is my witness, I will slay you where you stand."

Vicarrio just laughed. "You studied at Oxford, so I suggest your intelligence should recognise the position which you find yourself in. You must assess if I am a man of my word."

"A man of your word. You are not even a man. It is impossible for you to let us go, so I shall tell you nothing."

"You are right of course. Perhaps it is time for absolute honesty between us. Once your cousin is dead I shall untie her and place Antoines gun in her hand, and mine into Gabriels. It will appear that there was a confrontation in which neither person won."

"That will still not force me to talk, so you may as well kill me now."

"You are indeed a brave and feisty one, I like that. However, you shall talk Ms Chapman. Antoine, you must pull yourself together and end this charade. let us take this English fool to the waxworks and find out what she knows. I am sure that she will be more agreeable once she is wearing a pair of wax slippers."

....

Billy looked up from his computer with excitement. "When Abadie was at his apartment his GPS location showed him as being in Harare, Zimbabwe."

"How the hell is that going to help?" Said a tense and frustrated Anthony. "That's precisely where it indicated his current location is."

"Not quite." Said Billy. "Five hours ago it placed him precisely 7915 km away from somewhere in Zimbabwe. Now it indicates that he is 7946 km away from Harare."

Jack and Anthony both looked to each other for inspiration, but Charles grasped the importance immediately. "What about this Antoine chappy, supposedly in New York?"

Billy smiled again. "Again, five hours ago that indicted he was 5851 km in the big apple."

"And now?" Said an animated Worwood leaping to his feet.

"Now he is 5821 km away."

"Could you two brainiacs please enlighten those less

gifted among us." Said Jack, but Anthony was on the cusp of figuring it out.

Charles Worwood ran to his attaché case and withdrew a plastic map of the world and a compass from his military issue leather instrument case and began drawing two circles. "Oh my god." He said. "We should leave immediately; they are at the Chateau...hiding in plain sight as the saying goes."

Nobody questioned Worwood as they clattered down the stairwell and into the waiting MI6 car."

"Jesus Charles, I think I get the idea, but math was never my strong point. Could you at least give us a clue?" Said Anthony, speaking for both himself and Jack.

"Of course dear boy. Both locations of the displaced phone locations are now precisely 31 kilometres adrift from where they were five hours ago. Harare being 31 km farther away and Ney York being 31 km closer. I drew two circles from both locations which both intersected at the Chateau. That is where they have taken Salonge and Kacey. I just pray that we are not too late.

Chapter 50

The Resurrection

I could barely believe that I offered no resistance as I was taken from the main chateau building, arms tied behind my back in plastic restraints. I was overwhelmed with a feeling of helplessness and defeat. My wonderful cousin Salonge had died for my ridiculous cause. That is not entirely true, it was not a ridiculous cause. It was a quest for the truth bequeathed upon me by Sir Grandads dying words.

For anyone approaching as we walked through the grounds towards the wax workshop, the scene must have looked like a father and son linking each arm of a soon to be bride and daughter-in-law. By raising my wrists higher up my spine to relieve the pain, and causing my elbows to bend, it created perfect loops through which their evil arms could link and transport me to their desired location.

We walked along twisting paths bordered by labyrinth like hedgerows, occasionally opening out into circular spaces depicting macabre waxwork scenes of cruelty throughout the ages. I wondered if one of the following displays would be of my ancestor being burned at the stake. We emerged from a leafy arch to reveal the outline of a huge barn-type space with sliding doors in the open position.

There was a glow from some sort of furnace or oven spilling light into the darkness. It became apparent that Joan and I were destined to suffer a similar fate, albeit centuries apart. I was thrust through the entrance and immediately identified the unmistakeable pungent aroma of boiling wax, confirmed by the regular sound of resistant bursting bubbles of air forcing free from the thick solution.

Despite the heat from the furness, a chill ran through my entire body as I glanced around the room at the reproduction clothing and armour strewn around, reminding me of my dear Grandfather and his tales of a chivalrous past. Nothing in this room seemed chivalrous to me; headless corpses with blood laden axes, and guillotine baskets filled with faces depicting contorted features. My eyes finally settled on a wooden ducking chair attached to a chain pully. I followed the string of links to a universal joint, and a wheel hanging centred above the oversized wax jacuzzi and had no doubt that I had just surveyed the intended method of my impending demise.

Sure enough I was led to the wooden chair and unceremoniously thrown into the seat. Antoine secured shackles around my ankles before slicing through the plastic wrist restraints only to re-secure my wrists to the arms of the ducking device; immediately I was hoisted ten feet into the air.

"Can you hear that Kacey?" Said Vicarrio.

"Hear what." I snarled.

"The drip drip drip sound."

"It sounds more like boiling hot bubbles of wax to me."

"Of course you can hear bubbling wax Kacey. The dripping that I was referring to was the lifeblood of your cousin trickling down her stomach, winding its way around her pelvis, down between her thighs and onto the floor with recurring gentle splashes. Actually, that is not true. Spilled blood thickens quite quickly under room temperature and also changes colour. The fresh blood by the bullet hole will continue to emit a bright red fluid of course, but as it slowly gravitates to the floor it will become gloopier and darker in colour. By the time they reach the parquet tiles they will resemble something similar to a balsamic reduction."

I was rapidly developing the worst migraine which I had ever endured; the fumes from the boiling wax overpowering all of my senses. My mind drifted back to my days at Oxford, a rare heatwave in the UK pushing the mercury past 35 degrees, or 98 degrees Fahrenheit. I remember the temperature in the lecture room far exceeding that due to the the failure of both the inadequate ceiling fans as well as the newly installed air conditioning. Back then it was the vaguely unpleasant aroma of teenage body sweat which threatened to bring on nausea...now it was the perfumed gases escaping from the waxy cauldron below.

"I don't think we need spend any more time here Antoine." Said Vicarrio. "It is clear that this stubborn one will not divulge anything of use."

"But what about the documents in their possession? They still pose a threat to France and the Catholic Church." Said Antoine.

"Oh I doubt that my young friend. I am quite certain that they have been hidden somewhere very secure by my dear departed ex FBI colleague, and I also doubt that this young fool has any idea of their whereabouts."

"How do you know that they are not in the possession of this AICAC organisation?" Said a nervous Antoine.

"Because my young friend, if they had possession of the documents then they surely would have intercepted us by now. And don't forget, I am also part of the AICAC hierarchy...they would have told me."

"So what do we do now?"

"I suggest that you go home, have a good rest, and begin the reorganisation of the Protecteurs de la France."

"And what about you?"

Al Vicarrio smiled as he pressed a red button on the wall. Immediately the pully system began manoeuvring my chair through the air and towards the wax bathtub.

"My work here is done. The bodily fluids of this young damsel will be evident on the surface of the wax. In the morning the workers will assume that the substance has been corrupted and simply let it cool. It was due for a fresh batch in a couple of days anyway so they will just send the giant soap-like bar to the Paris incinerators along with her concealed remains. As for me, I shall fly back to America on the first available flight."

Vicarrio glanced at a table where he had placed the three black gemstones, and then back at me. "I guess that your boyfriend will not be needing these anymore."

Al Vicarrio tossed them into the cauldron causing a few splashes of the piping hot liquid to scald the bottom of my feet which were already beginning to blister. I wished for the chain to simply break and end my agony, but the old pully was creaking along at a snail's pace. I watched as the two men left the building without so much as a glance back.

....

The helicopter was no longer an option as it was on another assignment, and by the time it would be available Anthony, Jack, Billy and Charles could make the journey to the chateau by car. When they had initially descended the stairs and reached their vehicle, Anthony and Jack were arguing over who should drive when they heard the engine fire up; Worwood was at the wheel with an expression which told them both not to argue; Billy was satisfied to sit in the back. In hindsight it was a good decision. Worwood had not only reduced the journey time from forty-five minutes to half an hour, but had maintained a ridiculously high speed through country lanes without the assistance of headlights: was there no end to this incredible man's talents? As they approached the entrance to the Chateau de Breteuil two sets of headlights could be seen exiting the residence. Worwood hit the brakes whilst simultaneously slamming the car into cover of the hedgerow, grateful that his choice of layby did not involve a deep ditch, as was more often the case on these narrow lanes. The first car to pass was driven by a young man weaving and swerving; he did not notice them. The second vehicle was approaching at a fast, but steady pace; far more controlled. It slowed down noticeably as it reached the point where Worwoods vehicle was rested, and the driver stared at our concealed vehicle. Worwood wound down his window and made a cutting gesture across his throat to the driver of the other car. Al Vicarrio caused his wheels to spin as he hit the gas pedal in shock.

"Quick, let's follow them." Urged Jack.

"No, I don't think so." Said Worwood. "The girls, if they are alive, will be at the Chateau.

"How could you possibly know that?" Urged Anthony. "They could be in the trunk of either car."

"I think not." Said Worwood. "The first driver was in a panic to leave. If he were transporting Salonge and Kacey, he would not want to draw attention to himself or risk a crash."

"Well what about the second car?" Said Anthony. "He was driving pretty steady until you gave the cutthroat gesture."

"That my dear boy was one FBI Director Allessio Vicarrio. He would never get his hands dirty by transporting our young ladies. Time is now very much of the essence I'm afraid. I just pray that we are not too late.

....

The pain was now excruciating as my medieval ducking chair slowly descended into the melting pot, yet I was somehow grateful. It gave me the time to say a prayer for Salonge, apologise to Sir Grandad for my failure, and even forgive my mother and father, hoping that we may soon meet again. In an instant all torture left my body, and a calmness replaced the agony. A white light filled the room and I strangely wished that I could have recorded the event in some way. I had heard of many stories of people feeling peaceful, and being drawn to a white light upon their demise; so it was true. I closed my eyes in acceptance of my fate and smiled, wondering if I may even meet my ancestor, Joan. I was jolted out of my daydream like trance by the thud of solid upon solid. I opened my eyes to see my chair resting upon a completely cold surface. In front of my shackled feet were the three gemstones. They were no longer black, and had returned to their magnificent white, blue, and red. The white gemstone was the one which had lit the room. The blue gemstone was covered in ice and mist, and I instantly knew that its power had cooled the wax. The red stone...the bloodstone as described by Joan, was pulsating as if delivering a call of urgency…I then knew what I needed to do, but how could I do it whilst still in shackles?

....

Worwood hit the accelerator causing the powerful Mercedes to leap from its hiding space almost vaulting into the opposite hedgerow, but his expert skills managed to regain control. The gates to the chateau were at the last throws of being fully closed when the front grill of their vehicle smashed them off their hinges. The engine began to over-rev as the rear wheels span on the pebbled driveway kicking tiny shrapnel stones through the air in their wake. Worwood was now weaving and drifting towards the rear entrance to the magnificent building when Anthony grabbed for the steering wheel.

"Charles, head for the wax workshop. If they are here, then that is where they will be."

"That does make sense young man." Said Worwood as he performed a handbrake turn and skidded onto the lawn, heading for the building via the most direct route. The two-ton vehicle made light work of the hedges and bushes attempting to block his path. Seconds later the windscreen was being assaulted by the torsos and contorted faces of the chilling exhibits. The scene was similar to that of a terrorist ploughing into a crowded street or shopping centre. The car eventually burst into free space and Worwood had to use all of his motoring skills to avoid smashing into the building. The four men were already exiting the vehicle even before it had completely stopped. Charles Worwood immediately restrained Jack and Billy, fearing that the scene inside the giant shed may well be one which Anthony should witness alone.

"Kacey, thank god you are alive." Said Anthony. "Where is my wife?"

"She is in the house." I said, but the fear for her wellbeing conveyed on my face was immediately interpreted by her husband.

Anthony dropped to his knees and began to sob. Jack Nichols knelt beside him resting a gentle hand on his shoulder; words not being necessary. I looked towards Charles Worwood hoping that he would not dismiss my next theory as crazy. He sensed the pleading in my eyes and approached the solid vat.

"Well this is most strange young lady, what. The Furness is still burning but the wax is no longer in a liquid form. Would I be correct in assuming that it has something to do with these odd-looking stones?"

"Yes Sir Charles." I said. "They have special powers. The blue gem, the lifeforce of water somehow cooled the wax." I then lowered my voice as he examined the controls for the ducking device in order to set me free. "Salonge has been shot...she is in the house and may well be dead."

With that his head snapped towards me, and then to Anthony, and back to me. The pain in his eyes was plain to see.

"Let's get you out of these shackles then we can go somewhere quiet to talk about it."

"No Charles." I said. "These stones really are magical. I believe, and please don't mock me, I truly believe that the red stone...the bloodstone as Joan called it, could save Salonge."

Charles told Anthony that we were heading to the main building, and it would be best if he did not accompany us. Anthony slowly rose from his crouching position and began striding towards the chateau. Despite our pleas, his pace increased until we were all sprinting to try and keep up. He bounded up the stairs of the grand entrance, grabbing a stone lion head from a pillar as he went.

I could feel the power of the red gemstone pulsating through my body as I carried it towards the building. I watched as Anthony launched the lion effigy through the magnificent glass entrance and vaulted into the interior. I summoned every ounce of energy I could in order to keep up. Jack Nichols was falling behind letting out expletives about meaning to give up cigarettes. Charles was keeping pace with me despite being the eldest of our entourage. We bounded up the ornate staircase and entered the bedroom where both Salonge and Gabriel Abadie had been shot. Anthony was covered in blood. He had clearly been attempting every method of resuscitation known to him. He eventually kissed her gently on the lips and left the room using furniture and walls to support his distraught and deflated shell of a body.

The red gemstone was positively vibrating now, and I knew that Charles could feel it too.

"Young lady, if those stones really do exude magic, then I urge you to put this one to good use with immediate effect."

With that he left the room to comfort Anthony.

I closed the door and walked over to the body of my dear older cousin who had been placed expertly in the recovery position. I gently rolled her onto her back and placed the red blood stone onto the bullet hole. I then closed my eyes and began to pray. After what seemed like an age, Charles knocked on the door.

"Kacey my dear, there is nothing more we can do. I shall call a team to clear up the scene and take Salonge's body to a location of Anthony's choice. Every ounce of energy and hope in my mind and body was spent. As I tried to rise from my kneeling position I was overcome by an overwhelming weakness, and collapsed unceremoniously on top of my cousin.

"Jesus Christ Kacey, you weigh a ton." Said Salonge, coughing and spluttering as she spoke. The bloodstone was no longer pulsating, and there was no evidence of any bodily fluids anywhere to be seen, nor any bullet hole.

Chapter 51

All roads lead to Rome

Antoine arrived back at Gabriels apartment building on the Champs Elysée, parked in the underground carpark, and made his way up in the elevator. Long before he discovered that his superior was his father, several of the Protecteurs de la France had been told of the precise location of a key moulded into the plaster architrave surrounding a painting of Napoleon Boneparte. If anything should happen to the chief aid to the President of France, the plaster should be shattered, and the key retrieved. Once retrieved, the person in possession should unlock another secret compartment hidden behind a marble effigy of Jesus.

Although Antoine did not possess a key to the actual apartment he had, over time, through his activities on behalf of the Protecteurs, honed the necessary skills to gain entry. Once through the door he was aware that he only had five seconds to enter the alarm code. Failure to do so would not alert any security company, or even the local gendarmerie, but would bring every soldier of the Protecteurs de la France to that location. At present he was the only one who knew that Gabriel was dead, and he wished it to remain that way...at least for the time being. With Al Vicarrio undoubtedly scuttling back to the United States, there was no one to verify that he was now the new leader of their organisation, and he could not afford the risk of a challenge to his authority.

Antoine stepped into the entrance hall and immediately punched in the necessary eight-digit code and stared at the tiny red bulb. The time allotted to enter the code was extremely tight and only Gabriel knew the override sequence should the five second timeslot be overrun; the tiny light remained dormant. Antoine strode across the main room until he was facing the magnificent oil depiction of the long-deceased Emperor of France.

It was a scene from the 1805 battle of Asterlitz, regarded to be Napoleons greatest victory whereby his vastly outnumbered army of around 68,000 soldiers cleverly outmanoeuvred the joint forces of a Russian and Austrian coalition. The Emperor is sitting proudly above his steed, Marengo, a small grey which was his favourite as it made him look somewhat greater in stature. The men in close battle are painted around the periphery of the artwork and engulfed in smoke, but Napoleon and his horse hold the centre stage, free from the encroachment of cannon and musket residue drawing ones eye to the central focal point. The Emperors left hand is gripping the horses reins whereas the right is thrusting a sword into the air at a forty-five-degree angle, urging his army to advance.

Antoine walked over to Gabriels huge desk, retrieved a heavy slate ashtray and returned to the painting. He trained his eye to the location of the plaster surround which corresponded to the compass point where Napoleons sword tip was pointing and thrust his make-do hammer to that location with all the force he could summon. Splinters of plaster flew in all directions and his vision was blurred by a plume of white powder, as if having been squeezed from a plastic bottle of talcum powder. Once everything had settled, Antoines shoes were covered with white dust, as was a six-foot circle of carpet. Glinting up at him from the epicentre of the residue caused by the mini explosion was a tiny, solid gold key.

Antoine stooped and picked up the unlocking device, blowing it free from dust as he did so. He slowly did a 180 degree turn to face the marble statue of Jesus adorning the opposite wall and tried to compose himself; the next part of the procedure was the most dangerous. He had never before noticed the subtle intricacies of the iconic piece of solid art. The marble was exquisite, which on first examination appeared to be a classical white with washes of grey blue. But on closer examination there were the feintest veins of red trickling down from below the figures hands and feet, eerily resembling blood. The nails which

pinned Jesus to the cross were of solid gold. In order
to insert the key into the compartment hidden
behind the bust there was a procedure to follow
which had to be executed with extreme precision.
Gabriel had told the chosen few that once the key
had been retrieved, the nails imbedded in the hands
and feet of the statue of Jesus needed to be
depressed simultaneously by the human flesh of one
singular person. This was a bit of a conundrum as the
two nailed hands pointing east and west were at least
a metre apart, and those in the feet, although side by
side, were over a metre due south. The only solution
was to place each of his own hands on those of Jesus,
and press his forehead upon the Lords feet. The
resulting image was not lost on Antoine. It would be
that of someone bowing, head lowered in reverence,
with arms raised in worship. This in itself would not
be a problem. The problem was that if all four nails
were not depressed in millisecond precision, the
person attempting to gain access would receive a
deadly charge of electricity.

Antoine positioned his thumbs a mere two
millimetres from the nails in Jesus's hands and slowly
lowered his head to those in the statues feet. After a
silent mental count of three he lunged forward. The
searing pain piercing through his body was
excruciating as he collapsed to the floor.

....

Al Vicarrio was relieved to be done with this situation. There is no doubt that his card was now marked by Charles Worwood, but who cares if he has to resign from AICAC; it was a stupid organisation anyway. Besides, once the super-heated wax had done its job on the British girl there would be no evidence which linked him to her death. And the the bitch Salonge would appear to have been in a gun battle with a respected French official; the Brits would not want that to come out. The real mission was to get back on American soil ASAP. Regardless of Worwoods position in British intelligence, or their so-called special relationship with America, his country would not stretch to the request for the Director of the FBI being extradited.

Vicarrio's request for any information on American diplomatic aircraft due to leave for the homeland got a hit. He was instructed to head for the tiny private hangar at the north end of Charles de Gaulle airport where he would be met by CIA operatives. Ok, he thought, it was not his own guys, the FBI, but at least they were American, and they had agreed to delay their take-off until he had arrived; God bless America. He had provided his vehicle type, colour, and registration so the security gates to the hangar were already swinging open as he approached. Vicarrio screeched to a halt and handed over the car keys to the man wearing a dark suit and sunglasses, despite it being well past sunset,... typical CIA.

"Boy am I pleased to see you guys." Said Vicarrio.

"We are all on the same team Sir. FBI, CIA, it doesn't matter, we are all Americans...the greatest nation on earth sir."

"Indeed it is." Said Vicarrio. But even so, he thought, there had always been a rivalry between the agencies, and this reception seemed a little too welcoming. Even for a lower ranked operative in the rival agency, a typical response would have been...*It's a pleasure for the CIA to come to the rescue again sir!*

"Our people will take care of your car sir. Could you please follow me to the aircraft, we are already thirty minutes behind schedule?"

Vicarrio smiled and relaxed. It was only a mild slight, but more akin to what he would have expected from the CIA.

No sooner had he ascended the aircraft stairs, the unmarked Boeing 737 was already taxiing for take-off. The CIA agent pulled aside the curtain and gestured for Vicarrio to enter the cabin. Immediately Vicarrio's instincts kicked in telling him that something was very wrong. The interior was even more elaborate than Airforce One. He felt a protrusion in his back and recognised the feel of the enlarged aperture of a silencer. He obeyed the gentle prodding which was urging him down the aisle of the cabin towards another three false agents dressed in identical attire to the man behind him, including dark sunglasses. Vicarrio was livid with himself. Perhaps the years of addiction to Jack Daniels had finally affected his perceptive abilities. Yes all of the men on the aircraft were in dark suits with dark shades; they could easily be mistaken for CIA. But how on earth did he not notice the cut and quality of the cloth? They were all wearing Georgio Armani, not state issue. The sunglasses were all Prada, not Ray-Ban's.

A door opened at the far end of the isle and a portly man squeezed through the tiny gap smoking a large cigar and holding a bottle of limoncello.

"Ah Mr Vicarrio...Buongiorno. Unfortunately, as I am sure you have already guessed, you will not be returning to the USA."

"What the fuck is going on? Stop this fucking aircraft now."

The portly man let out a tut tut expression using his tongue and teeth. "Please take a seat. We are going on a little vacation to your original homeland, Italia.

You have caused some considerable problems for my friends in Rome, and they would like to...shall we say...ask you some questions."

"I don't care if you are Italian secret service, but I doubt it. I don't care if you are Mafia. I don't even care if you work for the goddamn fucking pope! I am the director of the FBI and you let me off this fucking plane right now or there will be hell to pay."

Al Vicarrio crashed to the floor as the man behind executed a perfect pistol whip to the base of his skull.

....

Antoine rose from the floor and stared down at the blood dripping onto his white shirt from the bullet-like hole in his forehead. Hands being able to move faster than a heavy head, Antoine had launched forward with a bit too much gusto in order to synchronise the contact, causing the painful wound. He had initially thought that he had mistimed the procedure and been electrocuted. After stifling the flow of blood Antoine raised his head to see that the statue of Jesus has slid to one side revealing a steel safe with a tiny keyhole in the centre. He inserted the key and instructed his wrist to make a clockwise turn. The door to the shoebox-size safe popped open to reveal a small red telephone which instantaneously began to ring. It had a spiral cord indicating that this had been its home since the 1970's, except that there was no circular numbered dial with which to make a call. Antoine stared nervously at the receiver as its call to be answered grew so loud that it reverberated around the whole apartment. With a shaking hand, he eventually plucked up the courage to reach for the receiver having no idea who the caller could be.

"Hello, who is this?" He enquired gingerly.

"The procedure is that I ask the questions and you answer accurately and precisely. Is that understood?"

"Yes sir."

"The fact that you have opened this communication channel I assume that Gabriel Abadie is dead???"

"That is correct sir."

"And to whom am I speaking?"

"My name ins Antoine, the new head of the Protecteurs de la France."

"Ah, the illegitimate son of Gabriel. Well Antoine, you must fly to Leonardo da Vici Airport immediately. We shall book you a seat on the 11.05 this evening.

Chapter 52

The final piece of the Puzzle

As Salonge rose to her feet, Anthony simultaneously dropped to his knees in disbelief.

"Get up you silly American. You didn't even drop to one knee when you proposed."

Anthony slowly rose and took zombie like staggered steps towards the love of his life. At the same time Charles took me by the elbow, leading me outside of the room with a raised eyebrow, indicating that we should give them a private moment.

"Kacey, my dear friend, your quest is over I'm afraid." Said Worwood in a sympathetic voice.

"No it can't be. We have to join the stones together...Joan said so."

"Kacey, continuing this quest of yours has now reached a whole new level of danger, and at an international level. I have to approach the US government to tell them that their director of the FBI has another agenda than simply looking after his nations interests. Even putting that delicate situation aside, there will undoubtably be an enquiry by the French into the death of the Chief aid to the President of France. There is no way that they will be unaware of our involvement."

I rose my chin in defiance. "All interested parties may well be representatives of government organisations, but they are made of flesh and blood, as am I. I do not fear them, and my honour is at stake. I made a promise to Sir Grandad which I intend to keep. I also owe it to my ancestor, Joan of Arc."

"Very well Kacey. Get the stones and join them together. However, if nothing happens, then we get you and Salonge out of France and to safety. Do you really wish to see your cousin spend the rest of her life in a French prison?"

"We have an accord." I said.

When I walked back into the room there was plenty of tongue wagging going on, but it did not involve conversation. I placed the three stones back into the discarded canvas bag lying on the floor and prepared to leave the room before I witnessed any further development in their joy and amorous activity, but my sarcastic, jovial side could not be restrained. I turned to face the interlocked duo.

"Anthony, it is time that you embraced the power of the stones, there is no need for mouth-to-mouth resuscitation."

As my words went unheard, or were deliberately

ignored, I extracted myself from the love scene
declaring that they should get a room.

"How are they doing?" Enquired Charles.

"Put it this way." I said. "In around nine months you
are likely to have the youngest ever member of
AICAC to date."

"What????"

It was the first time I had ever heard Charles
Worwood begin a sentence with that particular word
as opposed to his unusual habit of using it to end a
sentence.

"Oh, I see. I suggest we take the stones down to the
main ballroom and discover what strange magic they
have not yet revealed."

I took them from the canvas bad and lay them side by
side in the centre of the grand dining table and just
stared at them nervously. My mind was drifting,
trying to find an excuse to delay the defining moment
of them being adjoined. What if nothing happened?
It would all be over, and for what?

Jack Nichols was slumped in one of the ornate chairs,
still wheezing heavily, but smoking a cigarette,
nonetheless.

"You can't put it off my dear. Do what you know

must be done." Said Charles.

I couldn't bring myself to face him. I did not want him to see the fear in my eyes. Not like the fear of facing death, nor the fear of the perpetual persecution that I had faced since birth. It was the fear of nothing happening with the stones. I nervously reached for the first gemstone, the blue one. I somehow instinctively knew that the water stone, the source of life, should form the base. The doubled crimped edge of the clear diamond artifact made that the obvious second choice; it slotted into place with ease. I then reached for the remaining red object, the bloodstone. I was fully expecting a surge of energy as I inserted into the top of the mini tower puzzle, but there was nothing. Suddenly a bright ray shot out from the clear centre stone sending a beam of light towards a spot on a giant ancient map hanging on an adjacent wall. Its focal point was the centre of the catholic empire, Rome.

"Look Charles, look. It is pointing us to Rome!" The excitement and exhilaration running through my body was immeasurable.

Charles let out a sigh and his head dipped allowing his chin to rest on his collar for a number of seconds. He then sauntered towards the crystal lead windows of the palatial doors that led to the gardens, or what was left of them. He pulled a silk cord which caused the velvet drapes to close and the beam on the map to disappear. Charles walked towards me and pulled me close.

"My dear Kacey. I know how badly you wished this to be a sign, but it was a simple diffraction of light. I am so sorry."

"Not so fast." Declared Salonge who had entered the room with her husband, unnoticed by both Charles and me.

Anthony looked a tad flushed in the cheeks, but his close shaved head gave no indication as to what had recently occurred. Salonge, however, was another matter. Her hair looked like it had been fashioned on Robert Smith from The Cure, or perhaps Siouxsie Sioux from the Banshees, both 1970's punk era icons. Salonge was awkwardly, or so I thought, trying to tuck her blouse back into the waistline of her trousers. I somehow managed to let out a laugh.

"I'm not a child you know. It is quite clear what you two have been up to,"

"Ok, we have established that we are all adults. I must say, those stones have more power that you can imagine. When this is all over, do you think you could use them on Anthony?"

Salonge continued to fidget with the rear of her

blouse, but appeared to be tugging as opposed to tucking. Her concealed hand eventually popped free, and she produced yet another ancient parchment.

"When you fled for the trees after we found the final stone, I spotted a tiny piece of fabric protruding from the fragments of stone. During my struggle with our abductors I managed to conceal it in my underwear."

I wanted to tell my cousin that this selection of hiding place seems to be her 'go to place' for concealment, but I was once again boosted by the revelation so held back from delivering the quip. I was certain that this parchment was the breakthrough needed to keep Sir Grandads quest on track.

"Let me see." I said

Salonge passed the muslin message to me, and I spread it flat upon the humongous rosewood dining table. Upon the discovery of previous messages from my ancestor, I could understand the basic gist of the text, but always needed clarification from Professor Field. Now, however, even though in the same format, I was able to understand every word as if it were my native tongue.

My Dear Kacey.

I pray for thanks to God that it is you reading

these words, as none other could possibly do so. My message would disappear as surely as steam from a boiling pot should this parchment be observed by anyone of unworthy morals or faith. If you have been successful in joining the stones of life together they would most assuredly have pointed to the location of the revelation, and shall continue to do so. However, what this revelation is can only be discovered by reassembling the stones upon the centre of the font of my christening.

I shall meet you one day, but I pray that this is many years from now. Your dear Sir Grandads stories are truly enchanting, although I have had to correct him on some of his more elaborate, or romantic exaggerations of the truth.

Joan D'Arc

I had no doubt that if the parchment were carbon tested, it would date from the early 15th century, so

how could Joan be talking about Sir Grandad. I
noticed the recognition of this fact of this same
anomaly on the face of Charles, but he was kind
enough to remain silent. He turned on his heels and
began marching at a pace towards the double doors
which led to the lawns and our vehicle.

"Well aren't you going to join me?" He said, looking
back over his shoulder. "It's quite obvious that I have
little chance of convincing you to leave France until
we have assembled the stones at Joans altar."

I disassembled the gems and placed them back into
the canvas bag before running to clasp Charles's
outstretched hand. "Thank you Charles." I said with
ever grateful eyes; no words were necessary.

We all sprinted back through the gardens with their
macabre wax displays until we reached our car. Once
again Charles took to the driver's seat without any
protestations from the rest of our party having
witnessed his superior road skills. The journey back
to the tiny church of San-Remy, close to Joans house
in the village of Domremy was made in silence. As
we approached the ancient place of worship Salonge
spoke up, addressing Anthony and Jack.

"I think that you two should conceal yourselves
outside in the bushes and keep watch. Charles, you
should guard the entrance to the church. Kacey and I

will assemble the stones at the altar."

"Under normal circumstances that would be a very sensible tactic Salonge." Said Worwood. "However, these conditions are far from normal. I suggest that we all enter the church, and you two ladies do what needs to be done. The three of us shall take up defensive positions inside the church. The crucifix style apertures in the structure were built as an ideal vantage point from which to mount a defence. I shall call in a helicopter to take us from this place. Where we go from here, be it to safety or some other location, very much depends on what is revealed. Besides, I think that this Antoine character will have problems of his own to deal with, and I have no doubt that Vicarrio is now somewhere over the Atlantic. I think we are safe for a time."

We walked along the stone slab path towards the entrance and Salonge tested the heavy oak doors which succumbed with ease. My eyes were transfixed on the spot where, on our previous visit, the old priest had seemingly withered to dust.

"Kacey, we do not have time to dwell on such things, hurry up!" Said Salonge, knowing what my mind was focussed on.

I joined my wonderful, wise cousin at the threshold to the aisle. Charles sat in the shadows of an alcove which gave a perfect perspective through the doorway to any approach from unwelcome arrivals. Anthony and Jack sprinted up each of the two creaking wooden stairwells either side of the main doors to the two small perches from where quire boys would have once sat. I was clutching the canvas bag to my chest like a bride clutching a bouquet. Salonge linked her arm through mine appearing to take on the role of a reluctant father about to give his precious daughter to another man, somehow knowing what was about to occur was inevitable. We began our slow walk towards the font of Joans Christening, unknowingly keeping a synchronized pace with each other; left foot, then right. I could hear Felix Mendelssohn's 1842 wedding march in my head, and wondered if I would ever walk down the aisle with the man of my dreams. Was there someone out there who could accept me for who I am now, and not perceive me as a freak of nature. Could it be possible that my quest could remove the ignorant phobias that have caused so much pain to so many loving, wonderful individuals over the centuries? The persecution, the beatings, the ridicule, the suicides...so much unhappiness for so many gentle people.

I increased my pace with a renewed vigour and purpose. Salonge sensed this and gave my arm a gentle, but perceptible squeeze.

I placed the bag at my feet and retrieved the blue water stone whilst staring into the empty font. There was a circle in the centre of the religious basin which looked to be the identical dimensions to the sapphire tube in my hand. I gently placed the flat end into the aperture, and it was a perfect fit. Immediately the basin began to fill with the clearest rippling water I had ever seen. Next I slotted one jagged edge of the diamond stone into that of the Sapphire; it did not fit. For a moment I was mortified, until I reversed the ends so that the Christmas cracker shaped crimp which had been pointing to the ceiling slotted perfectly into place. The water began to bubble and dance as if ready for pasta to introduced. There was only one last task to complete which would be the defining moment. I inserted the crimped edge of the ruby stone into place and my world changed forever.

Chapter 53

A reunion in Italy

Antoine had gone to the standard check-in for the 11.05PM, Air Italia flight AI 4514 to Rome. The man at the counter showed signs of recognition as he glanced from the passport photo to Antoine's face, and back again. He expertly slid his hand under the counter and pressed a security button; Antoine noticed.

"We shan't keep you a moment sir, the system appears to be malfunctioning."

Moments later two men appeared and took Antoine by the arm and led him to the golf cart type vehicles usually reserved for people with disabilities. One man took to the driver's seat whilst the other accompanied Antoine in the rear.

"Don't look so worried Mr Babin. We are simply taking you through the fast-track gate reserved for dignitaries, senior politicians and representatives of the Vatican flying on Air Italia. You are perfectly safe."

Antoine Babin plucked up a moment's courage and defiance. "I, as I'm sure you know, am the new leader of the Protecteurs de la France. I demand to know why you feel that you have the right to demand my presence in Rome?"

"What makes you think that your presence is demanded in Rome? This flight is indeed flying to that location, but from there you shall be transferred to a private plane and transported to Sicily."

The man could see the confusion on Antoine's face.

"You see, when your small operation is dealing with matters that solely pertain to France, we leave you alone. However, when they encroach on the integrity of the Catholic Church, then my family act on behalf of the Vatican to sort things out in a clean and efficient manner."

All courage and bravado drained from Antoine's body as the realisation sunk in that his escorts were most certainly Mafia.

"What is it Mr Babin? Are you surprised that the Holy men of Rome have links with my brotherhood? Even they understand that the Devil is ever present, and the Devil requires more than prayers to be held at bay. You won't be alone though. A friend of yours is already at our final destination."

....

Unlike Antoine, Al Vicarrio's unmarked aircraft had flown directly to Catania International Airport on the

island of Sicily and taxied to a private hangar at the
far end of the runway. Even though it was dark
outside, Vicarrio could sense that they had entered
an enclosed space by the change in sound of the jet's
engines which eventually wound down to silent. One
of his escorts manoeuvred the lever for the airlock
door and flung the heavy exit open with ease using
just one muscle bound arm. Vicarrio could hear the
stairway being rolled into place when the portly man,
puffing on yet another cigar, gestured for him to
leave the plane. As he walked down the steps, he
could see a line of some twenty men standing in
procession as if waiting to be inspected by the
Queen, or the President of America; each of them
were dressed in the same black attire, wore
sunglasses, and held Uzi's over their shoulders.
Vicarrio paused halfway down the stairs to assess the
scene, but his attention was drawn to the sound of a
motor vehicle approaching. A large black stretch limo
appeared as if from nowhere and drew to a halt
immediately in front of him. Two men left the line of
twenty, opened the passenger door of the limo, and
gestured for Vicarrio to sit in the rear of the car, both
employing an outstretched hand and bowing slightly,
like a waiter ushering him to a table. Vicarrio slowly
descended the remaining steps and entered the
vehicle; the death march seemingly playing in his
head causing his feet to move in time with an
invisible, slow set metronome; both guards took their

places either side of him on the rear seat. The portly man joined them in the luxury car and, in keeping with this type of transport, stretched out in the opposite seat which could easily accommodate three. Vicarrio knew there would be no point in asking questions, so just remained silent as the airport lights faded into the distance and the motorised cubicle filled with smoke from his abductor's cigar.

....

Antoine recognised the approach to Leonardo da Vinci International Airport from the tiny window of his first-class seat. His escorts had been reasonably pleasant during the flight, and he was able to begin constructing the series of events which he would possibly need to relay to whomever he was meeting. Once this was done, he would return to France and cut all ties with Italy, obviously part of some kind of collaboration orchestrated by his deranged father. There was one thing troubling him though. Although there was no way off of a plane, why did he hear the presence of someone outside the door each time he went to the bathroom? Yet, when he exited the tiny closet there was no one there, and one of his companions was re-settling into his seat.

Once they landed the steward invited them to be first to depart. As Antoine disembarked there was another type of buggy waiting. Not one of the tiny ones he had last used inside the terminal at Charles de Gaulle, a more powerful, speedy version driven by airport staff for traversing across aprons and runways at speed.

They were whisked towards a helicopter whose rotors were already spinning at a velocity just below that required for take-off. Without speaking the three men headed to the side aperture of the chopper, unnecessarily dipping their heads to avoid decapitation from the blades spinning fifteen feet above them.

Antoine held his nerve for the next three hours until he sensed the decrease in airspeed followed by a noticeable descending feeling in his stomach.

"Where are we?" Said Antoine. "We can't possibly be in Sicily yet."

"Relax." Said the obvious senior of his anonymous escorts. "We are refuelling."

Antoine instantly regretted breaking the silence; it was a sign of weakness. It was obvious that, if they were telling the truth about the final destination, there is no way they could have reached that point in the time which had passed.

Two hours later, after flying over a blankness of open sea, Antoine became transfixed on the fairy-like display of lights from cities, towns, and hamlets twinkling below. The terrain then morphed into a dark canvas devoid of human existence.

Fatigue was finally kicking in, and Antoine involuntarily began to doze. His partial slumber was eventually disturbed by a pyrotechnic display dissipating across the doubled glazed reinforced windows of his transportation, exaggerating the effect of each flash and spark being spurted into the air from the cavernous aperture in the earth below. Antoine rubbed his eyes and was momentarily transfixed, until realisation hit home.

"This is Mount Etna."

"Congratulations, you are correct." Said no1 escort. "We are about to hover over the the active crater."

"Is that safe?"

"Reasonably." Said the Mafia man. "The cabin is sealed, so no gases will come in, and the molten lava is quite sedate at the moment. We cannot stay this close for too long or our engine will overheat. We just wish for you to see something."

Antoine stared out of the window to see a long chain being retrieved from the depths of the hole. The crane to which it was attached appeared to be perched perilously close to the crater's edge.

Eventually a crucifix appeared with a chargrilled man pinned by nails as if he were Jesus.

"Your good friend Mr Vicarrio was unable to give us the information we required. Perhaps you will be more cooperative."

....

The three stones emitted a light and energy, the likes of which I had never experienced. An image projected itself onto the wall behind the altar. It was very basic, almost a crude outline of a naked male having been drawn by a homicide detective, except that the genitalia were included, and the arms were clasped together as if in prayer; this image had a slight blue hue to its edge. Seconds later a second image appeared alongside the first in an identical crude form of artistry. But this one had a slightly red hue and was unmistakably that of a woman; the unmistakeable pout of breasts being raised by the folded arms allowing clasped hands to be brought together in prayer. There was also a defined triangular pubic area with the subtle hint of a vertical dissecting line leading to the point where the top of the inner thighs met; clearly indicating a vagina. The energy continued to increase as the centre crystal stone began to rotate alone, defying the fact that the three-piece jagged puzzle should not permit this, until the two images had merged, and words appeared below the morphed outline, which was now neither a man or a woman, to form something that could only be accurately described as both.

I could sense that my cousin could not understand the scripture, but it was as plain to me as if an elementary school student had written it; I no longer required Professor Field's expert knowledge.

This is my true image, mother and father of all creation. Many centuries ago I placed a special person upon this earth in order to host my son, Jesus, into this world, her name was Mary. You may recognise this event as the immaculate conception. Since then the world has not been ready to accept that man and woman are equal. I have tried many times to bring this acceptance to the masses, and many have suffered, including St Joan. My true words have been changed and misinterpreted over time to suit individual purposes. But now the time is upon us when you should reveal the truth. The stones will reveal a message from my beloved son, Jesus, and you must take heed of these words.

The new words and images disappeared as magically

as the first had revealed themselves just moments ago. I had no time to dwell as the blue and red stones decided to join the performance. They also began to rotate in a contrary direction to the crystal. The incomplete ruby stone wording was projected to my left, and the blue gapped message to my right. The wall behind the altar had been replaced by another set of disjointed wording. Painfully slowly they crept across the walls of the ancient church of Saint Joan's christening until I could read the document in its entirety. ,

I the son of God hereby decree that those born as both a man and a woman shall be seen by God as the saviour of mankind. Only one who encompasses the virtues of both sexes can truly understand the good, and the bad which inhabits the earth. They shall suffer for millennium and carry the burden of our weaknesses until the day eventually comes when understanding wins through. Only then can the world live in harmony.

My Father and Mother be as one, and in one body are the creator of all things. I deliver this message to you, Joan D'Arc, in the form of three precious stones. You must hide them in separate locations until the day that one true of heart, and of your bloodline, shall reveal the truth. Only when they again be joined together, and placed on the crystal font at the altar of your christening, can this message be read in full and truly understood.

Your quest is to first embrace the words delivered by my messengers, Saint Michael the Arcangel, Saint Catherine of Alexandria and Saint Margaret. They will advise you on how to end the suffering of the oppressed in your land, and bring peace after many years of blood spilling. There are three orders which you must obey if you shall succeed and be accepted into our creators Heavenly Kingdom. You must lead the armies of salvation dressed in manly clothes. You shall remain carnally untouched but either man or woman. You shall give your life as the ultimate sacrifice, as did I.

Many years from now, when one of your bloodline be born in the bodily likeness of you and my mother will the truth be revealed to the world.

Amen

I was still drawn to the words upon the wall when Salonge pulled me to the floor, drawing her gun as she did so. She had clearly heard something which her trained ear had honed in to. From nowhere, the old Priest came shuffling out from an alcove, apparently having been resurrected from the dust recently piled at the entrance. This time though his cassock was concealing his face, and he was carrying an impossibly heavy looking roll of carpet. The old hunched man ignored us both as he rolled the rug out before us. Immediately a beam of light sprung from the centre, clear crystal and focussed on a point of the map weaved into the floor covering. It once again focussed on Rome but began to trace a line towards Sicily.

The old man walked towards the exit of the church and, just before he hit the threshold to the outside, he turned to face me.

"The stones will always show you the way my dear Kacey. They will lead you to the remains of the mother of Jesus. This will prove that Mary, Joan, and now you, are truly the special ones who can finally bring harmony and peace to the world."

My legs turned to jelly; I recognised the voice. The old priest removed his hood and smiled.

"I am so proud of you, and I shall always watch over you, and do whatever I can to keep you safe. Be strong my brave young knight."

All strength left my body as I fell to the floor, and the last words left my lips before I passed out. "Sir Grandad...please don't leave me again."

When I awoke Salonge was cradling me in her arms. I asked my cousin if Sir Grandad had gone, already knowing the answer.

Anthony appeared along with Charles and Jack. "What the hell was that? When that man who you called grandad left the building he just turned to dust and blew away into the wind."

Chapter 54

The Sistine Chapel

The helicopter banked away from the bubbling crater and settled at a safe distance. Instead of asking Antoine to disembark, two more men joined them inside the glass cabin. As soon as they had buckled their safety harnesses the first new arrival began to speak.

"So Antoine, you and your recently barbequed friend killed the FBI female and the young girl from England who have been causing my friends and me so many problems?"

"Yes, at the Chateau de Breteuil." Antoine saw no gain in lying.

"And the three stones which were in their possession?"

For a moment Antoine was confused, until he remembered the gifts for Kacey's boyfriend. "Oh, you mean the black stones with jagged edges. They are currently residing in the ashes at the city of Paris incinerator along with those of the girls burnt remains."

"And what of the ex-FBI Agent's remains?"

"Her body is in the main bed chamber of the chateau,

along with that of my father Gabriel. We made sure to stage a scene which will undoubtedly be construed as a deadly confrontation between the two of them."

"Is that so. What if I were to tell you that they were seen leaving the chateau with three gentlemen from various western secret service agencies, and they were very much alive."

"That's impossible." Said Antoine.

"If only that were the case. Now, unless you wish to be cremated in Mount Etna like your friend Al Vicarrio, you must make a telephone call to a Charles Worwood. You are required to offer him a deal whereby he will be provided with all the answers to their quest if he agrees to cease any future pursuit of yourself. You must inform him that the answer lies at the Vatican and, should he agree to leave you alone, he will be contacted soon."

"Why would the head of MI6 believe me?"

"Because young man, he knows that you are scared, and that your organisation is in disarray. Under those circumstances it is not unusual for someone to try and save their own skin."

Antoine was handed the oversized mobile phone, connected to the aircrafts communications system for uninterrupted calls whilst in transit, which was already dialling Worwoods number. He delivered the proposition, and listened for a moment, before hanging up.

"Worwood agreed to the terms we set out." Said Antoine, not realising that they were once again hovering high above the crater.

One man unbuckled his harness as another opened the sliding door to the helicopter. The third man gave a two palmed push projecting Antoine into the pyre below.

....

Deep in a secret crypt below the Sistine Chapel

The four keepers of the most guarded secrets of the Catholic Church were gathered around the 15th century coffin deep below the Sistine Chapel.

"Do you think that they will be convinced?" Said the no 1, Francesco.

"The mummified remains are most definitely that of a woman, and will pass any test as to being from the time of Jesus." Replied no 2, Paulo.

"And what about the stone tomb?" Countered Francesco.

No 3, Tomassi, walked towards the ancient coffin. "The stonework is of the same date. On close inspection the stonework would be identified as coming from Egypt, but this was not unusual to be found in Italy at that time due to the Roman Empires imports."

"And what about the addition...the new lock."

It was the turn of no 4, Michael. "We were able to make casts from the indentations in the cooled wax at the Chateau outside Paris. This gave me the correct dimensions for the jagged edges of the stones. I have been able to construct an unlocking device which will magically open the casket. I have attached the mechanism to the tomb and aged it appropriately. It would not, however, stand up to close scrutiny. I believe that their attention and forensic examination will be concentrated on the female's remains and not the container, especially given the allocated time afforded them."

"Tomassi, tell Lorenzo Visconti, the chief of the Italian secret police, to make the call. Worwood will trust his word. What is wrong Tomassi, I sense hesitancy?"

"Sir, it is just that we are true Catholics, servants of the church. It does not sit well with me to tell a lie ... It is blasphemous. We have promised that the actual body of Mary mother of Jesus is in a crypt below this chapel."

"Do not fear the wrath of God my brother for you are telling no lie. We have informed them that the remains are in a crypt below the Sistine Chapel, not this chapel."

"I do not understand, sir." Said a confused Tomassi, as were the other two guardians.

"Let me explain. Francesco Della Rovere was born in 1414 in Savona, north west Italy. In 1471 he was elected Pope Sixtus IV. I'm sure that you are all familiar with our papal history. What you may not know is that he constructed another Sistine Chapel in his place of birth next to the Cathedral of Saint Mary of the Assumption; quite appropriate don't you think?

As we speak, Mary's true remains are being transported to that location. So you see my brother, you will not be lying."

....

Charles had seconded the private apartments on the upper levels of the British security services situated by the river Thames. It had taken some persuasion, but with the assistance of Anthony and Jack, Kacey and Salonge had agreed to regroup in London.

"You must understand my dear, the people who wished you immediate harm are all but disbanded. But I fear that the next stage may well be even more perilous, so we must consider carefully what our next move should be."

"You don't think I am going crazy, do you? You saw my grandad, didn't you?" Said Kacey, addressing the entire group and not just one individual, eyes darting from one to the next for confirmation.

Salonge walked over to Kacey and placed her palms on her young cousin's cheeks and gave a gentle smile. "I have not seen your grandfather for many years, but there is no doubt in my mind that that was him. As for how he was briefly resurrected, that is just one more magical occurrence that I have witnessed since we met in Paris.

Anthony spoke up. "Do you have any contacts in Rome Charles? Kacey and Salonge are convinced that the answers lie there. And after what I have witnessed in the past few days, I think we should trust their instincts."

"There is no doubt that there are some magical things in play here which demand more investigation." Said Charles, clearly pondering how to deliver the next statement. "However, these revelations are not easily explained to associates who were not witness to the strange occurrences. Add to that the fact that the threat from corrupt officials in France has been removed and I have been informed that Al Vicarrio is missing in action at best, or perhaps simply gone to ground."

Worwood's phone began to ring, and his eyebrows perceptibly raised as he recognised the +39 prefix for Italy, followed by that of the region of Rome.

"Charles, how are you my friend?" Said Lorenzo Acconci.

"I am keeping well my friend. To what do I owe this pleasure?" Said Worwood to his Italian counterpart.

"We have been following this quest of yours with great interest and I believe I can be of help and put this ridiculous fable to rest."

"How so?" Said Charles, activating the speaker whilst simultaneously placing his index finger across his lips to demand silence in the room.

"I have been instructed by the highest echelons of the Catholic church to invite you and your friends to visit the Sistine Chapel in Rome."

"I see." Said Charles. "And what would be the purpose of this visit?"

"Oh I think you have a very good idea my friend."

"Well it would be much appreciated if you could indulge me with your interpretation as to the purpose of the invite."

There was a long pause before Lorenzo spoke again.

"Charles, we have known each other far too long to play games. We, or should I say, the Catholic church, have been aware of blasphemous rumours about Joan of Arc and her sexuality. The very same rumours have also, in the past, been spread about Mary mother of Jesus, and what the immaculate conception actually was, but these were suppressed many centuries ago."

More silence ensued as Lorenzo let his words sink in.

"Am I correct in assuming that people believed Mary impregnated herself? When was this rumour in circulation?" Said Worwood.

"It was most prevalent around 325AD when Emperor Constantine of Rome endorsed religious toleration, including Catholicism. However, many still remained loyal to the old Gods such as Mars, Jupiter and Saturn. It is said that Mary's body was entombed and hidden by the modern Catholics of the time and moved from destination to destination."

"And you are saying that her remains are currently in the possession of the Vatican?"

"That is precisely what I am saying. What is more, they have invited you to bring an expert to examine these remains and prove that Mary was a true miracle and not a monstrosity."

"If they know this to be the case, why have they not made this revelation known to the world." Said a dubious Charles."

"Because." Said a nervous sounding Lorenzo. "They have parchments declaring that the tomb in their possession is that of Mary mother of Jesus. However, the tomb has never been opened."

"This all sounds a tad incredulous Lorenzo. Why on earth would they have not examined the remains?"

"That is because there is a special mechanism to open the stone casket. The scriptures say that only a key of three precious stones can open the lid. Any other method would destroy the contents held within."

Everyone in the private apartment above his office at MI6 looked at each other in shock, but Charles was first to recover his composure.

"So, if the casket cannot be opened, what use is it for us to visit Rome?"

"Come come Charles, we know you have the stones.

We have been following the girl's progress. She seems to have a gift of discovery afforded her which we have never been able to attain."

"If we were in possession of the stones, and I am purely saying if, and the casket was opened to reveal something unsatisfactory to the Catholic church, what then?"

"These are modern times Charles. If the church is to survive, and the history books are to be re written, then so be it. They will accept the findings."

"Very well, we shall arrive in Rome tomorrow... myself, and six guests. Goodbye Lorenzo."

"Goodbye Charles, and don't forget the stones."

Chapter 55

The answers await

Salonge, Anthony, Jack, Charles Worwood and I had boarded a helicopter from the roof of MI6 and were on approach to RAF Northolt in West London. The mood was very sombre as Charles explained the sequence of events to unfold. I was deep in thought, clutching the canvas bag containing the magical, precious stones, hoping to sense a signal from their energy that we were doing the right thing, but I felt nothing.

"Ah, that is good news." Said Charles, looking out of a port side window. "The Hercules transporter plane already has her propellers turning. That must mean that our two guests are on board, and we will be able to take off for Rome immediately.

I snapped out of my trance. "Two guests you say. And who might they be?"

"One is your old mentor dear girl, Professor Field. We shall most likely need her assistance, as I am told part of the verification process involves some old scriptures."

My eyes lit up. "Elizabeth is coming with us?"

"Yes my dear."

"And the other guest?" I said, in a curious manner.

"That would be an old Etonian friend of mine, James Boothroyd, an eminent scientific archaeologist. He will make observations as to the authenticity of the casket and its contents. If permitted, he will take some samples of what we discover and analyse them at Lorenzo's laboratory in Rome, or preferably at the site."

"Can you trust him?" Said Anthony, immediately regretting the statement as Salonge dug her nails into his leg.

"You really should know better Agent Mazur. Just mentioning that he was an Old Etonian should be enough, but I also stated that he was a friend."

There was an awkward silence until the bump of the helicopter landing prompted a clumsy attempt by Anthony to recover from his gaff. "What I meant was, can you trust him to handle himself should things get nasty. I would not want an 'Old Etonian' friend to be embroiled in such a dangerous situation.

Salonge rolled her eyes in disbelief as Jack, and I tried to refrain from cringing. .

"My dear Salonge, could you please inform your devoted husband that James is the archaeologist so there is no need for him to continue digging holes."

This time all four of us let out a gutsy laugh before disembarking and running across the asphalt to the awaiting RAF Lockheed C-130 J Hercules.

There was no wheeled stairway leading to a doorway for us to ascend. Instead, the rear of the aircraft had a lowered ramp, usually used for armoured vehicles to roll up. The interior was also altered from that of a transport plane to a more comfortable setting for passengers devoid of parachutes or backpacks. There were three seats backed to the opposite sides of the aircraft's fuselage with a table placed centrally between them. I immediately spotted a smiling Professor Elizabeth Field sitting comfortably harnessed, drinking a cup of tea. She looked up and had barely managed to place her beverage on the table before I was hugging her.

"Easy Kacey. I'm still quite sore from the assault back in Oxford. You know that at my age our bones take longer to heal."

"But Beth…I mean Professor Field…why are you here. It's far too dangerous. You almost died because of me."

"Dear Kacey. Since I was a little girl, I have been obsessed with uncovering the secrets of the past. If you think that you can keep me away from the biggest revelation in known history, then you are very much mistaken. If I were not included in the conclusion of your quest then I may as well be dead anyway. An opportunity like this is precisely what I live for. It's a dream for me, regardless of the dangers."

I kissed Beth on both cheeks and settled into the seat next to hers, tucking the canvass bag below my feet. Salonge filled the final space on our side of the table whilst Charles, Anthony and Jack sat opposite.

I could sense the aircraft beginning to taxi when a nagging thought entered my mind… where was this friend of Charles…James Boothroyd?

"Charles, I thought your archaeologist colleague was joining us?"

"Indeed he is." With that Charles called his name into an intercom."

"Hi everyone." Came a voice through the tiny speaker. "I shall join you as soon as we are flying straight and level after take-off."

Charles addressed us all, but his eyes were focussed on me. "You will notice that the end of this compartment containing a door does not account for the full length of the aircraft. James has a one third section between us and the cockpit containing some of his tools of the trade. He needs a sealed section to use various sensitive equipment in order to examine artifacts correctly."

"But he has no artifacts to examine yet." Said Jack Nichols.

Charles's eyes remained on me. "Kacey my dear, James would like to examine the gemstones whilst we are in transit. As soon as we have landed you may have them back."

I was very unsettled. Would an Xray or other tampering somehow interfere with the stones powers which have guided and protected me thus far? Besides, logic told me that if mere mobile phones could not be used in flight for fear of interference, how could this James character be performing any examination of importance on the items. I reluctantly handed the canvas bag to Charles who, once he sensed the aircraft level out, tapped on the door to my left. A slender man came out and briefly introduced himself. He had slicked back hair, greying around the temples. His eyebrows were were of a bushy nature accentuating the frowned, wrinkled forehead. His eyes were of a kind, smiling nature though. James Boothroyd disappeared back into his compartment carrying the gemstones. My travelling companions could sense my unease and left me to my thoughts, believing that my only trepidation was that Sir Grandad's quest would soon amount to

nothing, but it wasn't that at all. It was that after all
of the events since his death, one would have
thought I would be as brave as any knight in
Grandad's tales, but I was not. If anything, I was as
frightened as any young girl in despair; a feeling I had
never really experienced as a tortured and frustrated
Kieth Chapman. The pilot's voice came over the
intercom informing us that we were on finals to
Leonardo Da Vinci Fiumicino International Airport, 25
kilometres south west of Rome. We all
simultaneously lurched to one side as the short take-
off and landing craft dipped its nose at a seemingly
impossible angle making full use of the flaps.
Seconds later we had landed on the smallest of the
four runways usually reserved for taxiing or
emergency landings. Once we had felt the almost
imperceivable bump of the wheels it was only
seconds before the Hercules pulled to a halt. I stared
towards the rear of the aircraft expecting the tailgate
to lower, but on this occasion it was a tiny running
track shaped door which was pulled open by Charles
allowing the continental sunshine to burst into the
cabin. I squinted my eyes as I followed him down the
gangway which contained no steps, just a long slope-
like ramp. As my pupils contracted and adjusted to
the bright light, I could see a figure standing in front
of a tinted stretch limousine waiting to greet us. I
deliberately slowed my pace in order to gauge the
interaction between the two heads of their

respective secret government organisations. Charles
extended his hand, drew the man closer, and then
gave a polite air kiss to each cheek of our host. I have
always been observant and fascinated by people's
quirks. I had only known Charles Worwood a few
weeks, but had already ascertained that if he really
liked someone, the formal greeting was always
followed by five intermittent pats on the shoulder; it
was his personal obsessive-compulsive disorder, or
perhaps a signal to his operatives such as Salonge.
Charles stepped aside and Lorenzo turned his
attention to me delivering a broad smile as he did so.
The whiteness of his teeth was exaggerated by the
surrounding, perfectly manicured black goatee and
tanned skin.

"Ms Chapman, Buen Journo."

"Hello kind sir. I assume that you are a certain
Lorenzo Visconti?"

"You can be assured that I am he."

I was instantly aware that he did not offer me the
customary cheek kiss, and wondered if his
intelligence gathering about my birth disgusted him.
His homophobia was confirmed when he did offer a
more affectionate greeting to the remainder of our
party, including the men; how hypocritical. I was
enraged, which instantly dispelled my nervousness

and gave me the courage to take command of the situation.

"My dear sir, it is so kind of you to offer your assistance. Having heard of your power and influence in Italy, I must say that I was surprised to be greeted by someone so handsome and youthful looking." With that I sprang forward and planted a big kiss directly onto his lip-balm greased mouth.

Lorenzo Visconti's face flushed as he ushered us into our next mode of transportation whilst vigorously wiping his mouth with the sleeve of his jacket.

"You are a wicked and naughty girl." Whispered a sniggering Salonge.

"He deserved it, the egotistical homophobe."

Shortly after we had set off I could hear Charles and Lorenzo pointing out landmarks to Jack and Anthony, and reminiscing about locations and restaurants where they had discussed collaborative missions or ate sumptuous lunches. I was aware of the conversations, but only vaguely. My head was dipped, and my arms were clutching the canvas bag to my chest waiting for a reaction or energy to emit from the stones, but there was still nothing. I was snapped out of my zombie like trance by the car pulling to a halt and Lorenzo declaring that our escorts were waiting. I looked up to see four armed members of the Swiss Guard standing to attention at the curb side. Their bright colours of red, blue and yellow stripes conjured thoughts of court jesters as opposed to skilled soldiers charged with protecting the Pope and the Vatican. Charles could see the confusion on my face.

"Do not underestimate the guards of the Vatican. Switzerland may be a wealthy country now, but five hundred years ago this was not the case. As such, many of their young men left for foreign lands as mercenaries. Their skill, discipline and resourcefulness was recognised by Pope Julius II who, in 1502, formed what is now one of the oldest, continuous military units in the world.

James spoke up for the first time since we entered the vehicle. "Lorenzo, who is transporting my dating equipment from the aircraft?"

"Do not worry Mr Boothroyd." Said Lorenzo. "When Charles detailed the scientific, archaeological tools of your trade which you desired to bring along, we arranged for the very same to be waiting for you in the crypt below the Sistine Chapel. The equipment has been suitably sanitised, and subsequently tested to ensure that the cleansing procedure had not affected their accuracy."

I could see one of the Swiss Guards inspecting our documentation that had been passed to him by our driver, identifying us as those who have been given given permission to access those areas of the chapel not afforded to members of the general public.

Lorenzo addressed the group. "When we leave the vehicle we shall be required to form a column of pairs; Charles and I at the front, followed by Salonge and Kacey, then Jack and Anthony, with Beth and James at the rear. We will be flanked by the four guards and led straight through the Sistine Chapel to a door marked private, and then down to a sanitation room before descending further to the crypt."

"You need to enter the crypt via the bathroom?" Enquired Anthony.

Lorenzo smiled, but not in a mocking way. "You will be required to enter cubicles, undergo a chemical shower, and then don sanitation suits. The crypt holds many ancient and priceless artifacts. Any outside contamination could destroy them, and they would be lost forever. This is why we have supplied our own equipment for Mr Boothroyd."

We formed a double column, flanked front and rear by the guards, and involuntarily fell into step with each other. It felt as if I were part of a military procession. Our escorts held their pikes forward at an outward forty-five-degree angle causing the tourists to spread like Moses dividing the waters of the Red Sea. There was a buz of confusion in the air, and an increasing flash of cameras from onlookers hoping to record the unusual event, thinking perhaps that it was an arrest of some sort. We continued on our way, passing the considerable tourist queues until I was eventually staring up at the ceiling of the Sistine Chapel causing Anthony to crash into my back. The rear guard urged us forward and through a small aperture at the rear of the magnificent atrium. We descended what must have been one hundred tiny stone steps with impossibly narrow walls causing us to adopt single file led by Lorenzo. The corkscrew-like passageway was dimly lit by iron candlelight mountings which had been refitted with flickering electric bulbs intended to maintain the original ambience. We finally reached a solid steel door. Lorenzo performed a complicated set of taps with his knuckles until we could hear locks being turned. The door swung open to reveal an impossibly white surgical type room. We were directed both left and right by two gender appropriate hosts: ladies in one direction and the men in the other. Once segregated, we were instructed to remove our clothes, enter the sanitation cubicles, and then don the white anti-contamination suits.

Kacey's Quest

Chapter 56

Crocodile Tears

The Sistine Chapel in Savona was packed to the rafters as the unusually oversized hearse drew up to its doors. As was common in the smaller, devoutly catholic provinces of Italy the whole city, albeit small when compared to Rome, seemed to have turned out to pray for another dearly departed. The only real difference is that there was no room for any locals within its doors; it was full of black clad strangers. Nobody from Savona recognised the name of this latest soul, only that she was extremely old and had left Savona many years before. Apparently her dying wish was to be returned and be buried in the place of her birth. One thing was certain though, she must have been very important to the church as she was to be interned in the burial chamber of their beloved Sistine Chapel commissioned in honour of Pope Sixtus IV's parents.

The hearse drew to a halt and its double height back door was opened as two men lowered a ramp and the huge coffin was rolled down using some sort of pully chain contraption. The chasse of the vehicle, and the links of the chains were creaking under the weight of the casket. The doors to the chapel opened as four men appeared and joined the six pall bearers, but there was no way that this body could be carried inside to where the wails from the mourners had risen by several decibels. Ten nautical strength ropes were affixed to attachments hidden beneath the tricolore flag covering the coffin, and the ten men pulled with all their might before the wheels upon which it was resting began to roll. The scene resembled medieval soldiers dragging a giant ramming post in order to breach a castles gates. After a supreme effort, the casket finally disappeared from view and down the central aisle of the chapel and brought to a halt in front of the altar, at which point the doors were closed to the outside world. Two hours later the mourners began to emerge, and the locals bowed their heads in respect whilst making the sign for the father, the son, and the holy ghost. Once everyone had left, and the respectful locals had returned to their families, the doors to the chapel were once again closed but ten men had remained.

The rotund head of the Mafia family who had recently disposed of Al Vicarrio approached the Cardinal Priest. "I can assure you that you have done a good thing Father. You may leave my men to the task at hand. They shall work through the night to remove the central isle slabs and lower the precious casket into the burial chamber. It is far too big, and far too heavy to negotiate the narrow stairs."

"This is most inconvenient Mr ......"

"My name is not important. All that matters is that you have had instructions from the highest level of the Catholic Church to comply, which you have verified. I can assure you that once you return in the morning, there will be no evidence of any disruption to the structure of this most holy of buildings."

With that the Mafia man handed over the one million euro for the coffers required to maintain the ancient structure.

The one hundred or so mourners from the service were now smiling and drinking champagne on their flight back to Sicily having completed their roles in the elaborate deception.

....

Our legs and arms made a crinkling sound from our brilliant white suits as we left the sanitation room to descend yet more steps until we were finally standing amongst corridors of religious artifacts from across the centuries; our destination was far from how I had imagined though. I had been expecting stone corridors full of dust and cobwebs, which was quite ridiculous considering the cleansing process we had endured. The scene was like a hybrid between the viewing gallery at the Louvre, and a Harley Street clinic. Four figures emerged out of the darkness in a ghostly fashion.

"Good afternoon everyone." Said the elderly of our hosts. "This is Father Paulo, my deputy so to speak. And this is Tomassi, the understudy to Father Paulo. Michael here is the junior of our group, but none the less of quite a senior standing within the Vatican. And my name is Father Francesco. As you can see, the artifacts here are of monumental importance to the Catholic Church, and as such, only the most devout, capable people with the necessary knowledge to preserve their integrity ascend to such a privileged position as keepers of these treasures."

Lorenzo stepped forward, bowed his head, and kissed Francesco's hand. "Thank you Father, for giving us this audience."

"The truth must be told, whatever the results of your friends quest." Father Francesco was looking directly at me as he said this. He continued. "I must admit to being very nervous whilst at the same remaining confident that we shall witness the opening of Mary's tomb and not the revelation of an impossibility which would change the history of the Catholic Church forever. Please follow me."

The four religious figures led the way with a respectful, but indifferent manner to those which these surroundings were commonplace. The others, including Charles, were stopping periodically to read the labels adorning the sealed and treasured artifacts stacked upon the shelves with the utmost care and protection. I, however, was at the rear of the group clutching the canvas bag thinking how disrespectful I had been by carrying Joan's precious stones in such a shabby receptacle. The corridor seemed impossibly long, much longer than the footprint of the Chapel above us. Eventually I could see a bright light ahead of us, like the opening of an underground tunnel. When we emerged into the space which contained the source of the light, my jaw dropped. It looked like a forensic laboratory with an enormous CAT scan type machine in the centre. Waiting on a conveyor belt, to be rolled into the high-tech tunnel, was a large stone tomb. The Vatican officials stood to one side, as did my colleagues, forming a guard of honour for me to approach the tomb. As I walked forward I could feel a tremble run through my body, but it was caused by adrenalin and my shaking knees, not the expected energy from the stones; they were dormant. At the foot of the tomb was carved an inscription in Aramaic. I felt an arm around my waist as Beth joined me.

"It says...Here lies the body of Mary mother of Jesus." She said.

I looked to my professor and back at the stone tomb. Below the inscription were three deep cylindrical indentations, two with a singular crimped end and one with a double crimp. I opened the canvas bag and retrieved the blue gem and, trusting my instinct, placed it in the left receptacle. Next I retrieved the red gemstone and gently slotted it into place on the right. Finally I took a grip on the final, double crimped, clear gemstone and held it above what looked to be its obvious destined resting place. A part of me did not want to release the pure crystal as I still felt that there should have been a signal, or energy from Joan; nothing. Eventually, encouraged by pleading eyes and a gentle nudge from Beth, I released the sone. It dropped snuggly into place and there was an immediate release of pressure of ancient CO_2 escaping from the tomb. It sounded like a desperate gasp of air from a free diver emerging to the surface of the sea after testing their lung capacity to the limits. The lid of the receptacle raised around four inches and began to slide toward me. Inside lay a body wrapped in bandaging. It looked somehow different to those I had seen on documentaries about the Egyptians, a heavier material of a much wider strapping.

Father Francesco stepped forward. "Mr Lorenzo will remain here with my brothers to ensure our conditions are adhered to whilst your colleague, Mr Boothroyd, conducts his tests. He will be permitted to perform a scan which will, I am certain, prove beyond doubt that the body in question is that of a pure woman. He will then be allowed to take one sample from the base of the foot which will verify the age of the bandages, and that of the body encased therein. In the meantime Mr Worewood, you, Professor Field, Ms Chapman, Mr Mazur, and Mr Nichols can wait in my office where the document declaring this to be the body of Mary mother of Jesus also awaits examination. I'm sure that Mr Boothroyd's tests will take some time, but I am afraid that I can only offer you fresh water as a refreshment. No food or steaming beverages are permitted in this sacred place for fear of contamination, or disruption to the climate control which protects our precious artifacts.

I felt an uneasiness on so many levels. If the gemstones bequeathed to me by Joan were designed to unlock this tomb, and they had been so alive with energy throughout my quest, why were they so dull at the conclusion of my struggle? I had also expected a far greater reaction from the four Vatican hosts. One would have expected them to fall to their knees in reverence at the revelation of the body of Jesus's mothers, but their eyes seemed to be focussed purely on us. Regardless of these concerns I trusted Charles Worewood and the man whom he trusted to uncover the truth. With a nervous reluctance I followed brother Paulo into a sparsely decorated office accompanied by the rest of our entourage. Once inside the office there was a singular desk which had a lead box placed upon it accompanied by a pair of white gloves. Behind the desk was ~~sat~~ a leather high backed chair. Directly in front of that, placed beside the box, was a name card with Professors Field printed upon it. Five smaller chairs were situated around the periphery of the desk with each of our names on the seats. In the centre of the desk was tray containing a large jug of water with six glasses.

"Ladies and gentlemen, please make yourselves comfortable whilst your professor, and only her, examines the document contained within the box. I'm afraid that you may be here for some time whilst Mr Boothroyd busies himself in the main chamber."

With that the Brother Paulo left the room and made no effort to hide the obvious sound of a key clanking inside the locking mechanism of the door.

"Ok everyone. I suggest you chat quietly amongst yourselves whilst I examine the document which is no doubt contained within this box."

We all rose and formed a circle in the corner of the room allowing Beth some space to concentrate. Inspiration for conversation did not come easy though. Everyone was angling their heads to afford a better view of Beths reactions. Eventually we all decided to hide the obvious pretence and shuffled towards my old mentor. I could hardly breathe as she donned the white gloves and gingerly opened the box set before her. Beth slowly lifted the lid and removed its contents. There was just a single page which she gently laid flat before her. I had expected to wait many anxious minutes, if not hours, before she would address the group, but it was almost instantaneous.

"The parchment looks to be of the correct period, as does the structure of the Aramaic text. It simply translates as:

Interned within this tomb lies the sacred body of Mary mother of Jesus.

As decreed by the Bishop of Jerusalem 451

Beth continued. "It certainly looks authentic, but they have made it quite clear that the document, and/or part of it, cannot be taken from this place. So I guess that everything relies on James's findings."

The next hours of waiting were excruciating. I have never worn a watch and my cell phone was devoid of a signal; it's world clock had frozen. I guessed it must have been something to do with the security protection within the Vatican. I could sense Charles irritation at me asking him to check his Rolex every five minutes. Although polite, his eyes were urging me to desist my repetitive requests to be notified of the precise hour, minute and second. Eventually we could hear the key being turned in the lock, and in walked James Boothroyd followed by the four officials. I stared pleadingly at the old Etonian almost dreading the results of the tests. James Boothroyd was holding a long sheet of paper and his head was bowed, as if he were re-inspecting the data before delivering the outcome.

Charles was the first to break the silence. "Come on man, let's have it!"

James cleared his throat. "I began with a study of the stone tomb. It revealed that the structure is made up from Egyptian material similar to that of the type used for the pyramids. The surface area, however, contained residue familiar to that specific to the terrain in Jerusalem where Mary was born, lived, and died. The scan of the mummified body is most definitely that of a female of slight to medium build for someone of that time. The sample taken from the foot of the body revealed that the said person, as was the case with the bandaging, date to a time concurrent with the life of Jesus."

I couldn't accept the findings. "So there is a female body dating to the time and place when Mary was alive, but it could be anyone. Why would Joan and the magic stones have brought me to this conclusion of my quest? And why have the gemstones been so dormant when on every other occasion they have been alive with energy?"

It was Beth's turn to interject as she rose and approached me with an almost bereaved look of sympathy. "My dear Kacey, perhaps there was no reaction because they had finally found their home. They slotted snuggly into the cavities for which they were designed, and the locking system immediately opened. Besides, the parchment which I have examined looks to be authentic also."

I felt Salonge place her hands on my shoulders and gently guide me back to my seat. She knelt before me and took my hands.

"Kacey, it's over. We have rid the world of a dangerous and sordid organisation, the Protecteurs de la France, and brought the stones to their correct resting place. Perhaps Joan was simply coming to the rescue of her beloved country once again. Why don't you come back with Anthony and me to Thailand and enjoy the rest of your gap year? We have plenty of room, and we could show you the delights of South East Asia."

I began to sob uncontrollably before eventually closing my eyes and clasping my hands in prayer. "My wonderful Sir Grandad, I did my best. I hope that I have not let you down. I have no doubt that I am the descendant of Joan as you stated. I am also sure that she will contact me again in the future. I miss you so much Grandad. I am going to spend some time with my cousin Salonge, and after that, perhaps search out other members of our estranged family. I love you grandad, your adoring Kacey."

Epilogue

Charles had exclaimed that it was an excellent idea for me to visit Thailand with Salonge. He kindly afforded my wonderful cousin two months leave from her AICAC duties whilst informing her husband that he would need to take up the slack. We left the crypt like museum and were driven back to Leonardo da Vinci airport by Lorenzo's driver; Lorenzo remained at the Vatican. We were taken to a private area and driven to the British Hercules by airport security. We all exited the vehicle with the intent of boarding the aircraft via its lowered ramp, but Charles halted our advance with raised palms.

"It shall only be myself and Mr Boothroyd taking this particular form of transport back to London. You Kacey, along with your adoring cousin and her husband will be taken to the Thai Air Dreamliner waiting to taxi for take-off to Bangkok. I have managed to delay its departure until you are safely on board. And for your information, I have taken the liberty of booking first class seats for the three of you, so be sure to turn left when you board the aeroplane. Mr Nichols, you will be taken to the American Embassy whereby you will no doubt be debriefed before assuming the responsibilities of a certain Allesandro Vicarrio."

With that Charles gave me a quick wink, touched his

hand to his lips, and blew me a kiss. As he and James walked away I could hear him saying..."What a remarkable young lady...what."

Salonge called out to Charles before signalling to us that she wished to speak with him. "Do you have a minute sir?"

"I have many minutes to spare. You, however, have about ten minutes before the plane to Bangkok leaves without you."

Salonge took Charles by the elbow and escorted him towards the Hercules, her voice eventually being drowned out by the aircrafts propellers.

"What did you do with the real stones Charles?"

"What on earth do you mean Salonge."

She knew that she had made the correct assumptions by her superior using her first name.

"You switched the stones on the plane when your friend was examining them, didn't you?"

Charles ushered Salonge a little farther away even though we were well out of earshot. "My dear friend, you are of course correct. But I have to always look at the bigger picture, and so must you."

"Why Charles, why?"

"We have weaned out a senior rogue agent from the United States. We have also rid ourselves of a fascist, extremist organisation who were led by a French government official... chief aide to the President of France no less."

"Agreed, but what about Kacey? Those stones belong to her. I have seen the magic they have produced to guide her along on her quest. Come to think of it, how did the fake replica stones fit the locking device on the casket?"

Charles Worwood let out a long sigh and then composed himself, suddenly taking on the aloof composure of a man with great responsibilities and one accustomed to making tough decisions. "Young lady, do you have any idea how much life has been taken in the name of religion? However sad it may be, if the Muslim world discovered that the Catholic Church was built on a myth, you could count every religious death through extremism, or war over the centuries, and multiply it by one hundred. In fact, you could add another two people to that tally, yourself and that dear young cousin of yours."

"So you colluded with Lorenzo and the Vatican to concoct this scam of an examination?"

"Not so my dear. We left a trail for them to follow. We were certain that they would make a fake casket, so we made sure we left perfect indentations in the wax at the chateau in order for them to manufacture a cleverly aged locking device. They believe that they have the original gemstones and will no doubt tuck them away in some hidden alcove of the crypt. Give your young cousin the life she deserves and remove her from this extreme danger. I'm sure I can arrange for a far longer period of compassionate leave for you. Once you are back in Thailand, and ponder the reasons that I have given you for my actions, I am certain that you will see the sense in it."

"So the Vatican think that they have fooled us. They produced a body and casket of the correct age and manufactured the locking device."

"That is correct Salonge. Goodbye my dear."

With that Charles Worwood turned and boarded his transportation back to London accompanied by James Boothroyd.

....

My eyes were everywhere as I took in the sumptuous surroundings of first class. I had initially walked into the wrong cabin section, being first to board and never having turned left upon entry to a passenger plane. The steward gently, but at the same time firmly, guided me to the correct section of the

fuselage and indicated the huge armchair size leather
seat whose number corresponded with my boarding
card. Salonge looked totally at home in these
surroundings and was already sipping champagne.

"Don't look at me that way Kacey, it's free. Just press
the button above your head and they will bring you a
glass. It's a long flight and will help you sleep."

"But I don't want to sleep." I said. "I want to soak up
every moment. I may have one glass though, and you
can tell me all about Asia."

Salonge began to describe the aromas, the climate,
the people, and the fabulous beaches. I did my best
to look enthralled. I realised it was naive of me to
attempt to fool such an intelligent, accomplished
agent as my wonderful cousin.

"Out with-it Kacey. Why are you pretending that you
are thrilled that the quest is over?"

"I know Salonge."

"What do you know?"

"I know that Charles and his friend switched the
stones."

"Now you are being ridiculous." She said, but this
time her face flushed betraying her years of training.

"When you were having a private word with Charles, I could see a red and blue light in my peripheral vision. At first I assumed they were just the port and starboard lights from the aircrafts wingtips. But when I turned my head, I could see that the light was coming from the tiny windows in the mid-section of the Hercules... the area where James Boothroyd examined my stones on the flight to Rome."

Salonge was initially lost for words until she finally spoke up.

"Kacey I am so sorry, but it's for the best...believe me."

"It's ok Salonge. I have had quite enough excitement for the time being. Besides, it would seem that the world is still not quite ready. Tell Charles to keep them safe. But also tell him, at some point I shall want them back. Now why don't you tell me more about Thailand. Did they ever have soldiers of honour like our knights of old?"

Salonge smiled. "You really are one incredible woman."

THE END

Printed in Great Britain
by Amazon

82765923R00312